"...ANOTHER MASTERPIECE..."
—CHICAGO TRIBUNE

Beginning with THE GOOD EARTH, Pearl S. Buck has written a succession of memorable and vivid books which have made China and Japan as familiar to westerners as their own communities.

Now she has done the same thing for Korea. THE LIVING REED is the story of four generations of a close-knit, powerful Korean family. We follow their struggles and sorrows and joys from the time of the last reigning Korean queen to the Second World War.

It is a story, in the words of the *Des Moines Register,* "Rich in Intrigue, History, Violence and Romance."

Those Americans who wonder why our soldiers were sent to this tiny peninsula to perish in what seemed like a futile struggle will find this poignant novel a revelation.

THE LIVING REED was originally published by The John Day Company.

Pearl S. BUCK

The Living Reed

A POCKET CARDINAL® EDITION published by
POCKET BOOKS, INC. • NEW YORK

THE LIVING REED

John Day edition published September, 1963

A Pocket *Cardinal* edition
1st printing..........August, 1964

This Pocket *Cardinal*® edition includes every word contained in the
original, higher-priced edition. It is printed from brand-new
plates made from completely reset, clear, easy-to-read type.
Pocket *Cardinal* editions are published by Pocket Books, Inc.,
and are printed and distributed in the U.S.A. by Affiliated Publishers,
a division of Pocket Books, Inc., 630 Fifth Avenue, New York, N.Y. 10020.
Trademarks registered in the United States and other countries.
                                                                  L

Contents

Historical Note

KOREA is a gem of a country inhabited by a noble people. Yet she is the Asian country least known to the western peoples, although to the three nations surrounding her, China, Russia and Japan, she has been well known for centuries and highly valued, and recent history has been only a continuation of that profound interest. When Stalin insisted that Russia have a share in the Pacific area of the second world war, he was fulfilling an age-old ambition of his land-locked people to secure not only the natural treasures of Korea but her matchless seacoast with harbors facing three sides of the compass. Had the Americans been sufficiently informed through history, we would have relentlessly opposed Stalin's demands. Instead we yielded, even to the extent of dividing Korea at the 38th parallel, a line of division which, ominously enough, Russia and Japan had once agreed upon in secret in the years when they were rivals for the possession of Korea. They were prevented from making the division only by certain western powers, who had hopes of their own regarding Korea.

China, of course, had long insisted that Korea must remain independent, a buffer state between herself, Russia and Japan. During the hundreds of years when China was the greatest power in Asia, and perhaps in the world, she was able to guarantee Korea's independence and in return Korea paid tribute to the Chinese imperial government, acknowledging the bond of suzerainty. The Chinese, nevertheless, were meticulous in maintaining the sovereignty of Korea. No Chinese were allowed to live in Korea or own land there, upon pain of death. It was only when China became weak as an old dynasty neared its end in the age of western colonialism in Asia, and with it came the rise of an ambitious modern Japan and a restless Russia, that China was no longer able to protect Korea and defend her from oppression.

1

Yet Korea, through no fault of her own a land of turmoil for centuries, was founded by a people in search of peace. Four thousand years ago many different tribes lived in Central Asia, that source of human life. In their nomad life these tribes wandered in different directions, the Han, or Chinese, southward to establish the country later called China, after their first emperor. Among those who went northward were the Tungu tribes, and one of these was the Puyo tribe, who settled in the region now known as Manchuria. There they became an agricultural community and there they might have remained except that to the west lived a fierce nomadic tribe, the Hiong-Nou, or Huns, the ancestors of the Mongols, and to the east the Mat-hat tribe, the ancestors of the Nuchen or Manchurians. Between these two barbarian peoples the more cultivated Puyo tribe found themselves oppressed, and soon they were forced southward into the peninsula now known as Korea. It was an ideal place for them, surrounded on three sides by the sea, and protected on the north by mountains, and here they developed a remarkable culture, rich in arts and crafts.

Legend says the origin of the Puyo was Heaven itself. A son of the Lord of Heaven was sent down to Earth, through miraculous birth from a union between bear and tiger, whose duty was to save human beings from chaos and destruction. With the help of his Heavenly Father, this Son of God ruled kindly and justly, serving always as a mediator between the Lord and human creatures. After his departure from Earth, he was followed by Tangun, the founder of the Korean nation, which was named Chosun, or Land of the Morning Calm. The name Tangun comes from the word *tangul,* or medicine man, and indicates a theocratic state. Korea was actually founded in the year 2333 B.C., and this is a date accepted by archeologists and historians, in spite of some lack of evidence, except that in ancient Chinese records, twenty or thirty centuries before Christ, the name of Chosun appears.

The people of that early Korea were not to find peace, however. In north China six powerful groups were fighting for control of that country. The Yen group attacked Chosun, whose power at that time reached far into north China. While fighting continued, the Ch'in group succeeded in conquering all others, in 221 B.C., and the country was unified although fighting still continued. The new rulers were oppressive, and many Chinese retreated into the peninsula of Korea. Struggle went on even into the Han dynasty, which followed the Ch'in, and then the strong resistance of the Koreans drove the Chinese away.

The history of Korea is too complex to follow here in detail, but the three kingdoms into which the country was then divided, Koguryo, Paekche and Silla, resolved their quarrels with one another and with the Chinese, ending significantly in pressure from Silla and Koguryo which forced Paekche, in the south, to a military alliance with nearby Japan, thus early dividing the peninsula between Chinese and Japanese influence. Silla conquered Paekche, however, with the help of Chinese in the T'ang dynasty, and then, eight years later, conquered Koguryo also. Thus in A.D. 668 Korea was unified, after three thousand years, and Koreans began to develop their own unique culture.

For two hundred and thirty years Korea enjoyed peace, and grew prosperous. Her arts developed indigenously and through her friendly relations with the glorious age of the T'ang dynasty in China. Like all successful dynasties, however, Silla too at last grew decadent. The ruling class began to neglect the welfare of the people, and the very brilliance of their cultural achievements emphasized the misery of the less fortunate. Revolt grew into revolution under the leadership of a great man, Wang Geun, especially in the north, where the influence of the Silla government was less strong, and the dissatisfied people from Silla joined them and thus was founded the dynasty of Koryo. This ruling group in the north did not, however, attack Silla, but waited in patience for decadence to bring submission. In A.D. 935 the King of Silla peacefully surrendered to the new dynasty. From its name is taken that of Korea.

Koryo began with many reforms. The civil service was revived and improved; land was nationalized and each farmer was given a piece of land for his lifetime; social securities were set up and universal education provided for. Movable

metal type provided for the printing of many books and as
early as 1230, thus preceding by some 220 years Gutenberg's
lead-cast printing type in Germany in 1450. In the next
dynasty, the Yi printing types were made of copper and these
Korean copper types and the production of them were introduced into China.

Another great cultural achievement of the Koryo dynasty
was the collecting, engraving and publishing of the Buddhist
sutra, the Tripitaka. The invasion of the Mongols in the
thirteenth century had so alarmed the Buddhists that a group
of devotees believed it essential, as an act of protection against
the invaders, to collect and preserve the best of the texts. During sixteen years the work went on, resulting in 320,000 pages
of such scriptures. This monumental work, Taijang-Kyung, is
now preserved in eternity in the Hal-in-sa Temple, Mount
Kaya, in the province of Kyong-sang, Korea.

In spite of a long period of peace and many reforms, the
dynasty of Koryo in its increasing decadence again brought
trouble to Korea. To the rising discontent of the people were
added attacks from Mongols and raids from Japanese pirates
and buccaneers. A revolution in Japan had overthrown the
power of the samurai and cost them their jobs. At the same
time a major economic depression fell upon the Japanese
people. Many turned into robbers by land and sea and these
made constant raids on Korean ports and ships. Added to such
disorder was the monstrous growing power of the Buddhist
priesthood in Korea, which encroached upon the rights of the
state and took over such political power that each king was
compelled to become a monk before he could reign and at
least one member of every family had to be a priest. The last
of the Koryo kings, under the influence of a corrupt monk, was
persuaded to attack China, then under the powerful Ming dynasty. General Yi, commanded to lead the attack, rebelled
and with a sympathetic people behind him, he overthrew the
King and established the new dynasty of Yi.

It is interesting, in view of recent events, to note that it
has been a tradition in Korea for the military to take rule
by a coup whenever the existing government becomes corrupt

and inefficient. Traditionally, too, the military force returns the government to civilians when essential reforms have been made. The *yangban,* or upper ruling class of Korea, is divided into two groups, the *tangban,* or civilian, and the *soban,* or military. Government belongs properly to the tangban, but should they fail, the soban takes over and restores the government and then returns it to the tangban.

The Yi dynasty, the last royal Korean ruling house (that is, the last "truebone" family, to employ a term which is in standard usage in Korea and which I have used in my novel in this literal translation), came to power with many great reforms, the most notable perhaps being the creation of an alphabet, under the decree and guidance of the great King Sejong. The new dynasty had been founded upon the principles of Confucianism and the improvement in the life of the common people was immediate and far-reaching. Any citizen could petition the King, and many reforms were made as the result of this communication. King Sejong, however, felt that the written language, based on the Chinese, was too cumbersome for easy communication with his people. With the help of a group of his finest scholars an alphabet was devised, the *hangul.* It is considered today the best and the simplest in the world. As King Sejong invented it, this alphabet had fourteen consonants and eleven vowels. It remains the same today except that one vowel has been deleted. These twenty-four letters allow for combinations which express every possible sound of the human voice in a remarkably accurate way, for King Sejong and his scholars studied the principles of phonetics, using the literature of many foreign countries as well as that of Korea.

Again, however, Korea was not to live in peace. While she prospered in all ways, including the arts, Japan was growing into a strong military power, under an ignorant but able man, Hideyoshi Toyotomi. He was the son of a peasant, ill-educated, boastful and ambitious, but able to unite contending war lords and rebels under his leadership. The Koreans had driven the Japanese pirates from their shores, and these pirates then attacked Chinese ports with such success that the

Japanese conceived the idea of making Korea a stepping-stone to mainland China.

With this dream Hideyoshi went to the Emperor of Japan, and as a reward asked only that when he had conquered it, the vast and ancient land of China be given him to rule as Viceroy. The imperial permission was granted and in 1592 he set out for Korea with a fleet of wooden warships. He landed in the south with 200,000 men and marched north. The Koreans were not prepared but they fought bravely on land. Meanwhile a Korean admiral, Yi Sun-shin, devised an iron-clad warship shaped like a turtle, with openings through the iron for the firing of blazing arrows. They were called turtle-boats and they were the first iron warships in history. With a fleet of turtle-boats, Admiral Yi destroyed the Japanese wooden ships in the Korean Straits and isolated the Japanese troops. Unfortunately the Admiral was mortally wounded, but his death was kept a secret until the worst of the war was over. At the end of seven years the Japanese were vanquished and so diminished in power that, although they never forgot their dreams of the conquest of China, it was centuries before they could invade Korea again with the same purpose.

The dynasty of Yi was brilliant and long. Opening with the end of the fourteenth century, it has been called the modern age of Korea, continuing as it does into the present. King Sejong, the fourth monarch of this dynasty, was not equaled, however, in all its history. He was a Korean Leonardo da Vinci in the variety and magnitude of his gifts. The Koreans have always been and still are a people of superb creative talents, but King Sejong, in the thirty years of his rule, became a deathless legend. The level of Korean culture under his rule reached extraordinary heights, great progress being made even in science, and especially in mathematics and astronomy. One invention, for example, was a water clock which showed automatically the time of day, the change of season, the hours of the rising and setting of sun and moon. Another invention was an accurate rain gauge for use in every part of the kingdom to serve as the basis for crop forecasts. Perhaps most important of all was the accumulation and codification of medical knowledge into an encyclopedia, *Vibang Yujip*, a work of three hundred and sixty-five volumes, finished in 1445. The Chinese have recently used this encyclopedia to recover some of their own sources of medical information lost in the war with Japan.

King Sejong also modernized Korean music and theory with the help of the famous musical theoretician, Pak Yon. Any visitor to Korea today realizes how extraordinarily talented the people there are in all the arts but especially in music. Perhaps the emphasis which Confucius placed upon the disciplines of music in the formation of moral character influenced King Sejong to provide for the publication of many books of music and for the arrangement of court music into beautiful compositions with divine themes.

Yet King Sejong did not suppress Buddhism. In his liberal spirit and under his personal approval, Buddhist scholars revised the Buddhist works of the previous dynasty and translated them into hangul and thus made them comprehensible to the people. As the centuries passed, the Yi dynasty grew in glory and achievement. The creative spirit of the people expressed itself in a vital literature. In this dynasty, too, the first western invasions took place. Catholicism entered in the seventeenth century, and French priests were murdered on Korean soil, as were shipwrecked sailors from foreign countries. Korea had had enough of invaders, and she asked only to be left a hermit nation, growing within her own skill. It was a wish that could not be fulfilled. Western expansionism was forcing the old nations of Asia into chaos. Portugal and Spain were engaging in active trade with Japan, and the crews of their ships, wrecked by typhoons in the Yellow Sea, often found refuge in islands off the southern coast of Korea.

Russia, too, was expanding. In the middle of the seventeenth century, a Russian regiment forced its way along the Amur River and fought the Chinese in Manchuria, near Korea. And Korean records tell us that in 1653 thirty-six "men of strange appearance," unknown before, with "blue eyes and yellow hair and high noses," staggered ashore from their wrecked ship. They were Dutchmen, and they were taken to Seoul, the capital of Korea, where they joined the army, married and lived for the rest of their lives, although in 1666 eight of them went back to Holland, and one of them, Hendrik Hamel, wrote of his life in Korea and so provided the first book about Korea in a western language.

In 1860 China went to war with Great Britain and France to protect her own sovereignty and her rights, with the result that Russia acted as mediator, and with the peace demanded a reward and was given the Maritime Provinces. This meant that at the northeastern tip of her peninsula Korean soil touched Russian soil—a significant portent for the future. In 1866 an American ship, the *General Sherman*, sailed up the Taedong River and relationships began between Korea and the United States, not always wise, not always peaceful, but established in 1883 by a treaty of amity and commerce.

It is shortly before that fateful year that my novel, *The Living Reed*, begins. The reader may well ask, as the story unfolds, how much of it is fact and how much is fiction. The basic Korean family is true in the sense of factual material passed through the creative process of a writer's brain. The historical material, however, is all factual, including the trial of the conspirators, the fire in the Christian church, and other such incidents—even, I add in sorrow, the events of the day the Americans landed at Inchon after the second world war. All American and other diplomatic persons, including Koreans, are factually presented. The political events are taken from history. The character of Woodrow Wilson is based on fact well documented, and whatever he says in the novel he said first in life. The way his words gripped the imaginations of the people of Asia is authentic, and a Korean delegation did call on him in Paris as did emissaries of other small nations.

But I have allowed my imagination, dwelling in Korea, to develop my Korean characters as I have known them on their own soil and as I saw them in the years when I lived in China and knew them there. To the Koreans, wherever we meet them in my book, I have tried to be true.

PEARL S. BUCK

March, 1963

PART I

THE year was 4214 after Tangun of Korea, and 1881 after Jesus of Judea. It was spring in the capital city of Seoul, a good season for a child to be born, and a fair day. Il-han, surnamed Kim, of the clan of Andong, sat in his library waiting for the birth of his second child to be announced. It was a pleasant room, larger than most rooms, and since the house faced south, the sun climbing over the walls of the compound shone dimly through the rice-papered lattices of the sliding walls. He sat on satin-covered floor cushions beside a low desk, but the floor itself was warmed by smoke ducts from the kitchen stove, after the ancient *ondul* fashion. He tried diligently to keep his mind on his book, open before him on the low desk. Three hours had passed since his wife had retired to her bedroom, accompanied by her sister, the midwife and women servants. Three times one or the other of them had come to tell him that all went well, that his wife sent him greetings and begged him to take nourishment, for the birth was still far off.

"Far off?" he had demanded. "How far off?"

Each time the answer had been a shake of the head, a vague smile, a retreat, behavior typical of women, he thought somewhat scornfully, at least of Korean women, silken sweet on the surface, but rock stubborn underneath. All except his beautiful and beloved wife, his Sunia! He would have been ashamed to show to anyone, even to her, how much he loved her, and this although he had never seen her before their wedding. For once matchmakers had not lied and fortunetellers had been correct in the forecasting of signs and dates. Sunia had fulfilled every duty as a bride. She had not smiled once throughout the long day of the wedding, in spite of the ruthless teas-

9

ing of relatives and friends. A bride who could not control her
laughter on her wedding day, it was said, would give birth
only to girls. Sunia had given birth to a son, now three years
old, and if the fortuneteller was right again, today she would
have another. Il-han's home, his family, made a center of
peace in these troubled times of his country. But when had
times not been troubled for Korea? In four thousand years
there had been scarcely a century of peace for the small
valuable peninsula hanging like a golden fruit before the longing eyes of the surrounding nations, proud China demanding
tribute, vast Russia hungry for the seacoast she did not have,
and Japan, ambitious for empire.

He sighed, forgetting home and family, and rose to walk impatiently to and fro across the room. It was impossible to keep
his mind fixed on books, although he was a scholar, not the
scholar his father was, poring over ancient volumes, but a
scholar for all of that. His book today was a modern one, a
history of western nations. His father would not have been
pleased had he known that he, Kim Il-han, the only son of the
Kim family of Andong, was engaged in such learning, his
father who lived in the classics of Confucius and in dreams of
the golden age of the dynasty of Silla! But he, Il-han, like all
young men of his generation, was impatient with old philoso-
phies and religions. Confucianism, borrowed from China, had
isolated this nation already isolated by sea and mountain, and
Buddhism had led the hermit mind of his people into fantasies
of heaven and hell, gods and demons, into anything, indeed,
except the bitter present.

He paced the tiled floor of his library, a tall slender figure
in the white robes of his people, and he listened for the cry of
his newborn child while he mused. Then, burning with restlessness at the delay and suddenly feeling himself hot, he slid
back the latticed wall. The clear sunshine of the spring morning poured its rays across his low table desk. The desk had
been his grandfather's, a solid piece of teak imported from
Burma, made after his grandfather's own design, and decorated with fine Korean brass.

"This desk shall be yours," his father had told him upon

the grandfather's death. "May the thoughts and writings of a great statesman inspire you, my son!"

His grandfater had indeed been a great man, a premier of the still existing Yi dynasty, and from the Yi rulers he had absorbed the doctrine of isolationism and the emotions of pride and independence.

"Situated as we are, surrounded by three powerful nations, Russia, China and Japan," his grandfather had memorialized the Throne half a century ago, "we can only save ourselves from their greed by withdrawal from the world. We must become a hermit nation."

His father had often quoted these words and Il-han had listened to them with secret scorn. The absurdity of his elders! He had kept his own secrets even from his father, his share in the first revolt against the Regent, Taiwunkun. He, Il-han, had been only a boy but a useful boy, carrying messages between the rebel leaders and the young Queen. The Regent had married his son, King Kojong, to her when he was far too young for marriage, and because he was young the Regent had chosen a daughter of the noble clan of Min, older than the King, a choice he had cause to rue, for who could believe the beautiful graceful girl was strong and of such brilliant mind, and determined that she could plot to set the Regent aside? He, Il-han, had seen her at first only by candlelight, at midnight, in stolen conference with the rebel leaders, he waiting at the door for a packet thrust into his hand which he must take to the young King when he went to play chess with him the next day. Even then he had known that the Queen was the one who must rule, and that the King, his gentle and amiable playmate, could only be the buffer between the arrogant Regent and the Queen.

But Il-han had told his father nothing. What could his father do, the handsome aging poet, dreaming his life away in his country house and his garden? For his father, unwilling to wound his grandfather, who had served the Regent, by taking the part of the young Queen who loved China, had early withdrawn from the royal conflict. Queen Min, it was said, though how truly none knew, was herself partly Chinese and her most powerful friend was Tzu-hsi, the Empress Dowager now ruling in Peking. From that capital the Queen still insisted upon buying the heavy silks and satin brocades she enjoyed wearing, and though some censured her for extravagance, he, Il-han, had not the heart to blame her for anything she did. Now in the joy of awaiting the birth of his second child, he thought of the Queen's only son, heir to the throne, who had been born of feeble mind. In the center of her being, proud and beautiful and brilliant as she was, there was emptiness, and he knew it.

His absent mind, always pondering affairs of state, was presently controlled by his attention focused at this moment to hear the cry of his child fighting to be born. He paused, listening for footsteps. Hearing none, he returned to his desk, took up a camel's-hair pen and continued to write a memorial he had begun some days before. Were this document to be presented to the King, he would have been compelled to use the formal Chinese characters. It was written not for the Court, however, but for the secret perusal of the Queen, and he used the symbols of the phonetic Korean alphabet.

"Furthermore, Majesty," he wrote, "I am troubled that the British have moved ships to the island of Komudo, so near to our coasts. I understand that they wish the Chinese armed forces to leave Seoul, with which I cannot agree, for Japan is demanding that she be allowed to send troops to Korea in case of emergency. What emergency can arise in our country which would need Japanese soldiers? Is this not the ancient and undying desire of Japan for westward empire? Shall we allow our country to be a stepping-stone to China and beyond China to Asia itself?"

He was interrupted by the opening of a door and lifting his head, he heard his son's voice, a subdued wail.

"I will not go to my father!"

He rose and flung open the door. His son's tutor stood there, and his son was clinging to the young man's neck.

"Forgive me, sir," the tutor said. He turned to the child. "Tell your father what you have done."

He tried to set the boy on his feet but the boy clung to

him as stubbornly as a small monkey. Il-han pulled the child away by force and set him on his feet.

"Stand," he commanded. "Lift your head!"

The child obeyed, his dark eyes filled with tears. Yet he did not look his father full in the face, which would have been to show lack of respect.

"Now speak," Il-han commanded.

The child made the effort, opened his mouth and strangled a sob. He could only look at his father in piteous silence.

"It is I, sir, who should speak first," the tutor said. "You have entrusted your son to me. When he commits a fault, it is my failing. This morning he would not come to the schoolroom. He has been rebellious of late. He does not wish to memorize the Confucian ode I have set for him to learn—a very simple ode, suitable for his age. When I saw he was not in the schoolroom, I went in search of him. He was in the bamboo grove. Alas, he had destroyed several of the young shoots!"

The child looked up at his father, still speechless, his face twisted in a mask of weeping.

"Did you do so?" Il-han demanded.

The child nodded.

Il-han refused to allow himself pity, although his heart went soft at the sight of this small woeful face.

"Why did you destroy the young bamboos?" His voice was gentle in spite of himself.

The child shook his head.

Il-han turned to the tutor. "You did well to bring him to me. Now leave us. I will deal with my son."

The young man hesitated, a look of concern on his mild face. Il-han smiled.

"No, I will not beat him."

"Thank you, sir."

The young man bowed and left the room. Without further talk Il-han took his son's hand and led him into the garden, and then to the bamboo grove by its southern wall. It was plain to see what had happened. The young shoots, ivory white and sheathed in their casings of pale green, were well above ground. Of several hundreds, some tens were broken off and lying on the mossy earth. Il-han stopped, his hand still clasping the small hot hand of his son.

"This is what you did?" he inquired.

The child nodded.

"Do you still not know why?"

The child shook his head and his large dark eyes filled with fresh tears. Il-han led him to a Chinese porcelain garden seat, and lifted him to his knee. He smoothed the child's hair from his forehead, and pride swelled into his heart. The boy was straight and slim and tall for his years. He had the clear white skin, the leaf-brown eyes, the brown hair of his people, different from the darker Japanese, a living reminder that those invaders must not be tolerated in Korea.

"I know why you did it, my son," he said gently. "You were angry about something. You forgot what I have taught you— a superior person does not allow himself to show anger. But you were angry and you did not dare tell your tutor that you were angry and so you came here, alone, where no one could see you, and you destroyed the young bamboos, which are helpless. Is that what you did?"

Tears flowed from the boy's eyes. He sobbed.

"Yet you knew," the father continued with relentless gentleness, "you knew that bamboo shoots are valuable. Why are they valuable?"

"We—we—like to eat them," the child whispered.

"Yes," the father said gravely, "we like to eat them, and it is in the spring that they can be eaten. But more than that, they grow only once from the root. The plants these shoots might have been, waving their delicate leaves in the winds of summer, will never live. The shoots crack the earth in spring, they grow quickly and in a year they have finished their growth. You have destroyed food, you have destroyed life. Though it is only a hollow reed, it is a living reed. Now the roots must send up other shoots to take the place of those you have destroyed. Do you understand me?"

The child shook his head. Il-han sighed. "It is not enough to learn your letters or even enough to learn the odes of Confucius. You must learn the inner meanings. Come with me to the library."

He lifted the child from his knee and led him in silence to the library again. There he took from the shelves a long narrow box covered with yellow brocaded satin. He unhinged the silver hasp and lifted from the box a scroll which he unrolled upon the table.

"This," he said, "is a map of our country. Observe how it lies between three other countries. Here to the north is Russia, this nation to the west is China, and this to the east is Japan. Are we larger or smaller than they?"

The child stared at the map soberly. "We are very small," he said after a moment.

"Korea is small," his father agreed. "And we are always in danger. Therefore we must be brave, therefore we must be proud. We must keep ourselves free, we must not allow these other nations to eat us up as they wish always to do. They have attacked us again and again, but we have repulsed them. How do you think we have done this?"

The child shook his head.

"I will tell you," Il-han said. "Time and again brave men offer themselves as our leaders. They come up from the high-born yangban as we do, or they come from the landfolk. It does not matter where they come from. When the need arises they are here, ready to lead us. They are like the bamboo shoots that must replace those you have now destroyed. They will spring from the roots that are hidden in the earth."

The child looked up with lively eyes, he listened, stretching his mind to understand what his father was saying. Whether he did understand Il-han never knew, for at this moment he heard the cry of the newborn child. The door opened and the old midwife appeared, her face wrinkled in smiles.

"Sir," she said. "You have a second son."

Joy rushed into his heart.

"Take this child to his tutor," he said.

He pushed the boy into the midwife's arms, and heedless of his son's calling after him he hastened away.

. . . In his wife's bedchamber they were waiting for him,

the maidservants, the women who had come to assist, and above all Sunia, his wife. She lay on the mattress spread on the warm floor and the women had arranged her for his arrival. They had brushed her hair and wiped the sweat of childbirth from her face and hands and had spread a rose-pink silken cover upon her bed. She smiled up at him as he stood above her and his love for her rushed up and all but choked him. Her oval face was classic in beauty, not a soft face, and perhaps more proud than gentle, but he knew well her deep inner tenderness. Her skin was cream white, and at this moment without the high color natural to her. Her eyes, leaf-brown, were drowsy with weariness and content, and her long dark hair, soft and straight, was brushed and spread over the flat pillow.

"I am come to thank you," he said.

"I have only done my duty," she replied.

The words were a ritual, but through her eyes she had her own way of making them intimate.

"But," she added with a touch of her daily willfulness, "I enjoy having your sons. How can it be only a duty?"

He laughed. "Pleasure or duty, please continue," he said.

Had they been alone, he would have knelt at her side and taken her hand between his hands to cherish and fondle. As it was, he could only bow and turn away. Yet he paused at the door to leave a command with the women.

"See that you do not keep her awake with your chatter and make sure that she has chicken broth brewed with ginseng root."

They bowed in silence, and he returned to the library where in a few minutes, as he knew, his second son would be presented to him. He knelt beside the great desk and then rose again, still too restless to read or write. Once more he walked to and fro across the tiled floor, across the squares of sunlight from the open doors. He turned his face to the sun. It fell upon him warmly and he welcomed the warmth. His white garments shone whiter, and he enjoyed the sense of light and cleanliness in which they wrapped him. He was fastidiously clean and Sunia saw to it that every morning he put on fresh white garments, the loose trousers bound at his ankles, the long white robe crossed from left to right on his breast. His ancestors were sun worshipers, and he had inherited from them his love of light. White was the sacred color, a symbol of brightness and of life. True, it was also the color of mourning. Yet so closely were death and life intertwined here in his troubled country that he could not think of one without realizing the other. This too was his inheritance, now given to his sons.

He paused on the thought and stared down at the pool of sunlight in which he stood. It occurred to him that he had not asked his elder son why he had been angry, so angry that he had rushed into the grove and broken the tender bamboo shoots. It was important to know why a son in this house should be angry. He clapped his hands and as a servant entered the room he took his place on the floor cushions behind the desk. Casually, as though he had no other interest, he spoke to the servant.

"Invite my son's tutor to come here and for a short time take care of the child yourself. He is forbidden to enter the bamboo grove."

He did not explain why the child was forbidden. In a house of many servants everything is already known. The servant bowed and backed out of the room and closed the door silently. He busied himself as he waited for the tutor, pouring water on the ink block and rubbing the stick of dried ink into a paste upon the wet block before brushing Chinese letters on the sheet of thick white paper, handmade from silk waste. He moistened his brush in the liquid ink and smoothed the fine hairs dexterously to a point. Then, the reed handle between two fingers and thumb, he held the brush poised above the paper. Four lines of a poem shaped in his brain to announce the birth of his second son. Ah, but what language should he use? If his father were to see the poem it must be written in the ancient Chinese.

"No true scholar can stoop to use hangul," he declared whenever he saw what he called "the new way of writing."

It was true that men liked to write in Chinese to show that

they had received the education of a cultivated man. Sejong the Great himself had been a man learned in Chinese, but he had been also a wise ruler. A king, he had declared, if he is to govern well, must know what his people think and want, yet how can they write to their king if the letters they use are so difficult that years must be spent merely in learning them? That communication between himself and his subjects might be possible, he had then devised, with the help of many scholars, an alphabet so simple that it had no resemblance to the complex Chinese characters.

The book of Sejong's life lay open now on the desk for Il-han had reflected much, of late, upon this noble king. Oh, that there were a ruler today as great as Sejong had been, one who, though he was the highest, could think of the low ones, the people, those who worked upon the land to produce food for all, who built houses for others to live in, those who only serve! Il-han himself, growing up the beloved and only son in a great house of the yangban class, had never thought of these folk. It was his own tutor, the father of his son's tutor, who had first told him of the stir among the multitudes, the speechless revolt of the silent. Sejong the Great had been well named. He was great enough to know that no ruler can ignore the discontent of his subjects, for discontent swells to anger and anger to explosion. Alas, again, where was such a man now? Was the young King ever to be strong enough?

The door slid open and his son's tutor stood there, bowing, white robes spotless.

"Sir, forgive me for delay. I was in the bath."

He bent low again and waited.

"Enter," Il-han commanded. "And close the doors behind you."

He did not rise, the man being his inferior in age and position, though the years between them were only three. His father had complained that the tutor was too young, but Il-han had persisted in keeping him, saying that his old tutor was too old, and he did not wish to entrust his son to a stranger whose forbears he did not know.

The young man came in and waited again.

"You are permitted to seat yourself," Il-han said kindly.

The young man knelt opposite to him on a cushion before the low desk and looked down modestly. He was agitated, as Il-han could see and, he supposed, prepared for reproach because of the child's destructive anger. Therefore he spoke mildly, aware of the anxiety on the sensitive youthful face which he now examined.

"I wish to consult you about my son," Il-han began.

"If you please, sir," the young man replied in a low voice.

"It is not a question of blame or punishment," Il-han went on. "It is only that I must be told about my son. He is with you day and night and you understand his nature. Tell me— why should he be angry here in his own home?"

The young man lifted his eyes to the edge of the table. "He has fits of anger, sir. I do not know what causes them. They come like sudden storms at sea. All is as usual, we are without quarrel, and then with no warning, he throws his book on the floor and pushes me away."

"Does he hate books?"

"No, sir." The young man lifted his eyes a few inches higher so that now they rested on Il-han's hands, folded on his desk. "He is very young, and I require nothing of him in the way of study. I read him a story from history, then a legend, a fairy tale, something to amuse him and please him so that he may understand the pleasure to be found in books and later will seek them for himself. This morning, for example, I was reading the story of 'The Golden Frog.'"

Il-han knew the story from his own childhood. It was the tale of King Puru who, because he had no son, prayed to God for a male child. On his way home one day, for he had ridden horseback to a place called Konyun, he was amazed to see a weeping rock. He ordered his retinue to examine the rock, and under it they found a golden frog which looked like a baby. He believed his prayers were answered and he took the frog home. It grew into a handsome boy, and he named the boy Kumwa, that is to say, Golden Frog, and this son succeeded his father and became King Kumwa.

"At this point," the tutor was saying, "the child tore the

book from my hands and dashed it on the floor. Then he ran from the room. I searched for him and when I found him in the bamboo grove he was wrenching the bamboo shoots with both his hands and all his strength and throwing them on the ground. When I asked him why he did so, he said he did not want a golden frog for a brother."

Il-han was amazed. "Who put that in his mind?"

The young tutor lowered his eyes again. A red flush crept up from his neck and spread over his cheeks. "Sir, I am miserable. I fear it was I who did so, but unwittingly. He had heard of his brother's approaching birth and he asked me where this brother would come from. I did not know how to reply, and I said perhaps he would be found under a rock, like the Golden Frog."

Il-han laughed. "A clever explanation, but I can think of a better! You might, for instance, have replied that his brother came from the same place that he himself did. And when the child inquired where that was, you could have said, 'If you do not know, how can I know?'"

The young man forgot himself and raised his eyes to Il-han's face. "Sir, you do not understand your own son. He is never to be put off. He pries my mind open with his questions. I fear sometimes that in a few years he will be beyond me. He smells out the smallest evasion, not to mention deceit, and worries me for the truth, even though I know it is beyond him. And when in desperation I give him simple truth he struggles with it as though he were fighting an enemy he must overcome. When he comprehends finally and to his own satisfaction, he is exhausted and angry. That was what happened this morning. He insisted upon knowing where his brother came from, and how could I explain to him the process of birth? He is too young. I was driven to use wile and persuasion and so I fetched the book. But he knew it was only a device and this was the true reason for his anger."

Il-han rose from his cushion and went to the door and opened it suddenly. No one was there and he closed it again and returned to his cushion. He leaned forward on the low desk and spoke softly. "I have called you here for another purpose, also. Your father, as you know, was my tutor. He taught me much, but most of all he taught me how to think. He grounded me in the history of my people. I wish you to do the same for my son."

The young tutor looked troubled. "Sir, my father was a member of the society of Silhak."

He lowered his voice and looked toward the closed door.

"Why be afraid?" Il-han inquired. "There is good in the teaching of the Silhak that learning which does not help the people is not true learning. It is not new, mind you. It is made up of many elements—"

"Western, among them, sir," the tutor put in. He forgot himself and that he was in the presence of the heir of the most powerful family in Korea.

"Partly western," Il-han agreed. "But that is good. Were it now treason to the Queen, I would say that we have been too long under the influence of the ancient Chinese. Not that we should allow ourselves to be wholly under the influence of the West, mind you! It is our fate, lying as we do between many powers, to be influenced to an extent by all and many. It is our task to accept and reject, to weld and mingle and out of our many factions to create ourselves, the One, an independent nation. But what is that One? Ah, that is the question! I cannot answer it. Yet now for the sake of my sons an answer must be found."

He leaned against the backrest of his cushion, frowning, pondering. Suddenly he spoke with new energy.

"But you are not to repeat your father's weakness with me. He told me of evil in other great families, but not in my own family of Kim. Yet in some ways we are the most guilty of all the great families. We early built ourselves into the royal house so that we could acquire benefits. Fifteen hundred years ago, and more, we married three daughters into the eighth monarchy, Honjong. Through three reigns, one after the other, our daughters were married into the truebone royal house. We fed upon the nation, both land and people. The best posts in government went to my ancestors and for that matter to my grandfather, and even my father until he refused to

oppose the Regent and retired to live under his grass roof.
How else could we live in such houses as these? Palaces! And
how else could I be the heir to vast lands in this small country?
At one time we even aspired to rule the Throne. You know
very well that one of my ancestors so aspired and was crushed
—as he deserved to be!"

He spoke with a passion restrained but profound and the
young tutor was shocked at this self-humiliation. "These are
affairs long past, sir," he murmured. "They are forgotten."

Il-han insisted upon his ruthless survey. "They are not forgotten. Millions of people have suffered and do suffer because
of the name Kim. We are well named!"

He traced upon the palm of his left hand with the forefinger of his right hand the Chinese letter for *Gold*, which
was indeed the meaning of the name Kim.

"That is what we have lived for—gold in the shape of lands
and houses and high position! We have gained the power and
even over the royal house. Ah, you must teach my son what
your father did not teach me! Teach him the truth!"

He broke off abruptly, his handsome face furious and dark.

Before the tutor could answer, the door slid open. The midwife entered, carrying in her arms the newborn child, laid
upon a red satin cushion. She was followed by Il-han's two
sisters-in-law and they by their maids.

His elder sister-in-law came forward. "Brother, behold your
second son."

Il-han rose. Again his family duty claimed him and with a
nod he dismissed the tutor. He walked toward the procession
and stretched out his arms. The midwife laid the cushion
across them with the sleeping child, and he looked down into
the small perfect face of his new son.

"Little Golden Frog," he murmured.

The woman looked at one another astonished and then they
laughed and clapped their hands. It was a lucky greeting, for
the Golden Frog had become a prince.

"What did he say when he saw our child?" Sunia asked.

She had already recovered some of her natural clear color,

and her large dark eyes were lively. Childbirth was easy for her and with a second son she was triumphant. Three or four sons from now she could wish for a daughter. A woman needed daughters in the house.

"He smiled and called him little Golden Frog," her elder sister said. She was a tall slender woman in early middle age married to a scholar who lived in a northern city. Since Sunia's mother was dead, and Il-han's also, she came to fulfill the maternal duties for Sunia, and with her came her younger sister, who would not marry but wished to become a Buddhist nun, to which Il-han, in absence of father or brother, could not agree. No woman today, he declared, should bury herself in a nunnery. The day of the Buddhists was over. Without his permission, Sunia's sister could only wait.

Sunia received her child tenderly and hugged him to her bosom. "He thinks of clever things to say about everything. He is too clever for me. I hope this child will be like him."

She gazed into the sleeping face and touched the firm small chin with a teasing finger. "Look at him sleep! He is hiding himself from me. I have not seen his eyes."

"Put him to your breast," the midwife told her. "He will not suckle yet, but he should feel the nipple ready at his lips."

The young mother uncovered her round full breast.

"Put him first to the left where the heart is," the midwife said.

Sunia shook her head willfully. "I put the first son to the left. This one I will put to the right."

The child stirred when the nipple touched his lips but he did not open his eyes. She teased him then with the nipple, lifting her breast with her hand, brushing his lips lightly and laughing at him. The women gathered about her to enjoy the sight of the healthy young woman and her beautiful male child.

"Look at him, look at him," the younger sister exclaimed. "He is opening his eyes. Look—he is pouting his lips."

They watched, breathless. The child had indeed opened his eyes and was gazing up at his mother. Suddenly, newborn though he was, he seized the nipple between his lips and sucked.

"Ah—ah—ah—"

The women breathed great sighs. They looked at one another. Whoever heard of such a thing? To suckle so soon— even for a moment—yes, it was only for a moment. The child fell back into sleep, the clear liquid of the first milk wet upon his lips. The midwife took him then and laid him in bed beside his mother, for a child should sleep close to the mother when he is newborn, should feel the warmth of her body, so lately his home, and know the presence of her spirit with him as much now as when he was unborn. Then the sister smoothed the pillows for the mother and arranged the quilt.

"Sleep," the midwife commanded her. "We shall be near if you call, but now you must rest."

They withdrew to another room, closing the sliding door after them. Sunia waited until they were gone, and then she turned to her child. This was her first moment alone with him and she must examine for herself her own creation. She sat up in bed and took the child on her lap and undressed him, her hands warm and gentle in their movements, until he lay naked before her. Then with the most meticulous care she searched his entire body for a flaw, first his feet, upon which some day he must walk firmly, a strong man—but how small they were and how pretty, the toes perfect and in order, the number complete, the nails pink and already long enough to be cut, but she must not cut them, for it would be a bad omen for his life-span. The insteps, left and right, were high as her own were, and the ankles shapely even now. The legs were long like his father's and they would be straight when the baby curve was gone, for the bones were strong. The thighs were fat and the belly was round. The chest was full and the shoulders, already broad, supported the neck. The arms were long, too, and thus promised a tall man. The hands were exquisite, again the long beautiful hands of his father. Her own were small and graceful, but Il-han's were powerful, although he had never done more with his hands than hold a brush to write. The head was ample for a good brain, nobly shaped, high from the ears to the crown, signifying intelligence. The hair was soft, dark and plentiful. All the features were perfect in shape and arrangement. He looked liked his father, this son, whereas the elder was like her. There was no flaw. She had made him perfect and whole. No—wait, the little ear on the left—the lobe? She examined it carefully while the child slept. The tip of the left lobe was shortened, tucked in, imperfect!

What had caused this? She searched her memory. What had she done that could have created a child with even the smallest imperfection? The omens had been good, she had known that she would have a son, for she had dreamed one night of the sun rising over the horizon at dawn. To have dreamed of flowers would have meant a daughter. Then why the pinched lobe of this small left ear? While she was pregnant she had been careful to remember all her dreams and none had been evil. Best of all, she had even dreamed of seeing her father who died when she was a child of four, so young that she could see his face only dimly if she thought of him. Yet in her dream his face had been clear and smiling, a long kindly face, the nose neither high, which would have signified bankruptcy and death in a foreign land, nor low, which would have signified greed. She examined the baby's nose anxiously. It was neither high nor low, though somewhat more high, perhaps, than low. Impossible to explain the pinched ear! She must show it to Il-han when he came to visit her tomorrow. If he, too, did not know its meaning then they must consult the blind fortuneteller. She dressed the child again and wrapped him in the silken coverlet and laid him beside her in the bed and was too troubled for sleep until nearly dawn.

. . . She did not at once reveal the defect. Let Il-han discover it for himself. He came in at noon of the next day, after the child had been washed and clothed and she herself had eaten and in her turn had been washed and perfumed and dressed in fresh white garments, her long dark hair brushed smooth and braided with pink silk cord. Il-han too had taken care to appear at his best, as she could see. She knew him well. He could be careless when he was absorbed at his desk but this morning he was shaved, his hair combed and twisted tightly in a knot on the top of his head, and his white robes were freshly clean. Her heart beat at the sight of him, as it had the first time she had seen him, a bridegroom in his wedding garments, the formal dark coat of thick silk over the white robes beneath, the high black hat, the long heavy necklace and the wide brocaded sash. Everything the matchmaker had said about him was true. Her father had hired spies before the marriage contracts were signed, since matchmakers are greedy and for the sake of their fee will tell lies to bring about a wedding. But the spies had come back and spoken truly.

"He is a handsome young man. He does not gamble or search out willing women. His only fault is that he follows the Silhak."

Silhak? It was suspect, for included in its teachings was the stern demand for action and not learning alone. A man, even a king, the Silhak maintained, was to be measured by what he does, not by what he says. When this was explained to her, Sunia cried out that she would have such a man for her husband, for she was weary of men who did no more than boast about the glories of ancient times. Her father yielded at last and the contracts were signed and the moment she set her eyes upon Il-han's grave and handsome face she knew that she had done well.

"Come in, come in," she said now while he stood in the doorway gazing at her, admiring her beauty as she could see, while she thought of him. She knew very well the kindling light in his dark eyes when he saw her and the smile on his lips. Had they been of the older generation, he would not have come to her room so soon after the child's birth, and certainly not alone, but old ways were yielding to young demands. And they were close, he and she. Among her friends she knew of no man and wife who talked together as he and she did. Or, if some did, the wives did not reveal it. Yet who knows what passes between man and woman? Deep under the surface the living stream flowed between them and the more exciting because she had been reared in innocent ignorance. No one had prepared her for the possibility that she might fall in love with her husband. Her mother had told her that she must not complain of her husband, nor should she refuse his demands. Neither must she be angry if she did not please him and he found women outside his house. His duty was fulfilled if he acknowledged her his wife and paid her respect and supplied her with shelter and food and clothing.

"Your duty is to him and only to him, whatever he does," her mother had said briskly but vaguely, for what was that duty and that "whatever"? She had not dared to ask, and her mother had been occupied with the details of the betrothal, the receiving of the black box from his family wherein was red silk wrapped in blue cloth and blue silk wrapped in red cloth and such matters and with these the letter. Ah, the letter! She had not been allowed to be there when it was presented by a relative in the Kim family, but she knew it by heart.

> Since you give us your noble daughter to be our daughter-in-law, we send you a gift of cloth, in accordance with the ancient rules.

Thus the betrothal was fixed. Her home had been bright with lanterns that night and servants stood at the gates with flaming torches. She had hidden herself safely in her own room, but she went to the window and, standing in the shadows behind a screen, she had watched. And there she had stood again on her wedding day, when he came riding through the gate on a white horse. The horse was led by a man in a red cap and blue robe, and under his arm was a live duck to signify wedded happiness. The man was a small fellow, however, and the duck was large and lively and he had struggled with the creature and Il-han sitting on his horse had laughed. She laughed again now.

"Why are you laughing?" Il-han inquired. He pulled a low carved stool to her bedside and sat down.

"I am remembering you on that high white horse," she

said, laughing, "and the servants behind you with paper umbrellas and the little man carrying the big duck."

He smiled at her. "Were you watching?"

It was one of the joys of their life that he found surprises in her, thoughts, feelings, acts, which she never finished telling him.

"Yes," she said joyously. "Did I never tell you! I was watching and the moment when I saw you laugh—I—I—was glad."

He reached for her hand. "Glad of what?"

"Because I knew I must love you."

Their hands clasped. "What if the duck had flown away?" This he said to tease her, since it is a bad omen for a marriage if the wedding duck escapes.

"I would not have cared," she said. "I had seen you and I would have followed you anywhere."

"Now—now." He pretended to scold her to hide the excess of his persisting tenderness, after all these years. "Is this the way to speak to a man? You are too bold—you have not been well brought up!"

"I am very well brought up, and you know that," she retorted, pretending to pout. "All Pak women are well brought up. Do we not belong to the truebone? We have royal blood, too—as well as you Kims!"

"Truebone to truebone," he said and put her hand to his cheek.

She smoothed the cheek, and then, allowing this to go no further, she withdrew her hand.

"All the same," she said, "on our wedding day you bowed too carelessly at the table before the gate. Three times, I think, instead of four! You were still trying not to laugh at the duck."

"The duck would not stay on the table, as you very well know," he reminded her, "and I saw myself coming to meet my princess with a duck flapping after me. As it was, your father looked shocked when he led you out of the house!"

"You had not seen me until that moment and yet you thought of ducks!" Her words were mock reproach but her dark eyes rested on his face with such a look that he bit his lip.

"Shall I ever forget—" he murmured.

He rose impetuously and lifted her in his right arm and buried his face in her hair. For a moment they embraced and then she pushed him gently away.

"We are not behaving well, father of my son—This is not our wedding night."

"A month yet before we are free to—" he muttered the words restlessly, and broke off.

She fluttered her eyelashes at him and looked down at the satin bed quilt and pretended to pull a thread.

"You have not told me what you think of our second son."

He drew a deep breath. "Wait," he besought her. "Let me cool my heart for a moment." He got up and walked about the room, paused before a painting of the sacred mountain of Omei in faraway China. Then he returned to his seat.

"This second son," he said, "is not respectful to his father. He slept the whole time he was in my presence. Otherwise, I think well of him, although he is not so beautiful as the first one. He looks like me. Though I will not grant that the Paks, in general, are more handsome than the Kims, you being the exception to all women."

She shook her head. "I did my best to make him perfect but—"

"But what?"

"He is not quite perfect."

"No?"

"This—" She touched the lobe of her own perfect left ear. "It is pinched. It is not like the other one."

He heard this and clapped his hands. A woman servant entered.

"Bring me my second son," he commanded.

"What can this mean?" he inquired then of his wife.

She shook her head again and tears came welling into her eyes.

"Ah now," he cried and impetuously reached for her

folded hands and held them in his. "It is not your fault, my bird."

"It is the evil of some spirit on him before he was shaped," she sighed. "A touch on the lobe of the ear—I must ask the soothsayer what it means."

"Where were our *samsin* spirits?" he asked, half scornfully.

It was an old quarrel between them, never ended, a small battle in which neither yielded and neither won. The samsin were the three spirits whose duty it is to guard the conception and growth and development of children in the house. He did not believe in samsin, and she did not believe, she said when he teased her, and yet she had prepared the symbols.

"The threads, the papers, the streamers of cloth, they were hanging yonder on the wall the night that we—"

He put her hands down gently and walked to the wall at the far end of the room. Yes, they were still there, the material evident presence of the samsin, looking now somewhat dusty and torn. How could these poor relics have influence on the birth of a child? Gazing at them with contempt, he felt the old disbelief well into his mind and heart. Folk tales, the fumbling efforts of peasant peoples and ignorant priests to explain the miracles of life, even his sister-in-law wanting to be a Buddhist nun! He longed to know and understand in new ways, to find other paths than in the books of the dead. His father, sitting day after day in his study, poring over the ancestral history of the Kim family, proud of the dead and censorious toward the living—this was the curse of Korea, this slow dying while men were still alive, begetting sons for the future, but dreaming of the past. He put out his hand and tore down the dusty symbols.

"Il-han!"

He heard his wife's cry and he turned to her. "How many years I have been longing to tear down those rags! And now I have done it!"

"But, Il-han," she breathed, "what will happen to us?"

"Something new and something good," he said.

At this moment the servant entered with his second son. He took the child from her and dismissed her with a nod and he carried the child to the bed and laid him beside the mother.

"Show me," he commanded.

She turned the sleeping child tenderly and pushed back the soft straight black hair that fell against his left ear.

"There," she said, "see what happened to him, even before his birth."

He leaned to see closely. The deformity was slight. For a girl, who must wear jewels in her ears, it might have been a defect more grave. Nevertheless it was a defect, and he did not like to think that a son of his could be less than perfect. Yet what could be done now? The shape was made, the flesh confirmed by life. No use to see a doctor—herbs could not change this permanence. And the thing was so small, the lobe of the ear tucked in as though a thread had drawn it up, and could be released again. A quick sharp knife could do it, if one had the skill.

He touched the child's soft ear, and then covered it with the dark hair. "I have heard that the western physicians know how to correct by the knife," he said.

She gathered the child in her arms. "Never! A western doctor? You do not love your son!"

"I do love him," he said gravely. "I love him enough to wish he were perfect."

Tears brimmed her eyes. "You blame me!"

"I blame no one, but I wish he were perfect," he replied.

"And I," she cried, the tears streaming down her cheeks, "I will not allow a foreign doctor to touch him! As he was born, let him remain. I love him. He is my son, if you will not have him for yours."

"Be quiet, Sunia," he commanded. "Do you accuse me of being less a parent than you? It is simply that if the child can be made perfect, he should be perfect."

She cried out at him again. "You think only of yourself! You are ashamed of your child! Oh, you must always have everything—so—so perfect!"

He was amazed. Never had he seen her in such anger as this. She could pout and be petulant but her tempers ended

in laughter. There was no laughter in her now. Her cheeks
were scarlet and her eyes black fire, blazing at him.

"Sunia!"

His voice was sharp but she would not allow him to speak.
She held the child clutched to her breast and went on talking
and sobbing at the same time.

"Are you truebone? I think not! Whoever heard of a tangban
who because his son has a small, small, small blemish, at the
edge of his ear lobe—no, you are soban—soban—soban!"

He reached for her and seizing her head in the curve of
his right elbow he held his hand over her mouth. She
struggled against him, the child in her arms, but he held her.
Suddenly he felt her sharp teeth bite into his palm.

"Ah-h!"

He uttered a cry and pulled back his hand. The palm was
bleeding. He stared at it, and then at her and the blood
dripped on the satin quilt.

She was aghast. "What have I done?" she whispered, and
putting down the child she took the end of her wide sleeve
and wrapped it around his hand and held it.

"Forgive me," she pleaded, and fondled his hand in her
breast, her eyes wet with tears.

He smiled, enjoying the power of forgiving her. "It is true,"
he said calmly, "quite true that Korean women are stubborn
and independent. I should have married a gentle woman of
China, or a submissive woman of Japan—"

"Ah, don't," she whispered. "Don't—don't reproach me—"

"Then what am I?" he demanded.

"You are truebone, tangban of the yangban class," she said
heartbroken.

"What else?"

"A scholar who has passed the imperial examinations."

"What else—what else?"

"My lord."

"True—and what else?"

He took his hand from her breast and with it lifted her
face to his.

"My love," she said at last.

"Ah ha," he said softly. "Now I know all that I am—yangban, tangban and your lord and your love. It is enough for any man."

He laid his cheek against hers for a long moment, and then released her, but she clung to him.

"You hand is still bleeding?"

He showed her his hand, palm up. The bleeding had stopped but the marks of her teeth were there, four small red dents. She cried out in remorse, and seizing his hand again in both hers, she pressed her lips against the marks.

At this moment the child, who had slept through all this, began suddenly to cry. She dropped the hand she held and took the child into her arms and put him to her breast and he suckled immediately and strongly.

She lifted her eyes to Il-han. He had stepped back from the bed and now stood looking at them.

"See him," she said proudly. "He is already hungry."

"I see him." Il-han replied. He was silent for an instant, his eyes on the child at the full smooth breast. "If I can foretell," he said, "I would foretell that this son of ours will never be hungry. He will always find his way to the source of satisfaction."

With this he left the room and returned to his library, looking neither to left nor right at the servants who paused in whatever they were doing to stand, heads downcast in respect, as he passed. Once in his library however he felt no mood for books. Unwittingly Sunia had touched upon an uneasy point in his own thinking. These times into which he had brought his sons to life were repeating in strange ways the age in which his own grandfather had lived. Now why should Sunia at this moment hark back to the age when civilian nobles had held power and the military nobles were subdued to them? Yangban they both were in the dual aristocracy of the ancient Koryo era, and in theory the two divisions of the nobility, civilian and military, tangban and soban, were equal, although in practice the civilian tangban, to which his family had always belonged, were in ascendancy, since the soban could not rise beyond the third level in government service.

Yet whenever the ruling house became corrupt the soban, the military, took power by force to end corruption. Thus it had been with the decadent king, Uijong, the eighteenth ruler in the age of Koryo. That king, aided and applauded by his civilian associates, had devoted his life to pleasure and foolish living, and on a certain night, while he was surrounded by women and drunken companions, the soban military leaders seized power and only after fierce struggle had the civilian tangban regained the throne. Now the times had circled again to the ancient struggle between civilian and soldier.

How had such confusion come about? Suddenly and to his own surprise he was angry with himself that he had not studied more faithfully the history of the past. Perhaps now, when he was a grown man and father of sons, he might begin to believe what his father had so often told him.

"My son, the past must be known before the present can be understood and the future faced with calm."

He had listened without hearing, weary of the past, sick of the adoration bestowed upon ancestors. Even now when his father met with his old friends they discussed nothing but the past.

"Do you remember—do you remember—" every sentence began with the worn phrase. "Do you remember the golden age of the Koryo? Do you remember how we fought off that Japanese devil, Hideyoshi, who invaded our shores—"

"Ah yes, but consider the Yi dynasty—"

Well, it was not too late to mend his ignorance. He would go to his father and listen to him now, and hear.

. . . "Sir, surely you will not walk?"

The servant, holding his black silk outer garment, put the question with mild anxiety.

"I will walk," Il-han said.

The man tied the wide bands of a black silk outer coat at his master's right shoulder.

"Shall I not follow you, sir?"

"It is not necessary," Il-han replied. "The day is fine, and I will tell my father of my second son's birth."

The man persisted. "Sir, it has already been announced by the red cards. We sent them yesterday."

"Be silent," Il-han commanded.

He spoke with unusual impatience and the servant, feeling his master's mood, bowed and followed behind him to the door. There he bowed again, and waiting for a few minutes, he followed at a distance without making himself known, while Il-han walked briskly through the cool spring air, warmed now by the sunshine.

The stone-paved main street was busy with white-robed men and women, the women moving freely among the men. Once in his youth he had visited Peking. His father had been appointed emissary that year to present tribute to the Chinese Emperor and he, a lad of fifteen, had begged to go with him. Roaming the broad and dusty streets of Peking, he had been surprised to see no women except a few beggars and market-women.

"Have the Chinese no women?" he had asked his father, one day.

"They have, of course," his father replied. "But their women are kept in the house where they belong. In our country"— he had paused here to laugh and shake his head ruefully— "the women are too much for us. Do you remember the old story of the henpecked husband?"

They had been seated at their meal in an inn, he and his father, he remembered, and his father told him the story of that magistrate in Korea of ancient times who suffered because his wife was master in the house. The magistrate called together all the men of his district and explained his predicament. Then he asked those men who also were *pan-kwan*, or henpecked, to move to the right side of the hall. All moved except one man, and he moved to the left. The others were surprised to see even one man at the left and the magistrate praised the man, declaring that he was the symbol of what men should be.

"Tell us," the magistrate commanded him, "how it is you have achieved such independence."

The man was a small timid fellow and, surprised, he could

only stammer a few words, explaining that he did not know
what all this was about and he was obeying his wife, who
bade him always to avoid crowds.

His father finished this tale and he looked at Il-han with
roguish eyes. "I," he declared, "have of course always been at
your mother's command. When worse comes to worst, I
remind myself that women still cannot do without men, since
it is we who hold the secret of creating children for them."

He had blushed at such frankness and his father had
laughed at him. He smiled now, remembering, and a tall country wife, carrying a jar of bean oil on her head, shouted at
him.

"Look where you walk, lord of creation!"

He stepped aside hastily to let her pass, and caught a sidewise glance of her dark eyes flashing at him with warning and
laughter, and he admired her profile. A handsome people,
these his people! He had seen Japanese merchants as well as
Chinese. The Japanese men were less tall than his countrymen, and the Chinese men were less fair of skin, their hair
blacker and more wiry stiff. A noble people, these his people,
and what ill fortune that they were contained within this
narrow strip of mountainous land coveted by others! If they
could but be left alone in peace, he and his people, to dream
their dreams, make their music, write their poems, paint their
picture scrolls! Impossible, now that the surrounding hungry
nations were licking their chops, impossible now that the
civilian tangban had grown decadent and the rebellious soban
again were threatening from beneath!

He paused at the south gate, whose name was the Gate of
High Ceremony, and inquired of the guard to say at what hour
the sun would set, for then the gate would be locked and
no one, except on official business, could come in or go out.

The guard, a tall man with a cast in his right eye, squinted
at the western sky and made a guess.

"Where do you go, master?" he asked.

"I go to see my father," Il-han replied.

The guard recognized him for a Kim, as who did not, and

he lowered his spear and spoke with respect. "You will have time to drink two bowls of tea with your honored one."

"My thanks," Il-han said.

When he had passed through the vast gate he paused, as he always did, to look back. This gate was one of eight gates to the city, any of which the people might use for coming and going except for the north gate, which was kept locked, for it was the way of escape for the King if there were war, and the southwest gate, which was for criminals on their way to execution outside the city wall. The southwest gate was known also as the Water Mouth Gate because the river flowed through there. It was also the gate used for the dead on their way to burial. All dead must pass through the gate, except dead kings, who could pass through other gates. The gate was built of wood and painted with colors of red and blue and green and gold. It sat high on the great stone wall and there were two stories, the first one wider than the second, and in the wooden wall of the second story were holes through which arrows could be shot. The roof was tile and the corners were lifted as are the palace roofs and gates of Peking—the better, Il-han had been told as a child, to catch the devils who slide down roofs in play and then falling to the ground are mischievous and enter houses to annoy good folk and bring trouble to them.

Once when he was thirteen years old he had climbed the tower and he found, cut deep into the wood, the letters of an ancient name. It was the name of a boy prince, the second son of the ancient dynasty of Yi who, like all boys, desired to leave his name carved forever on some smooth surface. He remembered that he would like to have carved his own name under that of the prince, but some reluctance had held him back and when he looked up he faced a soldier guard, and he had run away from those hostile soban eyes. He turned away from the memory, and faced the mountains, and soberly he walked the dusty cobbled road while behind him, afar off, his servant followed in secret. The city sat in a valley two or three miles across, the valley encircled by mountains. Here in this city was the center of his country, the heart of his nation, enclosed by the craggy and pinnacled heights of bare rock. Yonder, highest of all, was the Triple Peak, and upon its triad crests the snow still clung in long white streaks. South Mountain, North Mountain, and the city wall wound in and out among the folds of these mountains, beginning at the west gate, which was called the Gate of Amiability—fitting enough, this name, for the Chinese, powerful yet amiable, came from the west —and curving to the east, to the Gate of Elevated Humanity, how wryly named, for out of the east had come from Japan, three hundred years ago, that villain Hideyoshi, that peasant, squat and brutish.

He walked slowly to enjoy the countryside now in the fullness of spring. Along the grassy footpaths between the fields, women and children were digging wild fresh greens for which they hungered after the long winter when vegetables were only dried and pickled. Beyond the fields the gray-flanked mountains were red with clustering azaleas. Even on the mountains there were people searching for fresh foods, the roots of bell flowers to be scraped and pounded and boiled, and then eaten with soy sauce and sesame seed, the delicate lace of wild white clematis and wild spirea, white dandelions, sour dock leaves, wild chrysanthemum tops, all savory with rice or for soups. How well he remembered his mother and her household tricks! Sunia was a clever housekeeper, but his mother had been the old-fashioned woman, unwilling to buy so much as a square of fresh bean curd. He had hung about her as a child, for where she was became the center of activity, and he dabbled his childish hands in the soybeans put to soak overnight in cold water and he helped her turn the mill to crush them in the morning and to strain it and boil it and then curdle it with wet salt to be drained and cut into soft white blocks of bean curd. He had described the process to Sunia, but Sunia had cried out willfully that it was enough to make kimchee at home nowadays and he must let her buy their bean curd.

"Nevertheless," he protested, "homemade is the best And my mother's soy sauce—"

Ah, that soy sauce! The crisp spring air made him hungry

to think of it. His mother boiled the soybeans until they were mush, and then pounded them in the old mortar made of a hollowed tree trunk, the pestle a pole with a solid wooden ball at each end so that either end could be used. Then she rolled the beans into balls and netted them into straw ropes and hung them on the kitchen ceiling. On a spring day such as this she fetched them down again and cut them into pieces and soaked them in water spiced with hot red peppers. He would never taste such homemade foods again. His mother had died in the first year of his marriage, and she had not seen her first grandson. It was her dying cry.

"I shall not see my grandson!"

She had tried to stay alive, but death overcame her. Thinking of her, he walked on soberly, forgetting the bright day and the fair countryside, and the afternoon was well along by the time he passed over a bridge that spanned a small river near his father's house. Along the banks the land women knelt on the earth and pounded the white garments on flat stones, their paddles sounding in crisp rhythm through the pellucid air. The country scene, dear and familiar, the atmosphere of peace, brought an ache to his heart. How long, how long could life remain unchanged?

His father put down his brush pen as Il-han entered. His son had been announced, but the elder did not lift his head until he saw the shadow across the low table upon which he wrote. Il-han then made the proper obeisance, which his father acknowledged by inclining his head and pointing to a cushion on the floor. Upon this cushion Il-han seated himself, a servant taking his outer coat from him.

The elder lifted his frosty white eyebrows at his son. "How is it that you are here?" he inquired. "Are you not supposed to be in attendance at court?"

"Father," Il-han said, "I have myself come to tell you that your second grandson is healthy and already suckling."

"Good news, good news!" the old man cried The wrinkles in his withered face turned upward in smiles and a small gray beard trembled on his chin.

"Yes," Il-han went on. "He was born before noon yesterday, as you know, and he is well shaped and strong, slightly smaller than the elder boy, but perfectly shaped. That is to say . . ."

He paused, remembering the child's ear.

His father waited. "Well?" he inquired at last.

"His left ear is not perfect," Il-han said. "A small defect but—"

"No Kim has ever had a defect," the old man said positively. "It must be the Pak blood from your wife's family."

Il-han wished to change the subject. He had married somewhat against his father's wish, who privately preferred the Yi family to the Pak, but no Yi daughter was of the proper age at the time. His father put up his hand to silence him, and went on.

"For example," he said, pulling at his scanty beard, "I have never heard of a Yi with a defect. High intelligence combined with great physical beauty—these are the attributes of Yi, even to this present day. Nor were they scholars only. This floor, for example"—he struck the floor at his side with his knuckles—"this ondul floor, designed not merely to walk upon, or to sit upon, but warm—"

Il-han listened patiently to what he had heard many times before. His father spoke of the inventions of the Yi dynasty; for example, the ondul floor, now to be found in any house, was laid a foot above the level of the adjoining room which was always the kitchen. From the kitchen fireplace five flues ran through the wall to this ondul room. The flues were made of low walls of rock and sealing clay, across which were laid slabs of rock. These rocks were laid over again with clay and then covered with a layer of sand and lime and over which more cement was spread. Over this again was laid a layer of paper, the last layer very strong and lasting, the paper, called *jangpan*, being made from mulberry wood. A polish made of ground soya beans and liquid cow dung was spread over the jangpan and dried, and the floor was then a light yellow color, of high polish, smooth and easy to clean.

When his father had finished admiring the ondul floor, he

would then speak of Admiral Yi's turtle ships with which he had driven off Hideyoshi. Il-han knew it would come and so it did, and then the loving learned discourse on his country's history. Il-han recognized the elder's mood. A great actor lost to the theatre! The familiar glaze would come over his father's eyes as he spoke of the past, and he would sit in a pose, motionless for a long moment. Then he would straighten himself, his thin face assuming the mask of nobility and hauteur, and he would lift his right arm as though he bore a weapon, and thus he would speak on. As he dwelt on the past even the voice was changed. A young man's voice came from the sinewy throat. So it continued through half the afternoon, until at last they were back to Admiral Yi and how he saved Korea from Japan.

"We were not conquered," his father concluded. "Kim or Yi, we shall never be conquered."

He struck the polished surface of the low table with his clenched fists.

"Then you are on the side of the soban?" Il-han inquired with mischievous intent.

The old man laughed. "You are too sly, you young men! No—no—I am a scholar and a tangban and therefore a man of peace. I learned at my mother's knee—" Here his father closed his eyes and recited slowly an ancient poem:

> *The wind has no hands but it shakes all the trees.*
> *The moon has no feet but it travels across the sky.*

"Then we need not fear the soban now?" Il-han asked.

His father pursed his lips. "I did not say that! The soban are not scholars, but not every man can be a scholar. We need both. It takes something in here to understand the books and the arts. The soban do not have it."

He tapped his high forehead and fell silent and in the silence, after so much talk, he closed his eyes to signify he had had enough of his son. Seeing his father's head sink upon his breast, Il-han rose and went quietly away.

And none too soon, he discovered when he left the house,

for as he approached the city gates in the twilight an hour later, he saw a cluster of men there, brawling and shouting. He went steadily forward and as he neared the gate he saw twenty or thirty soban beating upon the gate with staves and spears.

They did not notice when he came up to them, so engrossed were they in their determination to break down the gate, a vain hope, for the gate was heavy and bound with iron and barred inside with a length of iron thicker than a man's arm.

He shouted at them, "Brothers, what are you doing?"

They stopped then and turned to stare at him. A leader stepped out from among them. "That demon of a guard saw us coming and barred the gate against us, although the sun has not set."

They were pushing about him now, and Il-han felt their hot angry eyes upon him like flames.

"Tangban," he heard voices mutter. "Tangban—tangban—"

"You are right. The gate is shut too early," he said calmly. "I shall report the matter to the palace."

Silence fell upon them for an instant. Then the leader spoke in a voice yet more rough.

"We need no tangban help! We smash the gate down!"

They crowded against the gate again and jostled Il-han into their midst and he smelled for the first time in his life the sweat and the stink of male animal flesh. A shiver of fear, insensate and cold, ran through his veins. At this moment his servant pressed through the crowd, and Il-han knew that the man had disobeyed him and had followed him all the way, and he could only be glad.

"Master," the servant said, "I know the guard at the gate. I will knock at the wicket and he will let me through when he knows you are here."

So saying, he went to a small wicket gate at the side and made a special sound upon it with a stone that he picked up from the road. The gate opened a small space and the servant went in. A moment later the great gate itself opened suddenly and the soldiers fell in through it in a heap. While they were gathering themselves from the dust, Il-han passed by without their notice and went his way to his home, the servant following again in silence.

Spring moved gently toward summer, Sunia rose from the bed of childbirth and took her place again in the household. All went well. Her breasts were filled with milk and the child thrived. Her elder son, now that his mother was restored to him, was in better mood and with him clinging to her hand one fine morning, she sauntered into the garden of mulberry trees. The leaves were full and green, yet tender, and it was to discover their ripeness for the silkworms that she had left the house. Silkworms were only her pleasure, for the work of silk-making was done outside the city on the family lands and by the land people. Yet ever since she was a child and in the care of her old nurse, she had loved the art of making silk, from the moment when the web of tiny eggs, no bigger than the dots of a pointed brush on a paper card, were hatched in the warm silkworm house to the last moment when the silk lay in rich folds over her arms. Thus, though the weaving was done in the country, she kept a small loom of her own in a service house here in the compound, and with her women she performed the ceremony each year of making silk. It was more than a pleasure. It was also a duty. Even the Queen at this season must cultivate silkworms and do her share of spinning, while the King must till a rice paddy.

On this morning, bright and calm, she walked under the mulberry trees with her son, and she felt of the leaves and tested them on her tongue for their taste. They were not yet strong or bitter, but no time must be wasted.

"We must set the silkworm eggs today, my princeling," she told her son, and with him she went to the service house where the eggs had been kept on ice during the winter and through early spring so that they would not hatch before the mulberry leaves were ready. Now she bade her women prepare the large baskets for the eggs, and they made them-

selves busy, the little boy running between the women here
and there and everywhere at once in his excitement.

"I want the worms to come out now," he cried impatiently.

Sunia laughed. "They are only eggs! We must let them feel
the warmth and then the worm will begin to grow and when
the shells are too small for them, they will come out."

After a few days of such warmth, the child asking a
hundred times a day, they did come out, thousands of small
creatures, each no more than the eighth of an inch in length,
and no thicker than a silken thread, and the women brushed
them off gently upon the finely cut leaves of the mulberry
trees which now covered the bottom of the baskets. For three
days and three nights the women fed the small creatures every
three hours, and in the night again and again Sunia arose
from her wide bed, while Il-han lay sleeping, and walked
softly across the moonlit courtyards to see how her silkworms
did. When the three days were passed, the silkworms stopped
eating and prepared for their first rest. Now they spun out
of themselves silk threads, as fine as hairs, and they fastened
themselves upon the mulberry leaves, except for their heads
which they held erect. Slowly they changed their color.

"See," Sunia said to her elder son, "the silkworms are
putting on their sleeping robes."

Heads up, the silkworms slept for a day or two, while
Sunia waited with her son.

"What do they do next, these silkworms?" the child asked.

He had refused to study or to stay with his tutor during
these days, for he could think of nothing except the silkworms and what they did. They had become creatures of
magic to him, fey and enchanting, as indeed they were to
Sunia herself, for she could scarcely stay by her infant long
enough to suckle him, and she hurried the child to finish without dawdling so that she could thrust him into a servingwoman's arms and return to the service house.

"Now," she replied to her son, "the silkworms must push
off their old skins, for these skins have grown too small and
they are making new ones while they sleep."

"Shall I push off my skin one day?" the child asked in alarm.

Sunia laughed. "No, for your skin is made to stretch."

At this moment she heard Il-han's step, for though silkworms are women's business and he pretended no interest in them, yet he came a few times to see how they did and to observe the life process of which they are the symbol. He spoke now to answer his son's question.

"You will grow too big for your skin, too," he told his son, "and skin after skin you will cast aside, but you will not know it. Without knowing, you will change into someone tall and strong and you will grow hairs on your face and your body. Then you will be a man, inside and out."

The child listened, and his mouth trembled and turned down ready to weep.

"Why must I grow hair on my face and on my body?" he asked in a small voice.

"You scare him," Sunia cried and she gathered the child into her arms. "Don't cry, my little—you will like being a man some day. It is beautiful to be a man and strong and young and ready to make children of your own."

The child stopped his tears at the wonder of this new thought. "Who will be the mother?" he inquired.

"We will find her for you," Sunia said, and over the child's head she met Il-han's eyes upon her with the look that she loved.

Four times the silkworms ate until their skins grew too small and four times they slept and shed those skins, eating at last so heartily of the mulberry leaves that the trees were stripped and the worms themselves so large that the champing of their jaws could be heard even in the courtyard outside as they chewed upon the leaves. Meanwhile no man or woman was allowed to smoke a pipe of tobacco near the silkworm house, for such smoke kills the worms.

All this time Sunia hovered over her silkworms. "Oh, you special creatures," she murmured, in endearment.

At last they became a silvery white, a clear pure color, and this meant that they were ready to spin their cocoons and change to moths. The women prepared twirls of straw rice for the spinning and the spinners began their work, weaving their heads this way and that as they fastened a few threads of the silk to certain points of guidance, and this was the task of shaping the cocoons. They wove their heads this way and that inside the cocoon shape until it was a nest of silk, firm and soft, and each cocoon was made of a filament many thousands of feet in length and each worm became a chrysalid. Now was the time to choose the best and biggest of cocoons to make next year's seed, and these cocoons were not used for silk but, as chrysalids became moths, they were allowed to cut their way through and lay eggs upon paper cards, each moth laying four hundred eggs before she died. But the other cocoons were dropped into boiling water before the chrysalids were moths, and the cocoons were kept in water, boiling hot, so that the gum which held the filaments together could be melted and the filaments reeled off and spun into thread.

Yet Sunia did not allow these broken cocoons to be wasted either. She bade the women boil them, too, and remove the empty chrysalid skins. When this was done, the women pulled the cocoons into small flat mats of silk. These were dried and used to quilt the linings of winter garments and make them soft and warm. In such ways Sunia tended her household and faithfully she kept the old customs and the family lived as though peace were sure and life eternal, and Il-han watched her as she moved about his house, the wife he loved and mother to them all. He had no heart to tell her of the world outside her house until he must.

. . . Thus the spring passed in one glorious day after another. The rain fell in good season. The ancient land grew fresh and green and gay with flowers and the people prepared for Tano, the spring festival which falls on the fifth day of the fifth lunar month. True, Il-han was put to much discomfort during the festival, for Sunia was a zealous housekeeper and this festival was the time, by custom, for housecleaning and mending and renewing after winter. The paper on lattice walls must be torn off and fresh paper pasted on, and even the paper covers of the ondul floors must be changed.

"You must allow me my library," Il-han said every year and against the complaints of her women, Sunia obeyed him because she loved him and could refuse him nothing.

"We will watch for a day when he is summoned to court," she told her women, "and then we will steal into his library and work like magicians and clean everything before he comes back."

This was her usual ruse, and meanwhile Il-han enclosed himself among his books while around him the household was in a happy confusion. When the rooms were cleaned and the courtyards swept, the women washed their clothes and then themselves and the children. This was the season, too, when they gave special heed to their hair after the winter, and into the basins they poured the juice of changpo grass, which cleanses and leaves a fragrance exceedingly pleasant and rare, and as they dried the long thick locks they thrust leaves of the grass into their hair and on both sides of their ears. Women less learned than Sunia believed that the changpo grass kept away the diseases which the heat of summer brings, but she declared herself against such superstitions because Il-han would not allow them, although in her heart she did not know what she believed.

The time of the Tano festival was a time of joy and freedom, a festival of spring celebrated for thousands of years and long before the beginning of written history, and Sunia, though a wife and mother, had kept the girl alive in herself. Thus during the festival she joined in the sport of swinging, which belonged to the day. Il-han, knowing that she loved the sport, ordered the servingmen to hang ropes as usual to make a swing from the branch of a great date tree in the eastern courtyard. There he watched Sunia and her women swinging and she went higher than any of the women, until his heart stopped to see her high in the air, her red skirt flying and her hair, freshly washed, loosening from its braids. What if one day the rope broke and he saw her lying broken on the ground? But the rope had never broken and he tried to believe it never would.

When the festival was over, nevertheless, he ordered the

swing taken down and in the night he clasped her close again and again, with renewed passion until she could not bear it, dearly as she loved him, and she cried out at last against his arms so tightly holding her that she felt imprisoned, though by love.

"Let me breathe!" she cried.

He loosed her, but only a little, and she lay in his arms.

"Why are you so silent now?" she asked at last. "Did I offend you?"

"No," he said. "How could you offend me? I am oppressed by happiness—our happiness."

"Oppressed?" She echoed the word, uncomprehending.

"How can it last?" he replied.

"It will last," she said joyously, "it will last until we die."

Why did she speak of death? It was on his tongue to cry out against the thought that they could die, but he kept silent. Death was what he feared, not the sweet and quiet end of a long life, but sudden death outside their door, death waiting and violent. Yet the difference between Il-han and Sunia was only the bottomless difference between man and woman over which no bridge is ever built nor ever can be. Il-han's life was centered outside his house, and what went on within the compound walls was the periphery. Joyous or troublesome alike, the household life was diversion from his mainstream. He trusted Sunia with all that went on inside the walls, and when she complained that he did not listen to what she told him at the end of a day, he smiled.

"I know that you do all things well," he said.

She would not accept this smooth reply.

"What have you to think of, if not of us?" she demanded.

"Is night the suitable time in which to inquire of so large a matter?" he countered, and he made love to her so that he could divert her and be diverted.

Somehow the summer slipped past, the days hot, the nights cool, and Il-han was so perturbed and puzzled by the tangled affairs of the times that he did not count the days or the months. One morning, waking late and alone in their bedroom, he smelled the sharp autumn fragrance of cabbage freshly cut. Could it be already time again to make kimchee for the winter? He rose and looked out of the window. Yes, there in the courtyard were piles of celery cabbages, brought in from the farm, doubtless, the day before. Two serving-women were washing the cabbages in tubs of salted water and two more were brushing long white radishes clean of earth while still two others were chopping both cabbages and radishes into fine pieces. At a table set outdoors on this fine clear morning Sunia, wrapped in a blue apron, was mixing the spices. Hot red peppers, ground fresh ginger, onions, garlic, and ground cooked beef she was mixing to-gether, exactly to his taste and according to the Kim family recipe. He knew, for in the first year of their marriage she had made Pak kimchee, so bland a mixture that he had re-belled against it. He had laid down his chopsticks when he tasted it for the first time.

"You must invite my mother to teach you how to make kimchee," he told Sunia.

Her eyes had sparkled with sudden anger. "I will not eat Kim kimchee! It burns the skin from my tongue."

"Keep this Pak stuff for yourself," he had retorted. "I will ask my mother to give me enough kimchee for myself."

She had shown no signs of yielding but the next year, he had noticed, she made the kimchee according to Kim recipe. Now, by habit, each year he inspected the kimchee and tasted the first morsel. He smiled and yawned to wake himself and then began to wash himself and to prepare for the day. When he was ready, he sauntered into the courtyard and it was here that Sunia continued again her gentle accusations that he was always busy and apart from family life. The women had fallen silent when he appeared and they did not look up or seem to listen while their master and mistress talked, after he had tasted the kimchee and approved it.

"For an example, this morning," Sunia said, her eyes upon the thin sharp knife with which she chopped the spices, "where do you go now? Day after day you leave after the morning meal and then we see you no more until twilight.

Yet you never tell me where you have been or where you will go again tomorrow."

"I will tell you everything when I come home tonight," he said. "Only give me my breakfast now and let me go."

Something in the abruptness of his voice made her obedient. She summoned a woman to finish her task and washed her hands and followed him into the house. In usual silence Il-han ate his morning meal of soup and rice and salted foods, and Sunia kept the children away from him, the elder son given to his tutor, and the younger, now beginning to creep, to a wet nurse. She suckled her children until they were six months old and past the first dangers of life and then she gave them to a wet nurse, a healthy countrywoman, to suckle until they were three years old and able to eat all foods.

This morning she served Il-han alone and when he had eaten she ate her own breakfast quietly, glancing at him now and then.

"You are losing flesh," she said at last. "Is there some private unhappiness in you?"

"No unhappiness concerning you," he said.

He wiped his mouth on a soft paper napkin and rose from the floor cushion and she ran to fetch his outer coat and thus, with a warm exchange of looks, his kind, hers anxious, they parted. He dared not tell her what lay upon his heart and mind. His memorial which he had begun in the spring and then put aside as better left unsaid was now finished and in the Queen's hands, for as he had watched the tide of affairs sweep on he could keep silent no longer. He was now summoned by the Queen to come alone to her palace. At the same time the King had sent a summons to his father. Until now father and son had gone together in obedience to royal command. Did this separation signify a new difference between King and Queen? He did not know and he could only obey.

He left his house, therefore, dressed in his usual street garments, his robes whiter than snow, his tall black hat of stiff horsehair gauze tied under his chin. On so fine a morning it was his pleasure to walk, and he did so with the measured speed befitting a gentleman and a scholar. Many recognized him and gave him respectful greeting, and because of his height and appearance the people parted to give him room, not stopping to show servility or fear. Indeed they had no fear. Accustomed as they were to dangers and distress, since the gods had given them a land which surrounding countries envied and longed to possess, the people were calm but firm in purpose and they were not afraid. They gave their greetings and went about their business while Il-han went on his.

His father was wont to meet him at the palace. When he entered the gate, however, the guard, peering through to see who stood there, opened the gate hastily and closed it at once.

"Is my father here?" Il-han inquired.

"Sir, he is already with the King and has been since dawn," the guard replied, "but I have orders from the Queen that you are to go alone to her palace in the Secret Garden for audience. Meanwhile your father says I am to tell you that if his audience with the King ends first, he will await you here. If yours ends first, you are to wait."

Il-han hesitated. It puzzled him that the Queen should send for him privately in such fashion, and what would he say to his father, or even later to the King? Nothing is hidden in palace or hovel and all would know that his father was already in audience with the King while he was only now waiting upon the Queen, an inexplicable division. Yet what could he do but continue to obey the royal command? He followed the guard through the palace grounds without further speech.

It was the season of chrysanthemums, and everywhere the noble flowers lifted their brilliant heads. In the Secret Garden the path was lined with potted chrysanthemums in waves and clouds of color, and thus escorted he came to the steep stone steps which led to the high terrace before the palace. At the carved and painted doorway of this palace he waited until the gate guard announced his presence to a palace guard, who announced it in turn to a palace steward. Then the doors opened and he was ushered into the large waiting room he knew well from other times when he, but always with his father, had been summoned by the Queen. Low tables of fine wooden chests bound in brass and cushioned floor seats gave the room comfort. Upon the wall opposite the door were scrolls painted by ancient artists, and the corners of the room were banked with rare and beautiful chrysanthemums in porcelain pots.

"Sir, be seated," the steward said. "The Queen is finishing her breakfast and her women are waiting to put on her outer robes. She will receive you in the great hall as usual."

Il-han sat down on a floor seat and gave thanks for the tea which the steward poured from a pottery teapot into a fine silver bowl. The tea was an infusion of the best Chinese tea, the tender new leaves of spring unscented by jasmine or alien flowers, and he drank it with pleasure and slowly. In a few minutes the steward entered.

"The Queen," he said in solemn voice.

Il-han rose and followed the man into the next hall, a vast room bare of furniture except for the throne set upon a dais at the west wall, the hall itself facing south. No one was there, but he knew the custom and he stood in respectful waiting, his head bowed, and his eyes fixed upon the floor.

He had not long to wait. In less time than he could have counted to a hundred, the curtains at the north wall were put aside and the Queen entered. He saw the edge of her crimson robes moving about her feet as she walked to her throne, and lifting his eyes no further until she gave permission, he bowed low three times in silence.

It was for the Queen to speak first and she did so, and continued thus after suitable greeting.

"I have received your memorial," she said, "and doubtless you think it strange that I have sent for you apart from your father. But you are so dutiful a son that if the two of you come together, as you have always in the past, whether I am with the King or alone, your father speaks and you keep silent or you defer to what he says, and do not speak your own thoughts."

Her voice was fresh and clear and young. He did not reply, perceiving that she would speak on, and thus she continued.

"I have read many times your memorial. Why did you send it privately?"

At this word "privately" he felt hot blood rise up from his breast to his neck and even to his ears, and he cursed the trick his blood could play on him to turn his ears scarlet.

The Queen's quick eyes, all observing, now noticed his confusion. "Do you hear what I ask, you with the two red ears?"

She laughed and it was the first time he had ever heard that gay laughter. He dared not smile or reply and he felt his ears hotter than ever. In his confusion he let his eyes move toward her and saw the tips of her silver shoes beneath the crimson satin of her full skirts. Small silver shoes, so strangely like those of Turkish women. Where had they come from in the beginning? But who knew the wellsprings of his people? In that long struggle, covering how many centuries could not be known, the tribes of Central Asia who were his ancestors had mingled with others, and now these little silver shoes of a Korean queen were a lost symbol of woman's grace.

"And dare you dream in my presence?" the Queen now inquired. Her voice was playful but she put an edge into the words.

He lifted his head, startled, and then blushed anew because inadvertently he had seen her face.

"You need not turn so red," the Queen said. "I am old enough to be looked at without fear by a young man."

"Forgive me, Majesty," Il-han said. He fixed his eyes on her rounded firm chin and the royal lips went on speaking softly but with definition in shape and sound.

"Will you answer my question?"

"Majesty," he replied, and because he was angry with himself for his confusion in her presence, and especially for his wayward thoughts concerning her shoes, he made his voice low and stern. "I sent the memorial to you because I know your loyalty to China."

He needed not to say what they both knew too well, that he came to her because the King was torn between his father and her. This was to say the King was torn between the Regent's desire to balance one nation against another and so gain precarious independence for Korea, and the Queen's resolute faith in China. Therefore he continued to skirt direct speech.

"You have reason, Majesty, for your faith. Through centuries China has avoided anything that can alienate our people. But now when we must prevent Japan from landing soldiers on our soil can the Empress save us when it may be she cannot even save her own people? Remember the opium wars which China always lost to England, who is friendly to Japan, Majesty, and who will always take Japan's part. And remember that France has cut a huge slice from the Chinese melon and claimed it for her own—Indo-China, Majesty! And China cannot prevent it or take it back again."

Now the silver shoe on the imperial right foot began to tap impatiently.

"France! What is it? We have only seen French priests, bearing in one hand a cross, in the other a sword! I have heard that they are winebibbers, but they make their wine of grapes, not rice."

"I still regret, Majesty, that our people massacred the French Christians," Il-han said, "and even more, that in our anger we attacked the American merchant ship, the *General Sherman*. And the worst folly was that we killed the American crew."

The Queen waved this off with her right hand. "What right had an American merchant ship in the inner waters of the Taedong River, near so great a ctiy as Pyongyang? Are there Korean ships in the rivers of—of—of—what are some of the American rivers?"

"Majesty, I do not know," Il-han replied.

"You see," the Queen cried in triumph. "We do not so much as know the names of their rivers, much less sail our

ships on foreign waters! I see no difference in these wild
western peoples, and as for the Americans, who knows what
they are? A mongrel people, I am told, made up of the cast-
offs, the renegades, the rebels, the younger sons, the landless
and the homeless of other western nations!"

He could wait no longer. "Majesty, they are our only hope,
nevertheless. America alone has no dreams of empire. With
her vast territories it may be she has no need to dream
and so can be our friend."

"You hurry me," the Queen complained, "and I am not to
be hurried."

"Forgive me, Majesty," Il-han said.

His eyes caught sight now of her hands, elegant and restless upon her silken lap, and involuntarily he lifted his eyes
and saw her face, this time all in a glance, the dark eyes large
and glorious in the light of her intelligence, the black brows
straight and clear, the brilliant white of her smooth skin, the
red of lip and rose of cheek. He looked quickly at the floor.
If she noticed, she did not say so, and she went on musingly
and as though to convince herself.

"These western nations—have they anywhere done justly to
other peoples? Their pretense is trade and religion but their
true purpose is to annex our land. No, I will have none of
these western nations!"

Il-han continued in steady patience. "I will remind you,
Majesty, that when the diplomatic mission from Japan returned only recently from the western countries they reported
to their Emperor that these great new western nations would
not look with favor on a military coup in Korea by General
Saigo. We were saved by the western nations, Majesty."

He had gone too far. The Queen rose, took three steps
forward, drew a closed fan from her sleeve and struck twice,
once on his right cheek and once on his left, as he knelt before her.

"Dare to speak!" she cried. "Was it not six years ago—
only six, it is to remind you—that the Empress Tzu-hsi, my
friend, forced Japan to make treaty with us and recognize us

as equal with Japan? It is China, not the western nations, who saved us!"

Il-han could bear it no longer. He forget that she was the Queen and no simple woman. He lifted his head and glared at her and he lifted his voice and shouted at her until his voice roared into the beams of the palace roof.

"That Treaty of Amity? Treaty of Amity—a joke! When the ambassador came with four hundred armed men to convince us! Japan was given special privileges here on our soil, and how can we depend now on China, when Japan has invaded Formosa, and even the Ryukyu Islands?"

The Queen shrieked in return. "Will you not understand? Small as we are, and weak in numbers, we can be attacked— attacked, absorbed—there are a hundred ways, if China is not our suzerain! We can only live in freedom and independence if we are in friendship with a powerful nation, and pray heaven it will never be Russia or Japan—no, nor America!—and therefore it must be China!"

At this Il-han was speechless and in his anger he did what no man had ever done before. He left the truebone royal presence without permission and turning his back on the Queen, he strode out of the palace, his head high and heart beating fit to burst.

. . . His father was waiting for him in the entrance hall at the gate of the palace. They walked out together, and he waited for his father to speak. How could he say, "The Queen wished to speak to me alone"? But his father was complacent. He walked with measured steps, his toes turned outward as an old scholar walks, a smile on his face.

Seeing that his father was not disposed to speech, Il-han kept silent, too. The day was fine and the people on the streets were enjoying the mildness of the autumn. Each such day was precious, for there could not be many now before the snows of winter fell. Over the low walls of the courtyards between the houses, or in front of gateways, the persimmon trees were bright with their golden fruit, and piles of persimmons were heaped on the ground, ready for market. Children ate until they were stuffed, their cheeks sticky with the sweet juice, and for once no one reproved them. It was impossible, moreover, to speak of important matters in these crowds of people.

"I will come to your house now and visit my grandsons," his father said.

It was not usual for father and son to live separately, but Il-han lived in the Kim house in the city, that he might be near the palace, and his father preferred to live outside the city in the ancestral country home of the Kim clan. Here he could indulge his love for meeting his friends and making poems, subject only to the occasional summons from the royal family.

"I have only one grievance against your father," his dying mother had once told Il-han. "He has never visited other women nor does he gamble, but he cannot live without his friends."

It was true that these friends, themselves idle gentlemen and poetasters, gathered every day in his father's house to remember together the glories of ancient Korea, to recount the events of her heroes, to recall how even the civilizing influence of Buddhism reached Japan only through Korea, to repeat that sundry monuments of art and culture now in Japan had been stolen from Korea—was not the beautiful long-faced image of the Kwan Yin in Nara sculptured in Korea, although what Japanese would acknowledge it! And from such raptures came poems, many poems, none of them, Il-han thought bitterly, of the slightest significance for these dangerous busy times.

Yet when he had complained in private to Sunia, she refused to agree with him.

"Not so," she declared. "We must be reminded of these past glories, so that we know how worthy of love our country is and how noble our people are."

He walked in silence with his father now along the stone-paved street until they entered the gate of Il-han's home and there his father led the way to the main room while Il-han bade a servant bring the children to see their grandfather. "And invite their mother, also," he called after the servant.

His father sat himself down on a floor cushion and a maid-servant bustled in with tea and small cakes, and Il-han sat in the lower place, as a son should. In a few minutes Sunia entered with the children, the elder clinging to her hand and the younger in the arms of his nurse. She made the proper obeisance and watched while the elder son made his and the grandfather looked on with pride and dignity.

"Is it not time," he said, "to set up a proper name for my elder grandson?"

"Will you choose a name, Most Honored?" Sunia said.

She sank gracefully to a floor cushion, well aware that in an ordinary household she would not have appeared so easily before her husband's father, although it was true that here women were proud and never knelt before their husbands as women in Japan did, or had their feet bound small as Chinese women did, or their waists boxed in, as it was said that western women did. No, here husband and wife were equal in their places, nor were mothers browbeaten by their grown sons. In the royal palace, were the King to die and leave the heir too young to rule, the Queen Dowager ruled until the heir attained majority. Il-han, too, had accustomed Sunia to freedom, partly because he gave her respect as well as love and partly because he had heard that western women came and went as they wished. True, his mother, now dead, had talked much of the good and ancient times when women were neither seen nor heard, and he said often that she longed for the old custom of curfew when only at a certain hour could women walk freely through the streets. So severe was the custom in those days that if a man stole a secret look at the woman his head was cut off.

"And would you be willing to have my head cut off if I stole a look at Sunia?" Il-han had once inquired.

"I would have taught you better," his doughty mother had retorted.

Sunia kept her own modest ways, however, and now in the presence of her husband and his father she held her head down and did not look up to either face. Meanwhile the grandfather considered the name he would choose.

"My elder grandson," he said, at last, "is no usual child. He has a high spirit and a quick mind. These are signs of youth, but in him they are more. They are the qualities of his nature. Moreover, he was born in the spring. Therefore I will choose for him the name of Yul-chun, or Spring-of-the-Year."

Il-han and Sunia exchanged a look, each making sure of the other's approval, and then Il-han expressed what both felt.

"The name is suitable, Father, and we thank you."

All would have gone well except that at this moment the newly named child saw a small mouse under a low table beside which his grandfather sat. Winter was near and the crickets, the spiders and mice crept into the house, seeking escape from the coming cold. Crickets and spiders were harmless but mice were dangerous, for people believed that if girl children played with mice they would never be able to cook rice properly. The women servants therefore always chased mice away, and the little boy, seeing the mouse as courageous as a lion under the table beside his grandfather, gave a loud scream and pointed at the creature with his tiny forefinger. What could they think except that he was pointing at his grandfather with a look of terror on his face?

The grandfather was dismayed, and Il-han was ashamed. "Remove the child," he said sternly.

The child, however, tore himself free of his mother and ran to the table to peer under it. At this the mouse crept out, to the horror of the nurse who held the younger child. She in turn screamed and hurried from the room with the child, and even Sunia rose and stepped back. Seeing the fray, Il-han himself rose and caught the shivering creature in his cupped hands, and going to the door that led into the garden he loosed it there. Though he was no Buddhist, yet so deeply had Buddhist learning permeated his mind and heart that he could not kill any living creature. Even a fly he brushed away from his face rather than kill it and he blew upon a teasing mosquito to move it away.

When all this noise was over he threw a commanding look at Sunia and she caught its meaning and left the room with the elder child in her arms. The two men were then alone and after a moment of quiet, Il-han's father made an observation.

"It is a strange truth," he said, "that where women and children are, there is always commotion. Nothing useful can be done until they are removed."

When this was said, he then went on to important matters.

"The King," he said, "is determined not to carry on the policies of the Regent now in retirement. Yet he remembers that the Regent is his father, and he does not wish to proceed too rapidly to make treaties with western peoples. Now he is in confusion because the military premier of China wishes us to make a treaty with that new foreign power the United States in North America. Have we not seen the evils of such treaties? Because we made even that one treaty with Japan, six years ago, her greedy soldiers invaded the island of Formosa and attacked the Ryukyu Islands. Why then should we make another treaty with any nation? I advised the King that his father, the Regent, is right. We must separate ourselves from the world. We must continue to be a hermit nation, else we shall lose not only our independence but our national life. Our glorious history will sink into the sea of forgetfulness and we shall be no more."

His father's voice fell into its usual cadences, as though he were reciting poetry, and Il-han could not bear it. He had been summoned by the Queen, but it was his father who was summoned by the King. True, the Queen was strong, yet she was a woman and if she gave an order which was in conflict with the command of the King, his will must be obeyed before hers. In this matter Il-han's father was stronger than he. For the sake of the nation he must speak against his father now.

"Sir, the Regent is wrong, and so are you. I dare to say this with full respect to both. Li Hung-chang has purpose in what he does. The Americans are no threat to us. They are a new nation, far away, and I hear they have a vast country. They have no need of our small terrain. They come only for trade—"

Here his father broke in with some anger.

"It is you who are wrong. You do not read the times right. How did the English begin their possession of India except by trade? Oh, they were very innocent, they only wanted trade, and this trade they said would benefit the people of India. Innocent—innocent—but what was the end? India became a subject people and there is no end to their subjection. The English have grown rich and strong upon this trade while the people of India have grown poor and weak. No—no—you young men never study history! Yet only the past can illumine the present and foretell the future."

Il-han was not surprised at his father's outburst, which repeated what the Queen had said. There was some truth in what they said, but it was specious truth.

"The two countries we must fear," he replied, "are Russia and Japan. In both countries the rulers are rapacious and the people ignorant of what their rulers plan. Moreover they are not peaceful nations, and Japan is the more ambitious because she is small. Small men are to be feared if they are ambitious for they are dissatisfied with themselves. Japan is a small man with a big head. We must fortify ourselves against this small man by seeking friends who are large and not greedy. Even China cannot protect us now. We must seek a western friend. Li Hung-chang knows this, and to keep us within China's sovereignty, he too seeks help. Therefore he advises a treaty with Americans, and—"

His father would listen to no more. He rose up from his floor cushion, he adjusted his tall hat, he folded his fan and thrust it into the collar of his white robe. Without a word of farewell he stalked out of the house, his head held high and his underlip thrust out beyond his nose. Il-han watched him go and did not follow, recognizing with some rueful mirth that he had left the Queen in like manner an hour ago. Then he sighed and shook his head. If father and son could not agree, if Queen and subject came to quarrel, where could peace be expected in the nation?

As usual when he could not answer his own questions, Il-han retired to his books, and reading he came upon a poem of the late Yi dynasty written in the Sigo style.

> Stay, O wind, and do not blow.
> The leaves of the weeping tree by the arbor are fallen.
> Months and years, stay in your course.
> The fair brow and the fresh face grow old in vain.
> Think of man; he cannot stay forever young.
> There's the thought that makes me sad.

Would life be long enough for what must be done for his people? He was suddenly conscious that the bright autumn day had changed to night. The wind was rising and he heard the sound of rain upon the roof.

"I am sorry," Sunia said.

It was night. The house was quiet, the children asleep, the gates locked. Il-han took off his outer robes and she folded them and laid them upon the shelves in the wall closet.

"Sorry?" he repeated.

"This morning—the mouse—the child—"

"Ha—I had forgotten."

He went on disrobing, down to his soft white silk undergarments. She held a night garment for him and he slipped his arms into it.

"What are you thinking of these days and nights?" she inquired gently. "You do not see any of us even when you look at us. I think this is why our elder son is too often naughty. He worships you as a god, and you forget to speak to him. How long has it been since you have spoken even to me more than to tell me you were hungry or thirsty or that something must be done?"

She was right and he knew it. Yet how to explain to her his feelings of heavy foreboding? How to explain them to himself? He smiled at her over his shoulder and walking away he slid back the paper lattices and stood looking out into the night. The garden lay before him gilded by the autumn moon, now nearly full. The gardener had lit the lamps in the stone lantern to warn away thieves, but the moon outshone them. Over the stone wall he looked at the crests of the high mountains outside the city. Their bare and rocky flanks shone softly with reflected moonlight. His heart filled anew with love for his country, his beautiful country, encircled by the sea on three sides, walled on the north by Pakdusan, Mount of Eternal Snow, and strengthened by the spine of mountains running its length from north to south. What treasures of gold and silver and minerals those mountains hid! For generations people had washed gold from the river Han, alone, in inexhaustible supply. He had read of caves in the western countries dug by men's hands deep into mountains, and how they found gold and silver and lead and precious minerals hidden there by nature. The riches of his country were unexplored, secret, waiting.

Between the mountains lay valleys as rich in fruitful earth and rushing streams, fields tilled with ancient tools, men and women and children doing the work of beasts. Seasons came and went, spring planting followed by autumn harvest and it was treasure, too. This he knew, but he had not traveled far into the countryside beyond his father's house. He was the son of a scholar and he had never worked with his hands, for though the Kim clan held vast lands he had been half ashamed to think of those lands. How had the Kim clan become rich in houses and land except by royal favor and corruption and usury? Even his father—even his father—

He turned abruptly away from the window. Sunia stood there waiting, her lovely face half questioning, half sad, her white robes flowing away from her slender body like floating mist.

"Sunia . . ." he began and stopped.

"Yes?" she whispered.

He knew what she expected. Her warm smile, her voice, tender and shy, her dark eyes longing and soft, her whole being waiting for his invitation to love. He could not give it.

"I am troubled," he said. "I have the cares of our nation on my mind tonight."

She withdrew with instant grace.

"I think only of you," she said, and left him alone.

. . . He woke early the next morning. The sun filtered through the rice paper lattices and, seeing the morning was fair, he put on a robe and went out into the garden. The air was cool but the earth was warm and a heavy dew lay on the mossy paths and the rocks and the shrubs. Clumps of autumn chrysanthemums glowed among the pines near a small brook sparkling as it fell over a ledge. He walked the length of a path and sat down on a Chinese garden seat of blue porcelain and there contemplated the low and flowing lines of the roofs of his home. The buildings had stood there for centuries, the foundations of mountain rock, the walls of gray brick, the roofs of earth-dried tile. Yet its stability was only seeming. Peasant unrest, the division between young and old, and even war could destroy his possession. The house could become a prison if a foreign tyrant ruled the land. What powers lay in his people to save them from such attack? They must defend themselves. China, their ancient friend, was now too weak to save her own people, and Russia and Japan were only contending enemies.

How strong were his people?

There was no answer to the question except to discover its answer for himself. It was at this hour in the morning, while under the curving roofs of his home his household lay tranquil in sleep, that a new resolve took sudden shape in his mind. He would go on a pilgrimage, not for penance or for any of the reasons for which men usually made pilgrimage. He would not seek out a temple or search for a god. No, his search would be for himself, for his own answer to his own question. North and south, east and west, he would travel in search of the soul of his people. He must know them for only then would he know what to expect of them, what to demand of them, and what they would be able or even willing to do for their country if it were attacked.

With resolution came peace. He had been a man lost in a jungle of doubt and fear but now he saw a path opening before him to lead him out of the jungle. If he did not see its end at least he saw its beginning, and he was free to pursue it and follow it wherever it led—free except for the two women he loved, his wife Sunia and his queen, Queen Min. They must be willing to let him go. Which woman should he approach first? There were arguments for one and for the other. If he began with the Queen's approval, he could say to Sunia that it was royal command. Yet he knew Sunia's willful and stubborn nature, and he knew her love.

"All very well for the Queen," she would cry. "All very well for her to send you wandering alone through the mountains and the valleys in these troubled times! She has other men to heed her bidding. Of men she has a plenty, but I have only you. To me you are everything and without you I am lost and with me our children. What if you never come back? What if—"

He broke off this imagining. He would tell Sunia first. He could persuade the Queen more easily than he could persuade his wife. He must choose the time, a moment when Sunia was gay and tender and pleased about some family matter. He pondered a while and then remembered she had wanted a new icehouse. The old icehouse in the rear of the compound was falling into ruins, and last summer the stores of winter ice had melted too early so that when the heat of the late eighth moon month fell upon them, there was no ice. This he would do for her housekeeping, he decided. For herself, he would buy jade from China, a ruddy piece such as she had longed for and did not have for it was hard to come by and the jade dealers brought it only now and again. She had white jade hairpins and she had green jade bracelets and earrings, but red jade she had not, and she wanted a lump of it to use as a large button to clasp a gold jacket that she loved. He smiled at himself that he could stoop to such wiles, but he loved Sunia for her few smallnesses, since she was of noble nature. It even pleased him to find a weakness here and there in her.

That night, therefore, when he was about to tell her of the new icehouse, she forestalled him luckily by saying that the elder child had lost himself that day and the servants had searched and called his name everywhere for half the morning. They heard a faint voice at last and it came from the old icehouse. The child had crept into the half-open door and pulled it shut after him and the jar of its closing had tumbled broken stone into a heap against the door and locked him in.

"Oh, my heart beat fast enough to kill me," Sunia gasped as she told the story. "We might never have found him and then some day in the winter when we cut the fresh ice blocks to put into the house, there he would have been—dead! Il-han, you must build a new icehouse. What if we had lost the child?"

"Quiet yourself," he said, soothing her. "In the first place, where was the child's tutor?"

"I forgot to tell you that he went home for three days. He is to be betrothed."

"Then where was the servant whose business it is to follow the child wherever he goes?"

She broke in. "But you know this is kimchee time, and we need every hand to help! I had sent to the country yesterday for the last cabbages and turnips and—"

"Enough," he said. "I accept all excuses—"

"Not excuses."

"—as valid," he went on firmly, "and I will build a new icehouse immediately. But I must tell you, Sunia, that I must leave home for a space and while I am gone—"

"Oh, why?" she wailed.

"Let me finish," he said. "While I am away from home, how can my heart rest if I know there is not always someone watching our elder son? True, the old icehouse shall be torn away at once, but this child, being what he is, will only plunge himself into new peril."

"Then why do you go?" she demanded.

"I would not go," he said, "unless I knew it to be my duty." And as was his habit when he did not wish to speak further at a given moment, he rose and left her.

From Sunia he went to the room where his elder son slept. The child lay on the floor bed, his arms upflung, his face beautiful in peace. This stormy boy, this being of his creation, who could so twist and tear at his father's heart, lay there now in such calm innocence that Il-han could have wept. Yet this same child could turn into a devil of anger and mischief and destruction and there were times when Il-han wondered if he were possessed. Once, because a kitten would not come to him, the child had strangled it. Once he had bitten his baby brother's tiny hand so that blood came. Once he had taken a stone and broken a turtle's new shell. When he thought of these times Il-han shivered. Yet there were other times. Into the bitten hand the elder brother had pressed a favorite toy of his own. Once he had wept for a brood of birdlings when the wind blew down their nest and they were too young to take food from his hand. And there were the times, how many times, when the child had curled himself into his father's arms, hungry for love. Did he dare leave this child? Yes, for what he did was for the child, too. The country must be safe for his sons more than for himself.

That night he was so silent and so grave that Sunia did not dare to speak to him. She was afraid because of what he had told her and before they slept she crept close to him and he was won by her gentleness and dread and he took her to his heart.

When he announced himself next day at the gate of the Secret Garden, where the Queen's palace stood, he waited in the anteroom until the guard came back after a while to tell him that the Queen took her leisure today in the bower of the garden. There he was led when she declared herself ready to receive him and he found her in the small room under the triangular rooms of the bower. She stood by a carved table heaped with flowers and autumn leaves and to suit the season she wore a full skirt and short jacket of russet and wine-red satin.

She was in a good mood, he could see, for she did not demand ceremony and was not herself ceremonious.

"Enter," she said. "You see me in disarray. I am amusing myself. I hope you have not come with troubles. You are always so grave that I cannot tell what goes on inside that skull of yours. It is full of secrets, I daresay."

She spoke with willfulness and smiles, and it occurred to him again that beyond being royal she was also a beautiful woman. He wondered at himself that he could continue to have such thoughts about his Queen and he put them hastily away.

"Majesty," he said, "I have come not to disturb your pleasure but with a request."

"Speak on," she commanded. She took a pin from the knot of her hair and caught into it a golden chrysanthemum and then put the pin into her dark hair again and the flower glowed there like a jewel against the pale cream of her nape. He looked away.

"I ask that I be excused from attendance upon your Majesty for the space of months—a few months. I cannot declare the number of months, for my purpose is to travel everywhere over our country to observe the people, high and low, and measure their strength, their skills, their temper. Then when I return to give report to you, I shall know well what to say. Only thus can I know how strong our people are for defending our land."

He made his request in a low, even voice, measuring his tones with reverence for her royal presence although she deigned to appear before him as a woman. He was horror-struck to see the change in her. She took swift steps to him and seized his right arm in both hands and clung to him.

"No," she whispered. "No—no—"

He tried to step back, but she would not let him. He felt the blood drain from his head and he was suddenly giddy. What was the meaning of such behavior? His consternation showed in his face, and her eyelids fell under his shocked gaze. She released him and stepped back and clothed herself again in dignity.

"I have reason to believe—" she began in a low voice and looked about her. No, no one was near. At his entrance she had commanded her women to retire to the end of the garden, within sight but not within sound, but they were to turn their backs to her. He stood like stone, waiting, his eyes fixed now on the mossy path where she stood.

She began to arrange her flowers again. "I hear rumors that the Regent is plotting to return to the throne," she said over her shoulder.

Shame and relief, these were what he felt. How dared he dream that his truebone Queen could behave only as a woman? Was it her fault that she was graceful and beautiful? And relief, because he knew now that not even a Queen could tempt him away from Sunia, since his first impulse had been to step back, to leave the dangerous presence. His heart was insulated by love for his wife, and he was glad that it was so. He spoke with restored calm.

"Majesty, I have heard of no such plot."

"There is much you have not heard of," she retorted.

Her back was toward him now, but he saw her white hand tremble among the flowers. He went on.

"Nor has my father heard the rumor, for if he had, I am certain he would have spoken to me."

"Your father is a friend of the Regent," she said.

"My father is a man of honor, Majesty, and a patriot."

"Even the King does not believe me," she said in a low voice, "so why should I think you would?"

"Where do you hear these rumors, Majesty?" he asked.

"A young woman, who waits on me in the night, is married to a guardsman at the palace of the Regent, and he hears the rumors and tells her."

"Servants' talk," Il-han declared.

"Nevertheless, I wish you would not go."

He did not reply at once. She looked at him over her shoulder and seeing his face rebellious, she spoke once more.

"No, I lay no such command upon you. Go, enjoy yourself."

"Majesty—"

She would hear nothing more.

"Go, go," she said impatiently, and he left her there among the flowers, his heart troubled but resolute.

There are many ways for a man to see his country. Had it been his father, Il-han knew that the preparations would have been vast. Boxes of garments and rolls of bedding, food and drink, a small stove for cold, fans for heat and huge umbrellas of oiled paper for rain, servants and a train of horses and for himself a cart padded with deeply quilted cotton, all these would have been necessary. And when he arrived at a town, the chief family would assemble to welcome him and arrange for his entertainment and comfort and he would meet the scholars and the poets and artists and they would drink tea and sip wine and write their endless verses and his father would have come back knowing no more than when he went, for he carried his world with him and for him there was no other. Il-han was of another sort. His tutor with whom he had grown up from childhood to manhood had taught him to hunger after knowledge and to know he must make himself like other men if he wished to learn from them.

To Sunia's amazement, then, he insisted upon assuming the garments of a man neither rich nor poor and taking with him no more than one man, his faithful servant, could carry on his horse. The two of them set forth on horseback on a fine cool day in early autumn, five days after his audience with the Queen. In spite of knowing how large was the task he had set himself, Il-han was lighthearted. To go upon a holiday he could not, for it would have seemed like a boy at play, and he would not have left his family duties for play. Now, however, he went with purpose, and if he were also diverted such diversion could be enjoyed in good conscience.

The last farewells were said. He stayed alone with Sunia for a few minutes, the wall screens closed between them and all others. He took her in his arms and held her warm soft cheek against his.

"How can you leave me?" she sighed.

"How can you let me go?" he retorted.

She gave him a playful push. "Is everything my fault?"

They clung together again, as though they could never part.

"I wonder at us both," she said at last.

Then since they must part she drew away from him and they went into the other room where the children waited, the older with his tutor and the younger with his nurse. Again Il-han wondered why the love of country was deeper in him than any other. His elder son began to cry when he saw his father ready to leave, and he caught the child to him and reminded the tutor of his duty.

"I hold you responsible," he said sternly. "The child is never to be out of your sight."

"I am responsible," the young man replied.

With the elder son clinging to his waist, Il-han next took the younger one from the arms of the nurse. This child was tranquil by nature and placid, with content and good health. His face was round, his cheeks were pink, and his dark eyes bright. He smiled at his father and looked about at the assembled servants and at his mother.

"He never cries, this one!" his nurse said. "Whatever is, he finds it good."

"I am glad to have one like him," Il-han replied and gave the child to her again.

To her, too, he gave warning. "I hold you responsible," he said.

"I am responsible," the nurse replied.

Farewells were finished, and since Il-han had visited his father the day before, there was no need to disturb him again, and he left his house and went through the gate to the street beyond, the neighbors bidding him as he went to guard his health, to drink no cold water and to beware of bandits in the mountains. He left them all behind at last and giving rein to horse, he departed from the city by the northwest gate. To the north he would go first, then eastward and south, striking through the center of the great peninsula which was his country. Once more he would move slowly up the western coast northward again until he reached the island of Kanghwa, which lies at the mouth of the river Han.

This island was dear to Il-han, though he had never seen it, for here began the history of his people. On a mountaintop upon Kanghwa the people believed that their first king, Tangun, had come down from Heaven three thousand years before the era called Christian. For four thousand years after this sacred birth, the people lived in peace under many kings until, seven hundred and more years ago, the fierce men of Mongolia poured their hordes across the Yalu River and swarmed over the land. Then the King and his people retreated to Kanghwa, since they could not hold back the invaders. The King commanded that a wall be built on the landward side of the island, and the people said that Tangun, now returned to Heaven, sent down his three sons to help them build the wall, which thereafter was known as the Wall of the Three Sons.

Such was legend, and Il-han had heard it in his childhood, for his grandfather spoke often of Kanghwa, not only for the sake of history but because here the Kim clan had its beginning.

"Kanghwa is the stronghold of our independence and the birthplace of our clan," his grandfather had told him. "There in every battle a Kim fought to defend our country. When the Mongols had returned to their own country, their hands dripping treasure they stole from us, we had some hundreds of years of peace until certain lawless tribes from beyond China attacked again. Once more Kanghwa was our bastion. Alas, now the Wall was broken down by the enemy but we would not yield. We built the Wall again, a Kim in command under the King, and again we repelled the enemy. When they were gone, we came out to acclaim our land. Yes, my grandson, in Kanghwa is the secret of our undefeated spirit."

Indeed it had been so, for even in Il-han's memory Frenchmen had made effort to reach the capital city, Seoul, and might have succeeded except when they tried to come up the river Han, the only entrance to the city, the Wall of the Three Sons held them back and they too were repelled and the capital was saved.

Mountains and valleys, sea and farmlands and island, he would travel everywhere and see his country and his people as they were.

. . . With what words shall a man tell of love for his country? Before he was conceived in his mother's womb, Il-han was conceived in the earth of his native land. His ancestors had created him through their life. The air they breathed, the waters they drank, the fruits they ate, belonged to the earth and from their dust he was born. When he bade farewell to his Queen and to his wife and children, Il-han laid aside for the time being all other loves except this one pervading love, the love of his country, and he opened his heart and his mind, day by day, to the people he now met, the scenes he saw, the life he lived. With no other companion than his servant, he traveled by day and slept by night wherever he happened to be when darkness fell.

Northward he went in the beginning and in a score of days he was in the Kumgang-san or Diamond Mountains, the name given to them not because jewels were there, but because the Buddhist monasteries built in high places were such that they shed enlightenment more illustrious than any sun. He had never traveled into these mountains and had only heard of their tortuous shapes, carved by high winds and torrential rains. They were barren cliffs, and in the dark and narrow valleys between, white torrents of water leaped in waterfalls to join the great rivers that emptied into the surrounding seas.

He had read the record of the mountains, made some two hundred and fifty years before he was born, by a great geographer, Yi Chung-hwan. These mountains, he read, formed three strong ranges: the Taeback Range, which ran across the country from north to south like the spine of some vast animal; in the northeastern corner three smaller ranges were parallel; and in the southwest was a third range, running north. Rain and melting snows washed the soil down from the mountains and each winter it piled, rich and fertile, into the valleys. How fertile, Il-han saw every day as he rode northward on his horse, for the fields were already golden with the rice harvest, and persimmons, yellow and red, were ripening on the trees.

Against the gray cliffs of the mountains tall narrow trees of poplar rose like candles of yellow flame, few in number in the scanty soil, but each tree standing single and emphatic.

In the midst of this stern beauty the people walked like prophets and like poets, tall men in their white robes and high black hats, and women as tall in bright full skirts and short jackets, carrying baskets on their heads or jars of oil. Children were everywhere, the gay children of countryfolk. By night he saw them close, for he stopped each evening after sunset at the first village to which he came and asked for shelter at some grass-roofed house. Without fail he was made welcome to what the family had—a pot of soup, wheat with dried bean curd, a bowl of rice, a crust of wheaten bread, a dish of mixed herring and shrimps pickled together, kimchee for relish, and a cup of hot tea at the end of the meal. He made talk with the men while the women sat in the shadows and the children pressed about to stare and listen.

The talk was simple enough. "Have you enough to eat?" he asked first and the answer was usually, yes, enough, but sometimes not enough before the harvest.

"Have you other complaints?" he asked next.

They were wary at this until he assured them that he did not come secretly for taxes or for government. Yet their complaints were simple. Each farmer only wanted more land than he had, and each grieved because his sons had no chance to go to school.

"How can school help you with the land?" he asked.

An old grandfather leaned out of the shadows to make answer. "Learning clears the mind," he said, "and books open the spirit of man to heaven and to earth."

"Do you know how to read?" Il-han asked.

The old man touched his wrinkled eyelids. "These two eyes can see only the surface of what life is."

When darkness fell and the candle guttered, they slept and Il-han shared the mat upon the floor. Few houses had more than one large room and perhaps a small one or two, and the larger room was where life was lived. At night the family lay on mattresses placed on the floor, parents in the center and the youngest child against the mother, and the eldest son lay nearest the door. A miserable life it might have been and yet was not, he concluded, for he heard no child cry in the night without comfort. Even he, accustomed to a great house and many rooms and his own privacies, felt here in the humble houses of the countryfolk a safety, a creature closeness, which made the night less dark. When morning came, nevertheless, he was glad to be on his way.

As he went northward, the air changed. The valley grew more narrow, the fields smaller and the harvests were scanty. He heard of bandits in the foothills, and twice the men of a village went with him to the next village and he knew he was safe because their kinfolk were among the bandits. The answers to his questions now were rough and quick. No, they were not content with what they had. They starved too nearly, and the truebone King and Queen forgot them. As for the Regent, he was no better than a tyrant and they would not have him back. What did they want? They wanted food and justice and land.

"How will you get more land?" he inquired one night at an inn built for pilgrims to the monasteries. "These mountains rise like walls around you. Can fields be carved from rock?"

To this they had no answer until one ready fellow shouted that then they must be robbers.

"We rob the rich to feed the poor," he sang, "and is this a sin? Under Heaven I say it is virtue!"

It was true that rich pilgrims were often robbed, and for that reason Il-han was glad that he traveled as a common man with only his horse and one servant following. Yet even these men were not evil for evil's sake, or so he reasoned.

Riding through the clear pure air of mid-autumn, he reflected that in a country so mountainous as this, where tillable land was only a fifth part of the whole, the treasure was land. Who owned land held power, and this he understood even more clearly as he listened to the landfolk.

"Master," his servant said one morning, "today we must go on foot. We climb mountains."

They had spent the night at a small village built on a rock at the foot of the mountains. It was a family village and the folk subsisted on what the monks in the monasteries paid them for food they carried in from more distant villages. Since the monks ate no fish nor fowl nor flesh of any kind, not even hen's eggs, their meat was beans, wheat, millet and rice.

Il-han looked far up the cliffs ahead. The narrow country road became a ledge of rock upon which no horse could walk.

"Leave the horses here then," he directed. "Tell the head villager that when we return we will pay him for good care of our beasts."

The servant obeyed, and when the sun rose Il-han found himself on his way up the cliffside face of the mountain. Had he been fearful of heights, he would have turned back before the day was half gone, for the ledge, at times not more than eight inches wide, would have been more than he could bear. He kept his eyes on his feet, however, pausing now and again to stand and look about him. The sight was awesome. Above him the mountains pierced the sky, their heads hidden in silvery mists. Far below, bright waters leaped through narrow gorges and the echoes roared about him. Speech was impossible, for no human voice could be heard here. If water did not roar, winds whined among the cliffs.

All day they walked, stopping at noon to eat their packets of cold beans and bread. It was dusk before they came to the first monastery, where shelter could be found. All that was poet in Il-han's nature took possession of him as he made the approach. The monastery faced west, and he saw it first in the light of the golden afterglow. Out of the shadows of twilight among the cliffs, he saw a stretch of green against the dark rocks, and among the gnarled pines he saw a curving stair of rock. Then, like a jewel, the ancient temple was revealed, the roofs of gray tile, the pillars vermilion red, the walls white. He climbed the steps and waited before great carved doors in the center of the stone-paved veranda. The doors opened as though he had called and a monk stood there, a tall gray-robed figure.

The monk spoke the Buddhist greeting, "*Na mu ah mi to fu.*"

Il-han replied with the Buddhist prayer which his mother had taught him years ago, when he was a small boy and she took him to the temple with her.

"*Po che choong saing.*"

"Enter," the monk said. "You are one of us."

He entered the vast hall and into the silence, and confronted a great gold Buddha sitting cross-legged upon a golden lotus, the hand upraised, the fingers in position. The golden face, benign and calm, looked down upon him and he felt peace descend upon him.

. . . For a month Il-han lived in the monastery among the priests. He slept at night in a narrow cell, and daily at sunrise he went into the Chamber of Spirits where the abbot, in hempen robes dyed saffron, sat upon a black cushion on the floor and read the Buddhist scriptures.

This monastery, the abbot told him, was rich in treasures of the spirit, and had been since the beginning of the kingdom of Koryo, when the monk Chegwan had taught the King himself that the unity of the Three Kingdoms revealed the unities of Buddhism, of which there were also three, doctrines, disciples and priests. The power of Buddhism had increased through such unity, spreading into distant China from India to the surrounding countries, and thence to Korea, and from Korea to Japan. Under this influence the Buddhist scriptures had been translated into the Korean language. The great Buddhist Tagak, son of King Munjon, and the twenty-eighth patriarch in direct descent from Sakymuni Buddha, himself went to China in the Sung dynasty and collected these precious books.

"We were preparing for the future," the abbot told Il-han. "It was foretold even then that the Mongols from the north would invade our land. It is out of the north that the destroyers always descend upon civilized man. Did not China build the Great Wall against the north? The Mongols came from the north, but under our influence the nation stood as one people against the barbarous tribes."

"To yield at last to Genghis Khan," Il-han reminded him, "and the books burned—"

"Not to yield, only to submit," the abbot said sharply. "True, our king fled to the island of Kanghwa. But we, believing that Buddha would save us, cast new wooden types and working, hundreds of us, for sixteen years, we gathered together again the sacred books, printing three hundred thousand and more pages of them. They are here, the most vast collection of Buddhist books in the whole world. And our country has remained intact, united under Buddha.

"Chegwan, who founded the School of Meditation, sat for nine years with his face to the wall so that he could not be distracted in meditation. The truly valuable things he taught are attained only by that inner purification and enlightenment which come through quiet pondering and meditating. For the source of all doctrine is in one's own heart and therefore we who are Buddhist monks retire to the mountains."

"Can you believe in this?" Il-han exclaimed. "What refuge is there here when armies swarm into our valleys and over our mountains?"

"In the age of Silla," the abbot said, neither lifting nor dropping his mild voice, "an ancestor of your own, a prince, Hsin-lo, surnamed Kim, became a monk. He traveled to China and as he went up the river Yangtse he paused at the Mountain of Nine Flowers and received from the local magistrate as much silver as his prayer mat could cover. He then sat in meditation for seventy-five years, a white dog always at his side, and as he sat a radiance surrounded him and people realized his divinity. In the seventy-sixth year, the seventh month, the thirtieth day, he received the great illumination and was accepted by death. After death, his body did not decay, and tongues of fire flickered over his grave. Why? Because he had descended into Hell in love and pity for those doomed."

"Of what use is this now?" Il-han cried. "All this meditation has not saved us. And is it enough to descend into Hell, as my ancestor did? Better if he had stayed in the Hell we now have in our country. We, too, may be the doomed, and remember that under the Koryo rule the Buddhist monks and priests and abbots themselves grew accustomed to power and so to luxury and corruption."

The abbot was silent. The accusation was true. As rulers grew effete, even the religious days of ceremony had become occasions for feasting and carousing. Confucian scholars, fresh with the energy of a new philosophy, had denounced the Buddhists for their decadence and before this young and righteous energy the kingdom had fallen to the dynasty of Yi. Thereafter, Confucianism became the religion and the custom of the state and the nation, and the monks had retreated forever to these temples in the mountains of the north.

Il-han shared his day with the monks, and when it was finished he walked at twilight in the shallow gardens planted upon the ledges of rock surrounding the monastery. About him, wherever he went and whatever he did, the sharp dark mountains looked toward the sky. The hollows were filled with darkness even at high noon and the shadows were black.

One evening at dusk he heard a special chanting of priests, a melancholy music, the human cry to Heaven of despair and hope, and he drew near and looked into the Hall of Chanting. The priests sat cross-legged on floor cushions, their eyes closed, their fingers busy with their rosaries of sandalwood and ivory, the dim lights of candles flickering upon their unconscious faces. Not one was young—not one! These were the old, the beaten, men in retreat from life, and the peace in which they lived was the peace of approaching death. . . . Death! Yes, this was a tomb for men's minds and men's bodies.

He turned away and summoned his servant.

"We leave tomorrow at dawn," he told the man.

"Master, thanks be to God!" the man said. "I feared you would never leave this doleful place."

And yet, when he entered his cell to pass his last night he saw that the candle on the table was lighted, and someone waited for him, cross-legged on the floor. It was the young monk who had arranged the abbot's robes in the morning. He rose when Il-hand entered.

"Sir," he said, "is it true that you leave us in the morning?"

"Before dawn," Il-han replied.

"Take me with you, sir, I beg you take me with you!"

The young monk's eyes glittered in the candlelight, his face yearning with demand. Il-han was dismayed and surprised.

"How can I?" he asked. "You have taken your vows."

"In my ignorance," the young monk groaned. "I was only a peasant's son, and when I was seventeen I ran away and was found by Christians and put into their school. But my soul was not satisfied, and I sought the Lord Buddha here. Alas, my soul is still thirsty for truth. I have read many books, East and West. From pilgrims I have had books of western philosophers, Kant, Spinoza, Hegel, but I find no peace. Where is truth?"

"If you cannot find it here," Il-han told him, "you will not find it elsewhere."

And steadfastly refusing the young monk's pleading, he sent him away and drew the bar across the door.

When he went to the abbot the next morning to bid him farewell and to thank him for his hospitality, Il-han felt, nevertheless, a pang of separation. Much, very much of his country's past was embalmed in this place and in other temples like these in other mountains. Mountains had become hiding places for the remnants of a lost glory. What doom lay ahead? What force could hold his people together, now that the love of Buddha was forgotten?

"Pray for us," he told the abbot, "you who still pray."

"I pray," the abbot replied, and he stood up to bless Il-han. The man was tall, but the priest was taller, and he folded his hands on Il-han's bowed head.

"Buddha save you, my son! Buddha guide your footsteps! Buddha grant you peace! *Ah mi to fu—*"

With this blessing, Il-han left the mountain and went southward to the sea.

The eastern coast of Korea is smooth but the western seas eat away at earth and rock and this for eons, so that shores are cut in deep and narrow bays and coves and the tides are high and perennial. Along such shores Il-han traveled as roads would allow, following the rough and sandy footpaths of seafolk as they walked from their huts to their nets. These men of the sea were different from farmer or monk. They were hard, their voices were rough, their skin was encrusted with salt, their eyes were narrowed by sun and storm. They were fearless, setting forth in small sailboats upon high seas and at the mercy of the tides. When they came home all their talk was of the sea and the fish, the soft fish and the shellfish. While the men went to sea their wives and children dug ginseng roots in the hills behind the fishing villages, a good crop, for the best ginseng root was to be found near the eastern town of Naeson. Yet it was rare and it was the more precious for its tonic qualities in soup and tea. A root of ginseng in a broth of salted fish was medicine enough for any ill, and old folk drank it to loosen the coughs that racked their lungs. For vegetables the seafolk used the young shoots of wild herbs steamed and then dipped into vinegar and soy sauce. They seldom ate meat, and indeed in the many days that Il-han traveled among the fishing villages, he ate no meat. True, one day he saw some dried beef hanging before a house, but when he inquired how it came there, the owner said the cow had died of disease.

"Master," his servant exclaimed in horror, "let us eat only fish in these parts."

For liquor the seafolk drank a homemade brew, muddy to look at and of vile odor. For fuel, as Il-han saw as he rode through this shore country, men and women, too, gathered pine needles and fallen branches, straw and grass and dried seaweed, and this signified, he thought, how little the seafolk cared for land. The houses, too, were smaller here and more filthy than elsewhere, and the people more ignorant. One night in a small village inn where he had stopped he was awakened by voices shouting "Thieves—thieves!" and the villagers burst into his room, believing him to be a thief because he was a stranger, until his servant, berating them loudly, sent them away again.

"Yet we are more lucky than the land toilers," a fisherman told him one night when he sat by a fire in a hut.

"How are you more lucky?" Il-han asked.

The man spat into the fire and considered his next words.

He had two fingers bitten off by a shark, a small shark, he said, with a short laugh, else his whole hand and even his arm would have been off.

"We are more lucky," the man went on, "because the yang-ban nobles cannot seize the sea as they seize the land. The sea is still free. It belongs to us because it belongs to Heaven and not to our overlords."

The words were pregnant. In the fishing villages Il-han found the same anger he had found among the peasants, subdued by the same despair. To be poor, it seemed, was inevitable. None could escape. But here by the sea, poverty with freedom was tolerable, while a peasant without land was a slave to the landowner.

He slept ill that night. The smell of the seafolk was the smell of fish. The fragrance of the temple had been incense and sun-warmed pine, but here even the sea winds could not clean the air of the smell of fish drying, fish molding in the mists, fish salted for the winter, fish rotting on the sand. Even the tea these sea families brewed tasted of fish, and so melancholy was their life, between bare mountain and rolling sea, that he could not linger.

After he had passed Pusan, at the southernmost tip of the peninsula, he rested at an inn at Hyang-san, and when the long tables were laid for the evening meal for the guests, he found the same poor fare but he ate as best he could, in order that he might not be suspected of being a rich man or a government official in disguise.

When he came to the river Naktong, whose source is somewhere in the region of Andong, he found it could not be forded, and he crossed it by boat. These boats were of a shape he had never seen before, narrow in width but sixty feet in length, and this, he was told by the boatman, was because the river is sometimes wide and sometimes narrow. Fishermen cast nets into this river and caught koi fish and carp, and these fish had a different flavor from those caught in the sea.

Once on a fair day he met a procession of worshipers of Buddha, and was reminded of the temples. In the midst of the procession was a gold image of the Buddha. Three singing girls in palanquins rode ahead, but a bystander said they were going to the temple for amusement and not for worship, since the Lord Buddha, the man said, had died long ago. "You are right," Il-han replied, "for he lives no more in men's hearts."

There remained now his last stopping place and this was the island of Kanghwa. Thither he now went, staying no more than a night at any inn until he reached his destination. In a fishing boat he crossed the channel where river meets sea, and thus he set foot upon that illustrious island. He had determined to travel it alone and so far as possible in silence.

"Follow me at a distance," he told his servant. "Ask me no questions. When night comes, we will sleep where we find ourselves. As for food, buy such as we can eat as we travel, by foot or on horseback."

So it was, and Il-han went first to the mountaintop where, it was said, Tangun, the first King, had come down from Heaven. The road was steep and the grass was slippery with frost as winter approached, but Il-han was tireless, his body slim and his muscles hard with much walking. When he reached the crest of the mountain he formed a cairn of stones, and he stood beside it and gazed upward into the pure blue above him. His mind could not believe but his heart did, and he stood in meditation, receiving he knew not what except that he felt calmer and more strong for being there. Before he left he searched among the stones and found a curious pointed rock and he set it on top of the cairn as his own monument. Then he came down from the mountain.

He paused again to see the Wall of the Three Sons. Seven hundred years it had stood, built and rebuilt, but now it was history. The new invaders, whoever they might be, would come with new weapons against which walls could not prevail and the channel, though a mile wide, could no longer serve as moat to a fortress. Kanghwa was now only a reminder of a people's courage in the past, a source of strength for the spirit in a people's future.

He had thought that he would visit for a few days the ancient Monastery of Chung Dong, but now he found he could not. What use was there now in such retreats? He longed for home and was impatient to return to work and duty.

He went his way swiftly then, content to do so as he perceived each day now fully the quality of his people. They were brave, they were strong, enduring hardship not only with courage but with a noble gaiety. Expecting nothing either of gods or rulers, they were grateful for small good fortune. Their strength was in themselves and in one another. They could be cruel and they were kind. They fought nature in storm and cold and under bleak skies, but they fought side by side and together. He loved them.

The first snow fell as he turned his horse homeward to the capital. His first task was to wait upon the Queen and tell her what a people she ruled and how worth all sacrifice they were and how they must not be yielded up to invaders from foreign lands. At all cost the country must be independent and free. What cost? That must be determined.

Halfway to the capital, he received the evil news. It was a windless cold morning and he was waked by the sun streaming into the small window of his room at an inn. It fell upon his face as he lay on the floor mattress of his bed and he stirred and opened his eyes. He had slept well, for the ondul floor was warm and he did not hasten to rise. A maidservant, waiting outside his door, heard him nevertheless and she came in with a pot of hot tea. She knelt by his bedside and poured tea into a bowl and set it on the low table by his pillow. She was a woman of middle age, her hands gnarled and cracked with winter cold and, like her kind, she was a creature rich with gossip.

"Bads news, bad news, sir," she said cheerfully.

"What news?" he inquired, still drowsy.

"Runners passed by at midnight from the capital," she prattled. "The Regent has seized the throne back again. The King has yielded but the Queen will not. She has escaped into hiding but the Regent has ordered the army to search for her and put her to death."

He sat up as though fire burned him through the floor.

"Out of my room!" he shouted.

The woman, alarmed, scrambled to her feet and was running away but he caught her by the end of her skirt.

"Call my servant—bid him saddle the horses. We wait for nothing—no food—"

He gave her a push and she ran to obey.

While he hurried into his garments and fastened his boots about his ankles, his manservant thrust a tousled head into the door.

"Master, what is your haste?"

"No questions," he commanded. "Time enough to talk on the way. Get the horses to the gate. Settle with the innkeeper. Listen for what you hear the guests muttering."

"Master, who is up at this hour?" his man replied.

"All the better," Il-han retorted.

Sooner than he could have believed possible they were on their way. The morning was glorious and his heart ached. In so fair a country, why could there never be peace? Why was there continual turmoil within when they were pressed always from without? What discontent, what quarreling and dissension within this narrow lovely land, this sea-girdled strip of earth, rising out of the ocean into lofty mountains and now disaster! The Regent had ruled too long and why must he return to seize by force what was no longer his?

He rode his horse as hard as he dared while the sun moved toward the zenith. The sky was sapphire blue, and on the land the peasants did their winter work, mending roads and ditches and thatched roofs. His path led toward the central mountains, gray against the brilliant sky, their heads crowned with hoar frost and snow. Through them was a winding pass and to that place he pressed without thought of food until at high noon he chanced to see his servant's pinched wan face. The man was older than himself, grown when he was still a child.

"There is an inn beyond the pass," he told the man. "We will stop for rest and I may hear more news, since runners go through that pass from the capital to the coast."

They stopped at the inn, and while the man took care of the

horses Il-han sat at a table in the common room and listened to the guests. They were rude men, carriers and runners, and their talk was cynical and free. None knew where the Queen was. Perhaps she hid herself, perhaps she was dead. But the Regent would not spare her, that was certain, since it was she who had sent him out of power because she loved China.

Here he broke into the talk.

"Will not the King discover where she is?" he asked, pretending to be idly curious.

A clamour of voices hastened to reply. "The King? The King has given over the power to the old Regent. Is the Regent not his father? And will the Regent save the Queen when it was she who plotted against him and restored the throne to the King?"

He was amazed that these ignorant coarse men knew the details of the palace intrigue. Indeed they were not ignorant, although none knew how to write his name or could read a letter even of hangul writing. But they knew history from their ancestors, father teaching son, and they heard gossip from palace servants and guardsmen. Thus Il-han, listening, heard that scanty rice crops had made the people restless and since rice was short, the army rations had been cut and the soldiers were rebellious, too, and ready to listen to the Regent's secret messengers, and so he had been able to seize the throne.

Such lower folk as these carriers and porters and carters took relish in recounting the troubles of the great, and Il-han sat in silence, listening, pretending to eat and drink and yet not able to swallow food or tea when he heard what had taken place. A wind-burned carter, his voice hoarse with frost, talked loudest of all.

"The Queen was sleeping," he bellowed, a lean filthy fellow, his coat in rags.

"In her own palace or with the King?" another asked.

"In her palace!" the carter snickered. "He comes to her, you fool, like a beggar—crawls in on his knees, they say, crying and whining."

"Not so," another roared. "It is the Queen who goes whining and crawling to the King."

This Il-han could not bear. "Go on with the news, man," he shouted to the carter, and was glad once more that the clothing he wore was not that of a rich man but common, such as a traveling merchant wears. Had they known he was a Kim of Andong—

The man went on.

"She was sleeping, the Queen and her women, and a guardsman ran in to warn her the gate was seized."

"What of the King?" Il-han inquired.

"The King? He? Waiting at the gate, they said, bowing and knocking his forehead in the dust to welcome his father, the Regent."

"Tell me about the Queen," a young man clamored. "Was she naked? It is said she sleeps naked."

"If it is said so, then she was naked," the carter roared, "and when a Queen is naked she is no different from any other woman."

Again Il-han could not hear this monstrous talk. The Queen, his Queen, that stately beauty, stripped bare by these foul traitors here in the inn, for were not such men traitors when they took pleasure in her distress?

"She must be dead," he said gravely. "How else could she escape in such a circumstance?"

"Ah ha," the carter rejoined. "You do not know our Queen." He lowered his voice and went on with delight, "A maidservant stood there, wringing her hands together and moaning and making such woman noises. The Queen slapped her cheeks and bade her be silent.

"'Take off your clothes,' she told the maid. 'Dress me in your clothes,' she said. Yes"—here the carter paused to nod and grin—"so she did. She put on the maid's garments. When the rebels burst into the palace and into that very room where she had slept, the maid stood there naked, and the Queen was gone."

"Did they think the maid was Queen?" a young man asked. His eyes were glittering and his mouth hung loose, thinking of the scene.

"She was putting on the Queen's robes when they seized

her, and she said she was the Queen. 'Take your hands from me,' she cried, as the Queen might, and they let her dress and then carried her away."

Il-han took his bowl and drank it empty of tea. Then he said, as though he did not care, "I wish I had been there when they found themselves wrong. A maid instead of Queen! She made fools of them."

But the carter, fresh from the capital, knew everything. "They took her to the Regent himself and when he saw what they had brought him instead of the Queen he cursed and swore and had them put in prison. The maid he had strangled."

Il-han rose from his floor cushion. "I must get on my way," he told them. "I have business."

What he did not tell even his man servant as they rode on was the fear in his own heart. The Regent knew, he must have known, that the Kim clan had served the Queen. Since she had sat on the throne beside the King, the Kim had been favored above all others, and among the Kim, he himself was the most favored by the Queen. Would not the Regent now take revenge? And when he, Kim Il-han, was not found in his house, would he not put to death his wife and children and his old father? Revenge is the tyrant's right.

"We will not stop at inns," he told the servant. "Bargain for fresh horses. We ride until we reach the capital."

The city was quiet when he entered the great south gate. Upon the streets the people came and went as though it was their purpose to reveal no change. None looked at him openly as he passed and if he was recognized, none spoke. His robes were worn with travel and his beard unshaven but these could only be excuses. Here he must be known. Did none dare to speak to him?

He rode without stop through the streets, less crowded than they should be, he imagined, and yet the markets were open, the fish markets and the butcheries, the pastry shops and vegetable stalls. Persimmons were still piled in the streets and the children darted in and out among the legs of vendors and passersby. One small boy fell before his horse and lay screaming in the dust, but he did not stop when he saw the child run away unhurt. Straight on he rode until he came to his own gate. There he dismounted and threw the reins to his servant and entered. The outer gate was open, but when he tried the gate of the house it was barred and he saw the gateman peering at him through the window in the wicket. Even then the gate did not open, and looking in from where he stood outside, Il-han saw the man running toward the house to tell the news of his arrival, no doubt. He waited impatiently and then the man was back again, opening the gate only enough to let him in before he put the bar through the iron bolts again.

"You are home, master, thank Buddha," the man exclaimed.

"Is my family here?" Il-han asked.

"Yes—and your honored father with us," the man replied.

Il-han strode then into the house. The outer room was warmed but empty, and he stood listening. The house was silent. Not even a child's voice cried. He was about to pursue his way when the doors slid back and Sunia stood there, unbelieving. One instant she stood, and then cried aloud.

"Oh—"

She was in his arms, her arms about him, and her head on his breast. They stood close for a long moment. Then she drew back and looked up at him.

"You know?"

He nodded. The walls had ears in times like these. She stood tiptoe then and put her lips close to his ear.

"She is here."

She stood back to see if he understood.

He lifted his eyebrows. "She?"

"The Queen!"

For a moment he was speechless indeed. The Queen? How dared she take refuge here in his house and risk the lives of his children? Where were her guardsmen?

"No one knows she is here," Sunia was whispering again. "She tells them she is a lady from the court. She says she saw the Queen killed and she cannot eat. She lies in her bed all day, weeping as if for the Queen. No one goes near her. She has the curtains drawn. At night I take her food."

"How long will this be believed!" Il-han muttered.

No more could be said for by now the household had the news of his return. The young tutor came in with his elder son grown tall in these many months, and the nurse brought in the younger child, who now could walk, his two feet far apart in caution. Il-han could only hide his fears and make pretense at welcome and smiles and praise. The servants came to bow before him and to exclaim their joy at his safe return, and he was compelled to be the calm master upon whom all could rely. And not one spoke of secret fears or made report of what had taken place in the palace while he was gone.

He spoke to each and to each gave some token of his thanks for faithfulness. To the servants he gave gifts of money and to his two sons he gave small jade animals that he had found in his travels and to the tutor he gave an ancient book of poetry which the abbot had given him in the mountain monastery.

"Now I must bathe," he said, "and be shaven and put on fresh garments. It is good to come home and may I never leave my house again."

So saying, he went into his own rooms and bathed, and his barber came and shaved him and washed and combed his long black hair and bound it up again into its usual coil upon his head. After this, Sunia came to him and sat by him while he ate, and his sons were brought to him again before they were put to bed. So the evening passed until night fell and the house was still and all through the hours he thought only of the Queen hidden in an inner chamber, the curtains drawn about her bed. She must be taken to a safer shelter. Though his servants were loyal, he believed, yet some gossip might escape one of the women washing the family garments at the river's edge. It would be enough for such a woman only to say, "We have a strange lady in our master's house. She lies in bed all day and draws the curtains and she will not eat."

"Now," he told Sunia when the house was still. "Now take me to her."

The Queen, dressed in a common woman's garment, sat on her floor cushion by a small table, in her hands a piece of red satin which she was embroidering. The light of two candles shone upon her quietly moving hands and she did not look up when the door slid back, until he stepped inside.

"Majesty!"

The words rose to his lips and he spoke it softly. No word must reveal who she was. He stood looking at her in silence and she looked at him and then her hands fell upon the table, the red satin a gleaming heap between them.

"I am making your second son a pair of shoes," she said.

He did not reply. He came close and knelt before her on the other side of the cushion, and Sunia followed and knelt beside him. He spoke so softly that his lips moved almost without voice.

"We must leave this house tonight. You are not safe and I cannot protect you. I may not be able to protect even my family. Dress yourself warmly and put out the candles as though you were going to sleep. I will come here to fetch you and we will take horse and ride to some distant place. I have a friend in Chung-jo—"

She did not reply. For minutes she sat with her great dark eyes fixed upon him. Then she folded the square of red satin and thrust the needle through.

"I shall be ready," she said, and added not one word.

He and Sunia rose then and went away to their own rooms.

What was there to say in such a time, even between him and Sunia? She prepared a bundle of warm clothing and put in some dried foods, in case they dared not stop at inns or in case snow fell and held them back in some lonely spot.

She asked only one question while he changed his house robes to warmer ones. "Should you not take your servant with you?"

He hesitated. "He is a faithful creature but he has been

away from his family all these moons. There are certain dangers, too, if we are discovered."

She interrupted. "I cannot think of your being alone. If you were killed in ambush, who would come back to tell me?"

Her face was quivering with suppressed weeping and his heart yielded while his will rose to make her strong. He took her hands and held them in his.

"I need your courage," he told her. "All that I have is not enough for what lies ahead. Your tears undo me. It is my duty to serve the Queen, because in her is the only hope of our country. Do you think that otherwise I could leave you—or defend her? She must be kept alive, she must return, she must wile the King away again from his father. Fortunately, I hear that he loves her and leans on her. Fortunately he does not love his father. He longs to rebel against him and hates himself because he is too weak to rebel. Or so I hear. A few months, Sunia, and if I plan well, the Queen will be back and the throne secure for a while, at least."

"Why must it be you?" she murmured, distracted.

"Because she trusts me," he said.

She looked at him over her shoulder. "You had better wear your fur-lined coat, and I will fetch it," she said.

In the small cold hours of the night he went to the door of the room where the Queen waited. He had bade his servant to be ready with three horses outside the gate, for this much he had yielded to Sunia, but he commanded him to ask no questions, whatever he guessed. Now while Sunia slid back the doors, he stood outside the Queen's room until Sunia came out, her hand clasping the Queen's hand. None spoke. The Queen was wrapped in fur-lined robes and a silk scarf was wound around her head and fell over her face like a veil. He walked ahead and she followed with Sunia while around them the house slept. Outside the gate, in the fortunate dark of the moon, the horses waited. Even the gateman slept, for the servant had opened the gate secretly, and now he stood holding the bridles of the three horses.

Il-han helped the Queen to mount. Then he turned to Sunia. "Go into the house, core of my heart," he said. "Go and sleep warmly and dream that I am home again, as surely I shall be. As far as man may promise, I promise you."

They clung together for an instant in the darkness and then she turned resolutely to obey him. He waited until he heard her draw the iron bar against the gate. Then he mounted his horse and they rode through the night, the hooves of the horses soundless against the cobblestones because the man servant had wrapped the horses' feet in rags. When they reached the city gate, the guard held his lantern high to see who wished to flee the city. The Queen put aside her scarf, he saw her face, and speechless he turned and drew back the iron bar.

That night and for the next few days Il-han did not take the usual stone-paved highway to the city of Chung-jo. Instead he guided his horse through country roads and mountain paths, stopping not at inns when darkness fell but with some peasant family in a village. Never before had the Queen met face to face with these many whom she ruled, and Il-han found that he had not one woman to protect and hide but many women in one. Thus she was amazed to discover that a farmer's house had but one room, the other one or two being no better than closets, and suddenly she was all Queen.

"What," she exclaimed to Il-han the first night, "am I to lie among all these stinking folk?"

"Remember you are a commoner now, on your way to visit distant relatives, and I am your brother."

She yielded at once. "I have always wanted a brother," she said sweetly.

Lucky that he had warned her not to speak in the presence of any strangers, for her sweet voice and pure accents would have betrayed her anywhere as no common traveler.

"Be shy," he had told her, "remember that women should not speak unless spoken to by father, brother or husband. No one will suspect you if you do not speak."

Now that she was somewhat safe, the old mischief and gaiety glinted irrepressible in her eyes and smiles. He looked away. Steady and cool he must be with this powerful willful woman, and yet he knew that if he had not the safety of his love for Sunia she might have put him into torment. Were she no more than Queen, she would have been temptation, but she was also the most beautiful woman he had ever seen, and she used her beauty as only a Queen dares to use such a weapon, knowing that if a man makes trespass she can have his head cut off, or poison put in his food. He believed that she would not stoop to such evils, but he knew, too, that a man can never trust a Queen. He held her then in unfailing respect, not drawing nearer than a subject may, and this though she tempted him on purpose, as a woman will, though it was a game he would not play.

"And remember," he told her one night when she complained that she could not eat the coarse food of the country folk, "remember that these are your people and this food is what they eat until they die and they never see better than a bit of pork once or twice a year. And if the room they live in crowds you, and the smells are too foul for you to breathe, then remember that these are still your people and they have no palace in which to live."

"Nor have I," she said mournfully.

"You have," he said firmly. "If you hold to your courage, you shall be in your palace again within the year."

In these ways he kept her to her best, and was heartened because she grew less willful and more steadfast as the days passed. She learned to watch the people and see how they did, instead of turning away from them, and in so doing she became more the queen and less the woman.

They reached Chung-jo on a cold winter's night. Il-han went to his friend's house, and knocked on the gate with the handle of his whip. His friend opened the door himself, for he was poet and a poor man, and had no servant.

"It is Il-han," he told his friend.

"Il-han! Come in, come in quickly—"

His friend's voice was joyful, for they had once gone to school together and it had been years since they had met.

Il-han gave his horse's bridle to the servant and stepped into the gate and spoke to his friend's ear.

"I have a royal refugee with me. She must be safely hidden. I know the woman in your house will receive and hide her somehow."

The poet could not believe what he heard. Gossip from the capital had proclaimed the Queen's death. Yet, some said, no one had found her body, nor had the rivers cast up a body that could be hers, and though the wells had been searched, they had not yielded her. True, there was a woman dead who wore royal robes, but it was found that she was not the Queen.

"You are not saying—" his friend gasped.

"Yes, I am saying!" Il-han told him. "Let me bring her in now. She is half frozen, as we all are. She needs rest and food."

He waited for his friend to protest that he could not accept such danger as the concealment of a queen. But this poet was a true one. He revered learning and so he had stayed poor and having little to lose, he was brave.

"I will tell my wife," he said. "Meanwhile the door is open. Lead her into my house."

So saying, he went ahead and Il-han helped the Queen dismount and he led her into the house.

"I have chosen this hiding place for you because my friend is a good man," he told her. "And it is well that he is poor. He will not have many people coming and going. You will be safe. But I ask that you make yourself one of the persons in this house. You are not royal here. Imagine that you belong to this poor good family."

The Queen was humbled by now, through her many days of hard travel. For the first time she saw how her people lived and who they were. Never again would she be so wasteful of money and jewels and fine silks. She had the heart and mind of a noblewoman, truebone and clear, and she was changed.

"I will remember," she told Il-han.

He had not imagined how difficult, nevertheless, it would be to leave her there as the poet's wife came bowing and half dazed to receive them. Her husband had bidden her not to mention the name of the Queen and not to say Majesty and she obeyed but she was overwhelmed.

"If you will come with me," she murmured.

The Queen bowed her head and then turned to implore Il-han. "You will stay a day or two?"

"Not even an hour or two," Il-han replied. "I must return at once and begin my plans for your return."

"We have said nothing of those plans," she urged.

"Because I will not tell you something that will be a burden on you. You are to live here quietly, helping this family as a friend might. Share the duties of this housewife—they have no servants. Listen to her talk, but do not talk much for yourself. Use this time for learning what it is to be a poor man with no treasure except a love of learning and of beauty. These people, too, are your subjects."

"Is this farewell?" she asked and he saw fright in her wide eyes.

"We meet again soon," he said.

He stood and watched as the poet's wife led her away. Suddenly she turned and came swiftly to him again. He looked at her, questioning, but saying nothing, she reached into her bosom and then pressed something into his right hand.

He looked and saw what it was. "I cannot take it," he exclaimed beneath his breath.

It was her private seal, a piece of Chinese jade upon which was carved her royal name.

"You must," she told him, her voice very low. "You may need to use my name in some high place to save your life—or mine."

He stood amazed while she ran back to the waiting woman, and he marveled that she put such trust in him. His heart was moved and he knew himself forever her loyal subject, yes, and more.

He stayed then for a brief space with his friend while the servant fed and rested the horses.

"Why should you hasten away?" the poet urged.

"It is better if there are no horses at your gate when the dawn comes," Il-han said, "and better if I and my servant are not here in your house. A woman can be hidden more easily than a man. Ah yes—before I forget—let your wife lend her some plain clothing when she needs it. She wears all that she has. And if someone asks who she is, say that she is a distant relative, newly widowed, who has come to stay with you because she has no other home."

"I am still bemused," the poet said. "It will take time for me to get back to myself."

"I shall be here again before many moons," Il-han told him.

The poet held him by the arm. "Wait—my wife wants to know what she eats."

"She eats anything," Il-han said firmly, and went away.

The Queen was left much alone in the lowly house of the poet. She understood that this was not enmity but reverence for her royal person. The poet's wife was always near but speechless with awe unless the Queen encouraged her. The poet kept apart in a separate small hut where he sat upon a straw mat before a low table and read his few books and brushed his poems. Each morning he presented himself to her, bowed to ask of her welfare, and then withdrew.

The Queen mused often on her fate. She remembered that her mother had foretold her wanderings, for she had been born at sunrise one morning, and at the same moment a cock crowed. According to the four pillars of her destiny, the hour, the day, the month, the year in which she was born, she had lived thus far according to prophecy, a woman of willfulness she did not deny, but also of strength. When she thought of her own strength, she thought of the King. She had believed him to be weak, but there were times now when she was not sure. Perhaps he had hidden his true self from her. He was the son of a strong mother and through his childhood he had cultivated habits of secret resistance against his father, loving him and hating him, deciding what he would do but telling no one what it was until the act was complete. The return of the Regent—had it been perhaps with the consent of the

King? If it were only the Regent's love of power, could not the King have prevented the usurpation, since he had eyes and ears everywhere throughout the capital? And if he had allowed his father, the Regent, to return, was it because he hated her, his Queen, and rebelled against her as he had rebelled against his mother before her, and so because she favored the Chinese as suzerains, he had chosen his father who was against such suzerainty? When did the King become the man? And when did the royal family tangle become enmeshed with the troubles of the nation, and beyond that, with the declining strength of China and the dangerous strength of Japan made new by Meiji emperors.

She grew restless with such musings as the days passed. There could be no hope of messages from Kim Il-han. He had warned her that communication was impossible. "When it is safe for you to return," he had said as he left her, "your palanquin will be at the gate. Step into it without asking a question. It is I who send it."

Yet there was no palanquin. She was first impatient and then angry. Once she went to the gate, as she should not, and saw a brook tumbling out of the mountains, and beside it a wandering cobbled country road. The poet's house was outside the village, a cluster of glass-roofed houses belonging, she supposed, to landfolk and their families, except that out of villages came poets. Such men, four or five, gathered at the poet's house often, and then the poet's wife asked her to stay within the small side room.

"I would beg my husband not to allow his friends to come while you are with us," she told the Queen, "but they are used to coming, and were he to stop them now they would put questions."

The Queen heard this with interest. She who was accustomed to command! The poet's wife saw her unbelieving look, and went on in haste to explain.

"You do not know what poets are! They are so willful that they dare anything. They are children in spirit but in wit and wisdom they are already old men when they are born. What

I have to endure! I tell you, it is not easy to be married to a poet."

"All the more reason," the Queen said, "for me to hear these poets. Leave the door open a crack—"

At this very moment while she stood in the garden she saw the poets coming from the village. They wore their long white robes, those robes which their wives washed fresh for them every day, doubtless, as the poet's wife did in this house, and they wore their high black horsehair hats tied under their chins, the tapering crowns making the men seem taller than they were. They walked one behind the other, the smallest and the oldest first, so that she could see each head above the other. She waited as long as she dared so that she could see their faces, and then made haste into the small room, leaving the door open a crack.

Lucky the room was without a window, for she could sit in darkness and peer through the crack at the five men who crowded into the one room, each upon a floor cushion, the low table in the middle. Greetings were given and taken, the easy greetings of old friends, and she saw that they were contented men, though poor. Since she had been reared in the learning of ancient China, she remembered what Confucius had said: "Though I eat coarse rice and drink only water, though my bent arm is my pillow, happiness may yet be mine, for ill-gained wealth and empty honors are only floating clouds."

Yet these poets, she soon perceived, were men of mirth as well as wisdom. They were not dismayed when the poet's wife brought them only pots of weak green tea without cakes. Sipping the tea, they encouraged one another to begin the day's enjoyment by reciting the poems each had written since the last time they met, and with proper courtesy each waited on the others until the eldest took lead. Closing his eyes and placing his hands on his knees, he recited in a clear voice, surprisingly loud for so small and old a man, a poem about a beautiful woman who could change herself into a fox at night. When her husband, who was also a poet, went hopefully to bed with her, he woke to find the marks of tiny claws on his hands and cheeks, and the pillow beside him was empty.

It was the youngest poet whose poem was of sorrow and death in the shadows of a pine grove. The more she listened the more the Queen perceived that the old men dreamed of youth and beauty and the young men dreamed of melancholy and doom. Most confounding to her was the fact that none of them spoke even once of the terrors of the present age, the enemies pressing from without the nation and the quarrels and the wars within. These men, both young and old, learned though they were, seemed not to know that they lived in peril of the times or that the past could not save them, or that their future could be lost unless they bestirred themselves to save their people. When she perceived this, it was all she could do to keep from throwing open the door and revealing herself as their Queen. To what end? So that she could cry at them to wake their minds!

"How dare you," she longed to cry at them, "how dare you live in these mists of dreams and poetry while I, your Queen, am in danger of my life? Wake up, you men! Old and young, you are all children. Must I be your mother forever?"

She forbade herself such indulgence. She must be silent for the sake of more than these, and silent she was, biting her thumbnail and forcing herself to be quiet. She must wait and still wait until some night the poet's wife would rouse her and whisper to her, "The palanquin is at the door."

Kim Il-han was not idle although he was prudent and did not venture from his house so that he might protect his family if the Regent ordered violence. To his father he sent word that he was not well, that his illness was not defined by the physicians and he felt it his duty not to come near his father until he was sure he was harmless. Daily messages passed between the two houses, nevertheless, his father's and his own, his servant coming and going, and his father, too, was prudent, and he said he had slight disorder of the stomach and must stay inside his own gates. The old man knew, of course, that his son's illness was not of the body. These were dangerous times for the Kim clan.

Step by step, Il-han planned the restoration of the Queen. His tool in this planning was his son's tutor. He called the young man to his private room one evening when the household lay asleep, and without daring to explain his whole purpose, he sent the young man to summon a handful of other statesmen whom he could trust. These gathered, not all at once, but one by one, this one today and another one tomorrow, weaving a web between their houses, and the messenger was always the tutor.

"You must trust me," Il-han told him. "I am working to save us all."

"Will you restore the Queen?" the tutor asked. "The times are changed," he added.

Il-han looked at him sharply. The face he saw was lean and young, the mouth too gentle, but the eyes were clear and demanding.

"Nothing is forever," Il-han said at last. "If she returns, she too must change."

"I trust you, sir," the young man rejoined, "so long as you know there must be change," and taking up the letters that Il-han had given him, he went to obey.

The first step was plain. The Regent must be removed. He must be taken bodily out of the country and sent to a place across the seas from whence he could not return, because he would be in the hands of his enemies. Who were his enemies? The Chinese were his enemies and the chief of these was the Empress Tzu-hsi. Il-han would not plot to take the life of the Regent, nor would he allow others to do so, for to use such cruelty would inflame his people against the Queen. Once the Regent was gone, the next step would be to send the palanquin to the poet's house and restore the Queen to her palace.

From his quiet house, while the children played in the gardens and Sunia tended her flowers and directed her women, Il-han spun his web wide. He had the genius to direct without seeming to command. Thus among his fellow statesmen as he had opportunity, or made it, he put his thoughts into a question here, or he made a reflection there, a suggestion that others, following his words eagerly, took up and put into action. His friends were peaceful men, and to them, also, he knew he could not propose violent deeds. Instead he proposed a new friendship with the Chinese.

"Our neighbors in the Middle Kingdom," he said one day in conference in his own house, "are ever ready to help us. Let us now use their enmity against Japan, and make it our weapon."

It was a day in late spring when he so spoke. Outside the open doors a hum of bees gathering among the yellow flowers of a persimmon tree told him that a hive had split. These were the wanderers seeking a new life for themselves with their queen, a symbol, perhaps, of what he sought too for his own kind. He clapped his hands for a servant and when the man came he gave a command.

"Tell the gardener that bees are hiving. Let him catch that mass of bees hanging there from the branch of the persimmon tree and persuade them into a new hive so that we may have the honey."

The man obeyed and Il-han rose and drew the door shut so that the bees would not be disturbed. Then he sat down again on his floor cushion.

"A good omen," he said to his guests. "There is honey to be had if we snare the bees."

They laughed moderately in politeness and waited, a circle of gentlemen in white robes, their faces bland beneath the black hair coiled on their crowns. Il-han continued.

"Let us invite China to strengthen her armies in our city. With this new army we will silence the Japanese, now growing too strong under the Regent's favor."

"How will the Chinese restore order among us?" The man who asked this question was a scholar, one known to favor new ways and western learning.

"They need do one thing only," Il-han said.

"And that one thing?"

"Remove the person of the Regent. Take him to China. Imprison him—not in jail, but in a house. And keep him there, perhaps forever—until he dies."

He allowed his calm gaze to move from one astounded face to the next.

The boldness, the simplicity of this plan confounded those who heard it. They were silent, pondering what he had said, and he watched their faces. Doubt gave way to dawning hope and then approval. The older men thought only of the Regent removed and the house of Min returned and peace restored. The younger men thought of internal strife ended and room and time for new plans and ways.

"If you approve," Il-han said, "then nod your heads."

One after the other heads nodded. Il-han took up his cup and drank down the tea, and they all did the same.

"How will you do what you propose?" one asked when all had set their bowls down again.

"A messenger will be enough," Il-han replied.

"What messenger dares to go on such a mission?" another asked.

"I know a man," Il-han said.

Il-han spoke that same night to the young tutor, when all his guests were gone. "You are to leave at once for Tientsin. Here is my letter. I have signed it with the Queen's seal. Yes, I have the seal! She gave it to me when we parted. Put it in the hands of our emissary in Tientsin. He is a Kim, as you well know—my cousin thrice removed. Let him read it and then ask how long it will be before the Chinese army can reach us. Tell him not too large an army—we are to be helped, not occupied! Four thousand men will be enough, or a few hundreds more to allow for death and illness."

He opened the secret drawer in his desk and took out a small bag of rough dark linen. "Here is silver, enough to take you there and bring you back. Where will you hide the letter?"

"In the coil of my hair," the young man said.

Il-han laughed. "Good! Then you must take care that no enemy beheads you."

They parted and the next day when the tutor was missed,

Il-han said only that he had sent the young man to the north to buy ginseng root to export to China. Since ginseng was valuable and the dealers in China were never satisfied, and its export was part of the business of the house of Kim, he was believed. Indeed, this ginseng root was a treasure for all physicians, for according to an ancient Chinese prescription, ginseng fortifies the nobler parts of man or woman, fixes the animal spirits, cures the palpitations caused by sudden frights, dispels malignant vapors, and strengthens the judgment. When taken over the years, it makes the body light and active and prolongs life.

"I am married to you," Sunia said, "but you are not married to me."

The hour was past midnight. The house was silent. They were lying in their bed, in the quiet of the sleeping house. He had come into this room at the day's end, determined to give himself wholly to his wife for the next hours. He had done what he could for his country and his Queen, and now he could but wait. He knew Sunia's patience and tonight he needed her with all the richness and the simplicity of her being.

Without words, then, he had taken her into his arms and for a while they had lain in quiet. Then the deep tide began to rise from his innermost center, and with ardor he had fulfilled himself and her. She had first yielded and had then responded with such delicacy of understanding and such instinctive passion that he breathed a deep sigh of profound happiness. Was there ever such a wife, such a woman? She asked no question, she spoke no word.

Then, in the midst of his completion, she made this monstrous accusation. She was married to him, but he was not married to her!

He considered for a moment. In what manner should he reply? Should he be angry? Or witty? Or laugh? He chose to answer as though he did not believe her serious.

"Shall we make an argument?" he inquired, his voice indolent with content.

She sat up in bed and began to braid her long dark hair.

"There is no argument," she told him. "I am speaking truth."

"Then anything I say must be untruth," he countered, "so what shall I say?"

"Nothing." Her voice was small and far away and she was very busy with her hair. He waited until she had finished to the end of her braid and then he took her by the braid and pulled her back gently to his shoulder.

"Can it be," he inquired, "can it really be that you are jealous of a queen?"

She hid her face against his bare flesh.

"Can you imagine," he went on most tenderly, "can you for one foolish moment dream that I could ever take a queen into my arms and hold her as I hold you, and adore her body as I adore yours?"

She began to laugh. "No, but . . ."

The laughter died away and she still hid her face against his bare shoulder.

"If you will not tell me," he said at last, "will you blame me if I say I do not know what you are talking about?"

She sat up suddenly and turned her naked back to him, a most lovely back as he observed, the spine straight, the waist soft and small, the nape delicate, the skin fair and smooth.

"There is more to a woman than body," she said.

"Tell me what more," he said, half teasing.

She looked at him over her shoulder.

"If you make fun of me, I shall not speak a word."

"I am not making fun—I am only waiting."

She was silent, stealing a look at him now and again over her shoulder to see if he were laughing at her. He made his face grave and he did not put out his hand to touch her.

"You never loved me—so—" Here she paused for the word she wanted to use.

"How?" he asked.

"So—so—so strongly as you did tonight. You were feeling something new. Why?"

"Nothing new," he said, "only more. Remember that for

many days I have had not one moment to think of you—or the children."

"Something new," she insisted.

He sat up. "The wonders of a woman's mind," he exclaimed. "The tortuous, twisting corridors in which she loses herself—and the man! Speak out, Sunia! Tell me what you are thinking. What have I done? Are you trying to tell me that I am dreaming of a geisha or one of the maids?"

"No," she said, her voice a whisper. She got to her feet and went to the wall screen and opened it. Outside the rain was falling and she felt the mist against her face.

He went after her and closed the screen. "Are you mad?" he demanded. "Do you want to die?"

"Perhaps I do," she said.

She sat down again on the floor cushion beside the low table and lifted the teapot from is quilted cover. She poured the hot tea in the bowl and took the bowl in both hands to warm them while she sipped.

"Be sensible," he urged. "I have neither time nor heart for complexities between us. Have I failed you as a husband? Then I must ask forgiveness. But first I must know for what I am to be forgiven."

"It is not a question of forgiveness," she said, looking into her tea bowl. "And perhaps you yourself do not know what is happening to you."

"What is happening to me, wise woman?" he inquired.

She lifted her brooding eyes to meet his eyes. "You are being possesed," she said. "The Queen is possessing you by her helplessness—by her high position—by her beauty and her power—and her loneliness. A lonely woman is always tempting to a man, but a queen! When she comes into any room it is the Queen who enters. You are flattered, of course. But you are overwhelmed by such honor. You, singled out, set apart, by the Queen? How can one who is only a—a—woman —compete with a queen? She possesses your mind—yes— she does—don't speak!"

For he had leaped to his feet, but she pushed him off. "Stay away from me, Il-han! It is true. For a man like you, with your mind—oh, there are more ways of enchanting a man like you than by the body, I know it very well. And I am not clever like you, or—or witty or brilliant or even very intelligent beside you—and though you will never possess her, yet I am your possession, and you will think me a poor creature. You do so think, already! Whenever you see her, after every audience, you come home as a man returns from a glorious dream. And now, when it is you who have her in hiding, it is only you who know where she is—why, I daresay you are dreaming dreams!"

Her voice rose with anger and then broke into sadness.

He was confounded. He sank back upon the bed and clasped his hands behind his head. How could he reply to so monstrous an insult? And yet she could so penetrate by instinct that he wondered if indeed she had perceived some truth that he had not. He did think constantly of the Queen. Her person was sacredly dear to him, not as a man, he nevertheless believed, but as a symbol of the nation and the people to whom he was dedicated. Yet he was a man. And it was true that some enchantment always came into his mind when he was with the Queen. He could look at any beautiful geisha and feel no desire to look again. But when a woman, such as the Queen, spoke with grace and intelligence, when she had a mind, then her body was illumined and he looked.

He sighed and closed his eyes. He had no time for self-investigation. And did it matter? He had a duty to restore the Queen to the throne and he would do it. And when she was on the throne she was Queen, and only Queen.

"Will you listen to me?" he said to Sunia. "Will you hear me tell you what must be done and what my duty is? There must be unity among our people, else the great hungry nations who surround us can lick us up as a toad licks up a mouthful of ants by the flicker of its tongue. Will you hear me, Sunia? As my wife?"

She put down the tea bowl. "I will hear you."

"I must keep my head clear," he said. "I must listen to all factions, but I must choose, step by step, my own path. I believe, Sunia, that finally we must make friends with the

West. We must find new allies. Yet for the moment China must come to our help against Japan so that we may restore the Queen—and the King—to the throne."

She was shrewd enough, this wife of his! "Why do you falter when you speak of the King?" she inquired now. "Put the Queen first, and then you stammer. What of the King?"

"Come here to me," he said.

"Lie down," he said when she stood beside him. "Rest your head on the pillow by mine."

She obeyed, wondering. When her head was beside his, he turned and spoke into her ear.

"I believe the King is not loyal to the Queen. It is he who helped the Regent to return to the palace."

"The Regent is his father," she reminded him.

"The Queen is the Queen," he retorted, "and she is his wife."

They lay silent then, for enough had been said so that she understood, at least in part, that it was possible for him to be possessed not by a woman, not even by a queen, but by the love of his country.

In silence they lay close, without passion, but closer than passion could bring them they lay close.

In the poet's house the Queen lived through the long days and the longer nights. Summer changed to autumn and winter lingered. Never before had she had the chance and the time to ponder her life as a woman. Now as the hours of the day stretched endlessly long, she watched the poet and his wife as they lived through their simple round. The woman's whole life was in the man, the wife a part of the husband, and this the Queen saw.

"Are you never weary of tending this one man?" she inquired one day when she was alone with the wife, for the poet had walked to the village to buy paper and fresh ink and a new brush.

The wife was grinding wheat meal between two stones, and she stopped and wiped the sweat from her face with the hem of her skirt.

"Who would tend him if I did not," she asked, "and what else have I to do?"

"True," the Queen said. "But do you never find yourself weary? Do you not dream sometimes of another life?"

"What other life?" the wife replied. "This is my duty, and he is my life."

The Queen persisted. "Then what do you dream of?"

The wife considered. "I dream of having enough money to buy an ox. I could drive the ox in the field instead of pulling the plow myself. And I would get him a fine white robe such as he deserves to have as a poet, instead of the patched rag he wears now. Yes, I might even buy two white robes, and certainly he needs a new hat. I mend the one he wears with hairs I pull out of the tail of the horse our neighbor has, but it would be well for him to have a new hat. This one belonged to his father who died. He has never had a hat of his own, and his head is smaller than his father's and the hat rests on his ears. But what can I do?"

"Ah, what indeed," the Queen replied with sympathy.

In the long night that followed inevitably upon the day, she thought about the King for the first time as her husband. Would she be happy to tend him day and night? No, she would not. Nor would he wish her to tend him. He sent for her and she went when he commanded. That is, she went sometimes, but there were also times when she excused herself because the time was not her time. Then he could be angry, and insist that her woman bring him proof. If there were no proof she sent a cloth dipped in the blood of a fowl. Yet, though she did not love him, she did not hate him, and indifferently she went to him. She was a warm woman, and lucky that she was, for the King was ardent, and without love the two of them could mate well enough. But she was slow to be pregnant, especially since now she knew that her son, the heir, would always have the mind of a child. Had she loved the father she might have cherished the child nevertheless. As it was, she sent the boy to a distant part of the palace where servants cared for him. She saw him sometimes playing in some garden, and she spoke to him kindly enough but she left him soon and knew that in truth she was childless and alone.

She lay on her poor bed now in this poor house, and she would not weep. She admonished herself: Remember your vow; you promised your own heart that you would not weep any more, for any cause.

The long night ended and it was the last to be so long. For on the next day, rumor crept through the nation even to the village and then to the poet. The Chinese Empress had sent an army to rescue the Queen. The poet closed the wall doors and put out the lamp on the table. In the darkness he whispered the powerful news to her listening ear.

"The Imperial Chinese armies have marched into the capital! Forty-five hundred men armed not only with good swords, but with foreign weapons! They have overwhelmed the palace guards. They have seized the Regent himself and he is to be taken to China and held there in prison. Only the King is left."

She heard this in the early morning. The poet's wife had wakened her and led her into the other room where the poet stood waiting. She could not suppress her trembling. "How true can this be?" she inquired.

"True enough," he said, "so that I advise your being ready to return."

Six days the Queen waited and five restless nights. On the seventh day the poet's wife came silently into the room where she sat embroidering.

"Majesty," she said, "the royal palanquin is at the door."

And so saying she knelt and put her forehead down on her folded hands.

The Queen lifted her up then and let herself be dressed and led to the door. The time was evening, at twilight, a lucky time, for the villagers were busy with their meal, and the bearers, with their guard, had come by side roads and along the paths that pass between the fields. Moreover, a light snow fell, and this served to keep people in their houses, the doors closed. Nevertheless, when the Queen appeared the chief guardsman, after obeisance, urged her.

"Majesty, I am commanded to beg you to make haste. We travel by night, and there are enemies among the mountains, in the valleys and behind rocks."

The Queen acknowledged this by a slight nod. She turned to the poet and his wife and then she stood for a long moment, in pure pleasure. Yes, it was her own palanquin, her private conveyance, a gift from the King at her marriage. It was made of fine wood and the panels were lacquered in gold. Into each panel was a jeweled center of many colored stones and the windows were of Chinese glass, hand-painted. At her desire the King had ordered that at each corner there should be a Confucian cross of gold, "So that," she had told him, "I shall be safe wherever I travel in the four corners of the world."

So indeed she had been saved and now she made a sign that the front curtain of the palanquin was to be lifted so that she could enter. And she did enter, and she sat herself down on the thick cushions covered with gold brocade and she smelled the fragrance of the rose jar which was her favorite scent wherever she was. To her it was the atmosphere of home and she breathed it in deeply. Then the curtain was lowered and she felt herself lifted from the earth and carried away into the night.

It was night, too, when, days later, she reached the capital. The streets were empty except for the blind. By law only the blind were allowed to walk abroad at night and now they walked in silence, tapping their sticks in front of them upon the cobblestones. Suddenly her mood changed. She felt alone again and cold. She was returning to the palace, but could it be the same? And what of her servingwoman, who had exchanged garments with her, hiding her Queen in her cotton skirt and jacket and taking on herself the royal robes which meant her death? She had been killed, without doubt, and her gentle ghost would haunt the palace forever.

"Has the Queen returned safely?"

It was Sunia's first question in the morning.

"She has returned," Il-han replied.

Sunia was superintending the arrival of the first plum

blossoms sent in from the forcing house in the country. The blossoms were white and all but scentless, except for a delicate freshness. Before she put her question she had sent the two men servants away.

"You did not want to tell me?" she inquired, busying herself with the arrangement of a branch. Plum trees in the winter, in spring the cherry blossoms, in summer the hanging clusters of the purple wisteria, in autumn the golden poplars, these were the seasons named in flowers and trees.

"You were sleeping like a child," he replied. "And you know how I dislike waking even a child. Who knows where the soul wanders in sleep? I once saw a man wake demented because soul had left the body and could not find its way back quickly enough to the body."

She laughed. "And you tease me because I believe in the household spirits!"

The two children entered at this moment, running away from nurse and tutor. The nurse came panting after the younger boy. She caught hold of his jacket and held him fast while Il-han watched.

"It is time this younger one had a tutor of his own," he observed.

"Not until after the next summer, I beg you," Sunia said.

The elder son came to her side and leaned against her. He was taller by a head than he had been only a few months ago, but his willful face had not changed. The lively black eyes were still bold. Seeing that his elder brother was with the mother, the younger one approached his father while the nurse stood aside, in silence.

Il-han took the child in his arms. This was a slender child, gentle as a girl, obedient, smiling as he smoothed his father's cheek with his small warm hand.

"Are you going away again?" he asked.

"Only to the palace," Il-han replied.

"Why do you go to the palace?"

"Because the Queen has come back."

The elder ran to him as he spoke. "Shall you wear your court dress, Father?"

"Yes. That is why I came to find your mother. I wish her to help me."

"I will help you," the child said. "I and my mother."

And soon they were busy with his court dress, difficult to wear, and Sunia advised while a man servant and two women fetched the garments and put them on Il-han, standing like an image except that he groaned with impatience. Over his undergarments of white silk they put on him the long blue satin tunic which hung to his ankles and was tied on the right breast by a silk band. The neckband was oval and under it was fastened a collar of white cotton. A belt, rectangular in shape and protruding in front and back, was secured by a strong cord of silk. Below his chest was fastened a plastron finely woven, and made of satin embroidered in solid gold thread. Upon the gold were two cranes in flight, embroidered in silver thread. These two cranes were the symbol of his high rank, for lesser nobles were allowed but one crane. Upon his feet where white cotton socks and black velvet short boots. Upon his head, after his long hair had been combed and freshly coiled, he placed his high black hat shaped like a cone with visor both front and back. At the sides were two winglike ears, symbol of his readiness to hear quickly the royal commands.

When he was dressed and ready to leave for audience, his two sons were awestruck. They stood before him like two young acolytes before a Buddha.

Sunia laughed. "Is he your father or not?" she inquired of her sons.

"He is my father," the elder one said proudly, but the younger one wept and hid his face in his nurse's skirts. Meanwhile the tutor had entered in search of his pupil, and Il-han dismissed them all, except Sunia.

"Leave me," he said to them. "I must clear my mind and prepare my spirit."

When they had gone, he took Sunia by the hand and led her to the tallest plum tree, now in snowy bloom.

"Sunia," he said. "Have I your permission to attend the Queen?"

She looked at him amazed. "Are you teasing me?"

"No, I am asking you," he said.

"And if I refuse? You would go anyway."

"I would not."

She gave her sudden ripple of laughter. "There is no man in the whole of Korea like you," she declared.

"Why do you say that?" he asked, amazed in his turn.

"Because it is true," she replied, "and now go tell the Queen I command you to attend her. I push you out of the house, so—"

And pretending to push him, she sent him off while she laughed. She laughed, but something stung in her heart, for still she knew the Queen had a power over him that she could not comprehend.

As for Il-han, he went his way in his own palanquin, pondering upon the two women he knew best, his wife and his Queen. In his youth he had known a few women of pleasure, "the accomplished persons," as they were called, trained to sing and dance and converse with men. They were not indeed women so much as persons, something between man and woman, and apart from both. Yet besides them he had scarcely so much as seen any other woman before he was given Sunia for his wife. Ladies of birth and wealth rode hidden in covered palanquins, and as for the bareheaded women in street and field, no man looked at them unless he wished to be attacked. These common women had a fierce pride in their womanhood and their men stood by them. Only a boy or a man insane would have dared to approach them.

He sighed at such thoughts and wished that he were to enter the palace of the King rather than the Queen. But to the Queen he was committed and these royal two were as far apart as the Empress of China from the Emperor of Japan.

. . . He perceived as soon as he had entered into the Queen's presence that she was changed. She had grown thinner, and even the fullness of her brocaded skirt and the short loose jacket did not conceal the slenderness of her body. Her face was less round and girlish than it had been and he was awed anew by her beauty, by the gentle sadness in her eyes which he had always seen lively, and by the pallor of her fair skin. She was quiet when he entered, somewhat distant as she sat upon her thronelike cushion while he stood. For the first time she did not bid him kneel or seat himself. She let him stand, keeping him at a distance for her own reasons.

He made his obeisances nevertheless and gave his greetings and he waited for her to direct what he should say and thus she began:

"Everything here in the palace is the same. And everything is different."

"May I inquire if your Majesty has conferred with the King?" he asked.

"We have not met," she replied, "but I have been told that he will send for me today. Therefore I wished first for you to come before me so that I might learn what is the state of the nation as you see it. I know that you will speak the truth. Alas, I can say this of no other living soul. And I know, too, that I can no longer trust even myself. I am not wise enough. Who could have dreamed that I would be forced to flee from my own palace? I have been in a far country far away—very far—very far . . ."

She looked about the royal room as though she saw it for the first time.

"Majesty," he said, "I cannot wholly regret that you have seen how your people live, in grass-roofed huts, with meager food."

"And yet more happy than I am here," she put in. "The poet's wife—how fortunate she is to have no greater burden than the day's work in her small house and all for one man whom she loves!"

"She is fortunate that her life is suited to her nature," Il-han replied. "And you know very well, Majesty, that you could never live in a small house. You are truebone, and the palace is your home, your people are your responsibility. This is suited to your nature."

She sighed and smiled and sighed again. "You will not allow

me to envy anyone or even to pity myself. Proceed! Enlighten me! What must I know?"

Still she did not invite him to be seated and he stood, his head bowed so that he saw only the hem of her full skirt, beneath which peeped the upturned toes of her gold satin slippers.

"The Regent," he said, "is now imprisoned in a house in a city not too near Peking. He is comfortable, but he is guarded and he cannot escape. I am in communication with that great Chinese statesman—"

"Li Hung-chang?" she cried with some anger. "Among all Chinese he is one I do not trust!"

Il-han replied firmly, "He is only wise enough to see that, while China will not lose her independence, we may lose ours, for she cannot protect us. For this reason, upon his advice, we must accept the newest western country as our ally. The treaty with the United States, which we have let pause, must now be ratified so that the Americans may send a representative here to the court—"

"You tell me this—"

"I tell you because I must. We must have a friend to take China's place, for if we have not, Japan will encroach and possess us."

"Japan never! Remember that we drove back Hideyoshi three hundred years ago!"

"Will you never forget Hideyoshi? The Japanese are stronger than we are now."

"They were stronger then than we were but our Admiral Yi used his cunning brain and his iron turtle ships—"

"When will you forget those turtle ships? The Japanese have new iron ships and western weapons and they have not made a hermit nation of Japan as we have of our country. They have visited western countries and learned from them. And they are preparing to fight China—I so prophesy!"

"I cannot believe that a handful of islands could dream such folly against a vast continent—"

He interrupted her. "Majesty, I am no Christian, but the Christians have a quaint story about a giant whom no one dared to kill until a shepherd lad with a sling let fly a pebble with such good aim that the stone sank into the giant's forehead and ended him. Today it is not size that means strength —it is the youth with the pebble. Some day, Majesty, the new nations will devise a weapon no bigger than a child's playing ball, and that weapon will destroy a continent."

"Do not tell me about Christians," she retorted. "They are wanderers and troublemakers wherever they are. We should always put them to death."

"There are too many of them now, it is true," he agreed. "They swarm everywhere, and they carry the pebbles of revolution. But we can no longer kill them, Majesty. We must accept them, not because of their religion, but because they come from the West and they bring western learning to us. Let them come, Christian though they are. We must learn everything of them except religion. We cannot go to their country, therefore we must let them come here, for our own sakes."

"If they come," she declared, "I will not receive them. And I will see to it that the King does not receive them. They must live as exiles."

He gave her a long look, and she returned it. Then she rose. "I am more weary than I thought," she said. "You are dismissed."

And so saying, she clapped her hands and her ladies came out from the next room and led her away.

He stood there irresolute. He had made her angry and he was chilled to think so. But he had done his duty. There remained now the King. What of the King? Should he ask for audience? Was it possible that his father had already been in audience? He thought quickly, and decided that he would go to his father and see how far apart they were, father and son, before he asked audience with the King.

When he arrived at his father's house an hour later, unexpected, he was frightened to discover that his elder was ill. He was announced at the gate and his father's chief servant himself drew back the bar and bowed before him.

"Sir," he said, "we have been looking for you. Your father was preparing to go to the King this morning, at command, but when he had taken food, he suddenly fell unconscious and we have not been able to rouse him. The doctor is here—"

Il-han brushed the man aside strongly and strode through the gate and to his father's bedroom. Everything fled from his mind except the fear of what he might see. His father was old, and yet somehow he had never thought of death, so strong was his father's spirit, a brave stubborn spirit, difficult and yet one to be loved.

He entered the room and saw about the bed the servants weeping, and the doctor kneeling beside his father and feeling for the thirty-seven ways of the pulse. Il-han did not interrupt him. He stood waiting until the doctor rose and bowed.

"Sir," the doctor said, "your illustrious father is suffering from the fatigues of old age and drying of the blood. He needs a healing stimulant. I prescribe a brew of *sanghwatung*. Do not scorn it because it is cheap. There is no better restorative for chill and fatigue. Your father rose before dawn to prepare for the royal audience. It is no wonder that at his age he became unconscious."

Since all had long known the value of this brew, Il-han accepted the doctor's decision, and he sent word to Sunia that he would remain with his father until the elder became conscious again, his soul returned safely into his body. As the day wore on, however, the old man did not waken. Instead his left side became rigid in paralysis and he breathed in great gasping sighs. Even though he was moved into another room for benefit of change, he did not waken or improve. Il-han became more alarmed with every hour, and at last he decided upon the extreme measure. He summoned his servant who was waiting outside in the gatehouse.

"It appears to me," he told the man, "that my father is growing worse and not better. He is not able to swallow and therefore he cannot drink even the sanghwatung. You are to go now to the western doctor, that American who lives by the east gate. Invite him to come and give his opinion."

The servant was horror-struck. "Surely, master, you dare not—"

"I dare anything if it may save my father's life. Go, and do not reply to me," Il-han commanded.

The man bowed and went away, and in less than an hour by the water clock the foreign doctor entered the room. He was tall and he wore black coat and trousers, and on his face he grew a thick sandy beard. He was indeed a fearful sight, for above the unnatural color of the beard he had strange blue eyes, and short hair. His eyebrows were bushy, and in the candlelight thick hair glinted even on his hands. For an instant Il-han regretted what he had done. How could he trust a man whose appearance was so savage as this? The very odor of the man was wild, a strong meaty reek, like a wolf's musk.

The man himself was calm. He bowed a short awkward bow to Il-han and then he sat down beside his patient.

"What happened to this old man?" he asked.

He put the inquiry to Il-han in simple Korean such as ignorant people use, but Il-han was surprised that he could speak in any language that could be understood.

He turned to his servant.

"Explain to this foreigner," he commanded him.

While the man obeyed, Il-han observed the man closely. Though he knew there were these persons in the city, he had never seen one close. This, then, was an American! It was to such a breed that he and his countrymen must look for friendship! What had they in common? Could there be friendship between a tiger and a deer?

When the servant had finished, the man rose to his feet and addressed Il-han. "Your father is suffering from a blood clot in the brain."

Il-han was so surprised that he forgot himself and spoke directly to the man instead of through the servant, "How can you say this when you cannot see into my father's skull?"

"I know the illness," the man replied. "The symptoms are clear. I will leave you some medicine, but I must tell you that it is likely your father will die before the night is over. He is very near to death now."

Il-han was horrified at such speech. To mention death, to say that it must come, was almost to bring it down by force.

He turned to the servant in cold anger. "Remove this foreigner. Pay him his money and take him outside the gate and draw the iron bar."

"I ask no money," the foreigner said proudly, and lifting the small black bag he had brought with him, he took out a small bottle, set it on the low table and strode from the room with such great steps that the servant was compelled to run even to follow him. As for the bottle, Il-han threw it out the window into the pool in the garden.

In the night, two hours before dawn, his father died without waking. The hour of death was exactly known, for upon his father's mouth Il-han had placed a wisp of soft cotton. Kneeling beside the floor bed he watched the slight stirring of the cotton. Suddenly it stopped, and he spoke to his servant, who marked down on a ready sheet of paper the hour by the water clock.

Il-han rose to his feet and covered his father's body with a silken quilt. Then he beckoned the servant to his side.

"Instruct my father's household," he commanded. "According to custom, there must be no wailing for an hour, so that my father's spirit be not disturbed in its flight. Meanwhile you are to return to my own house and fetch my sons and their mother and such other persons as are needed to care for them. We will remain here until my father's burial."

"Sir," the servant replied, "before I obey, may I ask for the honor of inviting the illustrious soul to return? I have ready the inner coat of cotton cloth which was prepared for this moment when your father reached his sixtieth birthday."

Il-han considered this request. It was proper for a member of the household or a distant relative, who had never seen the dead, to perform this rite, and he might have refused his servant except that the man grew up in this house and had cared for Il-han himself as a child and had served him through his youth, leaving only when Il-han himself left to set up his own household after marriage.

"You may do so," he said.

The man then climbed to the roof of the house and standing exactly over the place where his old master lay dead, he prepared himself for the solemn rite.

The hour was dawn, and rays of the rising sun crept through the mountains in long bright shafts. The wind blew fresh and cooled by the night. It was indeed a beautiful day upon which to die. So thinking, the man lifted up the coat, and holding the collar in his left hand and the hem in his right, he faced the south and waved the coat three times. The first time he announced in a loud voice the full name of the dead nobleman. The second time he announced the nobleman's highest rank. The third time he announced his death. After this he cried out again, and this time to invite the departed soul to return. When all was done he came down from the roof and placed the coat over the body of the dead, and wailed in a loud voice again and again. Then with the help of others, he lifted the body upon a special bed which faced the south, and he placed around it a paper screen.

After such announcement and invitation, the household prepared for the ceremonies due the dead. Il-han's father had lived alone after his mother's death many years before. In spite of loneliness he had not taken another wife, not even a young woman. His servants had cared for him, men and women, and now they set about their sorrowful work. The women put away all jewelry, and men and women let down their long hair. In the kitchen the cook boiled rice into pots of thin soup, for no rice could be cooked dry during the days of mourning. In the death chamber, the dead man's body was washed with soft white paper and warm perfumed water. His hair was combed and tied loosely, not in its usual coil. The combings from the hair were brushed into the hair, and all that had been separated from the body during the long lifetime and had been saved was now restored, the nail parings, the hair droppings, and four teeth which had been extracted when they caused pain. These were put into two pouches and placed right and left beside the body so that in the next life the person could be whole as when he was born.

The mouth was opened with a spoon of willow wood and

into it was placed a pearl, which was held fast by three spoon-fuls of gluten rice. This pearl was the death pearl, grown only in the giant clams which are found in the Naktong River, a rare pearl, pure but without luster, found in but one out of ten thousand clams and without fault, for it grows of itself within the shell. Indeed, so rare is this pearl that it is removed before burial and handed down from generation to generation. The pearl in his father's mouth had belonged to a Kim five generations before and some day it would also be placed in Il-han's own mouth, and after him in the mouth of his eldest son. When the ritual was finished, Il-han left the room, and the servant finished his duty by putting balls of cotton into the dead man's ears and covering his tranquil face with a cloth of handspun linen.

Now the household busied itself. New garments must be made for the dead, and a new mattress for his coffin, new blanket and new pillow. The men who serve the dead must be summoned and also the geomancer, whose duty it was to de-cide upon the place of burial, a place suited to the winds and the waters. The coffin too had to be built, and of pinewood, for the pine tree is evergreen and is a symbol of manhood. It does not wither or cast its leaves until it dies. Serpents and turtles and lizards and all such reptiles will never nest near a pine tree. Nor does the pine tree rot at the core to remain an empty shell. It dies whole, and quickly, and begins another life, and this, too, is good. The old life should not cling to the new and hamper the growth beyond. What is finished is ended and if dust is the end, then may the end come entire when it comes. The parts of this coffin were put together with wooden pegs for nails, and the cracks were filled with honey and resin, the walls and bottom lined with white cloth, and upon this bottom a mattress was laid. Inside the lid the word *Heaven* was brushed, and at the four corners the word *Sea*.

Into this final home Il-han, in his position as master of mourning, now helped his father to lie and the coffin was lifted into the place of honor on a raised platform. By this hour neighbors and friends and relatives knew of the death and they came to mourn. With each guest Il-han made the wail of mourning the suitable number of times, and then the guests were served with wine and food. The next day at sunrise Il-han, still as master of mourning, lit the early incense and again wailed in mourning, and food was brought for the dead as though he were living. So it was again in the evening until all ceremonies were performed according to ritual.

Then Il-han sat alone in the room where as a child he had studied his Confucian books with his old tutor, and while he waited for Sunia, he was aware of a new loneliness. His mother's death remained in him still as a wound too deep, for he was her only child. But she had long been ill and feeble. His father was his family in those days, and his closest friend, and there had been no estrangement between them, for the elder man had declined political posts and had retired more and more deeply into his books as the years passed. To Il-han he had often said that he could not share the strife and dissensions everywhere, the struggles for power between this man and that, the treacheries of court life, the enmities between surrounding nations. He was content to keep his own spirit pure, and he believed that he could do nothing for his fellow patriots that served them better than to remain untouched by deceit and private profit. Yet he did not judge these faults in others, nor did he change the traditions. He did not, for example, consider sharing the Kim lands with the peasants who tilled it. When Il-han, in his impetuous youth, declared that his father should rectify those sins of the past whereby the Kim clan had, like other yangban clans, seized great portions of the nation's land, his father had merely replied that each generation must take care of its own sins, and he believed that he himself had committed no sins.

It was past noon of the next day when Sunia arrived with her retinue of children and servants. Il-han met her at the entrance and he saw her face was pale, but she allowed herself no outbreak of weeping. Instead she directed the children to embrace their father, and he lifted them into his arms, first the elder and then the younger. Their eyes were large and frightened and he comforted them, saying that he was glad they had come and that their grandfather could not speak to them now, but they might run into the garden and play with the little monkey chained there to a tree, and he could come to them later. Then he returned to his room and Sunia followed.

"Sunia," he said, as soon as they were alone. "You must wait upon the Queen, announcing my father's death. Tell her I will wait upon her myself as soon as the rites are fulfilled."

She was looking at him with tender and sorrowful eyes, but at these words her tenderness changed.

"Even now you think of her first," she said.

"Because it is my duty," he told her.

"Go to her yourself, then," she said.

With these words she turned away from him and walked to the end of the room which opened upon a small private garden. There in a pool no larger than a big bowl a few goldfish swam in the clear water, and the sun glinted on their ruffled fins.

Il-han was suddenly seized with rage for all women. Queen and commoner alike, they thought first of themselves and of whether they were loved by men. His reason told him that he was unjust, for surely women must think of love, else how can children be born? It is children they desire and for this they seek men's love above all else. Yet Sunia had no cause to complain of him for lack of love or of children. So his angry heart exclaimed, and then his reason reminded him that he had been many months away from home, and since his return his mind had been much troubled, and Sunia was quick to discern that his whole self was not with her. Yet, because he feared to rouse her jealousy—still inexplicable to him, for how can a woman be jealous of a queen—he had not explained to her the weight upon him, now that he had seen his country whole and the people clinging to its earth and scratching its surface for their food.

He turned his back on her, too, and thus they stood for minutes until his heart took hold again—yes, and his reason. Let these two meet, his wife and his Queen, this time in the palace, and let each take the measure of the other. Surely Sunia would come home to him again and know the depths of her folly. And he was stronger than Sunia, and as man should be stronger than woman he should make peace first.

With such feelings and reasonings, he went to her now and put his hands on her shoulders and turned her about to face him. Her eyes filled with tears and her lips quivered as she looked up at him.

"Do what I ask of you," he said. "Go and see for yourself. She is your Queen as well as mine."

His gentleness melted her as it always did, and he went on.

"I left her presence in anger, Sunia, such anger that I was about to ask for immediate audience with the King. Then I thought I should come to my father first, since it was he who had access to the King. When I came here, I found him—as you know. I cannot return to the Queen now, with my mind divided and my heart in sorrow. Do this for me, my wife."

She put up both her hands then and stroked his cheeks with her palms and he knew she would obey. When she went to prepare herself, he ordered his servant to precede Sunia and ask for audience with the Queen, declaring the emergency, and he ordered her palanquin to be made ready and to be hung with streamers of coarse white cotton, signifying a death in the family.

When she had gone, he escorting her to the gate and seeing her into her palanquin and the curtain lowered which hid her from public view, he returned to his father's house and gathered together the head servants. When they were assembled, standing before him while he sat on the floor cushion behind the table, he gave his commands.

"I have decided for reasons of state that we must hasten the burial of my honored ancestor. He would not wish to imperil the nation because of his death and our national affairs are not yet settled, although the Queen has returned to us. Therefore the burial must not be later than the ninth day after his death, for as you well know, it must then be delayed for three months. In that time it is possible that we may have war. Therefore we must arrange the funeral for the seventh day."

The servants looked at one another, stricken. They were elderly men, the four of them, long in the service of his father, and now that their master was dead they were afraid to disobey his son and heir. Yet they wished to do honor to their dead master and they wanted no undue haste.

"Young master," the eldest said, "to show such haste as this is unworthy of your honored ancestor, our master. In common families, yes, seven days are enough to make a few worthless mourning garments. But in this house it would be unseemly. The longer the delay between death and burial, the higher the family. It is only yesterday that he—left us. Only today is the priest of the dead here, and at this very moment he is binding the sacred body with the seven ceremonial cords."

Il-han interrupted him. "I trust this priest knows his business."

"He does, young master," the servant replied. "I stood by him while he bound the cords about the shoulders, elbows, wrists and thumbs, hips, knees, calves and ankles, all in proper order. True, I had to remind him of the evil spirits that enter even into such a house as this when the master dies. Under my own eyes then he looped the cord at the waist in the shape of the character *sim*, which—"

"I know, I know," Il-han said impatiently.

The servant, because of his age, continued inexorably slowly. He remembered Il-han as a lively mischievous small boy and an impetuous youth, and though his surface was courteous, his mind continued stubborn.

"As to the mourning, young master, consider what must be made. The cloth is to be bought and sewn into garments for the family, even to the eighth cousins removed, and after them for the household servants. I have written all this down—"

"Read it to me," Il-han demanded.

The head steward beckoned to the next in rank, who took a scroll of paper from his bosom which he unrolled and read aloud in a deep loud voice.

"For the chief mourners, yourself, young master, and your two sons, undergarments of coarse cotton, leggings of coarse linen, shoes of straw. On the upper body, a long coat of the same coarse cotton, a girdle of hemp about the waist, a hat of bamboo, a headband of coarse linen, and a face screen of coarse linen, one foot long and half as wide, upheld by two bamboo sticks. I trust, young master, that your two sons are able to hold the screens before their faces, but if not—"

"Proceed," Il-han said shortly. These old men were making a festival of his father's funeral!

The man obeyed. "The ladies of the first generation will wear coarse linen and straw shoes. Their jeweled hairpins must be taken away and they will be given wooden pins. As for the next female relatives, their mourning will be the same. They need not wear hats of bamboo and shoes of straw or headbands and their waist cords may be white. Distant relatives need wear only the leggings and a hempen twisted cord. But all must wear white. No colors, of course—even on children."

Il-han could endure no more. "In Buddha's name," he exclaimed, "how can all this be done?"

The four old men were wounded. They fixed their eyes on the wall behind his head and waited for the chief steward to reply.

"Master," he said with dignity, "all will be ready on the fourth day after death, which is the day of putting on mourning."

"Then let the burial be on the seventh day," Il-han commanded and he clapped his hands together to signify they were dismissed.

Meanwhile, Sunia stood before the Queen. She had upon her arrival been ushered into the anteroom, and there she waited a long time, too long she felt with indignation, and she believed it was because the Queen was making an ado over her apparel and jewels and hairdress. If so, she could not blame the Queen, for when she appeared at the end of an hour or more, she was beautiful indeed. Sunia had more than once begged Il-han to tell her how the Queen looked in her royal robes, and Il-han had always refused.

"How do I know how she looks?" he had replied. "I try never to look higher than her knees, and if possible no higher than the hem of her skirt."

"But you do look higher," Sunia had insisted, teasing and serious at the same time.

"Not if I can help it," he said sturdily.

"But sometimes you cannot help it?"

At this he had been angry or pretended to be.

"Whatever you are trying to make me say I will not say it," he had declared.

Now Sunia saw the Queen in full splendor, and it was as if it were for the first time, so changed she was by her royal robes and in her palace. The Queen entered, leaning upon the arms of two women, though she needed to lean on no one. She was not taller than most women are but she held her head regally. Her features were perfect and in proportion, the nose straight, the cheekbones high, the mouth delicate and yet full, the chin round, the neck slender, her eyes large and black, their gaze direct and fearless. Her skin was white as cream, her cheeks were pink as a young girl's, and her lips were red. She was too beautiful even for a Queen and yet Sunia was comforted, for it was a high, proud beauty, willful and passionate, of a sort that demanded a man's service rather than won his heart. Relieved somewhat of her jealousy, she looked at the Queen with lively interest, and suddenly they were two women together.

The Queen smiled. "I used to imagine you before I saw you in your house, but I was always wrong."

Sunia laughed. "What did you imagine, Majesty?"

"I thought you would be a small woman," the Queen said, gazing at her. "Small and soft and childlike. Instead—we could be sisters!"

Oh, what a clever woman, Sunia said to herself, how clever to destroy the distance between us, how subtle a way to win my heart! And yet in spite of this self-caution, how successful the way was, for against her own judgment, which indeed was never to trust a queen, she found herself drawn to this woman. Could a queen be so without pretense as this, and yet who but a queen could be so fearlessly frank?

"Majesty," she said, remembering. "I have come in obedience to my children's father. He has sent me here to announce the death of his own father."

The Queen waved her two women away and came close to Sunia. "Oh no," she breathed. "I heard the rumor and I did not believe it, thinking he would come at once to tell me, somehow—"

"He has his duties as only son," Sunia said. "And he asks forgiveness for sending me in his place."

The Queen came down the two steps into the waiting room and sat down beside the sparrow table, a square table of the time of Koryo. It was covered with embroidered silk, whose corners were hung with streamers of silk.

"Sit here beside me," she commanded Sunia. "Tell me everything."

Sunia obeyed, except what was everything?

"Death came yesterday, suddenly," she said. "Luckily he— my children's father—had just entered his father's house, and so he went at once to the bedside. Physicians were called, both our own and the western one."

"Not American!" the Queen gasped. "I cannot believe that my faithful courtier would—"

"He wished to try everything, Majesty. And the foreigner, though he could not prevent it, foretold the death."

"He would, he would," the Queen exclaimed, and she pulled a silk kerchief from her sleeve and wiped her eyes. "And how is he?" she inquired.

"He?" Sunia asked innocently.

"My courtier."

"My children's father is in mourning, but he knows his duty to you, Majesty."

Sunia spoke with some coolness and made as if she would rise to end the audience, but the Queen took both her hands and pulled her down again.

"You shall not leave me yet," she said. "Let us be friends. Let us be sisters. Do you know I am alone here in the palace? I have no friend except the Queen Mother, and she is old and lives only in ancient times. So do I, too, live alone, by my wish, but I am not allowed peace. I am told by him—your—your lord—that everything is changed and that I must be wary and alert from day to day, and even that I must receive a new ambassador from the West—an American. Does he tell you all these secrets?"

"No, Majesty," Sunia said.

The Queen put her palms to her cheeks in distraction. "I wish he did," she murmured. "I wish I had not to bear all these changes alone."

Sunia took courage. "Does not the King . . ."

"Oh, say nothing of the King," the Queen said impatiently, and let her hands fall. "When do we meet, he and I? If I am summoned you may be sure it is not for communication."

She looked for a long moment at Sunia. "Do you know," she said, "I lived for many days in the poor glass-roofed house of a poet. He and his wife, the two of them, lived there with me and they hid me. But I saw how they lived. They were friends, he and she. When I was in the small secret room where I was hid, I could hear them talking together and laughing. Such small things they talked about, as where the gray cat had hidden her kittens, or whether a certain wild bird had returned from beyond the southern seas, and whether the next day they could buy a bit of meat for dinner. And then he read her the poem he had written that day and she listened and said it was the most beautiful poem he had yet written. And at night they lay down to sleep together in the same bed—"

She turned her head away, she pressed Sunia's hand between both hers. "And why I tell you all this, I do not know. It is very silly. Return to your children's father. Tell him not to hasten himself. I will wait patiently until his filial duties are finished. Tell him I will make no move meanwhile."

She rose, smiled at Sunia, released the hand she held. Then her two women came to her, and leaning upon their arms again she left the audience room.

"Well?" Il-han asked when Sunia returned.

He was in the garden with his two sons, although until a short while ago he had been in the room of the dead where his father lay. He had examined the handiwork of the priest and then he had seated himself alone for some time with his father. According to custom, when a meal was served to the household, food must also be brought here to the dead, and only when the head servant came in with the bowls on a tray had Il-han left his father to go in search of his sons. They were still in the garden with tutor and nurse, and they had made friends with the monkey, laughing over his antics and feeding him with peanuts the nurse shelled as fast as she could.

Il-han had only finished saying to the tutor that the time had come when the younger son should also be under his care, to which the tutor had replied that he felt the younger should be under the care of another than himself.

"This elder son," he was saying, "is of such a nature, so brilliant and so strong, that he takes my whole strength. Your younger son, sir, is different, and I fear that I am not able to teach and nurture two such different—"

At this moment Sunia had come to the door of the house and Il-han left the tutor's words hanging and went to her at once. They entered the house together and he drew the wall screens shut as he spoke.

"Well," she replied, "I have seen the Queen."

"But did you give her my message?"

"Of course I did," she replied, "and she tells you not to make haste, but to fulfill your filial duties and she will wait patiently until your return."

"Is that all?"

She looked at him thoughtfully. What should she say? It was not all. She could say that the Queen was even more beautiful than she had remembered, she could say that the Queen behaved to her as though they were sisters, she could say—she could say nothing.

"That is all," she said. Now she paused to look at him between half-closed lids.

"Why do you look at me like that?" he demanded.

She smiled. "How am I looking?"

"As if you were not telling me something," he said bluntly.

When she only went on smiling, he turned away from her impatiently. "It is impossible for women to stop pretending or imagining or something or other. You delight in puzzling me!"

And with that he strode out of the room.

On the day before his father's burial he went to the site of the grave, since it was his duty to be present while the grave was marked and dug. The site was outside the city wall, for it was against the law for any to be buried inside the city wall of the capital. The day was warm with spring, indeed a day for life and not for death. He rode his horse ahead of his servant, who sat on a smaller horse behind him. The cherry trees were coming into blossom, their soft white and pink a mass of delicate color against the gray of the mountain rock. People were stirring from their houses, the children running about with bare arms slipped out of their padded winter garments. Old men sat in the sun smoking their pipes, and old women crouched close to the earth, searching for the early green weeds to cook with bits of flesh or fowl and to eat with the day's rice.

The city's most skilled geomancer had chosen the site for the grave and was waiting for him. Il-han rode across the valley and halfway up a low hill, and there in a sheltered cove open to the sun, he found the man already marking the grave. With him were the gravediggers. Il-han dismounted and after suitable greeting he examined every view and aspect and then gave permission for the grave to be dug. While this solemn work was in process, he stood looking out over the city, a great city, a vast huddle of the houses of the poor, the palaces of the royal family and the noble clans, these set in parks of pine and blossoming cherry. Here in the capital were the extremes of his country and his people. How long could such division continue, while outer peoples threatened? How could he compel his people to realize their folly? Only the closest union inside the country could fend off foreign attack. His troubled mind searched again for answers to the question, eternal and dangerous, and he reviewed the dangers. He heaved a sigh as deep as his soul and was glad that his father was dead. Yet of what use was death? His two sons were alive and must meet the future he dreaded, and how could he help them except by somehow preserving for them their country, whole and independent?

"Sir," the geomancer said. "Will you approve?"

He turned and walked toward the grave and looked into it. The earth was scanty, and rocks had been heaved out of it to make the pit and piled until the grave was rimmed with such rocks. To one side were the two gravestones upon which were already carved the high qualities of his father as poet and patriot, one to be buried at the foot of the grave and the other to be set up for the eternal future.

"You have done well," Il-han told the geomancer.

There remained now only to wait for the mourners who were to bring food offerings to the spirit of the mountain, who was now to receive the body of his father, and Il-han waited until he saw the procession coming on foot from among the rocks. The bowls of food were then set forth in proper arrangement and the rites were concluded. There remained but one more duty, and it was to declare to his dead father that the grave was ready for his body, which he did as soon as he returned to his father's house. In the presence of his father's dead body he made declaration.

On the morning of the seventh day, his servant reported to Il-han that the shelters had been built near the grave, the funeral bier was made, and this because the family was too high to use a rented bier, the banners were complete, and all was ready for the funeral. To this Il-han made no answer except to incline his head in acknowledgment. He had kept himself apart from his family during these days, and alone he had returned to the library of his father's house, dressed every day in mourning and eating only a little coarse food, while he studied the Buddhist scriptures and the Confucian classics in order that his soul and mind might be purified. He had so continued thus throughout the days until the hour came for the funeral procession to assemble.

In the late afternoon of this seventh day all gathered together in readiness to proceed to the mountain. Twilight was

near, the suitable time between day and night when his
father's spirit would not be disturbed. In his place as the son
and master of mourning, Il-han viewed the procession as it
formed. He was content with what had been done. The procession then set forth. At its head were the torchmen, who
held great torches made of brushwood branches bound together. These were lighted and were dragged along the
ground, firing as they went a trail of lively sparks. Now and
again the men lifted the torches and whirled them in flames
about their heads and then dropped them again to the earth.
Next came the lantern bearers in two lines, carrying lanterns
of ironwork covered with the best silk in red and blue colors,
and after those came a banner bearer on foot, carrying in
both hands a banner of silk on which was written the name
of the illustrious dead and the many honors he had accumu-
lated in his lifetime.

In the center of the procession was the shrine, carried by
bearers, and in the shrine, which was made of the finest wood,
carved in detail, was set the spirit tablet. On both sides and
following the shrine were the women mourners, and after
them other lantern bearers whose duty it was to illuminate the
catafalque itself, borne by a host of bearers chanting a mournful tune to keep their feet in step. Since the dead had been a
man of honor and wealth, a bell ringer walked in front, ringing
his bell as he went, and around the catafalque on all sides
were banner bearers carrying the banners sent by those who
wished to honor the dead. Behind the catafalque Il-han rode in
a sedan chair carried by bearers, and behind him in other
chairs were Sunia and his sons and the lesser relatives and
mourners.

Slowly the long procession went its way through the streets,
the people stopping to stare and to follow, and thus they approached the Water Mouth Gate, which was the gate for the
dead. The first darkness had fallen when at last they reached
the mountain and there they stopped for the night in the
shelters that had been raised for this purpose. They slept in
rude beds, but Il-han could not sleep. He lay down and got
up again, many times, and at last he walked outside in the

cold night air. The moon shone so clear that the whole world seemed to lie before him, as still in sleep as the dead.

Though it is in the course of nature that a son live longer than his father, yet a deep and solemn mood fell upon him as he realized that from now on, until he himself lay dead, he was responsible to his generation for the conduct of affairs inside his house and beyond its walls to the nation and even beyond to the world. An age had ended with his father, an age when his nation had chosen to be hermit, seeking only to hide itself from the surrounding nations and so to live in peace. Yet there could be no peace now, when foreign ships were sailing toward them across foreign seas, and quarrel rising between a new and young Japan and an old and dying dynasty in China. And what of the giant toward the north? He turned himself to the north, and there above the sharp and pointed peak of the mountain, above that solid rock, he saw the northern star, at this moment as red as blood.

In the morning, Il-han roused the procession and they went on and upward to the site. All was ready there, and with due ceremony the coffin was placed upon transverse poles and covered with a wide length of white cloth, while the geomancer stood near, a compass in his hand to make sure the position was exact. Had there been more sons, these sons would have lowered the coffin, but since there was only Il-han, others helped him at the task. The empty grave, cleansed of all evil vapors and plaguing spirits, now received its owner, while incense burned and women faced the east and the mourners wailed their formal wails of sorrow. Now Il-han, with the help of the men, slowly filled the grave with earth. Deeply as he had felt his father's death, this was the moment of most acute sorrow. The clods fell upon the coffin with sad dull thuds and he heard his sons scream in fear. Yet he did not turn his head nor speak to comfort them until the task was done.

Then he stood on the first terrace below the grave, and facing it in his clear strong voice he announced to the spirit of the mountain that the dead was now buried in its rock and soil. For a moment he stood, carving into his memory the scene he surveyed. His father's grave lay on the warm southern slope of the mountain, on a leveled place, the dug earth raised about it in a bank so that the grave itself lay in the hollow of a crescent. Here at its foot the earth was terraced down to the slope of the mountain and here he stood, saying in his heart the long farewell to his father. There remained but one more task and it was to appoint a caretaker for the grave. For this he summoned the chief steward, who accepted the charge with a deep bow and folded hands.

Thus the day ended and with his family and his retinue Il-han returned to his own house.

When the days of this mourning were over, Il-han asked audience of the King and not the Queen. During the long quiet hours of isolation which respect for his father demanded, he had considered carefully his duty. Without the title or high office desired neither by his father nor himself, independent as they had always been in wealth and family, he could refuse the obligations of position, and yet he had the right to approach the rulers when he had advice to give. So long as his father lived, he had not presumed to approach the King and he maintained his access to the Queen. Now, however, he had by death come into his father's place, and it was fitting that he should first approach the King.

He made known his wish by courier, and the King set an appointed time for private audience. It was at dawn on the seventh day of the seventh month of that moon year. The season was summer. At the set hour Il-han entered his palanquin and was borne to the palace, his servant riding on horse before him to announce his arrival at the gates.

King Kojong, the twenty-sixth monarch of the dynasty of Yi, was still in the prime of his manhood. His mother, Queen Cho, and his father, the Regent, Tae-wen-gun, were early separated in spirit and mind and fact, and he had grown up in the vacuum which existed between them. Each was strong, his father with a male aggressive will and his mother with a deep feminine immobility. He had been played upon by both and had therefore grown slowly to maturity. There were times when he still struggled against these conflicting influences, to which had been added a third, his marriage to a beautiful girl of the powerful house of Min.

His secret taste in women was for small soft yielding child-like females. Instead he was tied to a strong willful woman who seemed never to have been a child. Yet she fascinated him, that part of him which was still boy, the boy whom he tried so constantly to ignore, to destroy, to eliminate from himself, and who he yet feared was his essential being. There was no one to whom he could talk about himself. For while there were the conflicts in him, these secret influences dividing him and distracting him, he understood very well that he was at the mercy also of the conflicts outside him.

He was not an ignorant king. As a child he had been schooled in Confucianism and Buddhism, and in the history of his country. Of the West he knew little, for his father, the Regent, had but one purpose, which was to close the country and make it a hermit nation. Alas, he, the son and present King, knew that this was no longer possible. Incredible as it seemed, the persistent weapon of the West had been religion, a religion based, his father had taught him, upon superstition first proclaimed by a small local group of persons who called themselves Jews, who had killed a revolutionary among their own people, one named Jesus. The human race was always in turmoil from these revolutionaries, his father had maintained, and the Koreans had no need of importing foreign ones when they had plenty of their own. With this excuse, his father had approved the murder of all foreign priests who continued to penetrate into the country, in spite of doom. Now his father, the Regent, was imprisoned in China, and he, the King, could decide for himself what must be done. Certainly he must come to some understanding with his Queen, for she remained steadfastly loyal to China, refusing to realize that Japan was in the ascendancy. They had quarreled over this matter only the night before. He had sent for her, an unusual circumstance, for they had long remained apart. Yet when she returned from her flight she had, he thought, changed for the better. She had come before him formally upon her arrival, and he found her gentler than she had been since their son was found to be of weak mind. She was still beautiful, and he thought he could detect in her manner some slight wish, or longing, or perhaps only the inclination of desire in a woman who knows her youth is nearly gone. Therefore he had invited her to dine with him alone last night, with the thought that if her charm held, they might renew something of the past and she might conceive a son while there was yet time. He had subdued her more than once in the years when their passion had been strong, and it amazed him that something of that past still lived.

The evening had nevertheless been spoiled. They had fallen into the old argument, and had parted early with formal bows and with mutual impatience, and after she was gone he had sent for a palace lady of pleasure.

Now, the morning after, he heard the announcement that the son of his old friend and recently dead adviser waited for audience, and was ready to step into his father's place. He knew Kim Il-han to be an adviser to the Queen, and he did not hurry himself. Let the man wait! It was fully two hours before he sent his chief chamberlain to the Hall of Waiting to say audience was granted. The delay would calm his subject's possible arrogance, he told himself, and then, to mitigate or merely to confuse, he would himself be informal and friendly upon meeting.

At high noon he strode into the audience hall and seated himself upon the throne, which here was scarcely more than an ornate chair, set low to the floor so that he could draw up his feet in the Japanese fashion. Instead, he sat down and crossed his knees in the western fashion. He had never seen a white man, but he was told that they sat on seats and let their legs hang or crossed their knees and he knew that subjects observed every detail of a monarch's behavior, anxious to catch any straw in any wind.

Il-han entered now and knelt before the King. He placed his hands together flat on the polished floor, thumb to thumb. Then he bent his head until his forehead touched his hands and waited.

"You may stand," the King said pleasantly.

Il-han stood, his eyes on the floor, and again he waited.

"You may speak," the King said in the same kind voice.

Without raising his eyes, Il-han then spoke. "Majesty, I come as the son of my father, now deceased. I come, as he did, only as a private citizen, but as one responsible, with others, for the people, and therefore ready for service."

The King listened and then directed by a gesture of the hand that Il-han was to seat himself on the floor cushion before the throne.

"Let us forget ceremony," the King said when the ceremonies were finished. "I trust you because you are your father's son. He was a wise man. He told me once that the three nations who surround us are like the balls a juggler must keep in the air and in motion, and we must be the juggler. Do you agree?"

"Majesty, I would even add more such balls," Il-han replied. "The western nations are eying us across the four seas. How many balls there will be for us to juggle, I cannot tell. But there will be more than three, and some may have to be cast aside."

The King uncrossed his legs impatiently and crossed them again. He did not wear his garments of state today, but about his neck was a heavy chain of jade pieces strung on gold. At the end was a jade circle, carved with the emblem of cranes under a pine tree, and with this emblem his right hand was now busy. He had a full underlip, a sign of his passionate nature, and he pinched it now between thumb and finger, in deep thought.

"Will you accept office?" he asked at last. "Will you be, let us say, prime minister? Chancellor? What you will—"

Il-han raised his eyes to meet the royal gaze and was startled by the boldness he saw. The King's eyes were narrow, the corners sharp and the pupils very black under wide short black brows. They were not the eyes of a poet or a thinker but of a man accustomed to act. His hand, fingering the full lower lip, was dark and strong.

"Majesty," Il-han said, while he let his eyes fall again to the embroidered cranes and the pine tree on the King's breast, "forgive me if I decline office. I wait for your command, day and night. I am your subject. But if I am more, I shall not be free to speak, to move, to report, to observe, to ask for audience, to be of use to you, I hope, as your own hand is useful, obedient to your brain and heart."

The King laughed. "What you mean is that you prefer not to owe me anything! Well, that is rare enough."

He clapped his hands and servants entered.

"Bring us food and drink," he commanded.

While the servants obeyed, he went on, "Now, let us discuss the position of this jewel you call our country. I do not deceive myself as to why Li Hung-chang wishes us to receive an envoy from the United States. It is his weapon against Japan, who threatens war. In such a war we would be their point of departure for China. Tell me, what is the United States?"

He put the question suddenly to Il-han, who was embarrassed because he did not know the answer.

"Majesty, I shall have to inquire. I recollect that the sailors shipwrecked on our shores some fifteen years ago were Americans and I have heard that they were very savage. They molested our women, and our people, outraged, put them to death."

"Not immediately," the King reminded him. "The sailors were at first only arrested. Then others came out from ships to rescue them, and these men seized their shipmates from us, and with them certain of our men, as hostages. It was only then that our outraged people attacked the ship, killed eight of the Americans, and captured the others and burned the ship —all of this deserved, I was told."

Here the King paused and thought awhile and Il-han was amazed to hear such detail.

"Perhaps the truth does not matter now," the King said at last, "but I may as well tell it to you. It was my father who commanded that the ship be attacked. He feared that it brought more Catholic priests to avenge the death of those whom he had ordered beheaded in earlier years. My father believes, has always believed, that western religions disturb the peace wherever they go. This he has observed from such foreign persons in China and in Japan and while he ruled he forbade all foreign priests to set foot on our shores, and if they did so secretly he had them killed. Alas, some of our own people have been beguiled by them, and have themselves become Christian. I will not speak of this."

Here he paused, and Il-han knew the King was reminded of that Kim ancestor of Il-han's who had been killed because he was Catholic.

"I have followed my father," the King continued. "While I was very young I refused to see the American, surnamed Low, who arrived in our port with a fleet of ships. But today I do not know. . . ."

The servants brought the food now and set it on the table and stood by to serve. But the King sent them away again.

"They stand there like images," he complained to Il-han when they were gone, "but they are not images. Their eyes see, their ears hear, and their tongues carry tales. Proceed!"

"Majesty, I am honored that you tell me your thoughts. I am your subject and I ought only to listen and not to speak."

"Speak," the King commanded. "I am surrounded by men who will not speak. Sometimes I think everyone in the palace has cut out his tongue except the Queen. She has no fears! I daresay if Buddha himself were reincarnated here she would tell him how to behave and what to think."

The King spoke willfully, aware that this was no fit talk between himself and a subject and he enjoyed it the more for that reason.

Il-han made a small smile and did not reply. Instead he went on thus:

"Majesty, your father, the Regent, has done what he believed right in his time. For example, he resisted the Japanese as stoutly as he did all others. I must even say that he seemed at times to devise insults for them, hoping they would leave our shores. They did not leave. I beg you, Majesty, not to follow your father. I beg you to think for yourself, to decide for yourself what must be done to preserve our nation and our people. Of all the western peoples, the Americans seem the least vicious. They are young, they have no experience, and they know what it is to fight for independence for themselves. I have heard that over a hundred years ago they fought the country that ruled them, and won."

"What are you saying?" the King demanded.

"I am saying that we must accept the Americans, as Li Hung-chang advises," Il-han replied.

The King clenched his fists and pounded the table so that the dishes jumped. "By a treaty which takes still more from us!" he shouted.

"By a treaty," Il-han agreed.

The two men looked straight into each other's eyes. It was the King who yielded. He got to his feet. "I can eat nothing," he declared, and he turned his back on Il-han and strode from the room.

How then could Il-han eat? He also rose, and putting on his outer garment, he went away. The servants saw him go and came into the empty room. The dishes of delicacies had not even been uncovered, and the servants took them to the kitchens and there with great relish and high laughter they ate the meats prepared for the King.

In the night, when Il-han returned from the long conference with the King, he told Sunia that he had been offered a high post in government and that he had declined. He did not regret his refusal, yet he wondered if she, perhaps, being more simple than he by nature, or so he imagined, might secretly envy other women whose husbands were publicly known. He had a certain fame as a scholar, a thinker, one who did not fear to do what he liked or refuse to do what he disliked, but was this enough? When she replied, he perceived that he had been wrong, and again he marveled, as he had often before, how it is that a man can live with a woman and have sons by her and still know very little of what she is. For Sunia spoke at once when he finished what he had to tell.

"You did very well to refuse a post," she said.

It was night and they lay on the floor mattresses. A candle burned on the low table at his side. The house was silent and beyond the drawn screens the night was dark. He had talked for a long time, and she had listened.

"Why do you say so?" he asked now.

"For one reason," she said. "You always forget small things. You are a great man, but only in great things. You speak to kings and queens as though you were their brother, but you do not know one servant in this house from another, except your own man. And I wonder sometimes if you would even know your sons, if you saw them in a crowd of children. Now you will have time to know your sons—and me, too, I daresay!"

She broke off a laugh, and she had ready laughter, but he was surprised at what she had said.

"You describe a very foolish fellow," he complained, "and I think I am better than that."

She turned on her side then and leaned her head on her elbow and looked down into his rebellious face. "You are only foolish, I say, in small things. If you were clever in small ways you would be foolish in great ones and I am satisfied with what you are. More than that, I know very well that I am a fortunate woman, a lucky wife, a blessed mother."

"Now, now," he said, laughing in turn. "You blame yourself too much. A woman gets what she deserves."

This banter went into sudden passion between them, he aroused by the sight of the lovely face so near, her eyes lustrous and dark in the candlelight. In this way he knew her very well, for when she was ready a peculiar fragrance came from her body. He had learned, but not easily, that while without this fragrance she could submit, it was without response, and then he was robbed of half his joy. While he was a bridegroom, a husband too young, he had not been able to restrain his passion, or suit its timing to hers, even though he cursed himself because, if he did not, they were further apart afterward. But with the fullness of manhood he learned, and he was rewarded. Better to have her whole, at her own time, than resisting when she was not.

Now her fragrance came sweet and strong, and he held her long and close. When they drew apart, they were closer than ever before, and they lay in peace and silence, she thinking while he fell asleep.

He woke after an hour or so and was thirsty and she poured a bowl of tea and then came out with what she had been thinking.

"While we are in mourning, you can do nothing outside, and you must promise me to learn the difference between our two sons. I feel each is different from the other, each not ordinary, but I have not the wit to know what the difference is. This is the first thing I have to say."

He drank the tea and held his bowl for more.

"Then there is a second? And a third, doubtless! When a man has a little time to be idle, be sure his wife will fill it for him."

She pretended to snatch the bowl away from him.

"Dare to think I am like other wives!"

"Fortunately you are not." He was suddenly wide awake, relaxed, amused, and wondering whether, if he indulged her, her fragrance would flow again. She had changed her garments, he could see, and the odor was that of clean freshness.

"You are to stop thinking your own private thoughts," she retorted. "You are to listen to me, if you please! Il-han, I say you should know some of these Americans before you advise the King again. You are in a high, responsible place. You advise rulers. Yet how do you know if Americans are good or evil? What if you lead the King into wrongdoing and our people suffer because you know too little of what you are talking about?"

This was the surprising woman. While he could have sworn she had no concern for anything beyond her household, she came forward with this simple wise conclusion. Unpleasant though it was to consider consorting with foreigners, what she had said was true. Chinese he knew, and Japanese, and a few Russians, but he knew almost no Americans.

All inclination for renewed lovemaking ebbed out of him.

"Go to sleep," he told Sunia. "You have said enough to keep me awake the rest of the night and for many nights to come."

And he pinched out the flame of the candle between his thumb and forefinger.

In these days of mourning for the one dead, Il-han devoted himself to the living. Each morning he sat near while the tutor taught his elder son and he was pleased by the boy's quickness where he was interested and then displeased because where he had no interest he idled. Nevertheless he did not interfere and as the days passed he saw that the tutor understood the child well, and when the child looked away from his books he did not reproach him. Instead he bade the boy run in the garden or he gave him a brush and colored inks and let him paint a picture.

"In a picture," he told Il-han privately, "I discover the child's hidden thoughts and feelings."

"What does he paint?" Il-han asked.

The tutor was troubled. "He paints violence," he said at last. "In this gentle and noble household your son paints a cat with a bird in its teeth, or a devil peering out from the bamboos, or a hawk with a mouse bleeding in its claws."

Il-han heard this with surprise. "No one has ever treated this child harshly. Why should he have such thoughts?"

"I surmise that it comes from the times in which we live," the tutor replied. "He hears of robbers in the city and of bandits in the mountains and he has asked me many times why the Queen was all but murdered, and he is aware of the quarrels among the noble clans. When he is in the country at your honored father's house, as he has always wished to be in the summer, he makes friends with the sons of the farmers who till your lands, sir, and they are wild children. I try to keep him away from them, but he escapes me and I find him there in the village, his good clothes torn and dusty, and his face and hands as black as theirs. He is often rude to me then, and he uses coarse language that he has heard them use. Indeed, he has told me more than once that he wishes he were the son of a peasant, so that he could be free to run the streets and do what he likes."

This was grave news, and Il-han was pricked by his conscience. While he had been concerned with the Queen and the King, his son had found companionship among the ignorant and the poor. That very day, when the morning's lessons were over and the noon meal eaten, he took his elder son by the hand and led him toward the bamboo grove.

"Let us see whether the young shoots are ready to break through again," he coaxed.

The season was too early, he feared, but no, when they came into the shadows of the grove, the bamboos so thick together that the sunlight fell through in drops of light, they saw the earth was loosened by the uprising shoots. Here and there a pointed sheath of palest green, feathered at the tips, showed above the earth.

"Do you remember," Il-han asked his son, "how once you broke the shoots and killed the trees?"

"You said they were only reeds—not trees." The boy spoke willfully, but Il-han could see that he did remember. Still holding the boy's hand he explained what he had said before.

"You were too small to understand what I told you. Although they were only hollow reeds they were living, and they spring anew from old roots. I said that in our country the bamboo shoot is the symbol of the strong uprising spirit of a man. Perhaps the man is a great poet, or an artist, or perhaps he is a leader among the people, even a revolutionist. It is easy to crush these bamboo shoots. You could do it even when you were very small. It is easy to destroy but hard to create. Remember that, when you want to destroy something."

The boy was struggling to pull away his hand, but Il-han would not let him go until he had finished what he wanted to say. Now he loosed him and the boy, as soon as he felt himself free, ran swiftly away. Il-han looked after the flying slender figure, and was deeply troubled. From then on he kept watch of this son, and when he saw him push his younger brother, or tear down what the younger son had built of stones or small blocks of wood, he took the elder firmly by the hands and held his hands behind his back and reminded him again and again. "It is easy to destroy, but it is hard to create. Do not destroy what your brother creates."

Sunia observed this one day. "It is not enough merely not to destroy," she said. "Why not help him to create something himself?"

Again she had said something to stir his mind, and Il-han thought of his ancestor Chong-ho, surnamed Kim, who was the first mapmaker. This ancestor, as a boy in the province of Kuang Hwang-hai, had been restless, too. He had wandered over mountains and beside rivers, and he began to wonder where the rivers had their sources, and how the mountains lay, and what the shape was of the winding coastlines, and how many islands were beyond.

Il-han told his elder son one day of the mapmaker. "This ancestor of ours asked everyone where he could find a map of our country which would tell him all these things. There was no such map. He promised himself then that he would be a mapmaker when he grew up, and he studied every map he could find, traveling here and there to see whether the maps were true. They were not true. Mountains and rivers were in confusion and the shorelines were straight where they should be curved into bays and coves, and the sources of the rivers were only imagined. When he was a man he came here to Seoul and asked the rulers to help him, but no one cared for maps or knew their usefulness. He was discouraged but he did not give up. He traveled everywhere again, measuring and drawing pictures and writing down what he found, until he had made the first complete map of Korea. Then it had to be printed. Still no one helped him and he worked and saved and bought blocks of wood and carved the shape of the map upon them. He inked these blocks and stamped them on paper and there was the map! Alas, the King in those times only thought that our ancestor was helping some enemy, and he had the maps burned with the blocks of wood. But our ancestor had memorized the map, and then the King decided that he should be killed."

The boy listened to this, and his face turned pale. "How did they kill him?"

"Does it matter?" Il-han replied.

"I want to know," the boy insisted.

"They cut off his head," Il-han said shortly.

The boy thought for a moment. Then he said in a cool voice, as though without interest, "There must have been much blood."

"Doubtless," Il-han answered, "but that is not important. I tell the story because I want you to know of our ancestor, and how brave he was to create something so good and useful as a map, and how foolish it was to destroy him. Even the King was ignorant."

He did not know whether his son heard him. He thought he had not, for he felt the child's hand on the back of his neck.

"What now?" Il-han inquired, and pulled the young hand away from his neck.

"The bone," his son said, his great eyes staring and dark. "They must have used a saw to cut the bone."

At this Il-han pushed the child's hand aside and went away. But in the night he woke suddenly and fully heard in the distance the sound of the night watchman in the street, on guard against fires. Among the huts of the poor a fire burning in the middle of a room could set a thatched roof ablaze, and even in the houses of the rich a faulty flue or rubbish thrown out by a careless servant could destroy the city. All night the fire guard walked the streets, striking his two bamboo sticks together so that folk, waking, would know that he was watching over their safety. Il-han listened to the man come nearer, until the clack-clack was loud and clear and then it faded again into the distance. It was not this sound that had waked him, for he slept through it every night of his life. No, he was waked by a deep worry inside his mind and his heart, a worry he had set aside in the day, and which now rose up in the darkness of the night. From this time on, he swore to himself, he would spend some part of every day with his elder son. For he could not forget the hand feeling the bone in his neck, the small cold hand.

. . . The younger son was another creature. This child could not bear to crush a fly or pull a cat's tail.

It was Il-han's habit that, until a child was free of his nurse, he took no great notice. Indeed the first notice he gave to this second son, beyond the worry of his shortened ear, was on his first birthday, one of the three highest days in a man's life, the second being his wedding day and the third his sixtieth birthday. True, he could never forget that this baby son had looked as pretty as a girl on that day. For Sunia had ordered her women to make special garments for him, light blue silk trousers, a peach-pink short coat, the sleeves striped in red, blue and green, a blue vest buttoned with jade buttons, and on his head the pointed cap on the sides of which were the Chinese letters for long life and prosperity. Il-han had noticed that Sunia had cut the sides of this hat long to cover the child's ears. She could not forget, and in her persistent grieving that her child was not perfect, he recalled again that he had heard of foreign doctors who could mend such faults. He had not reminded her, however, for he wished not to add a sadness to the bright day. Guests had come bearing presents for the child and feasts were prepared for all, the best for the relatives and guests and lesser dishes for the servants they brought with them, as well as for his own. What he remembered now was his small son seated on the warm floor, while before him Sunia placed the objects for his choice, a sword, short and square-bladed, a book, a writing brush, a lute, and other such things. The child had looked at them for a while, seeming even at so young an age to know what they meant. Then he had put out his hand and grasped the handle of the sword, but he could not lift it and he cried and again he had tried to lift the sword and each time he failed and cried again. Sunia had coaxed the child with other objects, but he refused and hid his face in her bosom, sobbing.

This younger son, Il-han now observed anew. The child was delicately shaped, the bones fine and the flesh soft. From which ancestor the elder child had drawn his square shoulders and unusual height none knew, but the second child looked like Il-han's father. He had the same large poetic eyes, and fine brows and high forehead. There were times when Sunia said she believed that the old man's spirit after he died had entered into the child, so quiet and staid were the child's movements, and yet graceful. He liked to play with small animals, with birds, butterflies and goldfish. Especially he loved lighted lanterns and flying kites and music. Sunia could play the Black Crane harp, so-called because in the time of Koguryo a musician had made a new instrument from the ancient Chinese harp, and while he played a hundred melodies upon it, a black crane had come down from the sky and danced. This harp could persuade Il-han's second son to come out of any melancholy or fit of weeping if he fell down or were ill.

These were the qualities that Il-han observed in his second son but the child was still too young to reveal his individual mind and soul. Nevertheless, when he sat with this child on his lap and if the child followed him into the garden and clung to his forefinger, Il-han always saw the deformity of his ear and he determined that one day he would ask a foreign physician to mend it. He examined this ear carefully himself, and he concluded that the necessary flesh and skin of the lobe were all there, but that it had been crushed, perhaps by some position the child had taken inside the mother's womb. His son's folded ear lobe now became a reason for Il-han that he should bestir himself when the period of mourning was over and acquaint himself with men of the West, through whom he might find one to be a surgeon.

Yet before he could fulfill this purpose, Il-han received a courier from the King's palace, commanding his presence. Since the period of mourning was over on that very day, Il-han could not refuse. He put on his court robes and went to the palace and was there received by the King.

"Do not stand on the ceremonies," the King said when Il-han prepared obeisance. "You are to ready yourself to go on a mission to the United States."

Il-han was already kneeling before the King, his head bowed on his hands, and when he heard these words over his head he could not move. He, go across the wild seas to a country that for him was no more than a few words he had heard spoken! His mouth went dry.

"Majesty," he mumbled, "when must this be?"

"If we are to make a treaty with the Americans," the King

said, "then I must know what their country is and what the people are. I have appointed three young men on this mission, but you are to accompany them and see that they behave well and that they observe everything. You may stand."

Il-han rose to his feet and stood with folded arms and bowed head. "Majesty, is this to be done in haste?"

"In some haste," the King replied, "for it is our wish to move quickly. We ratify the treaty with the United States at once, and before you and these others leave our country. I hear that the old Empress in Peking is displeased with Li Hung-chang, and declares that all treaties must still be made through China. But we must deal directly now with the Americans and establish our right as a sovereign nation so to do."

"Whom then do you send, Majesty?" Il-han next inquired.

"First," the King replied, "I have appointed my brother-in-law, Prince Min Yong-ik, Heir Apparent to the throne."

This prince Il-han knew very well. He was by adoption a nephew to the Queen, and was her ally. In the revolt the Regent had ordered him killed, but he had escaped his murderers by putting on the robes of a Buddhist monk and hiding himself in the mountains.

The King proceeded. "The second is Hong Yong-sik, the son of our Prime Minister. I send him because he has already been ambassador to Japan, and he is not ignorant of other countries than our own. The third is one whom I keep constantly near my person, for I trust him. He is So Kwang-pom."

This young man Il-han also knew. His family was an ancient one, whose members through centuries had been known as wise and just. In this generation So Kwang-pom believed zealously that Korea should be independent of China, and he had headed a party of other men who so believed. He had even once gone secretly to Japan and had returned to tell the King fearlessly how Japan was changing into new ways, and was making new weapons, and dreaming even of making war upon China. The young man was a baron, and by inheritance, and this gave him the right to have access to the King.

All three men were young, about thirty years of age, but this third one was the most modern and bold, while Min

Yong-ik was the leader of the Min and the favorite of the Queen.

"Besides yourself," the King was saying, "I have chosen two others, Chai Kyung-soh, who is skilled in military affairs, and Yu Kil-chun, who has also lived long in Japan."

Il-han bowed his head. "How can I refuse the royal command?"

The King accepted this decision and with a brief nod, he strode from the room. Il-han could only return to his house, his mind in a daze that the King had moved ahead of his advice and with such speed.

On a certain day in late spring of that same year, sixteen days after the King had told him that he must go abroad, Il-han was again on his way to the palace by command. He wore his court robes, on his breast the square of silver brocade embroidered with three cranes to signify his high rank. The day was fine and he had commanded the front curtain of his palanquin to be raised so that he could enjoy the mild air and the light of the sun. The occasion of the royal summons was the ratification of the treaty with the United States, a solemn ceremony. True, ratification had been long delayed, but preparation had begun even before the revolt of the Regent and all the sad events that had taken place until he was safely exiled. The important first steps were taken when Shufeldt, an American officer whose rank was Commodore, had negotiated the treaty under the approval of the Chinese statesman Li Hung-chang who, wishing at that time to remain in his own country, had sent his representative, Yuan Shih-k'ai, to live in Seoul and uphold China as suzerain over Korea, and this although the treaty asserted that Korea was a sovereign nation and needed no conference with Chinese before it was ratified. Thus far affairs had proceeded until the Regent routed the Queen from the palace and disturbed the nation. Now that the King was again in power he commanded ratification on this day.

For Il-han the day was the beginning of his long journey abroad. He had not yet told Sunia, knowing that her woman's heart would immediately set up a clamor concerning his health, the strange foods he must eat, the foreign waters he must drink, the wild winds he must breathe, all different from those in his native land. Yet today, after the treaty had been ratified, he would have to tell her, for there could be no delay in the journey.

Two hours after noon, then, on this nineteenth day of the fifth month of the solar year of 1883, and the sixth month of the lunar year, Il-han stood in the great hall of the Royal Office of Foreign Affairs. With him were Min Yong-wok, president of this office, and the chiefs of the four royal Departments, each with his retinue. Il-han was present at the King's command as special representative.

The day was mild with approaching summer, the wall screens were drawn, and the gardens lay in full view in the clear sunlight. At the appointed hour all were ready and ten Americans entered the hall. Il-han had never seen them close and he could not forbear staring at them. They were all tall men and they wore naval uniforms of red and gold jackets over black trousers. One man wore gold wings on his shoulders, the sign of highest rank. The ten came forward and the court crier announced in a loud voice the name of the leader.

"General Lucius H. Foote, Envoy Extraordinary and Minister Plenipotentiary of the United States of America to the Kingdom of Korea!"

The name Foote, translated, astonished the Koreans, and for a moment Il-han himself was confounded. Was this a mischievous trick of the announcer, a design to embarrass the foreigners? Foot? Could a man of high rank be so absurdly named? He caught the eye of Min Yong-wok, and they exchanged a questioning look. But no, the Americans were not angry, since they understood no Korean, and they presented the treaty in English to President Min, and the president presented, in return, the Korean copy. The ratified treaties were exchanged between the two men and thus a bridge was raised between two countries on opposite sides of the seas. The ceremony took no more than a few moments. The Americans then withdrew and Il-han returned to his house, marveling that in so short a time two nations could enter into friendship, their millions of people tied together by a piece of paper and written words.

"I shall die while you are away," Sunia said.

"You will not," Il-han said.

It was the middle of the night. They were in their own room and the house was silent about them. Outside in the garden pools the young frogs piped their early song of love and summer. He had told Sunia that he was going to America at the King's command. She had listened without a word, and now she said simply that she would die.

She did not answer his denial. There beside him she lay, her hands locked under her head. He looked down into her face, pale in the moonlight.

"You will not have time to die," he went on. "While I am gone, you must take my place with the Queen. You must visit her, hear her complaints, advise her, watch over her, consider her."

"I will not," Sunia said.

"You will, for I command you to do it," Il-han replied. "Moreover, you are to become acquainted with the wife of the new American ambassador. You are to know her, you are to present her to the Queen as your friend."

"I do not know even her name," Sunia said, not moving.

"She is Madame Foote," Il-han said.

Sunia heard this and suddenly she laughed. "You are making jokes! Foot? No—no—"

He let her laugh, glad of the change in her mood, and she sat up and wound her long hair around her head. "How can I call her Madame Foot? I shall laugh every time I see her. The female Foot! How did the man Foot look?"

"Like any man," Il-han said, "except that he had a short red beard and red hair and red eyebrows over blue eyes."

He was glad that Sunia was diverted, and he went on to describe the Americans, their height, their high noses, their great hands and long feet, their trousered legs and clipped hair.

"Were they savage?" Sunia asked.

"No," Il-han said, "only strange. But they understand courtesy and they seem civilized in their own fashion."

In such ways he led her to accept the matter of his crossing the sea and entering into foreign countries. It was no easy task, nevertheless, and all through the summer months, while preparation was made, she busy with his garments both for heat and cold, with sundry packets of dried foods and ginseng roots and other medicinal herbs, there came dark hours in the night when she clung to him, weeping. She insisted that at least his coffin must be chosen before he went, lest he die while he was abroad and his body be sent home with no place to rest. So to humor her he chose a good coffin of pinewood, and had it placed in the gatehouse, while he laughed at her and told her he would come back healthy and fat and far from dead.

The day of departure drew near, in spite of everything, and Il-han made his last visit to the palace, appearing before the Queen and then the King. To the Queen he commended his wife Sunia.

"Let my humble one take my place, Majesty," he said. "Accept her service, and let her do your bidding. Tell her what you would tell me, for she is loyal and has a faithful heart. I have only one request to make for myself, before I leave."

"I shall not promise to grant it," the Queen said. She was in no good mood on this last day, for she did not favor friendship with the Americans and had mightily opposed the journey.

Il-han ignored her petulance. He proceeded as though she had not spoken.

"I ask, Majesty, that you invite the wife of the American ambassador to visit you here in your palace."

At this the Queen rose up from her throne. "What," she cried. "I? You forget yourself!"

"The time will come when it must be done, Majesty," he said with patience. "Better that you act now with grace and of your own accord than later by compulsion."

She walked back and forth twice and thrice, her full skirts flowing behind her. On the fourth time she drew near to the end door of the audience hall which led into her own private rooms. There, without looking back at him, or pausing to speak one word, she disappeared.

For a long time he waited and she did not return. Then a palace woman came out and bowed to him and folded her hands at her waist and spoke like a parrot.

"Her Majesty bids you farewell and wishes you a safe journey."

She bowed again and turning went back from whence she had come. Il-han left the palace then, amazed that in his breast he felt a strange sore pain of an unexpected wound struck by one he loved. He hid it deep inside himself, and refused to allow himself to examine his own heart. He had no time, he told himself, to fret about a woman's ways, queen though she was. He bore the monstrous burden of his people and carrying this burden always with him, he bade his household farewell, accepting the anxious hopes for his safe return. The last moments he spent alone with Sunia and their sons and to comfort her he stood before the ancestral tablets and together they lit incense and she prayed, her voice a yearning whisper.

"Guard him all the way," she besought those dead. "Keep him safe in health and bring him home again living and with success."

The second son, whom Il-han held in his arms, began suddenly to cry, but the elder stood as stiff as any soldier and said nothing. There was no time left for child or wife. Il-han held Sunia to him for a long instant and tore himself away. He stepped into his palanquin while a crowd stood by to watch and cry farewell. Then he felt himself lifted from the ground and borne swiftly on his way.

On the fifteenth day of the ninth month of that solar year, Il-han and his fellow compatriots arrived at the capital city of the United States. During the long sea journey he had studied the language of these new people, the only one so to learn, for the others saw no need to know a language they would never use. But he, with the help of a young Catholic interpreter, shaped his lips to the unusual syllables, and when he reached Washington, a city named for the first President of these people, he was able to read signs and the large print of newspapers and even to understand a few words spoken.

Already Il-han knew that his own people had much to learn from the Americans. Even the ship in which they traveled had been dazzling in marvels and he had made friends with the captain, a bearded man whose life had been upon the seas. With this man he had climbed upon the bridge and watched the turning of the wheel that steered the ship, and he descended into the bowels of the ship and saw the great furnaces where naked men threw coal into the monstrous maws to make steam that drove the ship with power. The train in which they had crossed the continent had provided further marvels, the engine powered by the same steam, and at such speed that even he was dizzied, though not vomiting as his fellows did. Five days they sped across mountain and plain, and he was overwhelmed by the vastness of the country, and astonished at the fewness of its people.

Here in the American capital he met the greatest marvels, especially the water, hot and cold, that gushed from the wall, and lamps whose fuel was an invisible gas. Much discomfort there was too. He could not sleep well in a bed high from the floor, and twice he fell out as though he were a child and bruised his shoulders, and after such misadventure he pulled the mattress to the floor. The food was unpalatable and tasteless and he missed Sunia's kimchee, and the spices and the richness of his own foods. Moreover, there were those eating implements, a pronged fork, a sharp knife, and he could not cut the slabs of meat, nor down it running red with blood. He chose a spoon and such foods as he could sup.

These were small matters, and soon he learned his way about the city, though only with the help of a young naval officer who had been appointed to stay with the delegation from Korea, an ensign named George C. Foulk. Seeing the name printed, Il-han spoke it complete until the young man had laughed.

"Call me George," he said.

This George Foulk had lived four years in China and Japan and once had even spent a few months in Korea, so that he spoke Chinese and Japanese and some Korean. Il-han was fortunate that he himself was not official in rank and could go or not go on official calls. While the others waited here and there, he walked about the city with George and listened with lively interest to what the young man explained of history and science and art in the streets and museums and buildings. All that he, Il-han, saw and heard he stored in his mind, to be used for his own country when the time came.

Nevertheless, the formal meeting with the President of the country, whose name was Chester A. Arthur, Il-han must attend as special representative of the King of Korea. It took place not in the capital but in the city of New York in a great hotel where the President was staying, for what reason Il-han did not know. Thither they went and were installed in palatial rooms, where they waited for the appointed time. The day arrived and the hour, and Il-han prepared himself. He wore his richest robes of state, a loose coat of flowered plum-colored silk over a white silk undertunic. Over these he put his ancestral belt of broad gold plates. Upon his breast he hung his apron of purple satin embroidered with two cranes in white silk thread, surrounded with a border of many colors. On his head he wore the tall hat traditional for yangban noblemen, made of horsehair woven upon a bamboo frame and tied beneath his chin. Besides himself only Min Yong-ik, the head of the delegation, wore such robes. Two others could wear aprons with one crane embroidered on them. The rest wore no breast aprons but the coats of plum-colored silk and the white silk tunics in blue or green with tall hats.

Shortly before noon, word came that the President was ready to receive them. He stood in the center of the parlor of his private suite, and Il-han, entering first, saw a thick-bodied man wearing tight gray trousers and a long dark coat cut back from the waist. On his right was his Secretary of State, a man surnamed Frelinghuysen, who stood quiet and apart. On his left was his Assistant Secretary, surnamed Davis, and several others, among them George Foulk. Il-han and his fellow Koreans entered in single file and formed themselves in a line before the American dignitary. Then at a signal from Min Yong-ik they knelt at the same moment, and raising their hands high above their heads, they bent their bodies forward slowly in unison until their foreheads touched the carpeted floor. They remained in this position for moments, and then rose and went toward the President, who, with his suite, had bowed deeply as they entered and so remained until the Koreans had risen.

Now Frelinghuysen came forward and he led Prince Min to the President and introduced him. The two clasped their hands together, Prince and President, and they looked deeply into each other's eyes, murmuring compliments, each in his own tongue. One after the other the Koreans were introduced to the Americans, and then the Prince and the President exchanged formal greetings, each in his own tongue, translated in turn.

After the ceremonies, the Koreans retired, and on that same day they took ship. With the American officers delegated to accompany them, they went to the city of Boston, there to inspect buildings and manufactories.

Time fails me [Il-han wrote to Sunia in the days following] to tell you of the many sights I have seen. My head is crowded with sights, my mind is enriched, and I shall need the rest of my life to tell you everything. I have seen great farms where machines take the place of men and beasts, and these I have observed most carefully, for you know my concern with the life of our landfolk. Alas, we are centuries behind these Americans! But I have seen the factories where textiles are made, especially in a city named Lowell, and there, too, I perceive how far behind we are with our handlooms. I cannot deny that our stuffs are finer, especially our silks, but can we compete with machines? I have seen hospitals and telegraph offices and shipping yards, the great shops of jewelers and merchants of all kinds. Tiffany in New York is a mighty name in jewelries, and I was glad I had not you

beside me as I examined their baubles, else I could not
have contained you, or myself for that matter, who wish to
give you all you long for. The post office—ah, that we had
such speed and exactitude, a letter posted today hundreds
of miles away by tomorrow, and this not by foot but by
train! And I saw sugar refineries where the whitest sugar is
made, all by machines, and fire vehicles, whereby fires in
great cities are put out before they destroy a hundred houses,
and great newspaper offices, and above all, I saw the military
academy at a place on a great river, where young men are
trained as officers of the national army here. These and
much more I have seen, and when you and I are old, Sunia,
and sitting upon our ondul floor together, I shall still have
new things to tell you, for a lifetime is not enough for all I
have seen.

When the mission was ended, the Koreans bade farewell
to the President in his palace, for they were in Washington
again to observe how the government performed its duties.
On the last day, they divided themselves. Some went to
Europe and homeward by the Suez Canal, some went home
directly by the way which they had come, but upon the
President's invitation three went homeward on an American
warship, and with these went Il-han, for George Foulk accompanied them, and Il-han wished to stay by this young
man and with his help gather more information concerning
the history and political life of the western peoples. By now
Il-han could read books in English partly by himself, but
George Foulk was there to help him when he could not understand, and Il-han made translations of such works for the
King to read, and for the Queen, if she would. Only Prince
Min would have nothing to do with such works. He declared
that Korea could never match the western countries and
therefore her strength must remain in her own old ways. So
saying, he retired to his cabin on the ship and returned to
the Confucian books he had brought with him.

The warship carried Il-han and three others and George
Foulk to Europe, where they disembarked at Marseilles, and
for seventeen days they traveled through other new countries
and saw still more new sights, until Il-han, fearing that by

now one sight would be confused with another, spent every evening writing down what he had seen during the day and where he had seen it.

It was spring again before he reached home, and indeed all but summer, for it was the last day of the fifth month of the solar year, 1884, when the ship weighed anchor in the harbor at Chemulpo. From there they were escorted to the capital in sedan chairs and on horseback, and Il-han chose a horse, and so did George Foulk. Side by side they rode through the sunlit landscape, but neither saw the surrounding beauty. They talked long and quietly together, and the burden of their talk was Il-han's fear that Prince Min's influence might be against reforms.

"Our only hope," he said, "is to leave the past and move into the present. I have hope, for I understand now that a small country can grow strong by means of science and machines. We must search out our best young men and send them to your country to learn, and return them here to teach. We must open colleges for our youths. Yet how can I persuade the King when Prince Min is so powerful? And certainly I shall not be able to persuade the Queen, whose relative he is. I make a prophecy and I pray it will not come true. The Prince, I prophesy with fear and sadness, will pretend to have interest in what he has seen, but it is only pretense. He will pretend to suggest reforms and then he will prevent them in secret. This is my fear."

He gazed far across the land as he spoke. The season was the planting of rice and in the valleys the farm families, young and old, were thrusting the young plants into the shallow waters of the rice fields. In the bamboo groves the new shoots were waist-high. So fair a country!

At the entrance to his own house Il-han descended from his horse and beat upon the gate with the stock of his whip. He was alone, for Foulk had parted from him at the city gate to go to the American Embassy, and the others had stopped earlier at their own homes. Il-han's house was the farthest and so he was last and he stood waiting. The gate opened a crack and he saw his servant peer through, and then fling the gate wide and fall to his knees to put his forehead in the dust.

"Master—master—you sent no word! We did not know when to expect you."

"I did not know the exact hour or even the day," Il-han replied.

He lifted the man as he spoke and then strode through the gate into the gardens and to the house. Silence was everywhere, and he inquired of the servants, who now came running, where their mistress was and his sons.

"Master, your sons are flying kites on the city wall," his servant told him, "and our mistress waits upon the Queen."

"Does she go often to wait upon the Queen?" Il-han inquired.

"Indeed she is the Queen's favorite," a woman servant put in.

Il-han could but go to his own rooms then to await Sunia's return. Meanwhile he sent for bath water and fresh garments and for the barber to shave him, and while he made himself clean, he rejoiced in his return to his own house. All seemed better even than he remembered, and when he was finished with barber and bathboy and servant, he strolled in the gardens, and saw how the trees had grown, how the plants flowered. The blossoms on the persimmon trees were yellow and in full bloom and the goldfish were merry in the pools and a bird sang in the bamboo grove. Here he waited for Sunia, and suddenly he saw her, her full skirts of apple-green silk flying behind her in the speed of her coming. He opened his arms, for none stood by to watch them, the servants hiding themselves kindly, and she ran into his embrace. Oh, good it was to feel her in his arms, her warm body pressing against his, her sweet cheek against his!

"You should have told me," she breathed. "I have missed all the expecting. How can I believe you are here?"

She drew back to look at him, to feel his arms, press his hands, clasp his waist again. "You are older," she exclaimed. "I think you are thinner." She paused to stare at him aghast. "You have cut off your hair!"

He had not told her that he had cut his hair. "I cut it—" he said and was stopped by her stricken look.

"You mean you are not—you wish you were not—married to me!"

What could he say? It was true that when a man married it was old custom that on the crown of his head he must erect the coil of his long hair.

"There are new times," he said somewhat feebly.

She looked at him with doubt and then a smile caught the corners of her mouth.

"You want to look different from other men here, you want to be anything that is willful and stubborn. Oh, you are not changed, not a whit, hair or no hair."

They embraced again, with passion, and hand in hand they walked into the house.

"Before the children come home," Sunia said, "let me tell you why I am so late."

She proceeded then to tell her tale and Il-han listened, marveling how she too had changed and was no longer the shy girlish woman she had been. Here then was the gist of her story.

While Il-han was in foreign lands, the American General Foote had endeavored to present himself to the King and the Queen, but the Queen had refused to receive him, and she forbade the King to receive him.

"What," she had exclaimed to Sunia, "shall the King show himself divided from me? Let the chief of the Foreign Office receive this Foote, not we who are truebone royalty. We are too high for him. Is he a yangban in this country or even in his own?"

When she was told that Americans had no yangban she grew more willful. "All the more reason," she declared, "for not receiving one of them in our palaces."

Thus it went until Sunia devised a clever scheme of her own. She had become friends with the Queen in her own woman ways, and she perceived that the Queen liked new sights. Thereupon she herself went one day to call upon the female Foote, and quite alone except for a woman servant, she entered the mansion where these Footes lived. All was strange to see. The tables and chairs were high, the floors were covered with thick wool mats, and the walls were decorated with foreign scenes and portraits of unknown persons. The female Foote received her kindly, nevertheless, welcoming her with both hands outstretched and leading her to sit upon one of the high chairs, from which her feet swung clear of the floor, it was so high, and she was afraid of falling off, until the lady Foote saw her distress and bade a servant put a stool under her feet.

This foreign lady could speak some Korean, much to Sunia's surprise, though with a strange twist of the tongue, and she was free and gay and she asked many questions which Sunia answered, until soon they were two women talking together. The lady then asked Sunia if she would like to see the house, and when Sunia said she would, for her curiosity was sharp, the lady Foote took her everywhere upstairs and down but the worst was when Sunia was compelled to come down the stairs again, which she could do only by sitting and sliding from step to step lest she fall headlong, since never before had she been that high. She saw many things in that house, a machine that could sew fine stitches, another machine that could write letters, beds on posts and surrounded by nets to keep off mosquitoes, an iron cook stove, and such things, more than she could count.

All this she told the Queen, and when the Queen asked how the lady Foote was dressed, Sunia said, "She wears a full skirt held out by a thin hoop, and her upper body sits on top like a Buddha on a mountain."

At this the Queen laughed aloud. Then she looked thoughtful. At last she spoke. "Perhaps I will invite her to come here and show herself."

"Majesty, I pray you will do so," Sunia replied. "It is more diverting than a play to see her walk. Her feet are hidden and one would think she went hither and thither on wheels. And her waist, Majesty! It is small like this." She measured a little circle with her two hands.

The Queen marveled.

"How can that be? Is she divided in two?"

Sunia had wondered for herself how it could be, and she had inquired privately of a woman servant in that home, who had told her that the lady Foote encased her middle in a steel-enforced box. So she told the Queen.

"She boxes herself in at the waist, to make herself small."

Upon this the Queen could not restrain her curiosity, and the lady Foote was invited and the Queen sent her own palanquin to fetch her to the palace. Alas, as the bearers told everywhere, the lady could not squeeze into the palanquin because of her wide skirts.

"However high we raised the front of the palanquin," they told, grinning at every word, "she could not get herself inside. Even her husband stood there laughing, and we all laughed. But she was not put off one bit and, laughing with us, she backed in like a mule between shafts. Then her skirts stood out so far that we could not put down the front curtain and so we carried her through the streets. The thousands stood to watch us, for word flew from mouth to ear everywhere and people ran out from their houses. Some even hid beneath the palanquin and we beat them out with bamboo sticks."

Thus the foreigner was carried through the streets until they came to the palace. There she had new difficulty in descending from the palanquin and she must be pulled out and set straight, whereupon her skirts belled out in a vast circle, a pretty sight, Sunia said, for her gown was made of rich golden silk, long in the back like a tail, and the front was hung about with wide lace and there was lace falling from her sleeves over her hands. Only one part of her was unseemly, and this was her front, where her breasts stood out like hillocks under the silk. This, Sunia concluded, was the misfortune of the foreign women, that they had big breasts.

At this moment she paused and looked at Il-han sidewise. "And did all the women in America have such swollen breasts?" she inquired.

Il-han looked sidewise at her in return. "I did not look at them," he replied.

So she went on with her tale.

When the King heard the female Foote was coming he declared that he too must see her, which he could not unless the Queen allowed. She granted his wish, however, and Sunia met the guest in the reception hall and led her through the antechamber and into the throne room, where the King and Queen sat on their thrones, with a nephew prince at their side. Sunia had taught the guest how to salute the truebone royal pair and she, though foreign, performed the salutations very well and then stood while the King and Queen rose. The King wore a long robe of dark red silk, the Queen wore a long flowing skirt of blue silk and a jacket of yellow silk most exquisitely embroidered with multicolored flowers and fastened with buttons of amber and pearl. Her long black hair was fastened in a smooth coil at her neck with pins of filigree gold set with jewels. Upon her nobly shaped head she wore an ornament also of jewels, and from her waist hung jeweled baubles fastened to bright silk tassels.

The King and Queen exchanged speeches with the lady, their guest, and she responded so freely and with such spirit in her simple language that soon they were laughing together. The royal pair then sat down again, and an ebony stool was brought for the guest since she could not sit upon a floor cushion, so upheld was she by her hooped skirts.

"The Queen," Sunia told Il-han, "was by then so pleased with the ease and freedom of the lady Foote, that she declared she would make a *fête champêtre* for her in the palace gardens, and she invited her on that very day to return another day for this *fête*."

"And did she so?" Il-han inquired, marveling at the ease with which Sunia had accomplished such a victory over the Queen.

"Never was there such a *fête*," Sunia exclaimed and she described it, her hands flying like birds while she talked.

The *fête*, she said, excelled all *fêtes* that were ever heard of in the capital. Two hundred tall eunuchs in splendid uniforms escorted the Queen and the guest through the gardens. All the trees had been brought to blossom at the right day, apricots and plum and cherry, and great displays of chrysanthemums, out of season, glowed among gold-lacquered pagodas and pavilions. Fairy teahouses and miniature temples the Queen had commanded built for the occasion, and music sounded through the groves of bamboo and flowering trees and among willows drooping over ponds. Bright-hued birds the Queen had commanded to sing and fly had been brought from the southern islands and servants in garments as bright flitted everywhere like butterflies.

The guest wore new garments, Sunia said, the skirts wider than she had before and her arms were bare, but she wore gloves of soft white leather so long that they clothed her arms like sleeves. The court ladies clamored to try these gloves on their own hands, but their hands were like baby hands inside the gloves. These ladies played with the guest's diamonds and felt her boxed-in waist and asked where she bought the creams that made her skin so white and smooth.

Thus the day wore on, for it took all day to see the many sights the Queen had commanded for the astonishment of this foreign guest. Musicians sat inside the pagodas and strummed their lutes and two-stringed violins, gongs sounded their mellow notes. Near the bank of a lake where lotus bloomed, a bud opened to reveal a small naked child whose waiting mother lifted him from his rosy bed. A sailing boat on another lake carried girls who danced old legends on the decks, acrobats swung from branches of the trees along the shores, and everywhere about the vast gardens troupes of actors made playlets for amusement of the Queen and her guest.

"Indeed we all went mad with merriment," Sunia said, laughing at her memories, "and when the lady Foote parted from the Queen the two embraced as though they were sisters and the Queen could not bear to let her go. And a good lucky thing it was that the *fête* came first—"

Here Sunia's face grew grave and she paused.

"What next?" Il-han inquired.

"You know how suddenly the Queen can change," Sunia said. "One moment she is all kindness and gaiety and the next she is a cruel witch."

He nodded. "So what did she do?" he asked.

"You know how many of the Queen's kinsmen were murdered by the Regent," she said.

Il-han nodded again.

"Well," Sunia went on, "even before all this merriment the Queen made up her mind in secret that she would command the death of all those who had taken part in the return of the Regent."

"No," Il-han cried, aghast.

"Yes," Sunia said. "As soon as you were gone she commanded them to be killed. Some had already fled beyond her reach and she commanded that their wives and children should be slaughtered."

Il-han covered his eyes with his hands at this, but Sunia went on, her voice steady.

"Yes, she did, and it would have so been done except that I went to the lady Foote after the *fête*, when I heard of it. I went that same night and begged her to move the Queen's heart."

Il-han lifted his head from his hands. "Who told you?"

"Your man servant," she said, "and he heard it from a eunuch in the palace, whose sister was among those doomed by the Queen. Upon that the lady Foote came in haste, uninvited and unannounced, only two days after the *fête*, and she faced the Queen."

Sunia paused to sigh and shake her head and bite her underlip.

"She had asked me to accompany her, and I saw and heard all. Oh, that Queen! Her face was hard as white marble, and her heart was not moved, not by one word that the lady Foote could speak. 'Why have you come here?' she screamed. 'Who bade you come? Leave the palace!' This she commanded. And then she screamed, 'I will see your face no more.' Such screams she made but the lady Foote only grew the more gentle. At last she knelt before the Queen, she took her hand, and she began to speak of the Lord Buddha who bade us take no life, not even the life of a worm, lest it be hindered on its upward way, and she spoke of the noble Confucius, who taught us that the great are always merciful to the small, for in such mercy is their greatness."

Il-han broke in. "Did the Queen listen?" His throat was dry and his voice came in a whisper.

"At last she did," Sunia said, "but only when the foreign lady spoke of our own gods. She listened and her eyes grew soft and after a long while she said that the lives of all should be spared. At this the foreign lady wept and then the Queen wept, and they clasped hands and the Queen begged the lady never to leave Korea. And she sent her home in her own royal palanquin and she gave her that palanquin as a gift, the same one which you sent to bring the Queen home to the palace from exile in the poet's house."

So long had Sunia talked that the sun was setting over the wall and now they heard the voices of the children at the gate.

Il-han looked at her with eyes not only tender but proud. "You have done well, my wife, better than I myself could have done. From now on I share all my life with you. Man and woman, we are equal, partners in everything. I shall have no secrets from you, ever, so long as I live."

They clasped hands and Sunia's eyes brimmed with tears. Better than words of love were his words of acceptance and praise.

"Alas, that my prophecy must be fulfilled!" Il-han exclaimed.

On this day he had met with George Foulk to renew their friendship, which they now did in a teahouse beside a small lake where lotus bloomed. Sitting on their floor cushions beside the low table, while a singing girl played the bamboo harp, George Foulk told him in low tones that the Prince, Min Yong-ik, had come the day before to make a private call upon the American Minister, Foote.

The Prince had come, George Foulk said, with only three in his retinue and he had commanded even these three to stand outside the room where he was received by the American. Foulk had been summoned to act as interpreter, and so only he knew what had taken place. The Prince, he said, had seemed in a dark mood. His face was pale and his eyes were sunken as though he had not slept. He let his head hang, after salutations, and when the American inquired kindly whether he had enjoyed his journey to the West, the Prince replied that he had come home deeply troubled and in sadness.

"Why sadness?" the American inquired. "I hope that my people did not show you discourtesy."

"No," the Prince replied. "Everywhere we were given honor. My sadness is because I do not believe that my country can ever equal yours. We are oppressed and divided, and without hope. How can we survive as a free people, when we are crowded by these surrounding powers? Sooner or later they will cut us up and eat us in three parts, or one, triumphant, will swallow us whole. We are doomed by destiny, I and my people. I was born in the dark. I went into the light. I have returned into the dark again. I cannot see my way clearly. I hope, yet even hope is feeble."

When Il-han heard this now, he could only repeat his fears. "You will see," he told George Foulk. "The King will announce many reforms, but none will take root. The Prince will not allow it."

Il-han's fears became reality. At first the King could not move fast enough to make reforms. He sent for Il-han again and again, inquiring into every detail of all that he had seen in America, and when he learned how the Americans lived and how they were governed, he sent requests almost daily to the Americans, begging for military officers to show how a new army could be raised and trained and he asked for teachers of machinery and teachers in government and in every way of life, until George Foulk told Il-han privately that the Americans were distracted by such demands, and even put to embarrassment before the other western nations.

"The other western nations are looking at us askance," Foulk said. "They imagine that we are trying to settle into your country and take it for ourselves, whereas we have no such intent."

They parted in gloom each time these two, Korean and American, only to meet again and again, each to learn of the other in private ways. Il-han did not tell what he knew from Foulk to anyone except Sunia, and he and Sunia agreed that it was too soon to speak to the King, and not safe to speak to the Queen. Let the King swing his nets far, and when they saw what fish were caught, it would be time enough to act. So, although Il-han called upon both King and Queen in duty, he was cool in what he said, and gave no advice, nor was advice asked. But he knew that while the King worked feverishly for quick reforms and the building of a new nation before Japan grew strong and before a war broke out between Japan and China, or Russia and Japan, for Japan was set for war and conquest, the Queen worked in secret with Prince Min to stop each reform before it became real. In spite of such intrigue, the King persisted, never believing that the Queen worked against him. She was always gentle with him and came docile to his command, and he thought her as changed as he was when in the privacy of the royal chamber, one night after rare intercourse, he told her of what he had done and what he pleased to do. She listened, admiring and agreeing, and giving him encouragement, only to return to her own palace and plot with Prince Min. This she did not in evil intent, but because she and the Prince loved their country, too, but in their way, and what they did was in true conviction that they must stay with China, their protector and suzerain from ancient times.

Even Il-han was deceived to a degree that later astonished him when the revelation of all this took place at a great dinner given by Hong Yong-sik to celebrate the new postal system which the King had commanded to be established throughout the country. Since this Hong Yong-sik had been among those who went on the mission abroad, on return he had abetted the King and urged him on, until the King had made him the head of the new national post office. Hong had not only accepted the position, but he had become the leader of all those who opposed the old regime and, above all, Prince Min himself.

Who could believe that Hong Yong-sik would go to such lengths? On the day of the dinner, when the guests were assembled in the great hall, all was merriment and music. The guest of honor was the American ambassador, Foote, and the next guest of honor was Prince Min himself, and after him Il-han and then George Foulk. Below these were other Americans, among them a physician surnamed Allen, and below him other Korean yangban.

In the midst of the feast suddenly there was a shout.

"Fire!"

The word rang through the hall. "Fire—fire!"

All started to their feet, but Prince Min rose first, for it was a law that a high military official should attend any fire in his neighborhood and give all aid to put it out before it spread elsewhere. But Il-han guessed that the cry was only a signal and he ran after Prince Min to warn him. Alas, it was too late, for certain among the guests in the lower seats were running after the Prince. They tore off their brilliant robes of many-colored silks as they ran and showed themselves in common cotton garments underneath. These men pursued the Prince and caught him at the open door and they drew out short swords and hacked him again and then again and then they escaped, climbing over the walls and leaping down the other side.

Prince Min staggered back into the hall. Seven cuts had gashed his head open and one cheek had been carved out and hung down over his jawbone. His several arteries were cut and blood poured from him. Il-han sprang forward to catch the Prince as he fell, but he was not more quick than the American ambassador, who lifted Prince Min's feet. Together they laid him down upon the cushions. The servants were wailing and running here and there in uselessness, but General Foote shouted to the American physician, Allen, and this man in a short time stopped the flow of blood with tourniquets of cloth torn from garments and held fast with the same chopsticks with which a few minutes before the guests had been eating the delicacies.

The Prince by now knew nothing. Whether he would live

or die could not be told, but after some time the physician Allen declared that there was hope for his life, and he sent for medicines and for instruments to sew up his wounds, and thus the life was saved. Il-han stayed near throughout, and when at last there was some assurance that the Prince would live, he urged the American ambassador to return to his Embassy.

"Your lady will be frightened to see you," he said. "If you will permit me, I will go with you myself."

The American accepted this and the two men then went on foot, for by now there was no bearer or any equipage to be found, and George Foulk followed. Total confusion was everywhere and Il-han did not tell the American that he feared this attempt at murder was only the beginning of new revolt against the Queen. Together they walked through the crowded streets, pushing their way between the people, the snow crunching and cracking under their feet, until they came to the Embassy. Here when the gates opened Il-han saw for the first time the lady Foote. She stood in the doorway of the house, her full skirts of crimson silk flowing about her, and he saw her clearly in the light of a lantern a servant held behind her.

She screamed when she saw her husband, for he was covered with blood.

"You are hurt!" she cried.

"It is not my blood," he replied. "It is the blood of Prince Min. They have tried to murder him, but they have failed."

So much Il-han could understand, and he prepared to withdraw, yet when he looked again at these two he was impressed by the intelligence he saw on their faces, and he remembered how good the lady had been and how she had kept the Queen from the folly of murder. He lingered a moment.

"Your Excellency," he said to the ambassador, George Foulk translating. "I must warn you now that this is indeed the beginning of a fire which we may not be able to put down. Let me ask the King to send his royal guard here to escort you to the palace where we can protect you."

Bloodstained as he was, the American was still proud. He

drew himself to his height and he took his lady's left hand and put it in the curve of his right elbow.

"I thank you, my friend," he said, "but we must remain in our own place, my wife and I. In all circumstances I must insist upon the inviolability of my government's embassy. Here there must be a center of peace, however the mob riots outside our walls."

When George Foulk had repeated this in his own language, Il-han could only bow and withdraw. He looked back once, at the gate, and he saw those two, man and wife, standing side by side in the doorway. The woman's face was as calm in determination as the man's, and he could but envy them their faith in themselves and in their government.

. . . When he returned to his house, he found Sunia gone. His man servant waited for him, weeping and distracted.

"I begged her not to go, master," the man wailed. "I told her that you would find your way home."

"Surely she did not go in search of me!" Il-han exclaimed.

"She went to the Queen," the man wailed. "She thought you might have gone to save the Queen."

The tutor now ran out. "Sir," he said, "it is the King who is in danger."

"How do you know?" Il-han demanded.

"I am told—I am told," the tutor said urgently. "Never mind how, but it is said that the King has asked the Japanese minister for help and Japanese soldiers have surrounded the palace. A battle is taking place at this very moment."

Il-han turned at once. "Take care of my sons," he commanded, and he ran into the street followed by his servant. On foot he made his way through the crowds now shouting and screaming, some for the King, some for the Queen, most of them only adding to the noise and madness. Steadily he pushed his way among them and between them, they too maddened to see him or care who it was that burrowed here and there and always toward the palace. At the palace gates he spoke to the chief guard and gave his name. All knew him as loyal to the King and allowed him to pass. He entered then and saw in the gardens before the palace the bodies of the dead, some bleeding into the snow beneath a pine tree, some lying on the ice of a frozen lotus pond, and others scattered, twisted and crumpled. He bent and searched each face as he passed, and recognized one and another. They were all followers of the Queen, upholders of her determination to stay with the Chinese and oppose the reformers. Pools of blood lay in every crevice and low place, on stones and frozen ground, as he made his way toward the palace, expecting as he went to see the Queen herself bound with ropes and dragged out to her death. Then he lifted his eyes by chance and in the distance beyond the palace walls he saw the American flag flying in the wintry wind. At this sight he took courage, and he wondered if the Queen, hiding somewhere inside her palace, saw that flag, too, and took courage with him.

Suddenly, before he could reach the entrance to the palace, he heard a fresh uproar in the streets, and the sound of cannon. He stopped and listened and heard Chinese voices crying their war cries, and he knew what had happened. Yuan Shih-k'ai, the Chinese general sent by the Empress Tzu-hsi to maintain the power of her throne over Korea, had ordered soldiers to protect the palace and the truebone royal King and Queen. What could this mean but a battle between Chinese and Japanese, here in the palace itself? Il-han ran into the palace then and into the King's throne room. There the King sat on this throne, and by him sat the Queen, both in their royal robes, surrounded by a handful of Japanese soldiers.

"In Buddha's name," the Queen cried, "why are you here?"

"Majesty," Il-han gasped, and threw himself before them, "I came to see if you were hurt."

"Your wife was here first," the Queen said, "and I sent her home again under guard. If I am to die, I die alone."

"You will not die alone," the King said.

Before he could speak another word, the doors burst open and the Chinese soldiers swarmed in, carrying foreign guns and short Chinese swords. At the sight of them in such number, Japanese soldiers fled, leaping through windows and crashing through doors. Hundreds of Chinese followed them as they struggled to get to the Japanese warship that was in the harbor, but the Chinese cut them down until few indeed reached the safety of their ship. Then in fury the Chinese fell upon the wives and children of all Japanese in the city and cut them to pieces, too, and threw the parts into the water surrounding the ship.

So violent was the battle that even the British left their quarters and ran to the Americans for safety, and in that whole city only the American flag still waved in the wintry wind. Inside the Embassy the Americans took counsel, for they believed that they too would be attacked in the senseless frenzy of the mob, and they planned that if the mob broke through the gates and tore down the flag, only the lady Foote could save them. She alone was well loved by the people, for all knew how she had persuaded the Queen not to kill the families of those who had rebelled against her, and how she had done this by reminding the Queen of her own gods. If the mob broke in, therefore, it was planned that the lady Foote would sit in a chair in the middle of an empty room with all the valuable documents beside her, and she would ask the people to spare her and for her sake all her fellow citizens. This Il-han did not know until afterwards, when George Foulk told him. For in the end the mob did not enter the American Embassy, and the flag continued to wave above its walls.

While this was going on Il-han remained with the King and the Queen, for by now they were surrounded by the Chinese, and Il-han stayed with them until the city was quiet. When the Queen rose to return to her own palace he knelt before her and said nothing until she spoke.

"Lift your head," she commanded, and he lifted his head.

"Get to your feet," she said, and he rose to his feet.

She gave him a long steady look.

"There will be another time," she said. "Watch for it—and come earlier to save me."

"Yes, Majesty," he said.

He waited until she was gone, and then he turned to the

King, preparing once more to kneel but the King stopped him with lifted hand.

"Here is sorrow," he said, "when a kingdom comes between a man and his wife."

He dropped his hand then and bowed his head, and Il-han knew himself dismissed.

When Il-han reached his own gate, it was barred as though for siege. He beat upon the gate and he waited but there was no answer.

"Beat again with me," he commanded his servant.

They beat four-handed, raising such clatter that doors opened along the street and neighbors put out their heads. When they saw what was going on, they shut their doors again in haste.

In such times every small sign was of significance, and Il-han felt his heart grow cold with fear. Had some vengeance been wreaked upon his family by unknown enemies? Enemies he knew he had for he had been friend first to the Queen and then to the King, and in his double duty doubtless he had made enemies on both sides. He was casting about in his mind to know what he could do, when suddenly the gate opened a crack and the gateman looked out. When he saw who was there he beckoned to Il-han to come in, but he held the door so that only he and the servant could enter and then he barred the gate again.

"What is this?" Il-han asked.

He looked about as he spoke. Silence was everywhere. The usual bustle of servants, the shouts and laughter of his children, and Sunia's voice of welcome, all were gone.

"Master," the gateman whispered. "We had warning just before sunset that this house would be attacked in the night."

"Warning?" Il-han exclaimed. "How did it come?"

"The tutor told our mistress," the man replied. "He was away all day, after you left, and he came in at noon and he told."

"But why?"

The man shook his head. "I know nothing. Only my mistress

bade us make all haste to leave and under her command we put clothing and food into boxes and baskets and as soon as darkness fell all went to the country except me. She bade me stay here until you came and to saddle your horse ready. I have saddled the two horses for I am to go with you."

Il-han was astounded and somewhat vexed. "How can I leave the city at this time? All is in confusion and I do not know at what moment I shall be sent for at court."

The servant interrupted. "Master, these questions can be answered when you are with our mistress again. Now we must leave, for who knows what lies ahead? You could be seized at any moment. You must retire now to your grass roof, otherwise you will lose your life, and if the Queen is angry with you, your family, too, will die. Who knows whether she will listen a second time to the American woman?"

When Il-han still hesitated, the servant began to weep silently but Il-han would not allow such pleading.

"Do not distract me with tears," he said sternly. "I have more to consider at this moment than my own life, or even the lives of my sons."

Upon this the servant sobbed aloud. "And can you serve if you are dead? Your father stood here even as you do. I was only a boy but I stood beside him. But he was wise—he chose to retire to his grass roof and live and protest, rather than to let his voice be silenced in death."

"My father?" Il-han exclaimed.

"Go to his house," the servant said. "Search his books and you will find what he was. You never knew him."

Why this moved Il-han he himself did not know, but he bowed his head in assent and the man went to the stables and led out the two horses, saddled and ready. Il-han held in his restless horse until he heard the gate of his house barred behind him and then he galloped into the night.

It was soon after midnight when he drew rein before the wooden gate set into the earthen wall which surrounded the farmhouse where his father had lived for so many years, alone except for his few old servants some of whom still lived here

and would until they died. The ancient gateman sat outside
on the stone step, staring into the darkness and huddled in his
padded jacket. The night wind blew chill and the moon was
dark when Il-han came down from his horse and the old man
wakened and lit his paper lantern and held it up.

"It is your master," Il-han's man servant told him.

"We are waiting for you," the old man said, coughing in the
night wind.

With this he opened the gate, and Il-han strode into the
courtyard. The sound of the horses' feet told Sunia that Il-han
had come and she opened the door of the house and he saw
her there, her head lifted, the candles burning in the room behind her. He entered and closed the door.

"I thought you would never come," she said.

"The road was endless," he replied. "Tell me what happened."

Before she could reply they heard a knock on the inner door,
and she called entrance and the tutor came in.

For the first time Il-han saw this man was no longer young.
He came in, not shy or hesitating, and he looked Il-han full in
the face.

"Sir," he said, "shall I speak now or shall I wait until you
are bathed and have eaten and rested?"

"How can I rest or bathe or eat when I know nothing of
what has happened?" Il-han replied.

"Can anyone hear us?" Sunia asked, her voice low.

"I have my men on guard," the tutor said.

"Your men!" Il-han exclaimed. "Who are you?"

The tutor motioned to Il-han to be seated, and Il-han sat
down on the floor cushion at the table in the center of the
room. He was suddenly very weary, and he braced himself for
whatever news he must hear. When he sat, Sunia sat also, and
he gestured to the tutor to be seated. Had he been only the
tutor he would not have dared to seat himself, but now he did
and face to face with Il-han who had been his master, the
tutor spoke.

"I do not know whether you have heard that a new revolution is growing everywhere like fire in the wild grass. Yet it is

so. The landfolk are ready to rise up in every village and on every field. They can no longer suffer what they are suffering nor will they any more pay with their life and their strength for what is being forced upon them."

A dark foreboding fell upon Il-han. "I suppose you mean the Tonghak."

"Only a name for being in despair, sir," the tutor said. "I must tell you that it was I who gave your household warning. I am grateful to you for sheltering me all these years in your house, as your father sheltered mine. Now I must warn you that the turmoil has only begun. The landfolk have lost hope. They have come together under the Tonghak banner and no one can foretell what they will do."

"Tonghak!" Il-han cried. "Are you a Tonghak?"

"I am," the young man said. He stepped back and folded his arms and looked straight into Il-han's eyes.

"I cannot understand this," Il-han exclaimed. "You have had ease and courtesy in my house. None has oppressed you or watched you. Why do you join with those Tonghak rebels?"

"Sir," the man said, "I am a patriot. I take my place with our people. And who knows them better than you do, sir? The landfolk are the ones who pay for everything. They only are the taxed, for we have no industries such as you say the western nations have. Here all taxes fall upon the land. When the King wants money for these new ventures of his, the new army, the post office, the trips abroad, such as the one you made, not to speak of the diplomats and the delegations, the new machines he wants to buy, where does the King get the money? He taxes the landfolk! And as if this were not enough, who pays for the corruption inside the Court? And outside as well, for every petty magistrate has his little court, and the Queen has her relatives and her favorites, and who pays—who pays? The countryfolk who till the land, even the land they cannot own, which they can neither buy nor sell because it belongs to some great landlord, and he does not pay the tax, oh no, it is the lowly peasant who only rents the land who pays the tax! Sir, does your conscience never stab you in the heart?"

Il-han stared at the tutor as though he saw a madman. "Am I to blame?" he demanded.

"You are to blame," the tutor said, his voice and his face very stern. "You are to blame because you do not know. You do not allow yourself to know. You traveled through the country for many months, did you not, and you saw nothing except mountain and valley and sea and people moving like puppets. Have you ever heard of a Russian named Tolstoy?"

"I know no Russians," Il-han said.

"Tolstoy was a man like you, a landowner," the tutor went on. "Yet his conscience woke. He saw his people, the people whom he owned because they belonged on his land, and when he saw them he understood that they were human beings and he began to suffer. Sir, you must suffer! It is for this that I have saved you."

Il-han could not swallow such talk. It was enough for him to be amazed that the meek young man who he had thought was only a scholar, employed to teach his elder son, now showed himself a stranger.

"How have you saved me?" he demanded.

"I saved you as my father saved your father," the tutor replied. "When angry people were about to kill your father in his time, my father persuaded them to let him retire to this grass roof."

"My father was a good man," Il-han said.

The tutor was relentless. "A good man, but he did not lift his voice when others were evil. And you too, you are a good man, but you do not lift your voice. You have access to the King and to the Queen but you have not raised your voice for your people."

Il-han returned look for look. "What would you have me say?"

For the first time the man's black eyes wavered. "I do not know."

He waited a moment, biting his lip. Then he lifted his eyes again to Il-han's eyes. "For that, too, I blame you. It is you who should know, and because you should know, because you must know, I have saved your life and the lives of your family.

Today, in the congress of the Tonghak, I stood up and declared that among those who are to die you must not be killed. You—you are not to die! But I swore by my own life that you would be brave enough, when you knew, to speak against the corruption of the government, and against the taxes heavy as death, and the pushing men from Japan who are bringing their cheap goods here for our folk to buy because there are no other goods. And above all, you must speak bravely against the Japanese tricksters who by one means and another are buying land from the landowners because the landfolk can no longer pay even the taxes on their harvests."

These words fell upon Il-han like blows from an iron cleaver. For a while he could not reply, and indeed for so long that the tutor could not endure the silence and he cried out again.

"I tell you, it is only for this that I have saved you and your sons!"

To which Il-han again after a long silence could only answer with deep sighs and few words.

"Tonight I must rest," he said.

"But tomorrow?" the tutor insisted.

"Tomorrow I will think," Il-han promised.

The tutor rose then and bowed and went away, and suddenly Il-han was so weary that he could only look at Sunia, begging for her help.

"You need not speak a word," she said. "Your bath is hot, your supper is waiting and then you must sleep."

He rose. "You who understand—" He felt her hand slip into his and hand in hand they went toward the rooms she had prepared for their life.

"What shall I call you?" he asked the tutor.

It was noon of the next day when he summoned the man to come to him alone. He had not yet seen his sons, and he had told Sunia that he would not until he had spoken again with the tutor. His older son was old enough to have been shaped by his tutor beyond knowledge, and he must know not only what the tutor had to say further but also what he was. It seemed to him, after his sleepless night, that all his years until now had been meaningless. He had lived at the beck of the Queen and the call of the King, conceiving this to be his duty. Even his long journeys into his own country and then into the foreign countries had been in service of the truebone royal house, rather than for the sake of the people. Was it indeed true that people and rulers must be separate? When he served one, must it mean that he did not serve the other?

"I can no longer think of you as my son's tutor," Il-han said when the tutor came again into his presence. "You are some-one I do not know. Your surname is Choi but what is your name?"

"Sung-ho," the man replied. He smiled half ruefully. "I wish I could call myself after the great Ta-san of the past, but I am not worthy. I must continue merely to use the name my father raised for me when I went to school."

"Perhaps you will make a great name of it," Il-han said.

Sung-ho only smiled again.

"I have a question to ask," Il-han went on.

"Ask what you will," Sung-ho replied.

Il-han saw how confident the man was, how bright his look, how straight his carriage. He sat on his cushion without diffi-dence, eager and ready.

"Is it you who have shaped my elder son so that he prefers to live here in the country under this grass roof rather than in the city?"

"Inevitably I have shaped him," Sung-ho replied. "At first it was only that the city was hot in summer while here it is al-ways cool. But as I shaped him, I shaped myself. Had I not spent summers here with your father under this grass roof I might never have come to know the landfolk."

"Are the people on my land Tonghak?" Il-han asked.

"They are," Sung-ho replied. "At least all who are young."

Il-han smiled wryly. "Does this mean that you will all rise up in the middle of some night and behead me?"

"No," Sung-ho said sturdily. "It means that we look to you to speak for us."

Il-han was somewhat confounded at this. Was he then in duress? He poured two bowls of tea, so that he could have time to think, and he handed one to Sung-ho, but not with both hands as he would to an equal. To his surprise, Sung-ho also took the bowl with one hand, and not with both hands as he must from his superior.

Il-han went on. "Tonghak is a dumping pot for all sorts of rascals and rebels, debtors who will not pay their debts, thieves who will not pay their taxes."

Sung-ho did not yield one whit. "You know very well how common people insist upon tricks and conjurings from those whom they love and admire, and who they think can protect them, and is it just to demand that every Tonghak be free from corruption when the yangban themselves are corrupt?"

It was Il-han who must yield. "I cannot deny it," he said.

At this Sung-ho softened his voice. "I exempt you always from the corruption of your kind. I know you to be an honest man, and I swore this in order to save your life."

Il-han laughed. "You will not allow me to forget that I owe you my life!"

"I will not allow you to forget," Sung-ho agreed, and he did not laugh.

Before Il-han could proceed, he heard the voices of his two sons, one shouting in anger, the other wailing in pain. Both he and Sung-ho leaped to their feet, but the door burst open and Il-han saw his elder son walking toward him and dragging something behind him. This something was nothing else than his sobbing younger son, bound hand and foot with rope. In his right hand the elder son held a dagger-shaped stick of bamboo.

"What are you doing?" Il-han shouted and seized his elder son while Sung-ho lifted the younger child to his feet and pulled away the rope. Without stopping to inquire why his elder son had been so cruel, Il-han lifted his hand and slapped him first on one cheek and then on the other, and this so hard that the boy's head turned left and right and left and right. Now it was the elder one who began to roar loud sobs.

"You!" Il-han said between set teeth. "You, who are a savage!"

"No," the child sobbed. "I am Tonghak, and he is a yangban who takes money—"

The younger child was loosed by now and Il-han clasped him and lifted him to his shoulder. The two men exchanged looks.

"You have made my elder son into a criminal," Il-han declared.

Sung-ho returned his hard look with another as hard.

"Forgive me," he said. "I do not belong in your house."

With these words, he disappeared and from that time on Il-han saw him no more, nor did he know where he went or whether he would ever return.

Here Il-han was, then, left with the two children, both crying, and a servant ran to tell Sunia, and in a moment or two she was there. The child she comforted was the elder one, Il-han observed, and he protested.

"Do not comfort that one," he exclaimed. "He would kill his brother if he could."

"How can you say so?" she exclaimed. "He is only a child."

She put her arms around the elder son and murmured to him, and Il-han stood holding the younger one on his shoulder until suddenly he was impatient.

"Come, come, Sunia," he said, "let us make some order in this family of ours. Take the children away and feed them and put them to bed. Leave me alone for a while."

She obeyed, casting hostile looks at him as she went, to which he paid no heed. His own confusion must first be resolved before he could be father and husband again. Impatient to be alone, he closed the door after them, and sat down on the floor cushion facing the garden and sank himself into meditation.

The disorder in his family was the disorder of his people. How diverse were the elements! Here under the grass roof of his father's house, here where his father had lived out his long life as a scholar and a recluse, the spirit of the past descended again. Must he repeat the life of his father in his own life? He had endeavored to avoid the national disease of dissension. He had maintained a prudent and middle course, now with the Queen, now with the King, aware of old loyalties, yet ready for new. To live a floating life, swimming with the tide and never against it, ready for all change provided it was for the good of his country, he had nevertheless come to the same place where his father had come in the years before he himself was born, and this by a totally different path. His father had never wavered in his faithfulness to the past, and so had been hated only by those who dreamed of the future. Now he, the son, was hated by all, by those who clung to the Queen and by those who clung to the King. Was there no place for him in his own country? If not, what could he teach his sons? Here in his own house the Tonghak rebellion was brewing, while he unknowing had pursued his middle way. He felt lost and distracted and the day passed without clearing his mind or lifting his spirit.

"All that I know about myself," he told Sunia in the restless night, "is that I am Korean. I am born of this soil, I have been nurtured on its fruits and its waters. The blood and bones of my ancestors are my blood and my bones. Therefore I must know myself first."

She let him talk, his head on her breast. And after a while he said, "I have never had time to know myself. I have always been at the call of others. Now I shall answer no summons. I will close the doors of my grass-roof house against the world. I shall be alone with myself."

Womanlike, she listened to such musings and answered yes, yes, do so, whatever you think best, and when morning came she busied herself again about the old house, silk-spinning and making kimchee and keeping festivals. To live in this country house after the years in the city was in itself a task, for here nothing was convenient. The kitchens were old and the caldrons worn thin, mice and rats ran everywhere, lizards came creeping out of walls, and spiders festooned their webs among the blackened roof beams. In the wall closets the bed mattresses were mildewed, in the rooms the floor cushions were torn and their linings split. There were also her sons, and where to find a new tutor for them was a burden.

"You must teach them," she told Il-han one day, "or else you must find a teacher."

Who would dare come now to this house to teach his sons? In the end Il-han was compelled to teach them, lest they grow up fools and yokels. Yet he found the teaching a task, and he could only force himself to it, teaching them two hours in the morning and then setting them free for the rest of the day, and Sunia complained that they were twice as mischievous after he had taught them as they were before, the elder one always in the lead. At last she set Il-han's man servant to watch them and keep them from falling into the fishponds and smothering in the rice vats and running down the road to be lost.

As for Il-han, he did not know what to teach his sons and he could only teach them what he himself was trying to learn. As he studied afresh the history of his people, each day he made a simple lesson for his children of what he himself had learned the day before. His father's books were his source and his treasure, and how vast the library was he had not realized until now. Here in the shelves of four connecting rooms lay the rolls of manuscripts and books, a room for each of the subjects of learning, one for literature, another for history, another for philosophy, and the fourth for mathematics, economics and the calendar. With philosophy was also politics, for these two were inseparably together both in history and in the present, and one cannot be considered without the other.

He knew that his people were divided by geography. Those of the rugged north, where craggy mountains split the sky, were more rude, less cultivated, less learned than those of the south. Troublemakers they were called, revolutionary by nature, and the cause for this was partly in that most landfolk owned their own land. Moreover, they did not plant rice paddies but they grew wheat on dry fields. They were scornful of the people of the south, declaring them effete and lazy, scheming rascals without ambition, working on land that others owned. This division went so deep that even here in the capital city, south meant those nobles whose families lived in the southern part of the city, as Il-han's family had for many generations, and north meant those whose houses were in the northern part of the city. The Noron, or northern, faction, was sometimes in power in government, and sometimes the Namin, or southern faction, took power. The struggle in the capital was the symbol of the struggle everywhere among his people, and he himself was a symbol, for he and his fellows had as children been kept within the circle of the Namin, and Sunia's family had been Namin, like his, else neither his family nor hers would have considered it possible to allow marriage between them. Namin would not marry Noron. Yet it seemed to him sometimes as he continued day after day to study the books in the library and to express them in essence to his sons, young as they were, that this very division had its benefits. For while one faction was in power, the opposition in retreat fought it with vigor and device, and their rebellion was expressed in strong music and passionate poetry so that much of the great literature of his people sprang from the sources of dissension.

This conception seemed to him so apt, so correct, that he cast about in his mind one day as to how to express it to his sons in language which they could understand. It was autumn again, the season of high skies and fat horses. Sunia and her women were making kimchee, and the smell of fresh cabbage, of white radishes a foot long, of red peppers and garlic and onions, ground ginger and cooked beef scented the air. She ran into his room, he looked up from his book and saw her there, wrapped in a wide blue cotton apron, her hands wet with salt, her beautiful face pleading and impatient.

"Can you not keep the boys with you today?" she demanded. "We are distracted with their naughty ways. The elder one throws the cabbages here and there like balls, and the little one follows him. I cannot watch them and get the kimchee into the vats, too. That elder one—he hid in a vat and we could have smothered him without knowing it."

"Send them here," he said, his own patience tried. They came in then, the two of them hand in hand, dressed in clean garments and with hair freshly combed. His heart melted at the sight of them in spite of himself, but he made himself stern.

"Sit down," he said as coldly as he could.

They sat down, awed for the moment by his coldness, and he bit his lip, contemplating them as they sat facing him. Their brown eyes, so trusting and clear, their cream-white skin tanned by the sun, their red cheeks and lips, made him long to embrace them but he would not allow himself the pleasure. However his love welled up in him, he must control it and make the surface cool and firm.

"Today," he began, "I will tell you the story of Ta-san. Listen carefully, for when I have finished I will be able to tell whether you have understood, and I shall be angry if you show me that you have not listened."

"Is the story true?" his elder son asked.

"True," he said, "and full of meaning for us nowadays, although Ta-san lived before you were born or even I was born. But my father, your grandfather, knew him and learned much from him."

He then told the story of Ta-san, concerning whom he had found many notes written by his father. He would not confess to himself that it was the tutor's mention of Ta-san that had rekindled Il-han's interest and sent him searching among his father's notes.

"You must know," he told his sons, "that our country, Korea, was the first in the world to make the printed word—that is, with movable type."

Here Il-han paused. He paused to see if his elder son would ask what movable type was, but he did not. Il-han then went on without explanation, for he believed that to answer a child's question before it is asked is to destroy natural curiosity.

"There were many books when Ta-san lived and he read them. In this he was fortunate, for though our people have for a long time had books, common folk could not read them, first because they did not know their letters and second because they were not permitted to share knowledge. Our rulers controlled all learning. But Ta-san could read and he read not only the books in his father's house but also the books in the King's palace, because he had passed his examinations with such high honor that even the King noticed him, yet he did not read all day. As he grew older, the King asked him to do many great tasks. One of them, for example, was to build the second capital at Suwon, where the King could retreat if the capital itself were attacked by enemies, and while Ta-san made plans for the second capital, he also devised a way whereby big stones and trunks of trees could be lifted by a rope put through a pulley, and how a machine, called a crane, could be used. He made many such inventions.

"One day he found some books that told of what other countries did. Until now Ta-san had thought that all knowledge was in our country and in China, but in these new books he found such new thoughts that there was even a new god. Oh, but this made his enemies happy, for it was forbidden to read such books, and now they said Ta-san was a traitor and he had to leave his fine city house and move to a house in the country, far away. There he sat reading and reading and writing great books and speaking his mind—"

"Like you, Father," his younger son put in.

Il-han had been thinking that his son had not listened and when the child said this with such intelligence and understanding, Il-han looked at him with a scrutiny he had never before given him.

"Like me," he agreed, "and in some ways Ta-san was more useful to his country and our country than he had ever been before. True, the Noron were then in power, and he was a Namin, as our ancestors were, and so he could only write his books and keep them. But the day came when he was free again, and then the books he wrote could be read by all who could read. Some day you will read them, too, as I did, and as I am doing now."

"Why?" This came from the literal mind of his elder son.

"Because he did not sit in idleness," Il-han said. "Because he roamed the earth and went among its peoples, while his body was confined to his own house and gardens. He made beautiful gardens, too, and he even built a waterfall."

"Then we will build a waterfall," his elder son declared.

The notion seized upon both children and they were on their feet in a moment and making for the door.

"Wait," Il-han called after them, "wait! I will come with you. We will do it together."

They halted, astonished that he could consider such play, and he reproached himself that he had not shared their life but forced them always into his. So he took a hand of each and they went into the garden, far from the kitchen court where the kimchee was being made, and Il-han spent that whole day with his sons, choosing a place in the brook where the water could be debouched into another channel to make a pool fed by the waterfall. This work took days to complete, and Il-han found the key to the teaching of his sons. First they must sit and learn for an hour or so much more as he felt they could bear, and then they went to the building of the waterfall and the pool. He saw to it that the work went slowly and so the months passed toward winter.

To Il-han's own surprise, this life with his sons deepened his own life. No longer was learning apart from life. When he studied Ta-san's plan for the community ownership of land he considered how he could apply it to his own tenant farmers, who maintained this farm he had inherited from his ancestors. Ta-san had declared that farmers should work collectively, each pooling his land into the general community ownerships. The harvests, he said, were to be allotted, after taxes, to the farmers in proportion to the labor they had given.

Il-han could not approve the plan as a whole, yet he was amazed that within the stern controls of the Yi dynasty, so long ago Ta-san could conceive such changes, even though they were never used. And he pondered long upon the question of how his own tenants could be justly rewarded for their labor on his land. Here he sat inside his comfortable grass roof, shaded from the summer sun and warmed in winter by the ondul floors, and he drew in the money they earned for him, while they toiled in his fields and lived in crowded huts and ate coarse food. Wrong, wrong, his heart told him, and dan-

gerous, his mind told him, but where could one man begin?
Moreover, he had not the power that even Ta-san had, though
in exile. He assuaged his heart then by calling in his tenants
that year after the harvest, and he met them on the threshing
floor before the gate.

They stood in the late sunshine, a ragged crew of sun-
browned men, their horny hands hanging while they bowed to
him. None spoke, and all were anxious, for why should a landlord speak to his tenants except to tell them that the rent was
raised?

He perceived their anxiety and made haste to allay it.

"I greet you," he said, "to thank you for the harvests, which
are good beyond the average. This I take it is at least partly
because you have done your work well. For the rest, we must
thank Heaven for rain and sun in proportion to the need."

They still looked at him with sullen eyes, doubting his
intent, and suddenly he was afraid of them. The distance
between him and them was very far and there was no bridge.

"I will not keep you," he said. "I wish only to tell you that
your share of the harvests will be doubled this year."

They could not believe him. They still gazed at him in fear
mixed with doubt. Whoever heard of a landlord who doubled
the share of the tenant? Such good fortune was too rare.

As for Il-han, he saw their doubt and he was angry at their
ingratitude. No one spoke. He waited and when he saw that
they had no intent to speak, he felt his heart grow cold and
hard.

"This is all I have to say," he told them, and he turned and
strode into his house and barred the gate behind him.

Yet when he had time to think over their brief meeting, he
blamed himself for his anger. Why should they feel gratitude?
For years they had toiled to receive a meager share of the
harvest. Even to double that share was not enough. The injustice of their lives was the injustice of centuries. It could
not be mended in a day by one man on one farm.

On one cold New Year's Eve several years later, Il-han
reckoned that all he had done and thought and felt, added

together, showed only two accomplishments. One was that his sons grew well and he had developed their minds beyond expectation. They were passing from babyhood to boyhood, the elder edging into his youth, although at thirteen he was still turbulent and impatient and argumentative, and he chose to make many quarrels with his brother, who in defense drew apart from him and became solitary. In a way this was a comfort to Il-han, for his younger son sometimes sought his company alone, partly for protection against the elder brother, but also because he and his father were much alike in loving books and writing poetry. This younger son had besides a tender love of music and he learned to play upon the kono harp so well that this became a cause of jealousy in the older brother. The elder was the more handsome of the two, however, and a very handsome lad he was, tall and strong, his eyes bright and bold, his nose straight, his lips thin, and he made fun of his younger brother's light build. When he was angry, he even taunted the younger one for the imperfection of the lobe of his ear until one day Il-han, himself in rage, took his younger son to the American physician who had saved Min Yong-ik's life, and he asked him to make the ear right again.

The physician by this time was aged, and his hands trembled. Yet he examined the ear and then he called his assistant, a young Korean whom he had taught during the years.

"Your hand is better at this than mine," he told the man. "I will stand beside you and help you, but you must hold the knife."

Il-han stood watching. First they put his son to sleep, holding some liquid-soaked cotton to his nostrils as he lay on a table. Then when he was asleep, while Il-han was uneasy for the sleep was too much like death, the young doctor, his hands encased in thin rubber gloves such as Il-han had never seen before, took a small thin knife from a tray held by a woman aide, and he cut the boy's ear lobe and split it cleverly. Next with a needle and thread he sewed it into shape and attached it to the head. When all was finished, he tied on a bandage.

"Come back after a few days," the old American doctor said, "and in ten days or so, you will see your son's ear as like the other as his two eyes are alike."

Sunia made much ado when Il-han brought the boy home again, for he had not told her, knowing she would be fearful and forbid it. But the ear healed well, and then the boy was perfect. Il-han was glad, except that he thought the elder son was colder to him than ever after the younger son was made perfect.

So much for his sons. The second accomplishment was a book that Il-han had been writing all these years. In it he put down, day after day, every wrong deed he heard done in the capital or in the nation. Friends visited him, though not often, and always in secret, and unknown men came to tell him stories of their sufferings, and again and again unknown members of the Tonghak came to his house and he received them because of Choi Sung-ho, but Sung-ho himself never returned, and when Il-han asked a Tonghak where he was, that man shook his head or shrugged his shoulders and none seemed to know who he was or if any knew him, they did not know where he was.

From whatever he learned from such persons and from every other source possible to him now, Il-han wrote in his book. He wrote down what every yangban spent on bribes and trickeries, and what every soban connived. When new governors were appointed for the provinces, he found out what time they left and when they arrived, how much they spent on the way, what women they took with them, or slept with as they went, who was bribed for what, and who welcomed them when they came to their new places, and who paid for the feasts and the dancing girls, and whether Japanese spies talked with them, and whether they met in secret with Japanese or Chinese or Russians, and if they traveled and where and how long they stayed away from their posts and who were their hosts and what favors were asked and if they were granted. When each such evil was known and written down in his book, and he saw how corruption weighed more heavily year by year upon the miserable landfolk, Il-han then wrote pages of what he believed should happen and how righteousness and justice could still be saved.

In the long evenings Sunia, her day's work done, sat listening while he read aloud to her what he had written. Sometimes she was so weary with her household cares that when he paused to ask what she thought, he saw she slept. He never waked her, for he saw, too, in her sleeping face how much she had aged. The youthful beauty was gone, the lines of middle-age were clear, the same lines that he saw in his own face in the mirror in his bedroom. Seeing her, he only sighed and closed the book softly and let her sleep.

Yet there were other times when she did not sleep and when she listened, admiring, yearning for the world he wrote of in contrast to what was. On one such night he saw her weeping when he looked up to ask her if he wrote well.

"Now, Sunia," he said, "have I written something wrong?"

She shook the tears from her eyes and tried to smile. "No, you have written all too well. But—but—oh, why can you not be heard? Will anyone ever read this book? I cannot bear to think your life is wasted here under this grass roof."

He did not answer. Her question was the one he asked himself many times. Was his life wasted? Perhaps for his times and for his people, but not for himself. He had set the task of knowing what he was—he, a Korean. Now he knew. He closed the book.

"It is time to sleep," he said. "The night grows dark and there is no moon."

In the early evening of a certain night a messenger came on foot to the gate of Il-han's grass roof home. Since he was a stranger, the gatekeeper would not admit him until he had himself inspected the man's appearance. When he had looked at the man from head to foot, he let him in, but held him in the gatehouse under the guard of three other servants until he went to find his master and report the presence and the appearance of this stranger.

Il-han had finished his evening reading of the Confucian classics with his sons. In the mornings now their studies were in mathematics and history, in the afternoons their studies were in literature, and in the evening before they were sent to bed, Il-han read aloud to them the *Book of Poetry* or the *Book of Changes*, expounding in simple words the meaning of the sonorous, ancient words. Each learning period was short for he knew how easily the thoughts of the young wander afield, yet he believed that by this thrice-repeated period each day, his sons' minds would be permeated with learning and with knowledge of the good, and he dreamed that though his life might be useless, in the lives of his sons his own might continue with benefit to his people.

In the calm of such comfort, then, he had bid his sons sleep well while he settled himself to his own studies, Sunia being absent at the moment and in the kitchen supervising the brew of a ginseng tea which he found soothing to his inner organs at the end of the day. At this moment the gatekeeper was announced by a servant and Il-han nodded his head for the man to enter. The gatekeeper came in and standing near the door in respect he bowed and then spoke.

"Master, there has come a stranger to our gate. I did not let him enter until I had looked at him well. He is a foreigner."

Il-han let his pen fall from his hand. "Is he wearing foreign dress?"

"No," the man replied. "He is in proper dress like yours, master. But his face is not our face."

"Did he give his name?" Il-han asked.

"He said that you would know him if you saw him."

"How could you understand a foreigner's language?" Il-han inquired.

"He speaks our language," the gatekeeper replied.

They looked at each other, master and man. One thought was in each mind. Was this a ruse in order perhaps to stab Il-han? Of all those whom the King had sent to America on the mission, only Il-han remained free in his own house. Min Yong-ik, when he had recovered from his wounds, lived in exile, hiding here and hiding there, rejected even by the Chinese whom he had tried to serve. Hong Yong-sik, who had chosen not to flee with the Japanese when the Chinese soldiers entered the palace, had been cut to pieces before the King's eyes. So Kwang-pom escaped to Japan and had lived there in exile these ten years, and here in his own country he was now called a traitor. Others were in prison, or in exile in unknown distant villages and farms.

"Master," the gatekeeper said in a low voice, "I will put my knife through this stranger, and throw his body in the pond."

For a moment Il-han was frightened, but at himself, because he was tempted. It would be easy—a thing he would never do but if a gatekeeper, faithful to the family—who would know, or if knowing, blame the master? The next moment he recalled what he was and was ashamed. What—had the evil of the times permeated him, too, and to the soul? Because men were killed everywhere in treachery and in secret, was he to stoop to murder? Thus he inquired of himself, and the answer was no, and no again. He took his pen and fitted it into the silver cap and he closed his book and got to his feet.

"I myself will look at this stranger," he said.

He strode across the garden and down the winding path between the mulberry trees kept for the feeding of silkworms, and then he stooped his head, for he was very tall, and entered the low-roofed gatehouse. Inside, the candle of cow's fat guttered and in its wavering light he could only see a man leaning sidewise against the wall, his face in profile as he stared into the candlelight. He lifted his head when Il-han came near and then he spoke.

"Have you been here all these years?"

Il-han knew him instantly, though the face was haggard and the eyes aged. It was George Foulk. He put out both his hands and the American clasped them.

"I thought you were dead!" he exclaimed. "I was told you had been killed with all your family and your house sealed."

"Is my house sealed?" Il-han asked.

"You have never gone back?"

"I have not gone back," Il-han said, "but my servants have gone and the house was not sealed."

"Then it is only recently," Foulk replied. "I sent my own

guard to discover who lived in your house, and the gate was sealed and a soldier stood there. At first he too said you were dead, but when he felt money in his palm he said you were living but in exile here in the country. My friend, I must talk with you. Enough has happened in these years to fill a century."

In the shadow of the trees and the twilight Il-han led the American, still grasping his hand, into the house by a side entrance. There he bade his servant allow no one to enter the room where they would talk, and not even Sunia was to enter, for he did not wish her to have the burden of confessing, perhaps some day when confession might be extorted, that she had ever seen the American in his house. In the quiet of his study, the wall screens closed, he drew Foulk down to the floor cushion beside his, so that they might speak in voices too low for anyone to hear. He trusted his servants, and yet he trusted no one, not even Sunia, for she was a woman and to save his life or her children's she might one day tell anything.

"Speak," Il-han said. "The night is not long enough for me to know all you have to tell. Why do you come to me now after this long silence?"

"I want you to know that I am leaving Korea," Foulk said.

Now there was silence between them. Each gazed at the other in this silence.

"Even you," Il-han said at last. "Then, indeed we are lost. It means, does it not, that the Americans are giving us up?"

"Not the Americans," Foulk said. "My people know nothing of yours. This is our sin against you. We are ignorant. In ignorance my government has done nothing to save your people, for the result of ignorance is indifference, and indifference is a desert in which a whole nation can die. I cannot stay to see your people die. I—love Korea."

These words fell upon Il-han's ears, each a separate blow as he comprehended their import.

"Tell me what has happened," he said.

In reply Foulk then told such a story that Il-han could not have believed except that he knew this American was all of a piece, so loyal in friendship, so true, that anything he said was true.

The beginning, as Foulk told it, went back to the year of the treaty with the United States whereby Korea was declared by the Americans a sovereign nation, independent of China, her ancient suzerain. Independent, Korea could and did grant trade rights to Americans. Next was the arrival of Ambassador Foote, with his wife and secretary and the translator Saito.

"A mistake, that Saito," Il-han put in. "You should not have engaged a Japanese translator. Who knows what words he added or took away for his own benefit?"

"A mistake, that Saito," Foulk granted and went on with his story.

"The Americans discovered," he said, "that the King and his cabinet were too weak to exercise sovereignty, however many good men were with him. Men like you, Il-han Kim, even true patriots like you, were accustomed to subservience to the Chinese or the Japanese. You did not believe that you could be strong if you would be."

"I remember," Il-han said slowly. "The King said he danced for joy when the Americans came."

"Yet how can we Americans overcome your fears rooted in the centuries?" Foulk replied. "The King has leaned on us for everything. This has not only angered China, but it angers the other western powers. England and Germany would not ratify their treaties. My government was alarmed and they sent word at first to Foote and when he was gone, to me, that we could advise the King only personally, unless our government sent advice. Yet how could those men far away in Washington, those prudent local men, understand the vast troubles of your valuable country? Knowing too little, we do too little."

He turned his head away, he bit his lips, muttering, "My government has not even sent me enough money to pay the legation expenses. My ambassador had no money for hiring a clerk and the secretary was serving without salary. We have no money to buy land for a proper legation building—not even land! We should have consulates—other nations have their consulates, and they laugh at our parsimony. The great, rich United States of America! I chose land at Inchon for a beginning, but no money has come for the purchase. Do you wonder that other nations laugh?"

He sighed, and got up and walked around and around the room, his feet noiseless on the ondul floor.

"I should not tell you this—it is our family business—we Americans—and I could endure it all, but your King—he keeps pressing me, begging me to give him American advisers. He has a hundred plans—all good ones—a good man, this King of yours—he could build the nation if he had half a chance, and if our government only knew—if they could only see what they are throwing away—the chance to help him build a strong independent free Korea—a bulwark in Asia!"

"Why do you not go home and tell them?" Il-han asked.

He was embarrassed by many emotions, fear for his people, dismay lest the Americans were indeed unable to help them, and despair for the King. They must fall into the abyss of the greedy nations if no hand stretched out to them in friendship. Who could save them if the Americans did not?

"In addition to all else," Foulk was saying, "my ambassador was reduced in rank. He was no longer Envoy Extraordinary and Minister Plenipotentiary. He was only Minister Resident and Consul General. Of course he resigned."

Il-han could bear no more. "Stupidity—stupidity," he cried under his breath. "How could your government send us a minister of first rank and then degrade him?"

"He resigned," Foulk said, "and there is no one to replace him. I am the only one left."

"Shufeldt?" Il-han suggested.

"Shufeldt will not come," Foulk replied. "He knows too well what it means—a prudent man! I wish I were as prudent!"

"How old is all this trouble between your ambassador and your government?" Il-han inquired.

"Old—old," Foulk groaned. He sat down again. "Even before the dinner when Min Yong-ik was nearly killed."

"And you did not tell me!" Il-han exclaimed.

"I was ashamed," Foulk said, "and I still had hope that we could persuade those men in Washington."

"When did your ambassador leave us?" Il-han asked.

"The year after that dinner."

"And you?"

"I have been in charge ever since, without rank and helpless. And now I too give up. I want one Korean to know why —and you I can trust."

"I pray you, tell me everything," Il-han urged. "It may be that I—"

"No hope," Foulk repeated. "But if you—want to know the worst, here it is."

With this he enumerated, one by one on his ten fingers, the steps by which he had come to his present despair. Left alone, he had returned to the task of beseeching his superiors to send the American advisers for whom the King so urgently asked.

"The most pressing need of Korea in her present deplorable situation, I told Washington, is competent western instructors for her troops—many of them. Well, what happened? Three teachers were recommended by the Department of State! The King said he would pay for their expenses, but they were not permitted to come, except under private support. And where was I to find the money?"

Now that he had begun his confession to Il-han it seemed that Foulk could not stop himself. He wrung his hands together, he ground his teeth in anguish. "I had no money, I tell you! Because I was acting chargé d'affaires I couldn't even draw my navy pay—I was allotted half the minister's fund, but I couldn't draw the money. And then that German, that von Mollendorf, he got himself appointed head of customs in your capital, since no American advisers came, and he has worked against me continually, trying to get German advisers into Korea with the hope of establishing German influence here—"

"He did not succeed!" Il-han exclaimed.

Foulk went passionately on, as though he recited a program of doom and Il-han could only hold his head and groan as he listened.

"No, but failing to get German advisers, he employed Russian advisers, at least for your armies. Then and for once China and Japan united in pleading with the King that American advisers be sent—they being above all afraid of Russia. Well, the American military advisers are now scheduled to come next year—four years too late! The King has lost confidence in my country and my government and how can I blame him?"

Here Il-han opened his mouth to speak, but Foulk was not finished. "My pay drafts have been returned. Insufficient funds! Appropriations for Korea have been exhausted! And meanwhile I must handle affairs at Chemulpo as well as at Seoul, my country being the only one without a consul in Chemulpo! I resigned six months ago!"

"But you are still here."

Foulk made bitter laughter. "No one reads the dispatches I send, therefore no one is sent to replace me! In spite of this, your people—" Foulk paused here and leaned his elbows on the low desk, and shaded his eyes with his hands. His voice broke. "Your glorious people still look on me as the representative of the United States, the lodestar of their hope of independence! But I have had to tell them—the leader of the new independence group—a brave young man—I won't speak his name even here—I have told him that my government is interested only in collecting the indemnity for the *General Sherman*—lost so many years ago."

Foulk's voice was trembling. He paused, he pressed his lips together and went on abruptly. "I can no longer carry the burden of representing my government—and my people—without even clerical or secretarial help. But I haven't enough money to pay the most necessary bills for the legation. It has all made me ill. My health has failed. I—look at this."

He held out his hands and Il-han saw how thin his wrists were, the big bones gaunt and the skin drawn taut over the wasting muscles.

What could Il-han say? He clasped the hands of his friend in his own hands again and he bent his head down until his forehead rested on their clasped hands and his tears overflowed. Foulk waited a long moment and then without further word he withdrew his hands gently and left the room.

Some time afterwards, how long Il-han did not know, Sunia slid the door open. "Will you not come to bed now?" she asked but timidly.

"No," Il-han said, and did not look up.

She slid the door shut again and went away, and he sat the night through alone.

. . . Hours passed uncounted. Whether he was in the body or out of the body he did not know. Did he hate the Americans? He could have hated them except that he remembered them as he had gone to and fro among them in their own country, a kindly people, enjoying the manifold benefits of their life, and in their enjoyment and self-content exuding friendliness, though without friendship, as he now perceived. They were still too young for friendship, incapable of the deep bonds which bind one human being to others. Friendliness is shallow though pleasant, and it was unreasonable to expect a depth beyond their capacity. The mind must know, the heart must feel, before there can be understanding, and they did not know the long sad history of his people, nor could they feel the terror of being a small country set by chance among giants. The King had expected far too much. He and his fellows, Il-han himself, had expected too much of the Americans. It was their own ignorance of foreign peoples to mistake the easy promises of friendliness for the loyalty of true friendship. No, he could not hate them. Yet without them he knew his people were doomed.

What then could he do? His heart urged him to leave his grass roof and go to the King and the Queen and offer himself for their service, any service at any cost. Yet he knew this was only the longing to rid himself of the burden of his own knowledge. The King was no fool—he must know very well by now that he could trust no foreigners, the Americans having failed. And the Queen had never trusted them. The country was like a ship at sea, anchor lost, rudder broken, and captain helpless. He and all Koreans could only stay by their ship, wait out the storm, let destiny take its course. In kindness and forgiveness, he hoped that the friendly people in America would not know the opportunity they had lost and which would never again be offered them. Pray Buddha they would not some day be compelled to pay the costs!

"Father!"

Il-han heard his elder son's voice and was startled, as though he had never heard it before. It was no longer the high voice of a child. It had dropped halfway down the scale, it was cracked and hoarse, the voice of a boy ready to become a man. How had this come about so suddenly? Or was it sudden? He had been too engrossed in the even smoothness of his cloistered days to notice.

"Come in, my son," he said.

He stared at the lad as he entered the room. Surely he was taller today than yesterday, his hands bigger, his bones heavier. And his face was changed, the features thickening into adolescence—

"Why are you looking at me, Father?" the boy demanded.

"You are growing up."

"I have been growing up for a long time, Father."

"Why have I not seen it?"

"Because you are always looking at your books, even when you teach us. Father!"

"Well?"

"I want to go to school in the city."

"What are you saying?"

Il-han closed his book and motioned to his son to kneel on the floor cushion opposite him.

"You think I am not a good teacher?"

His son faced him with black eyes as bold as ever. "You teach old books, and I want to learn the new."

Il-han was about to reply sharply and then remembered as sharply. In his youth he had accused his father in the same fashion. In his son's voice he heard his own again. He kept himself calm. "Are there such schools in the city?"

"Yes, Father, and there are some teachers from America."

"They are Christians!"

His son shrugged. "There are also schools with Japanese teachers."

"You wish to learn from Japanese?"

"I wish only to learn," his son retorted.

What could Il-han say? He was wounded to the heart that his son considered him no longer fit to be his teacher, and yet he would not acknowledge his private hurt. He continued his argument.

"It is all very well to have new learning, but this does not mean the old is without importance."

His son replied insolently. "We have had enough of this old stuff!"

Il-han forgot himself. His right hand raised itself by instinct and he struck his son a blow on the cheek. The boy's face grew red, his great eyes flashed. He rose, bowed and left the room.

Il-han heaved deep sighs. He felt suddenly faint and his heart beat too fast. This son—as he strode out of the room he had looked a man, shoulders broad, long legs—ah, he should not have struck his son! What could be done now? Impossible for a father to repent to a son! The elder generation does not ask forgiveness of the younger. And what if the son was right and he was no longer a fit teacher for this time of confusion? What indeed did he himself know now of the world beyond this grass roof?

He pushed aside the book wherein he had been writing a poem. Of late he had found refuge for his troubled spirit in poetry—Oh, heaven, had not his father also taken to writing poetry, and what of the village poet in the grass-roof hut where the Queen had hidden from her enemies? Poetry was a drug, a vice, a cover for helplessness, or perhaps only indolence. He sat for a long time in meditation, searching his soul, accusing himself, submitting his spirit to a humility difficult indeed for a man so proud.

For days after that he did not speak to his son. He conducted the lessons for both sons as usual. The elder son took no part, asked no question, did not look at his father, but he came and took his place and remained in silence. After ten days Il-han told the younger son to leave the room, for he had something to say to the elder. The younger son obeyed and Il-han was left alone with his elder son. He called him by name now, for the first time.

"Yul-chun, I have considered your wish to go to a school in the city. You know I am in exile here in my own house. Is it not dangerous for you in the city when it is known you are my son?"

"No, Father," Yul-chun said. "I have friends there."

Il-han was amazed. "How can you have friends when I have none?"

"I have friends," Yul-chun repeated stubbornly.

The two gazed at each other. It was Il-han who yielded. So his son had friends of whom he knew nothing! A generation earlier a father would have insisted on knowing who his son's friends were and how they had been made. But this, this was a new generation, one very far from the past, and he did not ask. He could not, for what if the son refused to tell the father? What force had the father now to compel obedience?

"Well enough," he said at last. "Then go."

"I shall live with my friends," Yul-chun said.

"Well enough," Il-han replied again. "Only let your mother know where the house is. And you will need money."

He opened the secret drawer of his desk and took out a small leather bag where he kept money for daily needs and gave the bag to his son. "Let me know when you need more."

He held back the grim words in his mind—with all his independence he takes money from me. There was a bitter comfort in the knowledge and he needed any comfort.

When his son had left the room Il-han went in search of Sunia and found her in the storehouse, standing by the scales to watch the measuring of rice for the household. Her dark hair was powdered with the white dust of the rice, and her eyebrows and eyelashes were white. It is how she will look when she is old, he thought, and for a moment he was saddened. Then he spoke to her in a low voice.

"Will you come aside? I have something to tell you."

She lingered until the tenant had called out the weight of

the grain and then she followed Il-han into the garden where they sat down upon a stone seat in the shade of the bamboo grove.

"Our elder son wants to go to school in the city," he told her.

She was wiping the rice dust from her face with her kerchief and she did not reply.

"Are you not surprised?" he asked.

"No," she said. "I knew that he would go."

"And did not tell me?"

"I told him he must wait a year," she said. "I told him he was not to trouble you while he was too young to leave home."

"And you think he is not too young?"

"I think he is too old to stay," she said.

"So," he said slowly, "so you have known all along! You have kept it secret from me. How many such secrets have you?"

She laughed and then was grave. "I have only one purpose in all I do. It is to keep you at peace. If I told you every vagary and whim and ardor that these two sons of ours have, you would be in turmoil. You could not work."

"Work," he repeated sadly. "I am not sure I have a work. An occupation, say!"

"Work," she repeated firmly. "Some day all that you write down in your books will be of use. Who else is keeping the record?"

She had a way, most comforting, of making him value himself.

"I pray you are right," he said. "So then, we are to let him go?"

"Yes, because we cannot keep him."

He mused for a moment. "What has happened that the young no longer obey their elders as we did?"

"They see the havoc around about them," she replied. "They know that we have failed. They no longer respect us."

She spoke the cruel words with such calm that he was afraid of her. Then he rose.

"You are right. We must let him go, or he will leave us forever."

With that he went to his lonely room and took up his pen to brush the characters of a poem now rising to the surface of his mind. It was strange how these poems came to him nowadays, the distillation of his private emotions, of his disillusionment, of his solitude, of his yearning for a future in which, nevertheless, he could not believe. Nothing now could stay the doom he foresaw for his people and his country.

He was surprised that his household could so easily settle itself into a life without the elder son. Peace became its atmosphere, a peace sometimes too deep, Sunia said, for the younger son gave her no trouble.

"I miss that elder son's naughty ways," she told Il-han. "Nothing happens now that he has gone. Nothing is broken, no wild animals are brought in from the field, the floors are not dirtied, clothes are not torn, shoes are not lost. I hear no complaints about food. I am not used to such peace!"

"I trust he is not making a commotion in the city," Il-han said.

Yet he too was secretly pleased to see Yul-chun once or twice a month when he came home with all his garments soiled and needing to be washed, and with his pockets empty of money.

"I daresay you are full of new learning," Il-han remarked in his dry way.

"Your hair wants cutting," Sunia said briskly, and went to fetch her scissors.

Yul-chun shouted after her. "I will not have you cut my hair, Mother! They'll say I have a country haircut."

"I will cut it!" she called back.

And cut it she did, holding him by the ears and hooking his head under her arm, he half laughing, half angry.

"I will never come home any more if you treat me like this," he cried while he looked ruefully into the mirror on the wall.

"Then cut your hair before you come," she told him.

She knew very well that he came back for money from his father and for love from her. He still could not do without her tender scolding and teasing love, and he liked to have her examine his clothes and sew on missing buttons and cry how filthy his socks were and how worn his shoes. In short, he needed to know that however far he went away, she was still his mother. And Il-han watched half sadly, and pondered the difference between father love and mother love. With all his teaching and his concern for his son's mind and character, Yul-chun did not love him as he loved the mother whose concern was all for his body. Body love was deepest of all love perhaps—woman love in mother and in wife. Yet was it not this love that kept men forever children? Though for that matter, how could he himself live without Sunia? Who would feed him, keep him clean and tended and free of care if he had not her? In his son he saw himself again, and he did not like what he saw.

Because his son was in the city, Il-han began in his own way to take more cognizance of the changes in the times. He bade his servant go to the city now and then, not only to observe secretly, but also to see what was new and to listen to talk on the street and in teashops and gathering places. In this way he learned that the Tonghak rebels were growing in number and though they were repressed by the King and his forces, nevertheless they broke out here and there through the provinces with increasing success. At last their leader was caught and put in prison for execution, and this roused the landfolk to new frenzy and despair. By this time they had no trust in the government, for they saw how the foreign powers pressed upon the King, and they knew how the Queen plotted to keep the Chinese in power in the war that was about to break between China and Japan as in mutual anger these two nations quarreled in Korea.

In the early spring, in the third solar month of that year, while their young leader was still in prison, many Tonghak rebels gathered near the capital and they chose forty men from among them as their representatives, and those went to the King face to face to ask first that their leader be released and next for measures to better their hard lives. The King was wise enough to meet these Tonghak with courtesy and good promises, and so they returned peacefully to their homes. Yet the King had fresh troubles, for the foreign powers, whose envoys sat in the capital like vultures to watch all he did, were angry because he had received the Tonghak, for among the requests which they made was that he should set up an anti-foreign policy and expel all foreigners from the country. The King was caught between his people and the foreigners and so did nothing.

Months passed and when the Tonghak saw that the King did nothing, they rose in greater anger than ever. Twenty thousand came to the town of Poum pretending to make a religious festival there, but instead they demanded freedom from the corruption of their own yangban and oppression from foreign powers alike. Everywhere over the land cries were heard in one city and another. Alas, in the city of Kobu, in the area of Pyonggap, the magistrate outdid all other yangban in corruption, for here he compelled the landfolk to repair the walls of a great reservoir, whose waters were used for irrigating the fields. When these farmers had repaired the reservoir, he levied a heavy tax on the water, which they then used for their fields, and he kept the money for himself. This caused much fury and the landfolk tore down the dam they had repaired, and they stormed into the city and drove the magistrate away from his palace while they occupied the city.

The King and his cabinet then sent armies from the capital to rout the rebels, and hearing this from his servant, Il-han sent a man to follow the armies and watch all that took place. The man came back after many days to report that the government forces were overwhelmed and the Tonghak had moved on to conquer other cities. The King in distraction next begged for help from the Chinese, who sent their armies and only then did the rebels retreat against such force.

"And, master," the man said when he had related all this to Il-han, "whom do you think I saw there in the battles?"

Il-han knew in his heart and could not speak.

"I saw my young master, and he was with his tutor, who lived so many years in your house!"

The servant turned away in pity when he saw Il-han's face.

The times grew still worse. A Chinese army, fifteen hundred strong, with eight field guns, arrived at the Gulf of Asan and marched to the capital. When the Emperor in Japan heard this he sent an army of five thousand soldiers to meet them. There in the Korean capital they went into battle, Chinese and Japanese, and the treaties declaring the independence of Korea became dust. The greater numbers won. Japan drove out the Chinese and then attacked the rebels and put down the Tonghak. Not content with this, the Japanese soldiers dragged the Tonghak leader from his prison and put him to death and the rebels in dismay retired into hiding.

All this Il-han heard from his several men whom he regularly sent out to bring him news. They spoke no more of the tutor, and Yul-chun came home as usual and said nothing and Il-han said nothing, and in the frightful silence between them, he lived in dread. Now that the Tonghak leader was dead, he knew that indeed the Japanese were in power and the King was dependent upon them for his own place. But what of the Queen? It was of her he thought. She would never give up her love for the Chinese, and her hatred of the present confusion could only increase her love for them. She would not yield or bend her will. Her proud imperious heart was stubborn with love. Even Sunia grew afraid for her, and she paused near him one day on her way to some household task.

"I hope you will not think of the Queen," she said. "Let her solve the troubles she has brought upon herself."

He looked up at her quickly. "I am not thinking of the Queen," he told her and knew he lied.

Indeed, why should he think of the Queen? He could not help her and he would only be blamed if he came out of exile and went to her now. Nor could he keep himself secret if he

went. Where the Queen was, nothing was secret. Her every
word, her every look, was seen and pondered. Spies surrounded her, and though she was reckless and did what she
willed, he who was known as her adviser in the past, if he
left his house would be killed somewhere in a side street of
the city or in a secret corridor of the palace, and no one would
know. He did not lack courage but must he die, he hoped that
it could be for a worthy reason and with an effect that
lived beyond his death.

He continued nevertheless in dread of what he would hear,
for his private spies, now increased to eleven men, brought
him further reports of the confusions which were taking place.
China and Japan, these two, were in constant combat for the
prize of his country, its trade, its central position in that part
of the world, and the Japanese were carrying the war into
China itself, and with every victory they seized new territory.
Meanwhile they made this war an excuse for their armies to
pour into Korea as reserves, and every day Il-han heard of
fresh outrage against his people.

. . . "The strong have now become too strong," Il-han's
wise old man servant told him.

The day was hot, in the midsummer of that year, and
Il-han sat in his white undergarments under a persimmon tree
in the garden. The fruit was small and green and the tree
was overloaded so that some fruit fell to the ground, and
his younger son was throwing the fruit against a target fixed
on the trunk of the tree.

Il-han watched the game while he listened to his servant.
"I have been waiting for some other nation to see it," he now
said. He clapped his hands as he spoke, for his son had struck
the target in the middle. Then he went on speaking. "Yet
there may be a benefit for us in the rising jealousy between
the nations. None will want to see Japan grow too powerful."

"Ah ha," the servant said, "you have hit the target, too!" He
came closer and made his voice low. "The Russian Czar
today warned the Japanese Emperor through his envoy here

that the territories newly seized from China must be restored."

"Will it be so?" Il-han inquired.

"Is Japan strong enough to fight Russia?" the servant asked. "Some day yes, but not yet. That is what I hear said in the streets and in the shops. Japan must yield now but she will hate China the more, and this war will go on. As for Russia—perhaps war in another ten years."

He waited for his master to speak. Instead Il-han cried out in sudden pain. His son, misjudging distance, had let fly a hard green fruit and it struck Il-han just below the left eye.

Il-han pressed his hand to his eye and the boy was overcome with remorse and burst into tears. Sunia came running at the sound of sobbing, and Il-han hastened to explain that he was not blind, that it was a small matter, an accident, but between comforting the child and reassuring his wife he did not say what he had been ready to say. When the hubbub was over, his servant was gone and then he was glad he had not said what troubled him so deeply. He knew now that the Queen was doomed.

Two days before the mid-autumn festival, in the tenth month of that solar year, Il-han's spies reported that it was common talk in the streets that the guards in the Queen's palace were being replaced. Outwardly all was as usual, they told him, but those within who were old servants of the Queen said that arms and accouterments were being taken from the palace on the pretense that they were needed elsewhere, and useless weapons were put in their place. The King's palace was also thus weakened and this at a time when he needed the best defenses. On the afternoon of the seventh day of the festival, one of Il-han's spies observed that even the gates and doors of the Queen's palace seemed to be open and unguarded, and he returned with the news.

"Did you speak to anyone of this?" Il-han demanded.

"How could I speak?" the man replied. "It was seen, but no one cried danger."

"Saddle my horse," Il-han commanded, and dismissed the

man. He would go himself to inquire into what was taking place. Then he considered. Should he tell Sunia or should he not? Not, he decided. Quietly as a thief he went to his own rooms and changed his clothes to old garments Sunia had put aside for the poor. He clung by habit to certain garments and it was his demand that she should always let him see what she gave away so that he could reclaim what he would not part with. In the midst of this changing he heard her flying feet and the door slid back.

"So—you think to steal out of the house!" she cried. "And why do you drag forth those rags which are only fit for beggars?"

He looked at her, half rueful, half smiling. "How is it you smell out my least coming and going? What if I only put on old clothes to go into the garden and—plant a tree—or—"

"Make no games with me," she said, coming full into the room. "You never plant trees. Why should you plant one now?"

He saw that deceit was impossible and he gave way. "Sunia, the Queen is in danger."

She advanced on him. "Is she your concern forever?"

"She is our concern," he pleaded. "She is the concern of every Korean."

The red flew into her cheeks and the fire into her dark eyes. "And why do you think only you can save her?" she cried.

"At least I can see for myself—"

"See her for yourself, you mean!"

"Sunia!"

"Dare to call my name!" she cried. "I am no Queen—and if you care more for her than you do for us who are your family —you have two sons, if you care nothing for a wife, and are they to lose their lives because you hanker for a Queen? They will be caught and killed, but that does not matter, I suppose, although you will have no more sons from me— but you care nothing for that, either, I suppose!"

She was beside herself and he in turn grew angry. He let her rail and in cold silence he drew on the old clothes and tied a wretched hat on his head and pulled it low on his face.

She ran to the doorway as he came and stood there to prevent him. He lifted her as though she were a child and set her aside and went on his way, looking neither to the right nor to the left.

. . . It was late when he arrived at the city gate, but it stood open and unguarded, as though prepared for those who must flee. He passed through, none noticing, and guided his horse to the northern part of the city, where the Queen's palace stood at the far end of the approach to the royal palaces. This approach was a fine road three hundred feet wide and one third of a mile in length. On both sides stood the ministries of State, some of which he saw were newly built. And new, too, were barracks where Japanese soldiers came and went, marching and countermarching. The palaces were surrounded by a wall twelve feet high and the gates were, as the man said, open and unguarded. Il-han descended and tied his horse to a bent tree. He then went through the entrance which was in the western wall and came to the small lake and the foreign house belonging to the King and where he sometimes stayed. The palace where the King lived usually was close by and the Queen's palace was to the east but adjoining. To the left were the quarters where lived the Royal Guard. This afternoon Il-han saw no guards, but the sun was very hot, and it was possible that some were sleeping inside the palaces. Beyond all these was a pine grove covering some five acres of land.

Into this pine grove Il-han now went, and he sat on a rock behind a large leaning pine and waited. If nothing took place, he would return home again without making himself known, but if there was a misfortune he would be there to save the Queen if he could. The King he knew would not be killed for then the succession would be endangered, and the country thrown into swift revolution. Throughout the night he sat listening and waiting while the darkness deepened and the night creatures came out to creep and call. He heard, or so he thought, the sound of marching and countermarching, but remembering the Japanese guards, he supposed that this was part of their duty.

The black hours were passing, he guessed that day was not too far away and he was considering whether he should not return again to his horse and reach home before too many people were about the streets when a shout reached his ears. Then he heard screams and cries, and listening with ear to the windward, he knew instantly that the palace was under attack. He ran out into the darkness with all speed but he caught his foot on a root and fell. He got himself up again, although he had wrenched his hip, and he hobbled on. Now the Royal Guards were awake and shouting as they ran toward the palace. He was carried along with them, still hidden by the darkness when they paused, bewildered and inquiring, only to hear that there was no attack, and that what had been shouted was no more than the marching cries of the Japanese near the western wall.

At this the guards went back again to their barracks. Il-han, however, did not return to the pine grove. Instead he hid behind a shrine set in a rock garden. He had not long to wait, for the outcry had roused the Colonel of the Royal Guard, who, distrusting the commotion among the Japanese soldiers, was already on his way to the Ministry of War. When he reached the main entrance to the palace grounds he was surrounded by the Japanese soldiers, and Il-han, looking out from behind the rock, saw in the flare of torches that all he had feared was about to happen. Eight shots rang out and the Colonel fell, whereupon the soldiers drew out their swords and cut the dead man to pieces and threw those pieces into the small lake nearby.

Now indeed Il-han knew that he must find the Queen and quickly, if he was to save her. He came out from his hiding place and, much hampered by his wrenched hip, he hobbled toward the gate which led to her palace. Alas, he could make no speed. The Japanese soldiers were pushing forward in a shouting, bellowing, roaring mass, their bayonets pointed ahead of them as they met the fleeing hordes of palace servants. The Royal Guards were once more aroused and they let fly their bullets helter-skelter and killed some seven or eight of the soldiers before they were swept into the mass of others advancing and so cut down. Meanwhile the soldiers pressed on into the Queen's palace, followed by beggars and local ruffians bent on loot. Among these Il-han could hide and he burrowed his way among them, trying by every means to reach the Queen first, though what he could do now to save her he did not know.

The mob filled the palace, and the rough soldiers seized every woman by the hair as soon as they saw her, demanding to know whether she was the Queen. Whatever the woman said, the soldiers beheaded them and threw the heads aside or tossed them from a window. Still further the mob went until they reached the very last room, and now Il-han, pressed among them, heard two shots. Then he heard a low scream and he knew it was the Queen who screamed. The scream ended in a long moaning sigh. He bent his head and bit his lips until he tasted his own blood, but he could do nothing. She was dead.

The crowd stopped, men looked at one another, and then one by one they went away, the looters to loot and those who had committed the deed to escape so that none was known to be guilty. When all were gone and only Il-han was left, he went into the room where the Queen lay alone and he looked down into the lovely face he knew so well, still the same lovely face though aged now with the years during which he had not once seen her. He crouched down beside her and took her hand, still warm. Blood flowed from her left breast and from her smooth neck and he lifted the edge of her wide silk skirt and held it to the wounds. The silk was crimson and it did not show the stain except that the stuff turned a deeper crimson.

So he sat in the empty palace until sunrise and he sat on into the morning until at about the ninth hour a gardener came to the door, barefoot, so that Il-han did not hear his footsteps. He peered in and saw Il-han, whom he did not know, so long had Il-han been absent from the palace.

"Who are you, brother?" he asked.

"I am her servant," Il-han said.

The man came near and stared down into the pale face of the dead Queen. "She liked white lotus flowers," he said at last, "and now her face is as white as any lotus flower. What shall we do with her, brother?"

"Have you a cart?" Il-han asked.

"I have an oxcart," the man said.

"Bring it to the nearest door and help me lift her into it," Il-han said.

The man went away and in a short time came back again and they lifted the Queen, so slender that her weight was nothing for the two men, and they carried her to the cart and laid her there and the man covered her with the straw that filled the cart. Then he climbed up and the ox drew the cart away while Il-han followed far behind and slowly, for his hip was swollen and tears ran down his face for pain. Yet even this was not enough. Before the cart had reached the gate the dead Queen was discovered by soldiers and ragamuffins and they dragged her body out from under the straw and hacked it to pieces with swords and knives and piled the straw about the pieces and set all afire.

It was time for Il-han's heart to break. He covered his face with his hat and hobbled away from that fire and into the street. His horse was gone, but the oxcart was there and he climbed into it, and bade the man take him home.

. . . Of that beautiful queen all that was left, he heard afterward, was the little finger of her right hand. This escaped the flames and was found by the man when he went back next day at Il-han's command to see what bones were there, so that he might bring them together and give them honor. No bones were there, for dogs had wandered freely throughout the palace, but under a stone lay the little finger. The man took it up tenderly and wrapped it in a lotus leaf he had plucked from the lake. Then he took it to the King's palace and demanded entrance and was received.

"I went into the King's palace," he told Il-han when all was done, for Il-han had said he would pay him well if he came to his grass roof with the whole story. "I went into the audience hall and the King sat on his throne surrounded by his ministers, and the old Prince-Parent sat there again at his right hand. The King listened to what I told him and he covered his eyes with his hand and he would not receive the lotus leaf from me. But he bade a minister take it and embalm it in a golden box and he said the Queen must be given a great funeral and a tomb must be built."

Sunia was there while all this was told, and when the man was gone she took Il-han's hand and held it and said not a word, but only sat beside him in silence, her warm hand clasping his.

So they sat until at last Il-han gave a great sigh and he turned to her and said, "My wife—my wife of great heart."

Then he put her hand away and returned to his books.

. . . Two years passed before the astrologers could fix upon the place for the Queen's tomb and then they fixed upon a stretch of land a few miles beyond the city wall. A thousand acres were here sequestered by the King and all houses were removed, for the tract held villages as well as mountains, hills, brooks and fields. Thousands upon thousands of young trees were planted upon the King's command and fortunes spent in making a beautiful garden such as the Queen loved when she was alive. Her tomb was built upon the highest spot, a tomb of marble, encircled by a carved balustrade of marble. Before the tomb was a great table of white marble polished to shine like glass, and this was for making sacrifices to the spirit of the Queen. Beside the table stone lanterns miraculously carved were set into rock, and marble figures stood in graceful reverence.

When all was finished to his content, the King announced the day for the funeral, a fine fair day, and people came from far and near. In spite of all her whims and ways, the people had loved their Queen for her beauty, for her merriment, for her courage and her brilliant mind and even for her stubborn will. For them, now that she was dead, she remained as a symbol of what their country once had been and could no more be. Already the victorious conquerors were at work to stamp out the ancient ways, the language and traditions of the Koreans.

Il-han stood far off and alone, and he watched the splendid scene. With the Queen gone, could his nation survive? He asked the question and could make no answer. His heart lay dead within him. He could not feel its beat. The Queen whom he had reverenced, the woman whom he had—had he loved her? He did not know. Perhaps Sunia knew better than he, but if she did, he would not ask her. Let the secret lie within the tomb of all that was ended and could not live again. He had no faith in resurrection.

PART II

THE year was 4243 after Tangun of Korea and 1910 after Jesus of Judea. The season was near the end of winter, the day was the tenth of the first moon month, the hour was midnight.

Il-han woke sharply and by habit now well established. He rose, taking care to be quiet so that Sunia would not wake as he crept from beneath his quilt. The ondul floor was cold. Fuel was too scarce to bank fires at night and the only warmth was from the quick flame of dried grass when the evening meal was cooking. He went into the next room, his stockinged feet noiseless, and there he poured cold water into a basin set on the table and washed his face and hands. Then he unwound his hair, oiled and combed it and coiled it again on top of his head. This hair he had kept short ever since he had been in America, against Sunia's complaints that women would think he was not married, but when the Japanese rulers moved into the capital he felt compelled to let his hair grow in defiance of the command of the Japanese Prince, now Resident-General. He had sent out a decree declaring that no reforms could be made in Korea until the men cut off their topknots, for he maintained that in this stubborn coil of hair was the symbol of Korean nationalism which must be utterly destroyed since Korea had become a colony of imperial Japan. The Governor-General then announced that the King had cut off his coil of hair and that he, the King, commanded his subjects to follow his example. This the Koreans had at first refused to do, saying that the King had not cut his hair by his own free will but had been forced to do so by his Japanese masters. In the end many had refused to obey, including Il-han, and so his hair was long again.

He slid open the doors now and looked out into the night. A slight mist of rain was falling and the darkness was deep. He lit the stone lantern that stood by the door, and he waited until he saw those whom he expected. A man came out of the night leading some twenty children of different ages, all boys. They walked in silence until they reached him. The man looked left and right and then spoke in a low voice.

"We saw a distant light."

"In what direction?" Il-han asked in the same low voice.

"To the north."

"A moving light?"

"Yes, but only one. Yet one spy is enough."

"I will keep the children here until dawn. Then I will send them away separately," Il-han said.

The man nodded and disappeared again into the mist. Il-han led the children into the house, looking into each face. Accustomed to silence, they walked gravely past him and into the room. He followed them, first putting out the light in the stone lantern. Then he drew the doors shut and barred them fast. By now the boys were seated on the floor. He took his place before them on his floor cushion and opened his book and began to speak, his voice still low.

"You will remember," he said, "that last night I spoke of King Sejong. I told you of his greatness, and how under his beneficent rule our country grew strong."

He continued to speak of history for half an hour. Then he closed his book and recited poetry. For tonight he had chosen a famous poem of the late Koryo times, written in the Sijo style.

"And this," he explained to his pupils, "is a special style because those times were like our own, troubled times when poets could not write long poems in the ancient Kyonggi style. Therefore they put their feelings into short intense form. There are only about ten of these Sijo poems left to us, and among them I have chosen the one written by Chong Mungju, who was a minister of Koryo, loyal to his King. Listen to me, children! I will chant the poem for you, and then line by line you will chant after me."

He closed his eyes and folded his hands and began to chant:

> Though this frame should die and die,
> Though I die a hundred deaths,
> My bleached bones becoming dust,
> My soul dead or living on,
> Naught can make this heart of mine
> Divide itself against my King.

He opened his eyes and repeated the poem line by line, the fresh young voices repeated them after him, and he observed how muted these voices were from the habit of fear. For what he now did was forbidden. The alien rulers had changed the schools so that even the language was no longer Korean but Japanese, and the books were Japanese. Unless scholars like Il-han taught the children in secret in the darkness of the night they would grow up ignorant of their own language and their own past and cease at last to be Korean.

When they had learned the poem, which they soon did, each child intent to learn what was forbidden, he expounded the meaning of the poem and how they all, like that minister in the past, must be loyal to the King, even though he lived now in duress and was only King in name.

"Our King's heart is still with us," he told them, "and the proof of his being with us is in the disbanding of our army. The Resident-General of the Japanese Imperial Army commanded our army to be disbanded in a very rude and dishonorable manner as you know, and our King was forced to sign the order for the disbandment. Yet only a few days later our King appeared at his Japanese coronation, wearing the uniform of the disbanded army. Meanwhile our disbanded soldiers are wandering everywhere telling the people of their dishonor, which some day we must erase.

"Remember, children, lest it be not written down. Two years ago our army, seventy thousand men, was dismissed by the invaders. Each man was given ten yen and told to go home. Most of them went to other countries to wait until the time comes for our freedom and many thousands went to Manchuria, where there is land."

In this way Il-han, and many like him, informed the young of the greatness of their ancestors and the disgrace of their present, and how they, the young, must not cease to rebel in their hearts against the island invaders who had seized the country.

"We are far higher than these petty foreign rulers," Il-han went on. "Though they treat us as serfs and slaves, we are not what they hold us to be. Nor should we in justice believe that all Japanese are as small as these who rule us. They have not men enough to govern their own country with greatness and they cannot spare us their highest men. Here we have the low fellows, the ignorant, the greedy, and we must suffer them, but the day will come when they will be cast out."

"By what means?" a lad inquired.

"That is for you to decide," Il-han replied.

"Why should they come here and take our country?" another lad inquired.

He was a rebel born but Il-han was too just a teacher not to present to such a lad the other side of truth.

"Alas," he said, "there is always another face to everything. Imagine yourself a lad in Japan. Then you would be taught that it is essential for Japan to control Korea, else our country is like a dagger pointed to her heart. Russia, too, wants Korea—Russia has always wanted Korea, you remember. Ah, but you are a Japanese lad, imagine, and so your teacher would be saying, 'We Japanese cannot tolerate the Russians so near us in Korea and that is why we fought the war with Russia, we Japanese, and we won, and all the world acclaimed us. It was necessary in that time of war to send our armies across Korea!'"

"They could have taken them away again when the victory was won," a lad interrupted.

Il-han put up his hand. "Remember now, we are Japanese for the moment. The Japanese teacher says, 'Had we taken our armies out of Korea, Russia would have come back in secret ways. No, we must hold Korea as our fort. And besides, we need more land for our growing people, and we need new markets.'"

He broke off and gave a great sigh. "I cannot go on with such imagining. We are Korean patriots!"

"Why did we not fight the Japanese?" a bold lad demanded.

"Alas," Il-han said again, "our sin was in our many divisions. We quarreled over how to defeat our enemies, how to keep our freedom. One family clan against another has divided our nation and for centuries. Divided we fell. Our own people rose against our own corruption. Well, it is over. Gone are the great families, the Yi, the Min, the Pak, the Kim, the Choi, and besides them the Silhak, the Tonghak and every other such division. Now we are united in our longing for our lost independence high and low, and we have only the Japanese to hate instead of one another. Perhaps it will be easier."

So the hours sped on. Listening always for unknown footsteps, his eyes watching the door, Il-han taught them the Korean language and its hangul writing until dawn stole across the foothills and the mountains and the sun rose. He had meant to let them sleep for a while at least but the day came too soon. Sunia was astir in the kitchen and one of the two old servants left to them put in his head at the door to warn Il-han of sunrise. Il-han looked up, surprised.

"I have kept you all night, my children," he said, "and you will not do well in school today. Tonight do not come. Sleep, and we will meet again the night after. Now go, one by one, a little space between so that you do not seem a crowd."

He stood by then and let them leave, each alone and walking in different directions, so that none would suspect he had taught them in secret. When the sun rose high enough to shine on the mountains the last pupil was gone and he was suddenly weary, although it was Sunia who made him know it. She came in brisk and neatly dressed for the day.

"How long will you go on with this teaching?" she exclaimed. "You look like an old man."

"I feel like an old man," he said. "A very old man."

"You are only fifty-four," she retorted, "and I beg you will not call yourself old for then you make me old. Drink this ginseng soup. Why have you kept the pupils all night?"

He took the bowl of soup and blew it and supped. "There was a moving light, unexplained."

"If you had called me," she said somewhat crossly, "I would have told you that our younger son is here. He came in the back gate, carrying a lantern."

"Yul-han? Why did you not tell him to come in?"

"He forbade it," she replied.

She was tidying the room as she spoke, picking up bits of paper the pupils had left, smoothing the floor cushions, dusting the table.

"Forbade it?"

"You are getting the habit of repeating what I say. Yes, he forbade it!"

He looked at her mildly. The strain of the times, the constant living in fear of the knock on the door, the secrecy, the poverty, all were changing his Sunia into a weary, irritable woman. He felt a new love for her, tender with pity. She had not his inner resources, his place of retreat into the calm of poetry and music. He put out his hand as she passed him and laid hold of her skirt.

"My faithful wife," he murmured.

The tears came to her eyes but she would not shed them.

"You have not eaten," she exclaimed. "I forget my duty." She hurried to the door and paused. "Shall I tell Yul-han to come in now?"

"Do so," he replied.

Before she returned, his younger son entered. Yul-han was the name given him when he began school, and it suited him, in both sound and meaning—Spring Peace! Now at twenty-nine years of age, he was neither tall nor short but slim and strong, his round face pleasant without being handsome. He wore the western garments which many young men wore nowadays under Japanese rule, a suit of gray cloth, trousers and coat and under the coat a blue shirt open at the neck and on his feet leather shoes. It was a nondescript garb, proclaiming no nationality, and Il-han, saying nothing, was always displeased when he saw his son wearing such garments. Did it mean he avoided proclaiming himself Korean? Was this son a prudent fellow, escaping trouble and argument in this vague attire? He refused himself answers to such private doubts and questions.

"Father," Yul-han said and bowed.

"Son, sit down," Il-han replied and inclined his head. "Have you eaten?"

"Not yet. I came early because I must go back to my school."

Il-han did not reply. This son of his was a teacher in a school where, as in all schools now, the classes were conducted in the Japanese language and the curriculum was planned by the Japanese Board of Education. When Yul-han first told him that he had accepted this position, Il-han was more angry than he had ever been before in his life.

"You!" he had exclaimed. "You sell yourself to these invaders!"

He had never forgotten his son's quiet reply.

"Father, I ask you to consider my inheritance—the inheritance of all my generation. What have you left us, you elders? A government rotten with corruption, a people oppressed by the yangban, taxes on everything but never spent on the people! Is it a wonder that the people are always rioting and rising up? Is there ever peace in the provinces? Is it strange that we have for generations been split into a score of parties? What does it all mean except that we are desperate? Yes, I chose the Il Chon Hui because among our enemies I favor the Japanese! At least they are trying to make order out of our ancient chaos. And the worst chaos, as you very well know, is in our national finances. Two hundred Japanese are scattered throughout our country, collecting new figures. Why do I say new? There are no figures. No one knew how much money was collected in taxes or how it was spent. As for property—I do not know how you have held our own lands except that we are yangban, and you, too, had your special influence in court."

Here Il-han had stopped him. "If you insinuate that I, your father, am corrupt—"

"The corruption began long before your generation," Yul-han said. "Before you were born—or my grandfather was born—there was already no distinction made between Court and Government property or between State and private properties or State and Imperial household properties. Why do I tell you, Father? You know that magistrates collected taxes as they pleased and spent them as they pleased. Land tax—house tax—but have we ourselves ever paid taxes, Father?"

To this Il-han had not replied except to say, "You echo your brother's complaints."

Father and son were silent then for a long moment. It was the sorrow of this household that none knew where the elder son had gone, or even whether he had been killed as so many young men were killed when the invaders came. Even were he dying he must continue in exile, for the invaders knew the name of every man who had opposed them. During the war with China the Japanese had marched into Korea on the way, and when they were victorious, Russia, fearful lest Japan hold the country, had sent in her own armies to contend. Japan had trebled her forces only to declare war next against Russia, and this war she won, too, to the admiration of the western powers, and especially of the United States, whose citizens applauded the doughty small nation who dared to fight the Russian giant. In their approbation, the Americans forgot their treaty of protection, wherein they had promised to help Korea to freedom, for in that treaty the Americans had promised that if any country dealt with Korea unjustly or oppressively, their government would "bring about an amicable arrangement."

Such watery words were meaningless, Il-han had so told the King at the time and it was proved. For the King, in despair when the invaders came, appealed to the Americans and one good American, Homer Hulbert, who was head of the government school in Seoul, himself went to Washington to plead for the Koreans, whom, though a foreigner, he had learned to love. But the President, one Theodore Roosevelt, would not receive him, and his Secretary of State merely brought the message that the United States would not intervene in Korea. And later that same President openly made this declaration:

"Korea is absolutely Japan's."

Yet by treaty it had been solemnly covenanted that Korea should remain independent. Alas, Korea was helpless and Japan maintained that it was her own duty to her own children and children's children to override the treaty, and so Japan formally annexed the country. And the first Japanese Governor-General, when he came to rule the Koreans, tore up the treaty and threw the scattered bits of paper into the air.

"Yet we are civilized," he declared, and in proof he did not behead the King or his feeble son. Instead he gave them an annuity, and the two lived on in the palace.

Today, remembering the unanswered question, Il-han looked at his son half quizzically.

"It may please you," he said, "to know that yesterday the Japanese tax gatherers came here to collect tax from me."

The young man's face showed concern. "Did you have the money, Father?"

"No," Il-han said calmly. "Nowadays I have no money."

"So?"

"I gave them a deed to the big field at the north of the village."

Yul-han looked grave. "You must reckon on regular taxes, Father, land or no land. And we must admit that the money is being well used. The streets are much improved—you would not know the city now. We are not sunk in mud when it rains, the streets are no longer drains and dumping places, and roads are being made in the country connecting the villages. Even the side paths are being improved, and trees are planted."

"I do not intend to travel," Il-han replied, "so why should I pay for roads? I say again I have no money."

"At any rate, money will be worth more, whenever you have it," Yul-han urged. "The currency reform—"

"I beg you will not speak to me of such reforms," Il-han said coldly. "I had rather live with muddy roads and ill-spent taxes and all the old evils than live as we now do, crushed under the oppression of the invader, who is stealing lands from our people—"

"Not stealing, exactly," Yul-han said.

"I call it stealing when I give up my land under compulsion."

"Could you not borrow?" Yul-han suggested.

"No," Il-han said strongly. "I will not step into that pitfall. You know how our people are. They are always ready to borrow money; even when they do not need it they will accept an offered loan, with no thought of how it is to be paid. Then, when it must be paid, they lose their land."

"Yet this is the old way of the yangban," Yul-han retorted. "Can you deny that our own ancestors did so procure our land? How else could we inherit so much?"

Since he could not deny, Il-han could only be angry. "At least our ancestors were our own yangban nobility and not dwarfs from foreign islands!"

"Stop!"

Yul-han looked left and right as he spoke. He leaned forward. "Father, you think me a traitor. I am no traitor. I—we—my friends and I—when the present rulers have made the reforms we need, some day we will take our country back again. We must use them now—use these men, learn from them how to run a modern nation—and when we have learned . . ."

Father and son stared into each other's eyes, but before either could speak Sunia came into the room, carrying a tray with two bowls of steaming rice gruel. She set it down on the table between them.

"Have you told your father?" she inquired of Yul-han.

"No, we have spoken first of other matters."

"What else is there to speak of?" she retorted. She stood up, wiping her hands on her apron. "Il-han, he is ready to be married now, this son of ours! At last he is ready to be married."

Here was Sunia's complaint in these times. The Japanese Governor-General had commanded that the early marriages common to the Korean people must be delayed. Early marriages, he declared, made weak children. Therefore Yul-han had steadfastly refused to be married.

"What," Sunia had cried, when he first refused, "are we to have no grandchildren? Am I to have no daughter-in-law to help me in the house? And who will care for you, pray, when you yourself are old?"

"Mother," Yul-han had replied with his usual patience. "Your grandchildren will be the stronger and better for not being born of parents too young."

"You have an answer for everything now, you young men," Sunia had said bitterly.

"He is ready to be married at last," she repeated now. "Yet who will have him at his age? Twenty-nine! We should already have grandsons ten years old. Indeed we should be thinking of great-grandsons."

Neither man spoke. They exchanged glances in mutual male comprehension. Why was it that women could think only of giving birth to children and more children, their whole concern intent upon their one creative function? Even Sunia!

She stooped to pull a floor cushion nearer.

"Eat, you two! While you eat I will talk. Now whom shall we find for this son? I have in mind—"

Yul-han had taken up his chopsticks but he put them down again.

"Mother, you need not busy yourself. I have found the woman I want for my wife."

Sunia let her jaw drop. "You," she exclaimed. "How can you—"

"I can, Mother," Yul-han said in his pleasant way. "And you will like her. She is a teacher too, but in the girls' school."

"I will not like her," Sunia declared. "A teacher! What I

wish is a good daughter-in-law here in this house. How can I take care of your children if you live in the city?"

Yul-han laughed. "What haste! I am not married yet. And perhaps she will not have me. I have not spoken to her."

This only brought fresh indignation for Sunia. "How dare she not have my son! Where does she live?" she cried. "What is her name? I will see to it."

"She lives in the capital," Yul-han said. "Her family name is Choi. Her name is—"

"Do not speak her personal name—not yet," Sunia commanded. "Time enough when she is my daughter-in-law."

Yul-han yielded, smiling, and took up his chopsticks again.

"I shall be late for school," he said, and he ate his rice and kimchee quickly and bade them farewell.

He walked quickly and gaily along the country road toward the city. In spite of the evil times he felt lighthearted. The truth had been told. His parents knew that he had chosen his own wife. Until they knew, he had not felt free to break with tradition and approach Induk for himself. They had never even been alone, but in the teachers' meetings they had spoken to each other, and then, when he found out that her family was Christian, he had on several Sunday mornings gone to the Christian temple on the main street of the city. Men and women sat separately but he discovered that the Choi ladies sat in the second row from the front and he went early to sit as near Induk as possible. He saw only her smooth nape and the coil of her dark hair. Yet when she sang the hymns, sometimes he saw her profile, the small straight nose, the parted lips, the round, cream-white chin. She was tall for a woman, but slender, and she always wore Korean dress. Last Sunday he had lingered at the church door, watching for her, and had been waylaid by the American missionary. This man, a rugged priest, his hair and eyebrows and beard a rusty red, had taken him by the hand and then had spoken in a booming voice.

"Friend, you have been here several times. You are welcome. Do you want to know Jesus?"

Yul-han had been embarrassed by the question and he could

only smile. At this moment Induk herself came out of the door and seeing what was happening, she approached and introduced him.

"Dr. Maclane, this is Kim Yul-han, a teacher in the boys' school."

"Does he want to be a Christian?" the missionary boomed again.

Induk laughed. "Let me find out," she said.

Her eyes, dark and lively, exchanged a look with Yul-han's.

"Good—good," the missionary said heartily, his small blue eyes already following other persons, and he released Yul-han and hastened away.

From this moment of understanding, the two had moved quickly to meeting alone one afternoon in a deserted classroom. By chance Induk was walking through a corridor on her way home and Yul-han, seeing her in the distance, had followed her.

"Miss Choi!"

She turned, saw him, and waited.

"Should you not begin to make me a Christian?" he inquired with mischief.

He enjoyed her fresh free laugh.

"Do you want to be a Christian?" she asked.

"Do you think it would improve me?" he countered.

"I do not know how good you are, as you are," she replied, teasing.

He liked her frankness, her humor, and he had walked with her, both of them self-conscious in their determination to be modern. It was not easy to break down the wall of tradition between man and woman. He was too aware of Induk as a woman, dazzled by the whiteness of her skin, the sheen of her dark hair, the loveliness of her small ears close set against the handsome head, her lithe body moving gracefully in step with him, her fragrance, the sweetness of her breath. Everything about her was feminine, warm and strong.

They halted involuntarily at the open door of an empty classroom and moved by the same impulse, they went in and sat down in the back of the room. The door was open but anyone passing could not see them. Dangerous it still was, but they could not part, not yet in this their first enchantment. What they had said in those few minutes alone was simple, even inconsequential, and yet he remembered every word.

"Do you like teaching girls?" A stupid question he knew as soon as he had asked it, for whom would she teach if not girls?

"I like teaching," she said.

"So do I."

They had paused. Then it was she who began.

"Do not be a Christian unless you wish. One should follow his own heart."

"What is the advantage of being Christian?" he asked.

She hesitated. "It is hard to say. My family is Christian, and I have grown up Christian. We believe in God, and we are comforted. In the church we meet with others who believe."

"What are the doctrines?"

"I cannot explain to you in a few minutes. Have you read the New Testament?"

"I have read nothing Christian. To me Christianity is a foreign religion."

"Nothing that teaches us about God can be foreign. I will bring my New Testament to school tomorrow and you can read it. Then we will talk. Now we must go."

She rose and he could only follow. When they parted at the door, he walked away in a daze, and was already dreaming of tomorrow. Yet the next day he did not see her. On his desk was a small parcel addressed to him. He opened it and found the book. There was no letter with it.

He began to read it that same evening and now was nearly at its end. One more evening, he told himself as he came to the city gate, and tomorrow he would find her and tell her.

"I have read the book," he would tell her. "Now we must talk."

When their son was gone, Sunia turned to Il-han. "You must go privately into the city and see for yourself this family of Choi. See where they live, what sort of house it is, what the neighbors say—and which Choi it is. Choi is a name of the North. Shall we of the South accept a daughter-in-law of the North?"

Il-han had been deeply disturbed by all that Yul-han had said before she came in. He could not forget the accusations that his mild son had made against his father's generation, and he longed to make even small amends.

"Sunia," he said, "I will go. I will look at the house. I will consult the neighbors. But it is time to forget who is from the North and who is from the South. Let us only remember, North or South, that we are Koreans."

Since Sunia gave him no peace once her mind was set on some goal, he went three days later to the city where for so long he had not been. It was as Yul-han had said. The streets were new and clean, and there were many changes. Everywhere he saw new shops where Japanese merchants sold their goods, and this he had heard was true throughout the country in town and village. But what he saw first was that of all parts of the city the quarter where the Japanese lived was the most prosperous and that it had grown from a cluster of houses to a city within a city. And when he asked of passersby, he was told that the Japanese Legation was now the house where the Governor-General lived, the gardens enlarged and made beautiful, as he could see when he looked into the open gates, but guarded by Japanese soldiers.

"Pass on, old man," the soldiers cried when he lingered. "No one is allowed to stop at these gates."

He went on. Opposite to this new-made palace other new buildings were built on a low hill and here he lingered again.

"What are these new buildings?" he inquired of the guard.

"These are the offices and headquarters of the Governor-General, the noble Count Terauchi," the guard replied. "Do you not know the Tokanfu when you see it? You must be a countryman."

Il-han did not reply. What the ignorant guardsman himself did not know was that this place where the center of government now was, a foreign government established by invaders, had once before been the site of a castle belonging to these same invaders. In the time of Hideyoshi during the invasion of Taiko Sama, one Kato Kyomasu, his most able lieutenant, had built a castle here. The castle had been destroyed when the invaders were repulsed, but they had returned and now here again was the seat of that same government over a proud people but subject, his own people.

Could this be accident or was it fate?

. . . "How could you see so little?" Sunia inquired when he returned.

Her eyes sparkled with indignation. "You go to the city and stay away for hours and then come back only to say that the house looks like every other house, and though the neighbors speak well of this Choi family, you forget to ask where they came from—"

"I told you, they said the family has lived in the same house for six generations," Il-han replied.

He was very weary but he knew he could have no rest until he satisfied Sunia's questions.

"Did you see no one of them?" she asked next.

"You said I was not to ask to enter."

"You could have looked in the gate."

"I did look in the gate. I saw two servants and a young woman cutting some flowers."

"It might have been she," Sunia exclaimed.

"It might have been," he agreed.

"Was she pretty?"

"Now, Sunia," he remonstrated. "What can I say to that? If I say yes you will not be pleased with my sharp eyesight. If I say no you will blame me for seeing nothing. I can only say that she looked cheerful and healthy."

"Round face or long face?"

"I cannot tell you. It was a face with the necessary features."

"Oh me," Sunia sighed, "am I to have a daughter-in-law who has only a face with necessary features?"

He laughed and then, because he was so weary and worried with matters which he could not explain to her, he kept on laughing until she was alarmed.

"Did you drink while you were in the city?" she demanded.

"No, no," he said, wiping away tears. "I am only laughing."

"At me, I'll swear!"

"At women," he said. "Man's eternal laughter at woman! That is all—that is all."

Sunia sighed. "However long I live with you, I do not understand you!"

She looked at him earnestly for a moment, and quizzically as if to appraise him. Then she too began to laugh.

"And what are you laughing at?" he inquired, surprised.

"At you," she said. "Am I not allowed to laugh?"

"Certainly," he said. "Laugh your woman's laughter. Why not?"

He was not pleased, nevertheless, although he did not know why, and he took up his book as a sign that she was dismissed, which sign she obeyed still smiling, and her lively eyes were mischievous.

Early spring gave way to full spring. Plum trees bloomed and their petals fell and cherry and peach, apple and pomegranate followed, blossom producing fruit, and Yul-han walked in dreams. No longer did he make pretense of accident when he met Induk, and she did not pretend. They met with their eyes when they were in the company of others, but when they met alone they spoke from their hearts. Neither used words of love for none were necessary. Each knew that they had but one thought and it was marriage. He knew that in the West it was the custom for a man to offer himself to the woman, but this was a way too foreign for him and, he was sure, for her. Were the approach so naked, would she not, in modesty, be repelled by him? He thought day and night of what he could say or do to express his love and desire. The new way was too foreign but the old way was too public. A professional matchmaker was only a coarse old woman. Nor did he want his parents to approach her family. The bustle of mothers, the formality of fathers, belonged to a past age. And Induk was Christian and would want a Christian ceremony. It was a grave danger, this marrying a Christian. The Japanese rulers did not like the missionaries or their religion; missionaries were sympathetic with the Koreans, they said, and the religion in itself was revolutionary in content.

Suddenly it occurred to him one day how to ask Induk if she would be his wife. It was a Sunday afternoon, the first in the sixth solar month. They had met by arrangement in one of the new city parks, and had walked to a quiet pool under hanging willows. He spread his coat on the bench for her to sit upon and together they watched the goldfish darting among the water lilies. Now—now was the moment. He began diffidently, wondering if he dared to touch her hand.

"Induk, I have something to ask you."

She did not turn her head. "What is it?"

Across the pool a flowering quince tree, growing in the shade of the willows, was still in bloom. He saw the red petals dropping into the water. Goldfish darted up to nibble them and darted away again. He went on slowly, feeling his cheeks burning hot.

"Will you go with me to a fortuneteller?"

His voice was so low that he feared it lost in the ripple of the small waterfall at the end of the pool. But she heard.

"Do you believe in fortunetellers?" she asked, incredulous.

"To discover whether our birth years agree," he said.

She understood. He knew it by her sudden stillness. She neither spoke nor moved. He looked at her sidewise and saw a rose-pink flush mounting from her soft neck to her cheeks. She was shy! She who seemed always so calm, so competent, so sure of herself, was shy before him, and seeing her thus, his own diffidence faded. He sprang to his feet and held out his hand.

"Come," he commanded. "We will go now."

She looked up at him, hesitating. "Alone? The two of us? Will it not seem strange to the fortuneteller?"

"What do we care?" he asked, very bold.

He smiled down into her eyes, infusing her with his own

daring. She grasped his hand and leaped lightly to her feet. Hand in hand in the gathering dusk they went through the now lonely park and into a narrow cross street. There in a corner sheltered by an overhanging roof an old fortuneteller sat in the dim light of a paper lantern swinging over his head, waiting for customers. Before him was a small table, upon it the tools of his trade. He peered through his horn-rimmed spectacles at Yul-han and Induk.

"What do you seek?" he asked, his voice cracked with his sitting in wind and rain, snow and heat.

"Our birth years," Yul-han said. "Are they suited for marriage?" And he gave the years in which he and Induk were born.

The fortuneteller muttered and mumbled over his signs and fumbled in worn old books. They waited, hands clasped and hidden behind the table. At last he looked up, and took off his spectacles.

"Earth," he declared. "Both of you belong to Earth. Thus far it is yes. As to which animal . . ."

Here he pursed his withered lips and mused aloud whil> he pondered his books again.

"I can almost guess by looking at the two of you what your animal years are. People are like the animals under which they are born. You are not pig, or snake, or rat . . ."

He fell silent while his long dirty fingernail traced the paper.

"A-ha!" he cried. "You are safe, both of you! You, the male, are dragon; you, the female, are tiger. Dragon is stronger than tiger, young man, but tiger is strong, and she will fight you sometimes, though she can never win, for the dragon sits above, always in the clouds."

In spite of their avowed disbelief in the old symbols both Yul-han and Induk were relieved. Tradition was still powerful and a man may not marry a woman whose animal is stronger than his own, else she will rule him without remorse or tenderness. Yet each was ashamed to show relief.

"I must fight you, it seems," Induk said.

"You will always lose, remember," Yul-han retorted.

Induk sighed in pretended despair and Yul-han laughed. Then something occurred to him.

"Old Fortuneteller," he said, "are you not shocked that we make inquiry for ourselves?"

The old man stroked his few gray whiskers. "Not at all," he said. "Young ones come nowadays to inquire for themselves."

They were too surprised to reply to this and they went away in silence. But their joy was increased. When they parted, Yul-han held both her hands for a long moment as they stood in the shadow of a stranger's gate.

"So there are many of us," he murmured before he let her go.

... As for Il-han, he took no further interest in the marriage, which was, after all, women's business. Indeed, as he reflected upon it, the wedding might bring only dissension into his house, for the young woman whom Yul-han wished to marry now broke all tradition by coming herself one day to see Sunia, her future mother-in-law, and, to his surprise, himself, for when the girl arrived alone except for an old woman servant, she asked not only to see the house but her future father-in-law. He was disturbed by Sunia, who came breathless into his library to tell him the strange news.

"She is here," Sunia exclaimed.

"She?" Il-han repeated.

"The woman—the girl—Yul-han—" She paused, not knowing what to say. Betrothed she was not as yet and to use the word "friend" in relation to a son would have evil implication. "Her name is Induk," she finished.

"Well?" Il-han asked.

"What shall we do? She wishes to see us both!"

"Tell her I am busy," Il-han said promptly.

Sunia hesitated. "Will she not think it rebuff? Yet what will the neighbors say if you do see her?"

Yul-han now arrived by another way, in time to hear these words. He came in and slid the wall door shut behind him. "Father—Mother—" He had been running and he breathed hard. "Remember that everything is different nowadays. She teaches the girls and I teach the boys, but we see each other in the corridors and on the playground in passing. I asked her myself if she would have me and she said yes. She wants our wedding to be modern."

"What is modern?" Sunia inquired with some scorn.

"Well, she does not wish you to give her the usual red and green sets of garments. She says a ring on her finger at the time of our marriage is enough."

"How does she mean enough?" Sunia demanded. "The red garments signify the passion any marriage must have for happiness and the green signifies that you will grow together, you two young ones. How will you say such things except through these gifts?"

Yul-han shrugged his shoulders. He could not explain to his parents how such things were said nowadays.

Sunia's sharp eyes saw the shrug and immediately she went on. "Doubtless the girl is not serious. At any rate, we do not know whether the marriage will be propitious. Fortunetellers must be called. We do not even know your two birth years. How can we know the combination of your lives?"

Yul-han smiled. He went to the garden door and stood there. The summer peonies were in bloom, their red and white flowers were vivid against the young green. In the pond a frog croaked. "Only for fun," he said, "she and I did inquire of a fortuneteller. We were both born in the year of Earth and though she is Tiger, I am Dragon."

Sunia could not but be pleased. "Can it be so! Earth? Then as every branch of a tree bursts into flower, your children will prosper and grow." She turned to Il-han, suddenly radiant. "We will be cared for in our old age!"

"If we believe in such things," Il-han said drily.

Sunia refused to be discouraged. "There is something in such symbols. Do not forget that our ancestors lived by their belief and are we better than they?"

The two men, father and son, said nothing. Each had his thoughts—Yul-han that any happiness his mother could find would be well for himself and Induk, and Il-han that he would not at this time of her life disturb Sunia's faith and hope. They remained silent while Sunia prattled on.

"Now," she said happily, "it is a good thing that we do not need to pay fortunetellers. The wedding must be thought of next—a good wedding. We must prepare the wedding hat and belt for you, my son, and we must mend the old palanquin to fetch the bride home to this house after the three days of ceremony. The curtains are in shreds."

Yul-han turned. "Mother," he said. "Remember that she comes from a city family. And I, too, do not wish to have an old-fashioned wedding. What! I go through all that clownery?"

He spoke with unusual energy, and Il-han was surprised that his quiet son could for the moment at least again resemble his older brother. But Sunia was not patient.

"Are we not to have a decent wedding?" she demanded. "True, we are poor now as everyone is, but not too poor to see our sons properly married. Sons? That older brother of yours refused to be married. Alas, where is he these many years and he with no wife to care for him? We do not even know where he is. All the more then must we see to it that your wedding is performed according to law and tradition."

"Mother," Yul-han urged, "I beg you let it be as I wish."

It was now time for Il-han to interfere. "Sunia, we must consider. It is true the times have changed and I am not sure the change is evil. I remember our own wedding day with no great pleasure—all that folly of ashes thrown at me when I left this house to go to yours and all my relatives flocking after me as I went and that wedding chest carrier with his face blackened to make people laugh! And you, with your face painted thick with white powder and your yellow-and-blue coat and red skirt and your family bowing when I came in! And all through the wedding feast we were teased until I was afraid you would cry and streak your painted face. And then when they tied my two legs together and hung me from the beam of the house and they pretended to beat the soles of my feet to make me promise them another feast! Those three nights I spent in your father's house as bridegroom were not joy, I can tell you, what with teasing friends and neighbors listening at our door."

Sunia heard this with eyes growing wider as she listened.

"And all these years you have kept this inside yourself!"

Il-han laughed. "Until now, when I bring it out to defend my son!"

They stood, two men against the lone woman, and she could only yield unhappily. She looked at them mutely and Il-han nodded to Yul-han and he went out and brought back the tall handsome girl, whose fresh skin and dark lively eyes showed health. She was not bold, in spite of her composed ways, for she bowed to Il-han and and did not speak until he spoke.

He put on his tortoiseshell spectacles and looked at her in silence and then he nodded his head.

"Welcome to my house," he said. "We break custom here but the times are new." With this he took off his spectacles. "Forgive me," he said. "It is not discourtesy that makes me put on spectacles. My eyes are not what they once were."

This was true, for the midnight teaching by the light of flickering candle made his eyes dim.

"Necessity is no discourtesy nowadays, sir," she said.

There was no more to say, and in a few minutes she went away as gracefully as she had come, pausing at the door to look back at Sunia.

"If you please, good Mother," she said sweetly. "Come with me."

She held out her hand and Sunia could not resist the gentle voice, the pleading eyes. Hand in hand, the two women left the room.

Now Yul-han was left alone with his father and he knew the time had come to confess that Induk was Christian. He did not know whether his father would accept the marriage when he knew, and he had tried to prepare Induk. Indeed only yesterday they had talked long on the necessity and he had begun thus:

"How shall I tell my mother that our wedding will be according to the Christian ceremony? You know how women enjoy our old-fashioned weddings."

"Leave your mother to me," Induk had replied. "Tell only your father. If we are wise in what we say, we shall win them separately and each will help us with the other."

She had a calm assurance, this young female who was to be his wife, and sometimes Yul-han felt a certain awe of her. Where did she find this wisdom? Could it be that her strange religion did indeed communicate a power unknown to him? She never spoke of religion, not even to ask him if he had read the book she had given him, nor did she ask him if he would be Christian too. Yet he knew that she made her prayers to the unknown god, and she went every seven days to the Christian temple. Now and then, however, she spoke of the missionary, sometimes with laughter, for he was very foreign, yet always with respect.

"He is honest," she told Yul-han, "and he is incorruptible. Moreover, he is for our people. He risks himself for our sakes."

Beyond this she did not go, except to say her parents wished her to be married with the Christian ceremony, and she also wished this to be. But they had very little time to talk. It was difficult to meet, for old tradition still held in many ways, and if they were seen alone together, tradition might compel those above to dismiss them from their schools on the pretext that their conduct could lead their pupils into unseemly freedom. For this reason Yul-han had urged immediate marriage. Afterwards, as husband and wife, they could discover each other's minds and hearts in mutuality.

"Father," Yul-han now said, "I need your good advice."

Il-han made a dry smile. "Unusual, is it not, in these days, to hear such words? I try to be useful, nevertheless."

Yul-han ignored this irony natural to age. "What I have to tell you will not shock you, Father, for you know these new times, but I fear for my mother."

Here he paused so long that Il-han was impatient.

"Well, well, well?" he said sharply.

Yul-han forced himself on. "Her family is Christian, Father, and she wishes to be married with their ceremony."

He had said it, and properly he had not spoken Induk's personal name. Sitting motionless on the floor cushion, he took courage to lift his head and look at his father across the low table between them. What he saw was not comforting. His father's eyebrows were drawn down and beneath them the eyes were narrow under lowered lids. His father's long thin hand moved to stroke the scanty gray beard.

"Why have you waited to tell me?" Il-han demanded.

"Father, would it have made a difference if I had told you early?"

The long thin hand fell. "You are saying that you would have married her anyway."

"Yes, Father."

Father and son gazed into each other's eyes.

"You two," Il-han said at last, "you and your brother, inside you are alike. You are both stubborn and willful, he with outbursts of temper and wild words, and you Confucian, always mild in speech. Seemingly without temper, you are the worse of the two. I am always deceived by you."

"I am sorry, Father," Yul-han said.

"Sorry! Does that mean you will change yourself?"

"No, Father."

"I suppose you will be Christian too."

"I do not know, Father."

Il-han closed his eyes. He took a black paper fan from his sleeve and fanned himself for a while.

"These Americans," he said at last, eyes still closed, the fan still moving to and fro. "Do you know that they betrayed us? Have you forgotten that they broke their treaty with us? When we were invaded, they favored the invader. Do they speak now against our oppressors? They do not. They preach their religion, they declare that we must submit ourselves. They say they are not anti-Japanese. They even adjure us to do justice to our oppressors. They bid us remember Korea is the most exposed part of the Japanese empire. Japanese empire, mind you, no longer our country! The Russian base, Vladivostok, is very near, they tell us; it borders Manchuria and by steamboat it is only a few hours from the Chinese port of Chefoo. Therefore Japanese must be allowed to rule Korea!"

Yul-han interrupted. "They won the war with Russia, and—"

Il-han interrupted in turn. "The causes for that war still exist. Russia has no ice-free port on the Pacific."

"Father," Yul-han pleaded, "we were talking only of my marriage. Why are we quarreling about governments?"

"Nothing is private nowadays," Il-han retorted. "If you marry into a Christian family, you undertake their burdens. Do not forget that among the twenty-one Koreans who tried to kill the Prime Minister of Japan who was visiting here, eighteen were Christians!" Here Il-han paused to point his long forefinger at his son. "What was the result? Count Terauchi was sent to rule us without mercy, because he believed that desperate men among us were hiding themselves among the Christians. He surrounds himself with military officers and soldiers. When he goes into our peaceful countryside—I saw it with my own eyes. Only the other day he passed through our villages on his way somewhere, an army swarming about him. Your mother was wailing. She thought they were coming after me. I am not so important any more, I told her."

"I will not argue with you, Father," Yul-han said. "I ask only one question. Will you come to my wedding?"

Il-han's eyebrows shot up. "You insist upon this marriage?"

"Yes, Father," Yul-han said, very steady.

"Then I will not come," Il-han declared. "Nor will I allow your mother to come."

Father and son, they exchanged a long, last look.

"I am sorry, Father," Yul-han said. He made deep obeisance and went away.

. . . He met Induk the next day, a holiday. The date was the seventeenth day of the fourth lunar month and the sixth day of the sixth solar month. By tradition this day was for the transplanting of rice seedlings from dry earth into watery fields, and though this was done only by landfolk, the day was celebrated by city folk, too, for rice is the food of life.

They had grown wise, these two, in their knowledge of the city and where they could meet, and today they planned to walk outside the gates and along some country road. Their meetings until now had been brief and they had always to be careful of being seen. Today, however, they would be in no haste for they would be far from all who knew them. They met by the west gate, and Yul-han paused to buy two small loaves of bread for their noon meal. Then they turned toward the mountains and away from city and field alike. The sun was already hot as they climbed the unshaded flanks of the bare mountains.

"Here is shelter at last," Yul-han said.

He left the narrow path and stopped beneath an overhanging rock. Under it they could escape from the burning sun. He smoothed away small stones and lifted moss from the shallow cavern behind the rock and spread it as a floor cushion for her to sit upon. They sat down then, side by side but not too near, each shy of the other in this new loneliness, around them the noble stillness of the mountain and above them the deep and passionate blue of the sky.

In silence Induk poured a small bowl of tea for Yul-han from the bottle she had put in the basket and then one for herself. It was cool and refreshing. They sipped it, and gazed down upon the city they had left. The landscape was splendid, the high rocky mountains guarding the jewel of the city set deep into the green circle of a valley. The sun glittered on the roofs and hid the poverty of huts and crowded streets.

"I am hungry," Yul-han said.

She gave him bread and broke a loaf in half for herself, and they ate. He felt a peace he had never known before. She was so near that he could put out his hand and take hers, but he had no need to touch her. They were together, committed to a long life ahead, always together. Nothing must be hurried or transient. They were laying deep foundations for the future, even in this silence. He ate his fill and leaned against the bank beneath the rock in profound content.

It was Induk who spoke first. "I have not told you what your mother said when I told her my family is Christian."

"Tell me," he said without urgency, his eyes on her calm face.

"At first," Induk went on, "she could not believe me. Then she was puzzled and she asked me what it meant to be a Christian. Would it mean, she asked, that we would not let her see the children? Assuredly not, I promised her. I said that everything would be the same except that our children would not go to the temple to worship Buddhist gods. Instead they would go to the Christian church and learn the teachings of Jesus. 'Who is Jesus?' she asked. When I told her, she was unhappy. 'He is a foreigner,' she exclaimed."

His children Christian? The thought was new and Yul-han was not sure he liked it.

"I had not considered the matter of children," he said slowly. Far off against the purple-blue sky an eagle soared upward toward the sun.

"Do you not want them to be Christian?" she inquired.

"How can I tell? I know nothing about this religion."

"But it is mine!"

"Must it be mine?"

She looked at him thoughtfully, considering how to answer. "Have you read the book I gave you?"

"Some of it."

"What do you think?"

"It is a strange book," he said in the same slow voice, almost as though he were dreaming. "When one reads it—well, there is a short story in the last part—a revelation. Someone, I do not know who, says that he ate a small book. He had been told to eat it by a spirit from Heaven—or perhaps from Hell, I could not decide, since it is all a sort of poetry, but this man ate the book. It tasted sweet upon his tongue, but when he had eaten it the sweetness went away and the taste was bitter. That is how it was with me. When I read your book it was sweet to my taste, but as I think about it, I feel bitterness."

"Oh, why?" she asked softly.

"I cannot say," he replied. "I only feel. It is dangerous to take a new religion in an old country. It is an explosive."

He did not wish to tell her now what his father had said, not on this first day of their being alone.

"Do you wish me not to be Christian?" she asked after silence.

"I want you to be yourself," he replied. "Whatever you are, that is what I want you to be."

"If you are not Christian, I do not wish to be Christian. I will not be separated from you."

His heart flooded his being with tenderness. What? She would give up so much for him? He could not allow it but he felt his blood warm in his veins.

"Nothing can separate us," he said, "nothing—nothing! And I give you a promise. I will talk with the missionary. I will learn more about this God in whom you trust. If I can come to the same faith, I will not hold back."

"But shall we be married by my religion?"

"Yes! I have none of my own any more. The old beliefs have been taken from us and we have been given nothing in return. Why do I say they have been taken from us? Perhaps they have died of their own age and uselessness. Now let us talk no more of these matters. Time will guide us because we love each other."

He dared to put out his hand now and take her hand and they sat side by side, shy of more than this and yet yearning for more. But the old traditions held. The palm of a man's hand, they had been taught, must not touch the palm of a woman's hand, for the palm is a place of communication, where one heart beats close to another heart. It is the first meeting place of love between man and woman, and for these two it was a virgin experience. From it, love would proceed to consummation.

He sat holding her palm against his until he grew afraid of his own rising passion, to which he must not yield.

"Come," he said resolutely, "it is time for us to go back to the city."

. . . Their wedding day was set for the summer solstice, which is on the third day of the lunar month and the twenty-first day of the solar month. Yul-han sent word to his father, and to his mother, and he gave the name of the church where the ceremony would take place. Whether they would be there he did not know, and no letter came from them by servant or by the postal system which the Japanese had reformed and made useful again. Neither he nor Induk spoke of his parents but both waited during the closing days of their schools. In the few days before the wedding he did not return to the grass roof to visit his father, lest his mother insist that he must bring Induk there to live. For Induk wanted a small house of her own and in his heart he planned that he would ask for some of the land he would inherit from his father. He had saved money enough to build a house but he could not buy land, for the cost of land had risen since the Japanese were buying land everywhere. No Korean was able to buy unless he had influence to help him.

The wedding day dawned in mist. The season called the Small Heat was hotter than usual, and the sun hung in the sky like a silver plate.

"Shall I wear my Korean robes?" he had asked Induk.

She had hesitated. "I have never seen you except in this foreign dress, but yes, I would like to marry a Korean in Korean dress."

He put on his Korean robes, therefore, and his best friend helped him, a teacher of mathematics, surnamed Yi and named Sung-man, a secret revolutionist but a man of merry nature. Sung-man had never married and he made jokes as he helped Yul-han to put on the white robes, and the boat-shaped shoes made from Japanese rubber, and the scholar's hat of woven horsehair, the crown high, the brim narrow.

Sung-man stared at his tall friend. He himself was a short stout man, not handsome, and clumsy of hand and foot.

"Is it you?" he exclaimed.

"I feel strange to myself," Yul-han acknowledged, "as though I were my own grandfather."

Nevertheless thus garbed he walked to the church, Sung-man at his side and taking two steps to his one. So they arrived at the church and went in. The benches were already full of people, men on one side, women on the other. On the platform the missionary stood waiting, dressed in black, and a foreign music came from somewhere, of a sort Yul-han had never heard. He walked up the central aisle looking neither to right nor left, Sung-man behind him, and the missionary motioned to them to stand at his right on the platform. While they stood there waiting suddenly the gentle music changed to loud clear music, very joyous, and Yul-han saw Induk coming up the aisle beside her father. In front of her walked two small boys, her brother's children as Yul-han knew, scattering flowers as they came, and behind her walked her mother and older sister. But it was at Induk that he looked. She wore a full skirt of pink brocaded satin and a short jacket to match, and her face was half hidden behind a veil of thin white silk. She walked steadily toward him and up the two steps while he waited, trying not to look at her and yet seeing her all the way until she was at his side.

Of that strange marriage ceremony he remembered not a word, except that when he was asked by the missionary if he would have Induk for his wife he replied in a loud voice that he would indeed, and it was only for this purpose that he had come. He was surprised to hear stifled laughter from some women in the audience and he wondered if he had said something he should not have said. The missionary went on, whatever he had said, and in a few minutes, before he could recover himself, he heard the missionary pronounce them man and wife. He hesitated, not knowing what came next, but Induk guided him gently by her hand in the curve of his elbow and he found himself walking down the aisle with her, arm in arm.

He had all but forgotten his parents in the agitation of the ceremony but when he reached the door he saw his father standing at the end of the last bench and passed him near enough to touch his shoulder. Father and son, they looked at each other, the one in gravity, the other in amazed gratitude.

Now he and Induk were at the door and now they had passed through into the outer air. It was over. Yul-han was a married man.

"Why should you build a house?" Sunia demanded. "Our ancestral house is empty of children. When we die it will be yours."

Yul-han and Induk exchanged looks. How could they explain to his mother that they were different in this generation? Sunia had come to her husband's house when she was a bride, the house was the home of their ancestors, and where else could she go, or indeed where else would she want to go?

She continued, addressing herself to Induk. "It is because you think I will not have a Christian in my house?"

"Surely not, Mother," Yul-han said quickly.

But Induk reflected. "Mother, you are right—and wrong. Being Christian does indeed make me different from other young women. You are kind, but you would find me irksome in your house."

"How are you different?" Sunia demanded, doubtful but determined still to have her own way.

Induk turned to Yul-han. "How am I different?"

He stroked his head, considering. "I have not had time to find out, but different you are."

Sunia yielded then, complaining privately to Il-han. "She wants to take care only of her husband. Is that a good daughter-in-law? Who brought her precious husband into this world? Who but me?"

"You forget that I—" Il-han began thus but Sunia stopped him.

"Oh you men," she cried, "you never think whether what you do will produce a child. Yes, yes, you are necessary, else why would a woman spend her life taking care of you? But it is we who create the child and with no more from you than a few drops of water upon an open flower."

"Peace," he said with dignity. "Tell me what you want and I will see if it is possible, but do not make me promise that they live with us under our grass roof. These are new times. And I myself do not know whether I want a Christian under the same roof with me."

The compromise was that Yul-han was to build a house attached to his father's but with a separate entrance. During the summer months of his great happiness with Induk thereafter Yul-han began the building of his own house. With the help of the one man servant he brought gray stones from the mountains and he cut cedar trees from the forest lands for the pillars to hold up the roof, but to his father's annoyance Yul-han employed a Japanese roof company to make the roof of tile instead of thatch.

"What," Il-han exclaimed one day when as usual he walked into the garden to see the new house, "do you buy tiles of the enemy instead of using the good thatch grass from our own fields?"

"Father," Yul-han replied, not pausing in the work of making a window, "the thatch must be renewed every three or four years, whereas this red tile will last for a century."

"You are too hopeful," Il-han retorted. "It is enough to look ahead for a few years. Who knows whether any of us will be alive beyond that?"

"You are too hopeless," Yul-han retorted gaily.

The house-building was only for the summer until such time as the schools were open after harvest. He must continue his teaching and so must Induk, she at least until she had a child, and in this summer he and Induk lived in a part of the ancestral home, and it was during this time that they both began to understand the sufferings of their people. In the village near which they lived Yul-han heard one night a great wailing of a woman screaming and crying for help. He was working late and alone and was about break off his labor, for the mosquitoes were singing about his ears, when this voice came to him in waves of agony, borne upon the rising night wind. He put down his plastering trowel and listened.

What he heard were the sobbing words repeated again and again, "O-man-ee, O-man-ee, save me!"

Someone, a girl, was calling on her mother. He listened and then he went to find Induk. She was in the small porch outside the kitchen, pounding his clean clothes smooth on the polished ironing stone. Beside her was a jar of heated charcoal, upon which rested her small, long-handled, pointed iron. He paused to enjoy the picture she made, kneeling on the wooden floor in the light of a paper lantern, the wind blowing her hair as she pounded with two wooden clubs, one in each hand, the folded garment, his shirt as he could see. This wife of his, when she was about her housewifery, could seem the simplest of women.

The sound of women pounding the garments smooth was the rhythm and the beat of the Korean countryside.

Without seeing him, Induk lifted the iron from its bed of hot ashes and he spoke.

"A woman is wailing in the village. Something is wrong."

She put aside the hardwood ironing clubs and the iron. "Let us go," she exclaimed.

Here was her difference. Where a usual woman would have said it might be dangerous to interfere in another's troubles and thereby bring down trouble on one's own house, her thought was only to go and help.

They walked down the road quietly but quickly. The screams had subsided to low moans and these came from one of the village winehouses. Small as the village was, there were three winehouses in it where, before the invaders came, there had been none. These winehouses were places where men came to drink and to seek women. In the deep poverty of the landfolk it was easy to buy girls for such places and few indeed were the girls who dared to rebel when such employment was all that kept their families from starving.

"Let me go in alone," Induk said when they reached the door of this lowly house of pleasure.

"I will not let you enter such a place alone," Yul-han declared.

Together then they went in. A slatternly old woman came toward them from behind the gate.

"We are neighbors," Induk explained, "and we heard some-one wailing and we thought you might need help."

The old woman peered at them from smoke-blinded eyes and replied not a word. Before Induk could go further a young girl ran out of the house, her garments half torn from her body, her hair in disarray and her face scratched and bleeding. A man ran after her. Induk put out her arms and caught the girl, and Yul-han stood between her and the man.

This man did not at first recognize Yul-han since he had lived in the city for the later years of his life and the man pushed up his sleeves and made as if to attack Yul-han.

"Take care of yourself," Yul-han said to him with calm. "I am her husband."

The man was taken aback by this and he stared at the two of them.

"Then why are you here?" he demanded.

Induk stepped in front of the girl and it was she who answered. "We heard a cry for help."

The man looked at her insolently. "You must be Christians!"

"I am a Christian," Induk said quietly.

The man sneered at her, showing his teeth like a dog. "You Christians! You are everywhere that you should not be. One of these days something will happen to all of you."

"Are you Korean?" Yul-han demanded. "How is it that you speak like a Japanese?"

The man looked at him sullenly. "I paid money for this girl. She belongs to me."

The girl now spoke for herself. "I belong to no one. I was cheated! You told me I had only kitchen work to do—not that —ha, I spit on you!"

With this she spat on the man full face, and he bellowed at her and lunged for her but Yul-han pushed him aside and he fell to the ground.

"Do not forget that I am the son of my father," he said sternly.

The man clambered out of the dust and stepped back. "One of these days," he muttered. "One of these days . . ."

He brushed his clothes and turned his back on them and Yul-han led the way out of the gate and to his own house, in silence. He was too prudent not to inquire of himself what they should do with this girl. She was the daughter of a farmer, he supposed, perhaps even of a man on their own land, and he knew that this incident might bring trouble down on him from the capital. The Kim family was too famous to escape notice, whatever they did. Only his father's continued absence from the city and from the King had made them safe. Now he, Yul-han had married a Christian, and it could not be imagined that this was not known to the authorities, for they knew everything and penetrated to the smallest village and to the last corner of every house. Even the man at the winehouse might be in the pay of the authorities, for there were many spies among the Koreans, low fellows who would do anything for money.

When they reached the house, Induk bade the girl wash herself and smooth her hair.

"What shall I do now?" the girl asked.

"Wait for me in the kitchen," Induk told her.

With this Yul-han and Induk went aside into the bedroom to consider what they had done. Neither knew how to begin. It was Yul-han who spoke first.

"The time has come," he said thoughtfully. "I must declare myself on one side or the other. Either I am a Christian or I am not a Christian. If I am to follow you into every trouble where your religion guides you, then I must share your religion. When we are summoned, as sometime we shall be, I cannot say that you are Christian and I am not. They will ask me why I allow you to interfere in the lives of others, for you will continue to interfere, I can see that."

Tears came into Induk's eyes. "But we are told—it is the command of Christ that we must bear the burdens of the weak!"

"So we will bear them," Yul-han said resolutely. "Otherwise we shall be parted, you and I—you driven by your conscience in one direction and I—what? Prudently staying at home, I suppose! Then sooner or later you will hate me—or I may hate you. This is a Christian marriage. You made it so by being what you are."

"You are not to be Christian because I am," she insisted.

"I am Christian because I must be, if I am your husband," he retorted. "Otherwise our paths diverge, and that I cannot accept."

She let tears fall now. "You make a monster of me," she sobbed.

He took her hand and put the palm to his lips. "Not a monster," he said, "only a Christian."

He drew her to him by his hand. "I shall not enter blindly into your religion, I will study and understand. I must be convinced as well as converted. Now cease these tears. You should be happy."

"I want to be a good wife," she whispered against his breast. "I would die before I bring you into danger."

He did not reply for awhile as he smoothed her dark hair. Both knew what she meant. In the last few days they had heard fresh news of the increasing harshness of the ruling government toward the Christians. Whenever Christians sought to work against some evil circumstance, the rulers declared that by so doing they rebelled against the authorities, until all over the country helpless simple Christians were seized and accused of rebellion when what they did was only against an evil which, according to their doctrines, they must oppose, whatever the government.

"It is better if we face danger together," Yul-han said.

At this moment a voice spoke from the door. It was the girl, who had grown weary of waiting. She stood there, her two feet planted widely apart, her bare arms hanging at her sides, her hair neat and her sun-browned face red with scrubbing.

"What do you want me to do next, mistress?" she demanded.

Yul-han and Induk parted and Yul-han turned his back properly on the girl.

"What shall we do with you?" Induk countered. "Shall we not send you home again to your parents?"

"If you send me home," the girl said, her country accent thick on her tongue, "the wineshop owner will only get me back again, since he has paid for me. He has a license from the Japanese police. How can we escape him? I will stay here with you and do your work if you will feed me."

Induk was perplexed. She had saved the girl and now must be responsible for the life she had saved!

"What is your name?" she asked.

"I am called Ippun," the girl said, and stood waiting, her eyes, small above her high cheekbones, beseeching and helpless and her big mouth hanging open.

What could they do then but let her stay? Therefore she slept in a corner of the kitchen at night, and by day she worked without rest, as devoted as a dog to its owners. Not knowing what else to do, Yul-han and Induk accepted her as a member of the household.

"Though you call it a gospel of love, yours is a hard doctrine," Yul-han said one morning in late summer.

He was seated on a chair beside a high table in the vestry of the Christian church in the city. The missionary sat opposite him, the book open before him, and Yul-han thought secretly that he had never before seen so craggy a face, or one so ugly in features and yet so noble in spirit, the blue eyes deep-set under brushy red eyebrows, the pitted white skin, the high nose broken, it seemed, in the bridge, the wide mouth and big teeth. Altogether the face was formidable and so were the huge hairy hands and the strong hairy neck. Under its clothing, was that thick strong body also covered with red hair?

"So you think Christianity is hard," the missionary said.

"It is," Yul-han replied, "hard even in its doctrine of love. What is more cruel than the command to turn the right cheek to the enemy when a blow has been struck on the left?"

"What is hard about that?" the missionary demanded.

East and West faced each other across the table. "Imagine to yourself," Yul-han said earnestly, "if I am struck on this cheek"—he put his narrow, aristocratic hand to his right cheek —"and I turn this cheek"—he turned his head—"what am I doing to the man who strikes me? I am saying to him without words that I am his superior, one far above him in spirit. I am compelling him to examine himself. He has given way to evil temper—I am daring him to do so again and thus prove how evil he is. What can he do? He will be ashamed of himself, he will slink away, condemned by his own conscience. Is this not cruel? Is this not hard? I think so."

The missionary shook his head. "You make me see things I have not seen before."

He was silent for a while and then he took up the book and read aloud from the sayings of Paul. Yul-han listened and after some time he held up his hand for pause. He repeated the lines which he had just heard.

" 'Dare any of you, having a matter against his neighbor, go to law before the unrighteous and not before the saints?' Do you not see what burden this places upon your innocent Korean Christians?"

"Burden?" the missionary repeated.

"It puts them in danger of death," Yul-han said bluntly.

"Death?"

"Do you think the rulers will be pleased when our people come to you instead of to them?"

"There are many Christians in Japan," the missionary said.

"Ah, but there the Church is ruled by Japanese Christians, some of them of high rank. Here it is true that the Church is composed of Koreans—how many did you say? two hundred and fifty thousand—a good number, but the Japanese do not rule the Church here. And my people when they become Christians are altogether devoted—there is too little else in our life nowadays. I feel the need in myself for enrichment and faith and some sort of inspiration. There seems no hope ahead. Some of us, like my father, find refuge in writing poetry and studying ancient literature. But what of those who have no such learning and no such talent? They are finding their interest in the Christian Church and in strong men from the West like you, through whom they seek connection with that outer world, a stream of culture new and modern from which we are cut off by the invaders."

The missionary was listening, his blue eyes fixed on Yul-han's face with intensity and comprehension.

"Go on," he said, when Yul-han paused.

"Look at any town," Yul-han said. "Say there are some eight or nine thousand people there, such a town for example as Syun-chun. Half of the people there, are Christian. The church and the mission school are the largest buildings and the best. A thousand, two thousand people, go to church and to your other meetings. In the surrounding villages there are many Christians, too. What do the Japanese rulers think when they see the vast crowds of Christians and these meetings in which they themselves have no part? They smell rebellion and revolution and so they send their spies to the meetings to listen and to report. These spies hear your Christians singing 'Onward Christian soldiers, marching as to war.' What was that song you bade them sing in the church this morning? 'Stand up, stand up for Jesus, ye soldiers of the Cross.' And what did you preach, you American soldier of the Cross? You told us the story of a young man named David, who with a small sling and a few pebbles killed the powerful evil giant, Goliath. And how was it that David could kill the giant and whence had he his power? Weak as he was, young as he was, his heart was pure, his cause was just, and so with God's help he prevailed. This is what you teach us. And we, hopeless as we are, crushed and lost, how can we but believe you, since we have nothing else in which to believe, our past useless, our future hopeless?"

Here Yul-han stopped, moved by his own words. He struggled against secret tears, his head downcast. When he conquered himself and lifted his head again he saw across the table the missionary gazing at him and in his strange blue eyes was a burning demand.

"Will you be one of us?"

"Yes," Yul-han said. "I will be a Christian."

Sunia woke in the night. Someone was creeping along the narrow porch, feeling the latches of the paper-latticed doors. She was suddenly tense, listening. Yes, someone was there. She must wake Il-han. Then she hesitated. He needed sleep, for he had been sleepless for several nights, fearful lest Japanese gendarmes appear at the gate, demanding to know why he gathered schoolchildren into his house after midnight. He had been warned by Ippun that there was such talk in the village.

"It is that wineshop owner," she had whispered. "He is angry because your son has sheltered me. When I went to the market yesterday he shouted at me that I would soon be back in the wineshop and the Kim family would be in prison."

Il-han had refused to appear afraid and he had continued his midnight school until two days ago, when Japanese gendarmes had indeed marched into the village to get themselves drunk in the wineshop and lay hold on the girls there. He had then sent word secretly to the parents of his pupils that they must not come again until he told them. But he had remained uneasy even at his books and sleepless at night.

Leaning over him in the moonlight, Sunia saw now how wan his face was and how sunken his cheeks. No, let him sleep. She would go and see who the intruder was. Perhaps it was only a neighbor's dog. She crept out of bed and stole across the floor in her bare feet and soundlessly she slid back the door screen an inch and peered through the crack. A man stood there, a tall thin figure in a torn garment. She pushed the screen open a few inches more and spoke suddenly and strongly.

"Thief! What are you doing here?"

The man turned to her and she heard his voice subdued and deep.

"O-man-ee!"

Not since her sons were children had she heard herself thus called "Mother."

"You—you—" She pushed the screen open wildly, it caught and she could not get through the narrow space and she began to sob. "Son—my son—Yul-chun—"

"Hush," he whispered.

He lifted the screen from its runway and set it to one side, and took her in his arms. She clung to him.

"So tall," she murmured, distracted, "so much taller—your bones sticking out—and you are in rags—"

She drew him into the house, crying and talking under her breath.

"Where have you been? No, wait, say nothing—I must call your father—here, drink some tea—still hot—no, it is cold—I will heat some food—"

He took her by the shoulders and shook her. "Mother, listen to me! I have no time. I must leave before sunrise. I took a risk —dangerous for me and for you both, you and my father. I have been sent here to our country—I cannot tell you why— or where I shall be—I must not come home—perhaps never again—Nobody knows what will happen."

She was immediately calm. "Why have you not written to us?"

"I dared not write."

"Where have you been these many years?"

"In China."

China! She breathed the name of that unhappy country. She had seldom heard it spoken after the murder of the Queen.

"You must tell your father," she said resolutely and drawing him by the hand she led him into the room where Il-han still slept.

She hated to wake him, yet she must for he would not forgive her if he was not waked. She began with slow soothing touches on his forehead, his cheeks, his hands. He stirred, he opened his eyes. She leaned close to his ear.

"Our son is here—our elder son!"

His face, bewildered, changed to consciousness. He sat upright in his bed. "What—where—"

"I am here, my father," Yul-chun said. He knelt beside his father and Il-han looked into his face.

"Where have you been?" he asked as Sunia had.

"In China, Father—with the revolutionists."

Il-han rubbed his face with his hands and stared afresh at his son. "You," he said at last—"had you anything to do with the death of the old Empress? Was she murdered there as the Queen was murdered here?"

"No, Father. She died of old age."

"They overthrew the Dragon Throne, those revolutionists!"

"Father, it had to be overthrown. The dynasty was dead. The rulers were corrupt. The old Empress held the empire together by her two hands."

"Who are the rulers now?"

"The revolutionists will set up a republic like the American republic. The people will choose their rulers."

Il-han was suddenly sharply awake and angry. "Folly! How can people choose a ruler when they are ignorant of such matters? I have been in America and you have not. Their people know how to choose—they vote—they—they—"

Sunia interrupted. "You two men, you have not seen each other, father and son, for how many years? Yet you quarrel over governments! Il-han, this son of ours has only a little while to stay with us. He must be on his way—"

"Where?" Il-han demanded.

"I cannot tell you, Father."

"You are a spy?"

"I have a mission."

"Then you are a spy!"

"Call me what you wish," Yul-chun said. "I work for Korea."

Il-han got out of bed and tied his robe about him and coiled his hair as he went on talking. "You will be caught and killed. Do you think you are more clever than these rogues who have spies in every winehouse? Count yourself dead."

"I have stayed alive all these years, Father."

"I do not know how," Sunia put in. "You look starved."

With this she hurried out of the room and to the kitchen to heat food.

"Come into the other room," Il-han said. He led the way to his library and took his usual place on the floor cushion behind the low desk table.

"Now," he said. "Tell me all that you will."

Yul-chun knelt on the opposite floor cushion, his knees bare through his rags.

"Father," he said in the low hurried half-whisper which seemed now his habit, "I cannot tell you anything. It is better for you to know nothing. If one day you are asked if I am your son, say that you have never seen me."

Il-han's eyes opened wide. "That I will never do!"

The haggard, troubled face, the face of his son, softened. For a moment Yul-chun looked as young as he was. He forgot to whisper.

"Do you remember how we used to walk in the bamboo grove, you and I, Father, when I was so small that you held my hand?"

"I remember," Il-han said, and his throat tightened with pain. How had that soft childish face changed to this man's face? He tried to clear his throat. "That was long ago—you can scarcely remember."

"I do remember," Yul-chun said. "I remember the day my

brother was born, and I broke the bamboo shoots, and you told me they would never come up again. You were right, of course, those broken shoots did not grow again. Hollow reeds, you called them. I felt my heart ready to break at what I had done. But then you told me that other reeds would come up to take their place. And every spring I went to the bamboo grove to see if what you said was true. It was always true."

Yul-chun rose to his feet and Il-han rose, too. Face to face, at the same height, they gazed into each other's eyes.

"What do you tell me?" Il-han demanded.

"This," Yul-chun said, "that if you never see me again, or never hear my name again, remember—I am only a hollow reed. Yet if I am broken, hundreds take my place—living reeds!"

He hesitated, looking at his father as if he had something to say and would not say it. Then suddenly he did speak, but leaning forward close to his father and in the half-whisper.

"I cannot come again—not soon, perhaps never. But sometimes you will find under the door in the morning a printed sheet—read it and burn it."

He looked about him uncertainly then and muttered to himself. "The sun is rising. I must be gone."

The sun was indeed creeping over the earthen wall, and with these few words Yul-chun was gone.

A moment later Sunia came in weeping. "I had his food hot and ready for him, but he went away hungry. Oh Buddha, why was I born in these times?"

Who could answer the question? Il-han could only summon her to his side, and there they sat, hand in hand, an aging man and woman whose children had been swept away from them. They were alone in a world they did not know.

A dry hot summer after the rainy season led into autumn. The grass on the mountains ripened and the land people cut it with short-handled sickles and bound it into sheaves for winter fuel. Against the shorn flanks of the mountains again the tall narrow poplar trees burned like golden candles. Under their grass roof Il-han and Sunia lived each day like the one before, and each night Il-han taught his pupils. He seldom saw his second son, for Yul-han and Induk returned to the city during their days of teaching.

"Shall we not tell our second son that his elder brother returned to us?" Sunia asked.

Il-han had already asked himself the question and his answer was ready. "We do not know this woman he has married. A Christian? She is like a foreigner. No. It is better if no one knows that our elder son is alive. Let him be forgotten by all except his parents. He is safe with us."

In silence then Il-han and Sunia lived their lives, and when Yul-han came to visit them in duty they were courteous and made inquiry of how he felt and how he liked his work in his new school, and when he inquired of their health they said they were well and as for happiness, who could have happiness now?

In the eighth month of that moon year, the tenth month of the sun year, two days after the season date of Cold Dew, a fresh trouble fell upon the people. The Japanese Governor-General, Count Terauchi, then on a journey toward the north, barely escaped death at the hands of a Korean assassin at the railroad station in the city of Syun-chun. The news spread to every ear and silence fell upon the people, silence of dread and terror. All remembered the murder of the first Resident-General, Prince Ito, before Korea had been formally annexed to the Japanese empire. Though that price was a kindly man and one who endeavored to make his rule gentle and even just, insofar as he was able, he had been killed by a Korean exile in the city of Harbin in the country of Manchuria. In reprisal the Japanese put the whole of Korea under military rule. Each Governor-General was now surrounded wherever he went by a bodyguard of soldiers, ruthless in their duty to preserve his life.

In spite of this, however, it seemed that the Korean conspirators did all but succeed in their goal. There was a great gathering of people to greet the Governor-General upon his arrival at Syun-chun. Schoolboys from both Christian and public schools were in line on the platform among other Koreans and some Japanese. All Koreans were searched by police for weapons concealed on their persons before they were allowed on the platform. Yet, in spite of precautions, a man was able to hide a revolver somewhere on himself, or had another given to him after he was searched. Who could know?

The Governor-General walked up and down the lines of students, he shook hands with the school principals, among whom were two or three missionaries from Christian schools, one of them American. When he turned to enter the special armored train upon which he traveled, a slender tall man appeared suddenly from among the Christians, in his uplifted right hand a revolver. A shot pierced the air but too high to reach its target. Soldiers swarmed upon the students, pushing them helter-skelter, but none could discover who the assassin was, or whether he was in student uniform. All in the vicinity were arrested, both students and others, in the hope that one would confess the deed. They were thrown into prison, guilty or not, and there waited until trial was held.

This was the news, and Il-han learned of it from the small sheet he found one morning under the door. Ever since Yul-chun had left, Il-han had risen before dawn while Sunia slept to see if there was such a sheet of paper under the door. One morning there it was, a bit of cheap paper, the printing blotted. Who was the assassin? Was it Yul-chun? For this purpose had he returned to his own land? Il-han pondered the dreadful question in his own heart and could find no answer. He resolved that he would not divide his burden by telling Sunia. Let her live her woman's life, make her kimchee and mend their winter clothes! And if Yul-chun were locked in some cold prison throughout the winter, at least he was alive and safe. Safe? How could he speak the foolish word? His son would be beaten and tortured when he would not confess.

Now Il-han understood the lesson of the hollow reed. When one died, another took his place—if one must die!

Throughout the winter Il-han kept his own silence. His flesh fell away from his bones and Sunia fretted by day because he would not eat and by night because he could not sleep. He took to hiding himself from her when he washed or when he changed his inner garments, for she cried out when she saw him.

"Oh, your poor bare bones," she mourned. "When I remember you on our wedding night—"

"Be quiet, woman," he said. And then when he saw her face he tried to laugh. "If I do not please you, look elsewhere."

It was a grim joke, an aging man and woman, exiles in their own country, hair graying, faces lined, alone in their house. Still he did not tell Sunia his burden, nor did he tell his second son.

The winter wore on. Through snow and ice his pupils came in the black of the night, but now not every night. The attempt to assassinate the Governor-General had set the rulers into such fury that everywhere more spies roamed among the people. No village was free of them, no country road lonely enough to escape them. Even women were seized and questioned and punished, and this at first because they were Christian.

There was some reason here, for the girls in the Christian school were more daring than others, and again it was in the news sheet that Il-han read the story, without date or place:

In a Christian day school, in another city, the girls resigned their places. The American woman who was their principal was troubled when they did so, but her pupils laughed and said they would not have her whom they loved punished for what they might do. That same evening she was summoned by the Chief of Police. She made haste to go to his office and he led her to the main street and there were her pupils, waving banners they had made, demanding the release of the prisoners who were accused of plotting to assassinate the Governor-General. The girls had stirred up the citizens and men had joined them and began to shout against the Chief of Police.

Not all Japanese were cruel, and this Chief was in distress. "I cannot arrest them all," he exclaimed. "The prison is already full."

The missionary went out and pleaded with the girls to go

home, but they only embraced her and greeted her with cheers, and they would not listen.

"Arrest me, then," she told the Chief of Police. "I will take their place."

He was a man of good heart, however, and he refused, for the missionary was a small old woman, her hair white, her pale face wrinkled and her eyes very blue and brave.

"I will tell them you will arrest me if they do not go home and I demand that you arrest me if they do not obey," she declared.

What could her pupils say when she stood before them, her white hair blowing in the winter wind? They looked at each other, and their leader said to those men who had gathered to help them, "You men, fight on! At least we have shamed you into battle." And so saying, she led them home.

This story Il-han read in the early dawn, forgetting to shut the door while he read, and the cold wind blew through his thin garments and chilled the marrow in his bones. He took the sheet and put it in the kitchen stove and lit a match and held his hands to warm them over the quickly dying flame. All that day he thought of the woman Yul-han loved, and in spite of himself his heart softened toward his son because of the brave schoolgirls who were Christian.

Not all women were treated so kindly by the police. Students continued in many cities to rebel and girls were beaten and kicked by police wearing heavy boots. The printed sheets lay almost daily now under Il-han's door.

"I was cross-questioned three times," a girl student said. "A police officer accused me of wearing straw shoes. I said my father was in prison and for me it was as though he were dead, and I wear the shoes of mourning.

" 'It is a lie,' the officer said with his hands he pulled my mouth so wide that it bled. Then he forced me to open my jacket to show my breasts and he sneered at me, saying, 'I congratulate you.' Then he slapped me and struck my head with a stick until I was dazed, and he said, 'Did the foreigners teach you to rebel?' I told him I knew no foreigners except the principal of the school. Then he yelled at me that I was pregnant and when I said I was not, since I was not married, he ordered me to take off all my clothes. He said he knew the Christian Bible, and it teaches that if people are sinless they may go naked. Were not Adam and Eve naked in the Garden of Eden? Only when they sinned did they hide themselves. He tried to take off my clothes and I fought him. And while he said these vile things the Korean interpreter stood sorrowfully by, refusing to speak, so that the officer had to use his own broken Korean, and he was angry and ordered the Korean to beat me, but the Korean said he would not beat a woman and he would bite his hand off first, so the officer beat me with his own fists."

Il-han read this and he kept his silence, but he knew the storm that was rising among his own people. Out of the depths of their despair the storm was rising. Throughout the months of that dreary year many Koreans were taken prisoner and every Christian was suspect. If the women were among them, they were treated with obscenities, and those who were young were abused in special ways. All this Il-han read in the small sheets of paper thrust under his door. Still he kept his silence even with Sunia and with Yul-han.

In the fourth month of that sun year, when spring was come, trials were proclaimed for those who had been accused of the attempted assassination of the Governor-General. The day set to begin was the twenty-eighth day of the sixth sun month and Il-han prepared to attend the trials.

The morning of that day dawned with a red sun in a sky white with heat, and Sunia scolded him.

"Why must you go to the city this day of all days? Crowds, dust, noise—you are too old for such things on a hot day. And what if you are recognized? Though who will see in your bag of bones the handsome man you are—"

She scolded him through tears of tenderness and he knew the tenderness and said not a word while she helped him to put on the garments she had washed snowy white for him and pounded smooth and ironed until not a crease remained. She tied the strings of his hat under his beard and bade his old servant take the packet of cold rice and beans she had prepared for his meal and the jar of tea, and she stood at the gate and watched them walking down the village street toward the city. Il-han's skirt swaying from side to side as he planted one foot after the other in the fashion that old scholars walk, their toes turned outward. She felt a deep aching pain in her breast and watching those two she began quietly to weep, for what reason she did not know except that life had become a burden she could scarcely bear. And yet bear it she must, for what would Il-han do without her? Impatient with him she often was, and too quickly, and why, when she loved him, she said something unloving, she did not know.

"I am a sinful woman," she muttered, her eyes on his tall frame, dwindling in the distance, "but of all sins, there is one I will not commit. I will not die before you, my husband—I promise—I promise—"

. . . The sun was well over the horizon when Il-han reached the hall where the trials were to be held. It was a special building behind the district court and built for the purpose for these hearings, a large place some eight-four or eighty-five feet long and thirty feet wide. The door was open wide, but guarded by soldiers.

"Where is your permit, old man?" a soldier asked when Il-han came to the door. "You cannot walk in as though you were the Governor-General."

Il-han did not know such a permit was necessary. He drew himself up to his best height, and stared at the soldier.

"I am Kim," he said with strong dignity. "My name is Il-han."

The soldier hesitated, but seeing before him a gentleman of rank, he allowed Il-han to enter. Inside the hall Il-han now saw the prisoners already seated in two groups in the middle, each group divided into smaller ones of ten men, manacled together. On the sides were seats for the counsels and for reporters. At one end of the hall were the seats for the judges, and at the other end were seats for the people. The prisoners were separated from both judges and people by a barrier, and Il-han pushed his way as closely as he could to this barrier so that he might see the faces of the prisoners. He searched each face and cursed the dimness of his eyes because those in the center were not clear. Was Yul-chun there? He could only wait for the trials to proceed.

Alas, the whole morning was wasted in preparations. Impatiently he waited while after long delay the judges took their places, their interpreters beside them, one Japanese, one Korean. Impatience grew in him while the names of the prisoners were read. He did not hear his son's name and if Yul-chun was there, it could only mean that he used a false name. The indictment was then read, an hour in length, another hour in translation from Japanese into Korean.

By this time the judges were hungry and the Court adjourned for an hour. In the hour Il-han ate his food and drank his tea and made haste to return early and get himself a seat again next to the barrier, but on the opposite side from where he had sat before. Behind it the prisoners waited, unfed and thirsty. One man just inside the barrier, within reach of his hand, sat with his back toward him and his head bowed. His hair was cut short as all prisoners had their hair cut, so that this man's neck showed bone thin and slender as a broken bamboo. Through the holes in his ragged garments his shoulder blades stood out like wings. The garment was filthy and soaked with sweat, for heat filled the hall with a hot fog, a miasma of evil odors and stagnant air. Il-han, observing this prisoner, saw his body heave in great gasps, and with instinctive pity he seized his half-empty jar of tea from his servant, crouching on the floor at his feet, and he reached over the low barrier and held the bottle before the prisoner. A claw of a hand, a man's right hand, grasped the bottle, and in that instant Il-han recognized the hand. It was the hand of his son. It was the hand of Yul-chun.

He fell back into his seat, overwhelmed by a sudden giddiness. His thoughts whirled in his head, a mass of confused colors and shapes. What should he do? What could he do? He felt impelled to cry aloud that this was his son, and his son must be released. He put down the impulse. His son did not know it was he who had given the bottle. He watched while Yul-chun drank the tea in great gulps. Before he could finish, a guard saw him drinking and he came up to the barrier and snatched the bottle away.

"Who gave you this bottle?" he bawled.

"I found it in my hand," Yul-chun said.

The guard turned and glared at all those near the barrier. Since Il-han sat nearest, he fixed upon him.

"Was it you, old man?"

Il-han was too dazed to speak and before he could recover, his servant spoke for him. "This old man is stone deaf," he said. "He cannot hear you."

The guard, getting no better answer from the fearful people, satisfied himself with striking a blow on Yul-chun's right shoulder, and so heavily that blood trickled out from the broken flesh and mingled with the sweat, but Yul-chun did not move, not even to lift his head.

Now the judges returned and the trials began again and Il-han gathered his wits together to understand what was said. The first prisoner summoned was a teacher in a Christian school, a thin tall young man who had, it seemed, confessed the day before the trials that he had been compelled by the missionary American who was the headmaster of the school to appear at the place of the assassination. Now he denied what yesterday he had confessed. He denied, too, that he was a member of the New Peoples Society, to which yesterday he had also confessed. The judge, hearing these denials, was indignant.

"How can you deny before the Court today what yesterday you confessed to the procurator?" the judge demanded.

The man, who said he was once a corporal in the Korean army but was now a gymnastics teacher in a Christian school, replied, "I made false confessions yesterday because I was tortured by the authorities."

"What!" the judge exclaimed in further anger. "You, a teacher, demean yourself to make false confessions because of torture?"

The man said doggedly that he could not hold out longer, and so he had lied. To all further questions he repeated no, he had never been visited by a ringleader in the conspiracy; no, he had never heard the plot discussed; no, he had not told the missionary of such a plot; no, he did not know there was a party of conspirators armed with revolvers at the railroad station at Syun-chun on the day of the attempted assassination; no, he had not even heard that the Governor-General was passing there; no, he did not know whether students in the school had been approached by the ringleader in the conspiracy; no, neither he nor his pupils had revolvers—how could they, when all were searched before being allowed on the platform?

So went the questions and answers, the prisoner standing in dogged patience until the questioner for the Court grew more and more loud in his demands. He pointed to a large box on the platform.

"Do you not know that this box was kept in the Christian school and in it were hidden revolvers?"

"I only went to the school to teach gymnastics. I know nothing else," the prisoner replied.

The judge now lost patience and shouted.

"Next prisoner!"

The next prisoner, a squat, sturdy fellow who said he was thirty-eight years old and a farmer, answered all questions in the same fashion as had the first prisoner. He knew nothing of the New Peoples Society, nothing of the alleged meetings in the Christian schools; nothing of the purchase of revolvers or of assassination. He had never given money to buy revolvers, nor had he heard speeches against the Governor-General. Neither did he know whether the missionary headmaster had told the story of David and Goliath, and he knew nothing about the story, or about David or Goliath; no, he did not know which was the brave man, David or Goliath, yes, he had before confessed that he knew all these matters, but his confession was false and made under extreme torture.

The judge now became grim. He ordered the prisoner dismissed and the next man brought forward. Il-han had fully recovered his wits and he listened with both ears and his entire attention. The pattern of the trials was becoming clear. Under his son's instruction, for who but Yul-chun could conceive so clever a plan, each prisoner denied every charge to which he had before confessed, saying that he had confessed only under extreme torture. The judges, the entire Court, also perceived the pattern, and the trials went on in ominous calm until evening. Then the Court adjourned until the next morning.

"I will not go home," Il-han said to his servant. "Find me a bed in an inn and tell the mother of my sons that here I stay until the trials are concluded."

The man obeyed, and Il-han ate a hearty meal at the inn and laid himself down on a mattress in a room with three traveling merchants. Pulling his quilt to his neck, he reviewed the day and marveled again at his son's cleverness, and laughed under his beard, and then slept as he had not slept for many a night.

The second day of the trials proceeded exactly as the first, except that Il-han overslept and arrived too late to seat himself close to the barrier. He could not tell, therefore, where Yul-chun sat, and he could only stretch his head high to watch for his son's appearance in the prisoners' dock. All day he waited, listening to each prisoner deny the confession made before under torture. Most of these prisoners were young men, teachers or pupils from Christian schools, and the more he heard the more alarmed Il-han became for his second son lest he, too, become Christian. Fourteen men were examined on this second day. David and Goliath were also discussed, but all fourteen prisoners denied knowing these characters, although one young man of weak intellect said that he believed David was considered the braver of the two. Nothing else did the fourteen know. So ended the second day of the trial, and Il-han returned in high spirit to the inn, where his servant waited with a dish of kimchee from Sunia, who said the kimchee at the inn doubtless was not fit to eat.

The third day was not different from the first and the second. To the questions asked before, only a few new questions were added.

"Did the American Christian headmaster address the students, urging them to be bold and undertake a great effort?"

"Did you go to the railway station disguised as a Christian student?"

"Did you not see American Christian missionaries signal their pupils as the Governor-General walked along the platform?"

"Did you tell the students at the Taiyong Christian School to inspire one another with the same ideas that were declared by the assassin of Prince Ito in Harbin?"

"Do you not remember the names of the men to whom revolvers were given?"

"Do you not know that a man came from Pyongyang to Syun-chun to warn the members of the New Peoples Society that the Governor-General was coming?"

To all these questions the answer was no, and to the charge of previous confessions, the plea was duress under torture.

So it went until the eighth day. Nor were the prisoners only students. Some were Christian pastors, some were merchants, but all denied any part in the conspiracy. At last on the evening of the eighth day Il-han saw Yul-chun on the stand. He wore the same rags, but around his head he had wound a towel to hide his cropped hair. Now Il-han strained his attention to hear every word. He had come this eighth day at dawn, so that he might be as close as possible to the stand, knowing that this must be the day for which he had waited so long. His heart beat heavily in his bosom and he felt half choked as he heard the first question.

"What is your name?"

"I am called The Living Reed."

"In the eighth month two years ago you went to Kwaksan to tell the local members of the New Peoples Society of the arrival of the Governor-General whom it had first been decided to asassinate at Chanyon-kwan. Is this true?"

"I admitted it under torture but it is not true."

"You bought revolvers in Manchuria with money given you by the merchant Oh Hwei-wen. Is this true?"

"I admitted it under torture but it is not true."

"You went with others also to Wiju to assassinate the Governor-General there."

"I admitted it under torture, but it cannot be true. The platform at Wiju is too small—we would have been noticed."

"In the spring of 1909, when Prince Ito accompanied the King of Korea on a tour of inspection, did you not determine to attack the Prince at Chanyon-kwan? Then as the imperial train did not stop there, you took the next train and followed Prince Ito to another station. Is this true?"

"I admitted it under torture but it is not true."

"Do you know that the object of the New Peoples Society is to build a military school, to assassinate high officials, and to wage a war to establish the independence of Korea if war breaks out with China or America?"

"I do not know such a thing. If I admitted it under torture when I was half conscious it is not true."

At this moment the judge, a Japanese general of high rank, lost his temper. He pounded the table before him with his clenched fists.

"Torture—torture! What is this torture?"

In the same steady voice with which he answered all questions, Yul-chun replied.

"My arms were bound behind my back with ropes of silk. They cut into my flesh. Two sticks were put between my legs, which were then bound tightly together at my knees and ankles. Two policemen twisted these sticks. Pieces of bamboo, three-cornered, were tied between my fingers and tied so tightly that my flesh was torn from my bones. Day after day I was pulled out flat on the floor and beaten with split bamboo until my back was raw. Each night I was thrown into an underground dungeon where I lay in wet and slime. Each day I was taken out for torture again. I do not know how many days. I was not always conscious."

The spell of the clear steady voice, the strong simple words telling of terrors worse than death, fell upon all alike. When Yul-chun finished speaking, he turned his head and looked at his father. His face did not change, he made no sign of recognition, but, father and son, the two men met.

"Next prisoner!" the judge shouted.

When Yul-chun came down from the stand Il-han rose

from his place and left the hall. He had seen what he came to see, he had heard what he must know, and he walked the long road home to his grass roof. Behind him his servant followed, and in silence. Slowly and steadily the two men plodded their way home in the twilight. The evening air was still and hot, and the miles were many and seemed longer than they were. Il-han reached home at last and Sunia met him at the door and cried out in fright.

"You look like a mountain ghost! What is wrong?"

"Ask me nothing," he said. "It is better for you not to know."

And however she begged him and scolded him and argued with him, he would not tell her.

"It is better for you not to know," he said.

The trials ended and many prisoners were kept in prisons for long years, even for the rest of their lives, but some were beheaded. Whether Yul-chun was among these Il-han did not know, nor could he find out unless he asked Yul-han's help. This he would not do, for Yul-han was in danger, too, now that he had married a Christian. He bore the burden of his secret alone and continued so to do.

. . . Summer passed again, and Yul-han had nearly finished his house, the maid Ippun working like any man carrying rock and mixing cement and digging the ground under the ondul floor. Once more the time had come for school to open and Yul-han must return to his teaching. This year Induk was not to teach. She had conceived and Yul-han wished her to remain at home, and home now was this small new house. He would go alone to the city for his teaching days, and return here for holidays, and she could stay with Ippun, near his parents but independent. There remained only to tell the news to his parents, the expectation of a grandson for them, the plan that Induk would remain near them with Ippun. But above all, he must tell them that he had decided to become a Christian, that he was to be baptized, and that he had accepted the headship of the Christian school in the city. This was the one demand that Induk had made of him when he told her that he wished to be Christian.

"I beg you then to leave the Japanese school and stay with the Christians. Among them you will be safe: but alone, one Christian among the Japanese, you will be searched and examined and questioned and watched, wherever you are."

She had already inquired of the missionary, who gladly had offered Yul-han the headship of the school since the present head had a consumption in his lungs and should rest in bed for many months. Yul-han therefore sent his resignation by letter to the Japanese school and when he was called to the office of the Bureau of Education, he gave the true reason for his change of work.

The chief of this bureau was a young man, once an assistant professor in the University at Tokyo, and he had come because the salary here was three times what he had received there and since he had his old parents to support he had not been able to refuse. Now he sat behind a high western desk in an office barren of decoration, but with western chairs and a desk. He wore civilian clothes, western in style, and his hair was cut short and he had gold spectacles with thick lenses. He was courteous when Yul-han came in and invited him to be seated. Then he opened a document which lay on the desk.

"I note," he said, "that you have resigned your post at the city middle school. Have you a complaint?"

"I have no complaint," Yul-han replied. He hesitated and then said, with a slight smile on his round good-natured face, "I have changed my work because I am about to change myself. I have decided to be a Christian."

The young man continued to study the document. "You have been baptized?" he inquired.

"No," Yul-han said, "but I shall be baptized on the first day of next month."

"By immersion or sprinkling?" the young Japanese asked, still not lifting his eyes.

Yul-han was surprised. "Does it make a difference?"

"There is a difference," the young man said.

Yul-han summoned his courage and asked a question for himself. "Can it be, sir, that you also are Christian?"

"I attended a Christian school before I went to the university," the young man said. "You understand—" Here he pushed the documents aside and lifted his head to look at Yul-han. "You understand that we are not opposed to Christianity, in principle. It is only when rebels hide among the Christians that we must be severe."

"I understand," Yul-han said quietly.

"You appear to be a sensible man," the Japanese said. "Therefore I will allow you to transfer your post." He drew the papers toward him again and with his fountain pen wrote something quickly on the top. "Of course," he continued as he folded the papers and fitted them into the envelope. "I shall count on you to let me know whether you discover rebels among the Christians. You may report to me in secret and safely."

Yul-han heard this and debated with himself as to what he should answer. He decided to answer nothing, for though he had not attended the trials, he knew that Christians had suffered the heaviest judgments. He put out his hand and took the envelope and bowing, he went away.

On the next Sunday he was baptized. The day was cloudy and cold, the winds of late autumn blew leaves from the trees and wrenched persimmons from their stalks. Children in ragged garments ran to save the fruit and stood under dripping eaves sucking the sweet juice and shivering in the chilly air. The reek of fresh kimchee hung like an atmosphere over city and country.

Yul-han walked through the streets to the church, Induk following decorously behind. He saw everything with new intensity this morning, as though his entire being were alive and aware as it had never been, as though he were separating himself from all that had gone before, all that now was. The dusty street, the sad-faced people, the children merry in spite of cold and poverty and even in spite of the ubiquitous police ready to rebuke them whatever they did, and behind the crowded busy city the mountains soaring into a darker gray against the gray sky, barren and beautiful—all this pressed upon his mind and heart. As he entered the church, he knew that he would come out of that door a different man for he was taking his place today among those who were separate. No longer would he be only a Korean. He would be a Korean Christian and which would be the greater part of him, Korean or Christian, he did not know, or perhaps there would not be two parts in him, but one whole, a Korean permeated with the new religion.

He did not wish to speak and in silence he went to the men's side and Induk went to the women's side. Among the men he sat, a stranger to himself. He was giving himself away to a God he had not seen and yet he felt a dedication he had never known. The ceremony was beginning now and as usual with music. A man played upon a small western organ, and he played well. Yul-han loved music as all his people did, and he was easily moved by it, as they all were. Music was woven into the texture of their souls and some of the attraction for them in the new religion was the part that music had in worship, the grave organ music and the communal singing. Already Yul-han knew the hymns they sang and he recognized the one the man was playing—"Just as I am, without one plea, but that Thy blood was shed for me, Oh Lamb of God, I come to Thee—" Mystic words, symbolizing what he was about to do!

The missionary came into the church from the vestry and above his long black robes, his upstanding red hair flamed like a burning crown upon his head. He prayed silently before the gold cross under the window. Prayer—that Yul-han had not yet achieved. He had made tentative efforts when he was alone to come into this communication, but he had not found the way. No one answered.

"Do not expect to hear a voice," the missionary had told him when he inquired as to whether he had prayed properly. "Simply cultivate the habit of prayer and after a while you will find answer in the content it brings to your heart and the direction it brings to your mind. Wait upon the Lord."

"These are also the instructions of the Lord Buddha," Yul-han had said, remembering what his father had told him of the monks in the monasteries of the Diamond Mountains.

To his surprise the missionary had shown anger and he made retort.

"It is not at all the same. There is only one God and he is not Buddha. He is Jehovah."

Yul-han had considered reply, for did it matter, if it was true that there was only one Being, whether his name was Buddha or Jehovah? But he was peaceable by nature and he kept question and answer to himself.

The missionary turned now to the people. The church was crowded and men stood leaning against the walls. Women sat close together, many of them with children in their arms. Why were they here except to seek comfort and encouragement in their sorry lives? The missionary looked at them and his rugged face took on a rugged tenderness.

"Let us sing," he said. "Let us praise the Lord."

The church was filled with the music of human voices. His people could sing, Yul-han knew, and he listened to the mighty chorus. Tears suddenly filled his eyes. These men and women, these poverty-stricken, oppressed people of his, singing! With all their hearts they were singing, in harmony, in rhythm, born singers and lovers of song, singing like children in the dark and to the unknown God. Out of his heart spontaneously a cry rose to his lips.

"Oh God, whatever your name, help me to help my people, for I love them—"

He heard no voice, but words sprang clearly into his mind, "For God so loved the world—"

Immediately he too began to sing, his powerful voice leading the melody. Well-being surged through mind and body as he sang through the hymn. The missionary spoke in his usual simple Korean, struggling to convey great thoughts through imperfect language and the people listened, rapt, the intense silence broken only by the occasional cry of a restless child. What was this sense of health and calm in himself? For the first time Yul-han was sure that he had decided rightly in becoming a Christian. He was not sure what it meant in entirety but he believed now that he could learn and grow. He was humble as he had never been before. There were many poor people in the church, those who were ignorant and who were not yangban. At first he had been reluctant to think that he must mingle with these people and call them his brothers, he who was born of a proud and ancient clan. Now he was cleansed of that pride. It did not exist in him, swept away in a moment and by what means he did not know, except that it was not there. He belonged here, and these were truly his brethren.

The hour passed and he heard the missionary ask those who were to be baptized to come forward and, half dazed, he stumbled to his feet and went forward with a dozen others, men and women. He bowed his head as the missionary prayed and his heart beat fast. This was the moment that committed him wholly to the unknown future.

"You may suffer persecution," the missionary was saying. "You may be called upon to die even as Christ died on the cross."

Yes, it was true. There had been such crucifixions by the Japanese gendarmes. In a village in the north three Christians had been crucified.

"I baptize you," the missionary was saying, "in the name of the Father and of the Son and of the Holy Ghost."

He felt a trickle of cold water on his bare head. It ran down his cheeks and fell on his coat but he did not wipe it away.

"And Jesus took bread and blessed it and brake it and gave it to the disciples and said, 'Take, eat, this is my body—'

"And he took the cup and gave thanks and gave it to them, saying, 'Drink ye all of it—' "

The deep voice of the missionary intoned the words and Yul-han felt the unleavened bread dry upon his tongue and he tasted the sharp acid of the red wine. It was done. By a strange mystic ceremony, he was born again into a Christian, as surely as long ago he had been born into the family of Kim.

Yul-han had stayed away from the trials of the conspirators against the Governor-General's life, and this at the beseeching of Induk. He had yielded to her not for his own sake, but because she insisted that her parents and brothers and sisters would also be in danger if by any chance he were seen there as a Christian. This wife of his, so brave where a good deed was to be done, could be as frightened as a child of police or soldiers or any official person. She shrank at the sight of a gun, and would walk far out of her way to avoid any man in uniform. Nevertheless Yul-han read of the trials assiduously each day in the newspapers and on the walls, for on the walls there was more than news. In spite of watchful police, always during the night some rebel would steal to the wall and in the darkness he would scrawl secret messages. If Yul-han went early, he could read before the police washed the words away. Thus he learned how the trials went and how all prisoners made the same confession of guilt one day and denied it the next, saying that they had been forced to give false testimony under torture. On the day after his Christian ceremony he read of the man now called the Living Reed.

"Beware—beware the Living Reed!" the secret message proclaimed.

In the newspapers under the eyes of the rulers, he read too the full account of what had taken place at the trials on the twelfth day. On that day, the newsmen reported, Baron Yun, a Korean of high yangban family, confessed before the Japanese judge that he was indeed the head of the New Peoples Society.

Now Yul-han knew this aged noble man very well, for Baron Yun had been a friend of his father's, and the two had often drunk tea together in the best teahouses of the capital. Yul-han himself could remember such times, when his father had taken him, a boy of twelve or so, to the teashops to meet gentlemen scholars. He remembered Baron Yun especially, for he was such a man that his father would not sit in his presence until Baron Yun insisted upon it. The Baron was a slight man, his face always pale, and he moved and spoke with serene dignity wherever he was. Now in his old age he was on trial for his life. He made his defense in fluent Japanese, for he had studied Japanese in Japan in his youth, Chinese in Shanghai and English in America. He had traveled also to Russia, and upon his return to his own country he had held many high posts, especially as Vice-Minister of Foreign Affairs during the Russo-Japanese war. When the invaders entered his country he became a Christian, and was deposed by the newcomers and thereafter took a post in a Christian school.

It was morning when Yul-han read the story of the trial. He sat at his breakfast table alone, as head of the house. Question by the Court, answer by Baron Yun, he read on, forgetting that he had classes at the school.

"What were your feelings when you were compelled to retire from the Foreign Service?"

"I was overwhelmed with grief."

"Are you not the head of the New Peoples Society?"

"I am, but I told the members that I would not perform violent acts."

"Yet you must have been indignant at the annexation of your country."

"I would never have found myself in this court if I had possessed the power at that time to prevent Japan from becoming lord over my country."

"Would it not be reasonable, nevertheless, for you to have formed a plan to change the situation?"

"I was rather too old to do more than I did, but it is true that I felt bitterly indignant at the position of my country."

Yul-han, reading these brave words, could see before his eyes the gallant old gentleman in his white Korean robes, his long white beard streaming over his breast, his staff in his hand, his wrinkled face, his steadfast dark eyes. The warmth of fresh courage, fresh hope, new faith, reached Yul-han's heart. If young and old among his people could be so fearless, should he be afraid?

Induk came to the door at this moment. "Do you forget that you must go to your class?"

"I do not forget," Yul-han said, "but I have another duty. First I must go to my father."

Induk's hands flew to her cheeks. "What is wrong? Has something happened?"

"Baron Yun was tried yesterday," Yul-han said. "He is in

prison and he is my father's old friend. I must tell him—and I must tell him that I am Christian now. I trust it is not too much for one day."

. . . He found his father watering a young apple tree in the east garden. His mother held a hoe with which she loosened the earth so that the roots could drink.

"You two, my parents," Yul-han said when he had given greeting. "Do you expect to get fruit from this little tree?"

"You will get it," Il-han said, "you and your children. And I am glad you have come. I have a matter to discuss with you."

He put down the watering pot and led the way into the house and to his accustomed place. Then he waited, as though he did not know how to begin.

"Speak, Father," Yul-han said, when they had sat down.

"You speak first," Il-han directed. "What I have to say may have some connection with you."

Yul-han took a breath. "Father," he said. "I have become a Christian."

Rain had begun to fall, a slow autumnal rain. It dripped from the eaves and trickled in rills over the stones of the footpath in the garden. Sunia was running toward the kitchen, her apron over her head. Meanwhile Yul-han waited for his father's anger and with such foreboding that he was almost frightened when he heard his father's voice come not angrily but with unusual mildness.

"Had you told me this a short time ago, I would have reproached you for bringing our family into danger. But I have seen such sights and heard such words—"

And he told of the trials of the Christians, of their wit and courage. Each one he described, young and old, until Yul-han interrupted.

"Add to the noble list one more name, Father," he said. "Add the name of Baron Yun."

Il-han's jaw hung ajar. "Not my old friend!"

"Even he."

Il-han hesitated, inquiring of himself whether he should not tell Yul-han of his older brother.

"That man they call the Living Reed," Yul-han said, as though he read his father's mind.

Il-han did not move or lift his eyes. "What of him?"

"Do any guess who he is?"

"Do you?"

"I was not there. I did not see his face."

Ah, Yul-han did not know! Let him remain unknowing and safe.

"Why should I know when you do not?" Il-han said. "And for the rest," he added with pretended impatience, "if you wish to be Christian, then be one."

This was all that was left of his anger against his second son.

The winter of that year passed in dire deep cold. Cold was to be expected but this cold was the chill of death. Each morning the gendarmes collected the bodies of those who had frozen during the night, men, women, and children, and threw them into trucks and carried them away. The earth was too solid to bury them and they were stored in empty barracks or piled and covered with mats until the spring came. Nor were those who lived better off, for a long drought in the autumn had dried the mountain slopes, the grass was scanty and the rulers would not allow trees to be cut. The mountains, they said, must be covered with trees again as they had been in past centuries, and if a man were caught cutting a tree in the night he was flogged and put in jail. In every house the ondul floors were cold, except for the two brief times, morning and afternoon, when food must be cooked, and since in the past the people had depended upon warm floors upon which they could spread their mattresses and therefore needed no heavy quilts, they were cold as they had never been before.

The long winter passed into a scanty spring and the time drew near for Induk to give birth to the child, and her mother begged Yul-han to allow her to come to her family home for this event. Yul-han did not know how to reply. If he refused Induk's mother, that one would be wounded. If he agreed, then Sunia would be displeased. Indeed she was already displeased, for somehow she had wind of the request, and she laid hold of Yul-han one day when he was on his way to school.

"What!" Sunia exclaimed. "I suppose you think I cannot help my grandchild to be born? I suppose only a Christian will serve?"

"Mother, I pray you," Yul-han exclaimed. "Is it a matter for me to decide? Let it be as Induk wishes."

This Induk heard from an open window and she came hurrying out.

"Good Mother," she said, coaxing Sunia. "The birth is not so important as the hundred-day feast. Will you let us celebrate the feast with you and the grandfather?"

Sunia, having made protest, was willing to be mollified, and so it was decided. On a stormy night in early spring, Induk went into labor, her mother and her sisters about her. Outside in the main room Yul-han awaited the birth with eagerness and so with mild amusement, for Induk had said she wished the first child to be a girl.

"I am praying God for a daughter," she told Yul-han one night as they lay side by side in bed in married talk.

He gave a shout of laughter.

"Now here is confusion," he exclaimed. "I am praying for a son!"

Induk did not know what to say. At first she was inclined to be somewhat peevish. Then she thought better of it and smiled.

"Let us both stop praying and accept what God sends," she said.

The birth was not easy for Induk. The hours were many and Yul-han was about to be fearful when, as the early sun climbed over the eastern mountain, his mother-in-law came to the door and beckoned him with her forefinger. He went to her at once and she gave him a sly look, for Induk had told her of their conflicting prayers.

"You have prevailed," she said. "God has given you a son."

He went to Induk then and knelt on the floor beside her bed. There, resting on her arm, he saw a sturdy child whose eyes were already open. It was his son! He felt a strange new pride in himself, a conviction of achievement, an upsurge of life and hope. Then he looked at Induk.

"Next time, since I am so strong in prayer, I shall pray for you a daughter," he said, and weary as she was, she laughed.

. . . At first Yul-han thought of the child only as his son, a part of himself, a third with Induk. As time passed, however, a most strange prescience took hold of his mind and spirit. Babe though he was, he perceived that the child possessed an old soul. It was not to be put into words, this meaning of an old soul. Yul-han, observing the child, saw in his behavior a reasonableness, a patience, a comprehension, that was totally unchildlike. He did not scream when his food was delayed, as other infants do. Instead, his eyes calm and contemplative, he seemed to understand and was able to wait. These eyes, quietly alive, moved from Yul-han's face to Induk's when they talked, as though he knew what his parents said. He was a large child, strong and healthy, and he had presence. Yul-han, watching, felt a certain awe, a hesitancy in calling him "my son," as though the claim were presumption.

"If I were Buddhist," he told Induk one day, "I would say that this child is an incarnation of some former great soul."

They were together of an evening, and Induk was preparing for the child's hundredth day after birth, which was to be celebrated the next day. She was baking small cakes and while they were in the oven, she arranged upon a low table the objects for the child's choosing tomorrow. According to tradition whatever the child chose was a prophecy of his future.

She paused when Yul-han spoke. "I feel it, too," she replied quietly. "What it means I cannot say. I only know that this child will lead and we must follow. We must not try to shape him, though we are his parents. He will know what he is, and we must wait until he tells us."

She came to Yul-han's side then, and they knelt together before the child, who lay on a pillow on the ondul floor. He had been moving his hands as babies do, kicking his feet and making soft burbles as he discovered his voice. Now he turned his head to look at his parents, and he gazed at them with such intelligence, such awareness, that it was as if he spoke their names, not as his parents, but as persons whom he recognized.

"Oh, what is this—" Induk murmured in amazement.

The child smiled as though with inner joy.

. . . "Let no one speak," Il-han said.

They were gathered together for this celebration, the two families, Yul-han's and Induk's, in Il-han's house. For the first time Il-han and Sunia met with Christians, a meeting not possible if Il-han had not seen with his own eyes the steadfast courage of the Christians at the trials. Today, therefore, he greeted Induk's parents with courtesy and they sat in the seats of honor, the father in his white robes, and the mother, short and plain of face, in her best gray satin skirt and bodice. On the outskirts in lower seats were Induk's sisters and young brother, and Sunia's sisters, a family crowd such as there had not been since the funeral of Il-han's father.

All were intent upon the child. He, too, was in his new garments of red silk that Induk had made for the occasion. He was propped against a cushion, and he lay in calm content, smiling when he was spoken to.

"Let no one speak," Il-han said again.

All voices were hushed then, as they watched the child. Upon the floor around him Induk had placed the usual objects, a brush for writing, a small dagger, a piece of money, a bundle of thread. The child looked at Induk inquiringly, and she nodded and smiled. Then as though he understood what he must do, the child examined the objects carefully and after a moment he put out his right hand and chose the bundle of thread. All burst into joyful cries and exclamations. The child had chosen the symbol for long life.

Thereafter they ate the cakes which Induk had prepared and drank tea and made talk happily. And when this was done, they presented their gifts to the child. Some gave garments of gaily colored silks, some gave money, and some bowls heaped with rice to signify wealth. The grandparents gave the essential gifts of bundles of thread, a rice bowl of fine lacquer with a cover of polished brass, a set of silver chopsticks and spoon. Each gift the child received with such calm and seeming comprehension that all guests went away awed.

When they were gone Sunia took the child in her arms. "I am glad he chose the thread," she told Yul-han. "Else I might have my fears. He is too wise, this child."

"Wisdom is what we need in times like this," he told her.

"I raise a name for him," Il-han said. "I raise a Chinese name. Let him be called Liang. Later he may add another name of his own choosing, but let us call him Liang, which means Light—the light of day, the light of enlightenment."

They considered, looking at each other and at the child.

"It is a good name," Yul-han said.

Sunia nodded. "A name big enough for him to grow in."

But Induk snatched the child away from her. "He is only a baby," she cried. "He is only a little baby. You make him too soon a man!" And she hugged him to her breast.

Beyond the despair in Yul-han's own country, a turmoil appeared in the West. Out of the West, so long committed to peace, a war arose. At first no one could understand such a war, beginning, it seemed, in the single assassination of a nobleman in a country whose name the people here did not know. Suddenly like fire upon mountain grass, the single death was spread into multitudes. Europe was divided by war, and Germany, the nation most admired by Japan and where many Japanese had been sent by their Emperor for education in soldiery, Germany was the first to move to battle. By command of their ruler, a proud man with a withered arm, the German army moved swiftly across the nations.

"What is to happen to us?" Induk asked, in fear.

"We are helpless," Yul-han replied.

"But which side will these who rule us take in this war?"

"They will take what profits them best," Yul-han replied.

He longed to stay and comfort her, but the day's work waited and he went to it as he did on all days. Yet in his classes he could scarcely compel the usual tasks. His pupils were restless, afraid, excited, guessing and wondering how the new war would change their lives and hopeful that in the turmoil their country could find its independence again.

"Have no hope," Yul-han told them.

"How can a Christian say we are to have no hope?" a young man demanded.

Yul-han could not answer. He felt himself rebuked. "Attend to your books," he said sternly.

But the young could not attend to their books. They were distracted and rebellious and they broke rules and reproached their teachers. When Japan declared herself against Germany many were surprised, but Yul-han understood what the declaration meant. Korea was only the stepping-stone toward all Asia for that small strong island nation. Germany had taken territories from China, and Japan would claim them as booty of war.

One Sunday after the ceremony of worship in the church, Yul-han told Induk to wait for him under a date tree in the churchyard where were the tombs of Christians, for he had need of special counsel from the missionary. He went into the vestry behind the pulpit and there the missionary was taking off his robes of office. The day was cool with another autumn but this ruddy saint was always hot whatever the season and as he took off his black robes the sweat ran down his cheeks into his beard, now laced with white hairs.

"Brother, come in," he shouted when he saw Yul-han. "How have you been?"

Yul-han came in, pale and quiet and courteous. "I have need of counsel," he said after greeting, and he went on to tell the American his fears.

"No one is deceived," he told the missionary. "The Japanese will not fight in Europe, but they will take the territories of the Germans in China and there they will put down the roots of coming empire. Even as they came here to our earth with the pretext of war—ah, all their talk was only how they needed a place for their soldiers to encamp in the war against China and then against Russia, not against us, ah never, never against us! Will your President Wilson understand what Japan is doing?"

"Trust God," the missionary said.

"Does God know?" Yul-han retorted with a crooked smile.

"He knows all things and all men," the missionary replied.

Yul-han left the vestry room with questions unanswered. He longed for a man with whom he could talk and argue and by whom he could be enlightened, and in this mood he sought his old friend and associate teacher in his old school, Yi Sung-man. They had not met since he left the Japanese school, and he had no wish to return to that place. But he remembered that he and Sung-man used often to take their noon meal at a small cheap restaurant in a narrow side street and there he went the next day about noon. Yes, there Sung-man sat, untidy as usual and gulping down noodles and soup from a steaming bowl. His hair was too long and his western suit was unpressed and not clean. Yul-han sat down at the same table, and Sung-man looked up.

"You!" he exclaimed. "How long since I have seen you? You are thinner. I hear you have made a Christian out of yourself. I have been thinking I might do the same thing—but no, I would lose my job. You are lucky. Soup—soup—"

He snapped his fingers for the old woman who served, and she brought Yul-han a small burning brazier on which stood the brass bowl of hot soup.

More talk passed between them, small talk, questions of this old friend and that, while the restaurant grew empty.

"Have you a class?" Yul-han inquired then.

Sung-man shook his head and tipped his bowl to empty the last of the soup into his wide mouth. He set the bowl down, wiped his greasy mouth on his sleeve and folded his arms and leaned forward.

"Do you know the American Woodrow Wilson?" Yul-han asked next in a low voice.

"Who does not?" Sung-man replied. "He is our one hope, a man of peace, alone in the world, who has power. He will save us all, if he can stop the war."

"Have you a book about Wilson?" Yul-han asked next.

"Come to my room," Sung-man replied.

Yul-han went with him then to his bedroom in the school

building and Sung-man gave him a small thick book, printed on cheap paper. The title was one word, *Wilson.*

"Read it," Sung-man said, "but always in secret. Then become one of us."

One of us? Yul-han would not ask the meaning of such words. He put the book in his sleeve and went home and read the book all night. Out of dim blotted words he began to see, face to face, the figure of a man, a lonely, brave man, a man too sure of himself at times, but a man who tried always to do right. Could there be such a man anywhere in the world in these times? There was this one.

. . . Under his grass roof Il-han, too, was learning of Wilson. The sheets thrust under his door had continued, stopping sometimes as though the one who put them there might be in prison or killed, but before many days they were always there again. Now they told of Woodrow Wilson, Woodrow Wilson and the war, Woodrow Wilson and his own people, Woodrow Wilson and the subject peoples of the world.

Il-han read these pages again and again, pondering their meaning. His memories of America, once so clear and warm, had cooled when he conceived a deep contempt for that Roosevelt who had understood nothing of the significance of Korea in the world. Korea, this country, this gem of rock and earth, its mountains rich in mineral treasure, its rivers running gold, this flame of human fire thrusting itself even into the sea, surely it was one of the treasure countries of the globe. There were a few such places which, because of their strategic position, became the centers of human whirlpools, small in themselves but each an axis about which other nations revolved. Theodore Roosevelt could not comprehend the importance of such a country and in ignorance, admiring the courage of a small Japan over a vast Russia, he had ignored the very means by which Japan had won the victory, which was Korea. Was this Woodrow Wilson a wiser man?

Slowly, pondering every line, gazing at a dim photograph, Il-han created for himself the man Wilson. He was a scholar and this went to Il-han's heart and to his mind. Scholars could understand one another everywhere in the world. Roosevelt had been only a rider of horses, a hunter of wild animals, a lover of violence. Even Sunia had exclaimed when, his office over, he had left his home to hunt savage beasts in Africa.

"Poor wife of his," Sunia had said. "After seeing nothing of him during the years of his office, she must lose him altogether to the wild animals! You, at least, when the Queen was dead, retired here to our grass roof. In this way my true life began."

He had dismissed this as woman talk when he heard it, but her words came back to him now. And Wilson was more than a scholar. He was also a man of deep feeling for his wife and children, the head of his house as well as of his nation. Did not Confucius say that a man's responsibility was first to his own house? In many ways Woodrow Wilson was Confucian and could therefore be understood. He was a man of ideals and conviction, a man of peace. This Il-han concluded for on one sheet the writer had taken pains to put down certain sayings from Wilson. Thus when Wilson decreed a day of prayer for peace, in the midst of war, he had declared:

"I, Woodrow Wilson, President of the United States of America, do designate Sunday, the fourth day of October next, a day of prayer and supplication, and do request all God-fearing persons to repair on that day to their places of worship, there to unite their petitions to Almighty God that He vouchsafe His children healing peace and restore once more concord among men and nations."

And again: "The example of America must be a special example. It must be the example not merely of peace because it will not fight but of peace because peace is the healing and elevating influence of the world and strife is not. There is such a thing as a nation being so right that it does not need to convince others by force that it is right. There is such a thing as a man being too proud to fight."

Beneath these remarkable words Il-han drew a line with his inked brush. He did not understand them fully and he pondered them in the night. What man was this who could speak words so strong that they became weapons for peace? Swordsharp, bold and clear, the words struck into his own heart, accustomed to the love of peace, and into his mind, trained by the classic discipline of Confucius that the superior man leads not by violence or by coarse physical acts but by the pure intelligence of a wise mind.

From such meditation Il-han slowly created the image of a man ruling a great western country with calm conviction and high righteousness, maintaining peace in a world of war and evil. He began at first to trust this American, and then to idolize him.

Yul-han's second child, a daughter, was born in the early spring before the sun had warmed the earth, when the first plum blossoms appeared on the bare branches of the plum tree, a time which should have been a happy one, with ceremony to be observed. Alas, it was also the time when the great American Woodrow Wilson had after all taken his country into the war, in the fourth month of the solar year 1917. The Japanese rulers had forbidden the use of the lunar year, saying that none cared what year it was in Korean history and from thenceforth all must use the solar year, which was the modern system of counting time. The year therefore was 1917.

The newspapers during these times had printed much of what Wilson said, and as people read his words all Koreans had grown to think of him as saint and savior and a man who would never descend to making war. For months Yul-han, too, had read everything he could find that the Americans said, and he met often with his father to consult on the meaning of what was said, and whether the Americans in the end must fight. For slowly and against his first confidence and his own inclination, Il-han had come to believe that though peace was the proper way of life, it might now be necessary for the Americans to enter the war, lest far away in Europe a center of tyranny, conceived in the mind of an angry man, a man born with a withered arm and a slight body often ill, could light a fire that in some future time, joined with other minds, even such as ruled now and here in Korea, would put the whole world into darkness.

Il-han believed but Yul-han could not believe the necessity. "Father," he exclaimed, "how can Wilson persuade his people to war when all his persuasion has been for peace?"

Il-han shook his head and stroked his graying beard. "Do you not observe that these Germans mistake his words of peace for words of fear? What is their answer? While Wilson speaks of peace they declare that they will fight an unrestricted war by sea. Is this to be endured?"

Yul-han looked at his father curiously. "Why is it that you, sitting here under this quiet grass roof, are concerned at what happens halfway around the world?"

"I have learned that no grass roof can hide me or any of us," Il-han replied. "We are not like the crabs of the sea. We have no shell into which we can creep. Our ancestors spent themselves and grew frantic and quarrelsome seeking for such a shell. All in vain! The enemy sought us and found us, and we are without shelter or hope unless we become part of the world, as indeed we are, though unknowing, for it is only in the safety of a safe world that we can be safe. Who can rid us of these alien rulers? Not we, not our friends, not even their enemies. We have no hope from any except from all. This Woodrow Wilson is the one man who understands that this is true for his country, too, and in his shadow we must follow. When the war is won, he will prevail, and we shall be given our independence and under his leadership we shall have the freedom we long for and have never had, for all will be free."

His father spoke like a prophet, and like a prophet he looked, the old prophets of another age, of whom Yul-han read in his Christian books. He was silent and reverent before his father. Yet his father and himself were not the only ones. All over the country, in city and village, people gathered to hear someone who could read to them of Wilson, and all looked to that man as their hope and their savior. There was not one voice under heaven except his voice which spoke such words. Others spoke of their own countries but this man spoke of all nations, and they believed in him. Everywhere the people crowded into Christian churches with hope and eagerness, believing that the God to whom Wilson prayed would make him victorious and with his victory would come their freedom again. Indeed, because of Wilson's faith they joined the churches and many thousands became Christian for his sake.

Wilson declared that on the sixteenth day of the fifth month he would speak to his own people, and by now, such was his strength, when he spoke to his own, in reality he spoke to all peoples. Even before this day could arrive, however, the arrogant enemy in Europe sank three great American ships.

Yul-han hastened to his father's house when the news of the ships was told. Il-han was in triumph. His eyes, still black and lively, were bright with excitement.

"Now," he told Yul-han, his left hand slapping the newspaper he held in his right, "now Wilson must lead his people to war."

"Father!" Yul-han exclaimed. "I cannot believe you are a man of peace! Or have you been drinking?"

"I have not been drinking," Il-han retorted. "Hear this!"

He laid hold of Yul-han's arm and held him while he read aloud the words that Wilson had spoken, breaking in with his own exclamations of approval.

"He speaks to the German people, this man—he begs them to turn against their own tyrants. It is as if he spoke to us—to our people. He says—he says—" Here Il-han stopped to find the place with his forefinger. "He says, 'We have no quarrel with the German people. We have no feeling towards them but one of sympathy and friendship. It was not their impulse that their government entered this war. This war was provoked and waged in the interest of dynasties accustomed to use their fellow men as pawns and tools—'" Here Il-han paused to inquire of his son, "Is that not our people? Are we not being used as pawns and tools? He is speaking to us, I tell you—no, wait, there is more— he says—here, he tells the German people, 'We seek no indemnities, no material compensation, we desire no conquests—no dominion. We have no selfish ends to serve.' Is there another man like this one under heaven? No, I swear there is not—And then he goes on, he says, 'There must be a League of Nations, to which all nations should belong, and before which all nations may present their injustices.' There is where you must go, my son! I will go with you. When the war is won we will go to the League of Nations. We will present our cause."

Yul-han was alarmed. He had tried several times to stop the flood of his father's talk and could not. Tears were streaming down Il-han's cheeks, he was trembling, his lips quivered, he was half laughing, half weeping.

"Father, remember the war is far from won. The Germans are in the place of power. It is the last hope that the Americans are now in it too. We do not know—"

"I do know!" Il-han shouted. "I know that this man will win the war for us! When I read his words, I feel my own heart ready to burst. I grow strong again, I am young, I can go to battle myself!"

"I grant that his words are strong and skilled, Father, but words do not win a war."

Il-han was like a child, disappointed. "You are cold," he said passionately. "You are very cold. If Woodrow Wilson is not enough for you, then where is your God, this new Christian God? Is he not Wilson's God also?"

His father had cut him to the heart. "Yes," he said. "He is the same God."

He turned then and left his father's house. This was how it was on that day, and when he came to his own house Ippun met him at the gate. Her round frostbitten face was bright.

"Master," she said, "you have a girl in your house, your daughter."

Yes, Induk had become pregnant again, though neither of them had rejoiced. The times were too hard for children, and it was enough to have Liang, their son. He grew big for his age, a large child, benign, composed and yet radiant. He walked at eight months and talked before he was a year old. Yul-han too often forgot how young he was and spoke to him and considered him as a person. The child loved his father and was happy in his presence, yet when he was away he amused himself easily with whatever he found.

Above all, however, the child loved his grandfather, and

Il-han found such comfort in this as he had not expected to find again in his lifetime.

"Liang, my grandson," he told Yul-han, "repays us for every loss I have suffered." And again he said, his voice solemn, "Liang, my grandson, must never be punished. Whatever he does is with good purpose and with understanding too deep for us."

It was only natural, then, that Yul-han and Induk felt it enough to have one such child. Often, indeed, they doubted whether they knew how to be good parents, wise enough, learned enough, for Liang as he grew to manhood. Again and again Yul-han had been unwilling to think of another child to be born, even while he saw Induk's body swelling as months passed.

Nor did this unwillingness change now as he looked down into the small wrinkled face of his newborn daughter. In silence he knelt beside the bed upon which Induk lay. She looked at him with her delicate air of sadness and pleading, her narrow high-cheeked face as pale as ivory and her eyes long and dark. She had a tender mouth and a high smooth forehead, the combination just this side of beauty.

"Why have we dared to have this child and a girl, too?" Her voice was sorrowful and low.

He knew what she meant. In times like this, in the midst of hunger and gloom and lost freedom, how could they protect a daughter? He had felt his own heritage was unhappy enough, a country beset with quarrels and divisions and threatened war, but at least the country had still belonged to his people. Now they were no better than serfs, and the only ones who were not serfs were traitors who had sold themselves to the invaders. Only the Christians had solidarity in their hope that some day God, in whom they placed their single trust, would deliver them out of the hand of the enemy.

"We must make her childhood as happy as we can," he said at last. "Let us at least give her something to remember."

Induk did not reply and taking her long narrow hand, workworn as it was, and warming it between his own hands, he noticed for the first time how different their hands were, his strong and square, but well shaped as were the hands of his people. Then he laid her hand gently on the coverlet and took the tiny clenched fist of his daughter into his palm. "Perhaps when she is a woman the world will be better and our country free," he said. "Let us hope, for without hope we die."

Spring passed into summer. Across the eastern seas all knew that young Americans were being called from their homes to become soldiers. The Japanese morning paper reprinted the notice:

ATTENTION

Register Tuesday, June 5th

On Tuesday June 5th every male between the ages of 21 years and 31 years, whether a citizen of the United States or not, must register at the nearest voting place in his ward. Registration does not mean liability to military service unless you are a citizen of the United States or have taken out first citizen papers.

The American President himself issued a proclamation which was also reprinted in the Japanese papers:

CALL TO ARMS

Now therefore I, Woodrow Wilson, President of the United States, do proclaim and give notice to all—and I do charge that every male person of the designated ages is written on these lists of honor—

The great sonorous words rolled across the world and announced to the serfs and the slaves and to all who were not free, and to Yul-han himself, that those male persons whose names were to be written on the lists of honor would deliver not only his own people from the danger of invaders, but those who had been and were invaded.

In the church the missionary raised his hairy arms to

heaven and asked God's blessing on America and on the American President and from the thousands of the suppliant congregation of Koreans there came forth like thunder after lightning a great Amen.

... They were meeting in the church at night. In the night, when the lamps of the city were put out and the rulers slept, the Christians stole to the church and sitting in the darkness, listened to Yul-han who read aloud beside a single candle, hidden by a wooden shelter. What he read was news of the war halfway across the world. Japan had seized territories in China; yes, ships were sinking to the bottom of the sea; yes, young men were dying by the thousands, and then by the millions. Britain alone had five million young men dead; yes, but Woodrow Wilson was speaking again to the peoples of the world and the Christians crowding the churches in Korea listened:

" 'The military-masters of Germany who proved also to be the masters of Austria-Hungary, their tool and pawn, have regarded the smaller states as their natural tools and instruments of domination.' "

A long low moan came from the people. "We are also tools and instruments of domination!"

Yul-han read on. " 'Filling the thrones of the Balkan States with German princes, developing sedition and rebellion, their purpose is to make all the Slavic peoples, all the free and ambitious nations of the Baltic peninsula, subject to their will!' "

The people chanted in the same long moan, "We—we are the subjects of others' will!"

Yul-han lifted his head, his voice rang out, dangerous with hope. "Hear further the words of Woodrow Wilson! 'We shall hope to secure for the peoples of the Baltic peninsula and for the people of the Turkish Empire the right and the opportunity to make their own lives safe from the dictation of foreign courts!' "

"Make us safe, too, Woodrow Wilson! Make us safe from the dictation of foreign courts," the people chanted.

All over the world such words were sent by the magic wireless. All that Wilson said was sent, and set in the news of each day's fighting were the messages of Wilson, put on the air as they were spoken and within twenty-four hours heard everywhere, from the mountains of South America to the mountains of Korea. Three hundred newspapers in the vastness of China received the news and told it to hundreds more in the surrounding countries until the voice of Woodrow Wilson was known everywhere and all that he said was believed.

In the midst of winter, as the war wore on, when snow lay two feet deep in the streets burying the frozen dead under its white cover, Yul-han came home one day from his school. It was evening and his mother was waiting for him.

"Come to your father," she said, "he is weeping like a child and I cannot stop him, nor will he tell me why he weeps."

Yul-han went at once across the courtyard and into his father's library. There he found his elder walking up and down the room, sobbing aloud, and clutching against his bosom a crumpled newspaper. Yul-han caught him by the arms and held him.

"Father, what is it that makes you weep?"

Il-han freed himself, he flung out the newspaper. "See this!" he cried. "Fourteen Points—Wilson's Fourteen Points—"

He held the folded newspaper, his hands trembling, and then threw it down. "I cannot read it. You read it—no—let me read this one—this third one." And Il-han read in a loud voice. " 'National aspirations must be respected; people may now be dominated and governed only at their own consent. Self-determination is not a mere phrase; it is an imperative principle of action.' . . . My son—" Il-han folded the newspaper small and thrust it in his bosom. He pointed his long forefinger for emphasis. "My son, it is of our people that he speaks! He knows—he knows!"

The tears of the old come as easily as the tears of children, and Yul-han saw that his father wept for relief upon hope long deferred. Underneath his seeming confidence in Woodrow Wilson he had hidden a deep fear that again an American

President was not to be trusted. Now he could believe. Self-determination—was it not the same as independence?

"Sit down, Father," Yul-han said. "Let your heart rest."

. . . Il-han was not the only one to be overjoyed. Everywhere the people rejoiced in private, and Christians gave thanks in the churches. On the following Sunday such thanksgiving was made in Yul-han's church. He went alone that morning, for Induk had stayed at home to tend her younger child who was fretful and often ill. The day was fair, the mountains clear against the deep blue sky, and Yul-han felt a new cheerfulness as he came out of the church. As usual, beggars waited at the steps leading from church to street, for they had learned that Christian hearts were softer on a Sunday than on other days.

Now as Yul-han came to the street, a beggar stepped forward and caught his coat. Without looking at him, Yul-han reached into his pocket and found a coin and dropped it in the beggar's hand. He went on then and after a few minutes he heard footsteps and turning his head, he saw the beggar again. He waited until the beggar came near to ask why he followed. When the beggar came near, however, he saw the eyes and was silent, wondering. Where had he seen those eyes?

"You do not know me," the beggar said.

"No," Yul-han said, and suddenly it occurred to him that this voice he heard was not the beggar-whine he had heard at the church.

"Walk on," the beggar said. "I will follow, my hand outstretched, as though I were begging."

Yul-han obeyed, much amazed, and the beggar went on talking, his voice low but strong.

"How many years has it been? I cannot blame you for not knowing me. Yet I am your brother."

Yul-han turned involuntarily and was about to cry out Yul-chun's name, when he heard the beggar-whine again—

"A penny, a good deed, master—mercy, good master, to send you on your way to heaven.

"Put money in my hand," Yul-chun muttered. Again Yul-han obeyed.

"Good master, you have given me a bad coin."

Yul-han leaned to look at the coin lying in the beggar's hand and he heard these words: "Leave the gate open tonight—and do not sleep."

They parted, the beggar effusive in thanks and Yul-han as steady as though his head were not swimming. Yul-chun! Of course it was Yul-chun. He hastened home and told Induk, swallowing his words in his haste and then his eyes fell on his son. The child was listening as though he understood, an impossibility, and yet Yul-han fell silent.

. . . Somewhere between midnight and dawn, when the night was darkest, Yul-han heard the gate swing slowly open, not more wide than enough to admit the thin body of a man. He stood in the darkness and he put out his hand and felt his brother's shoulder and he slid his hand to find his brother's hand. Then stealing in such silence that their feet made no sound, they crossed the garden to the house, and Yul-han led the way to a small inner room, a storeroom with no windows, and where bags of grain stood against the walls. Induk brought floor cushions and a lantern and the two brothers sat and talked in whispers.

"I escaped prison two days ago," Yul-chun said.

"Prison!" Yul-han exclaimed.

The light from the candle flickered on Yul-chun's high cheekbones and shadowed the deep-set sockets of his eyes.

"Did you not guess I was in prison?" he asked. "Ever since the trials."

"The Living Reed!" Yul-han said in sudden comprehension. "You were the Living Reed."

"And am," Yul-chun said. He went on to tell his brother hastily what had befallen him since they had last been together.

"But how I escaped—you will not believe it, but a Japanese came to my cell that night. I thought myself doomed, and I spoke recklessly of my dream of independence for our people.

He listened, said nothing, and went away—and I saw the door of my cell ajar."

"What was his name?" Yul-han asked.

When Yul-chun spoke it, Yul-han remembered that it was the name of the young chief of the Bureau of Education who had given him permission to become the head of the Christian school, and who himself had once attended a Christian school in Tokyo. Was there not a miracle here, a Christian miracle?

Yul-chun was urging questions again. "How are our parents? Tell me what has happened in our family—but quickly, brother! By dawn I must be far away."

As quickly as he could Yul-han told him of their parents and of his own marriage and the birth of his children.

A flickering tenderness appeared on Yul-chun's harsh face. "I would like to see your son," he said. "Since I am not to have a life like other men, it may be that only your son will carry on the war for our independence."

At this Induk, still silent, rose and went to the room where Liang lay asleep. She lifted the boy from his bed, and carried him to Yul-chun. The child was barely awake but being amiable and benign by nature, he roused himself and smiled at his uncle at first without much concern. Suddenly, however, an inexplicable change took place. The smile left his face, he leaned forward in his mother's arms and gazed most earnestly into his uncle's eyes. He gave a cry of joy, he reached out his arms and leaned out so far that Yul-chun caught him to keep him from falling. The child clung to him, he put his arms about Yul-chun's neck, he laid his cheek against his cheek, then he lifted his head to gaze at Yul-chun again and laughed aloud, and this he did again and again while Yul-han and Induk stood transfixed in amazement.

"How is this?" Induk cried. "The child knows you! Why, he was never like this, even with us!"

"One would say he recognizes you from some previous life," Yul-han said, and was troubled, for a strange excitement had taken possession of Liang. He was between laughter and tears, he was struggling to speak and had not enough words, nor could Yul-chun soothe him except by yielding to him and holding him close. This he did for a few moments. Then he gave the child to Induk and he strode from the room.

In the dark garden the two brothers clasped hands and whispered a few last words.

"When shall we meet again?" Yul-han asked.

"Perhaps never," Yul-chun said. "But perhaps sooner than we dream. I am going back to China!"

"China! Why there?"

"The greatest revolution in man's history is brewing there. I have much to learn there still—and some day I will come home again to use what I have learned. Have you any money?"

"Yes, I thought you would need it." Yul-han had prepared a packet of silver coins, all that he had saved, and he gave it now to his brother. They parted then, but Yul-chun suddenly came back the few steps he had taken.

"I do not know why Liang behaved as he did, brother, but this I do know. A great soul came into him somehow when he was born. I am no Buddhist, I have no religion, but I know this is no usual child. Respect him, brother. He has a destiny."

With these last words, Yul-chun disappeared into the night and Yul-han returned to his house, his heart heavy with concern over what Yul-chun had said. Yet when he came into the room where the beds were spread on the floor, he saw Liang peacefully asleep while Induk, in her nightdress, braided her long hair.

"Is the child himself again?" Yul-han asked.

"Yes," Induk replied, "except to me he will never be the same again. I know now how Mary, the mother of Jesus, felt. Some day our son will say the same cruel words to me, 'Woman, what have I to do with thee?' "

"Now, now," Yul-han said comforting her. "We are overwrought and we communicated our feelings to the child."

But Induk would not be comforted. "Some dreadful future lies ahead," she insisted somberly.

"We must not run to meet it," Yul-han replied and did not dare to tell her what Yul-chun had said.

Yul-han was a man of quiet prudence and persevering patience. Had the times been as they were before the invaders came, he would have lived the life of a scholar and a country gentleman, his tenants farming his land, his children taught by tutors, and his wife a lady who busied herself only in her house. All his instincts were toward peace. It was revolution enough for him to become a Christian, and he was drawn to that religion because it advocated peace between peoples and kindness between persons and this in a time of war and violence and cruelty. Beyond becoming a Christian he might never have gone except for what befell Induk one spring day.

His small daughter was past a year old, a gentle intelligent child of clinging nature. She could not be separated from her mother, so that wherever Induk went the child was with her, grasping her skirt or holding to her forefinger. When Induk sat down to rest in the house or garden the child was in her lap, refusing even her father. For this reason Yul-han scarcely knew his daughter and he drew his son closer. Because of the difference in the two children, the girl demanding her mother and the boy following after the father, a distance had grown between the parents, imperceptible to both except in small ways. Yul-han in the evening withdrew from the fretfulness of his daughter and Induk's constant preoccupation with her, and he went into his study and his son followed while Induk and the girl sat in the central room. Nor would the girl go to bed without her mother, and Induk must sit beside her until she fell asleep. Then often she herself was weary and went to her bed, too.

Yul-han, drawn to make his son his companion, did so in adult ways. He told the boy his thoughts, he shared his knowledge and together they discussed what happened each day in the nation. The boy spoke of Woodrow Wilson as though the American were his grandfather, and he began passionately to love that distant country which he had never seen. He kept in a box bits of newspapers where he saw pictures of anything American, and he began to visit his grandfather, who once had been to that country.

"Tell me what America is like," he begged.

So he would coax Il-han and Il-han searched his memories and spoke of kindly people and tall buildings and big farms and great cities, and all that he could remember of America went into the fresh retentive mind of his grandson. And Liang, with that love of truth and goodness natural to those born with wisdom, absorbed into his being these qualities wherever they were to be found and he was enlightened from within.

Easily then did the boy come to believe in the greatness of Woodrow Wilson, and his image of this man as he thought of him was of a great kindly presence, someone like the Christian God of whom he heard from his mother and from the missionary, a being alive in a mist of music and brightness and righteousness and all hope and beneficence. Wilson, so he believed in his poet's mind, would come one day out of those heavenly clouds and he would make everyone free and happy. He dreamed how he himself would approach Wilson, with flowers in his hand or fruits. He began to save the best of anything he had for Wilson. If in the autumn he saw a persimmon larger than the others, or an orange more golden than others, or an apple more sweet, a pomegranate more red, he would put it aside for Wilson, however tempted he was to eat the fruit himself, until sometimes Induk would find the fruit rotted and then she would throw it away, reproving him for waste. But Liang never told her why he had saved the fruit. It may be that she was inclined to greater impatience with her son because he was his father's companion, and even, unknown to herself, because he grew so tall and strong for his age, escaping the ills of childhood, thriving on any food, and always quick to learn and understand, and all this in contrast to her sickly daughter. Yet in justice she knew she could not blame the child, for her own indulgence toward the girl was the means of her separation from Yul-han.

She was glad, therefore, when in the autumn once more she became pregnant, for she hoped that a third child would release her from the clinging girl and so mend the division between herself and Yul-han. She was almost three months pregnant when one day she went to the village market to buy fresh fish for the noonday meal while Ippun stayed to wash the family garments at the brook outside the gate, where women gathered for this task. The little girl went with her as she always did, clinging to a fold of her skirt, and slowly they walked to the village. The child grew weary before they reached the end of the road and Induk stooped and let her clamber to her back and she carried her thus until she came near to the market.

There had been some disturbance in the city the day before, but this was so constant that Induk had paid no heed to what Yul-han had told her, which was that some of the students of the Christian school had been arrested a few days before for shouting *"Mansei"* when the Governor-General had passed by the school gate on his way to his palace. This cry was the cry of old Korea, and hearing it the soldiers in the Governor-General's bodyguard fell upon the students and hauled them off to prison on a charge of plotting against the Governor-General. This was such a thing as could happen everywhere in the country and did happen every day and it only added to the rising revolt among the people, a silent smoldering which would burst into flames, if hope became opportunity.

When Induk came into the village she saw that it was swarming with soldiers today, a sight not usual in this quiet place. She argued in her mind as to whether she should not return unobtrusively to her house, but she remembered that Yul-han had especially asked about a fish of which he was fond and which was in brief season now. She walked on then, the child on her back, and as she passed the wineshop from which she had helped Ippun to escape, the wineshop keeper came outside his door to be among the soldiers. His face was red with drinking, although the day was not yet at noon, and he laughed and talked to the soldiers, who had also been drinking. Some could drink and remain themselves, but the peculiarity of the invaders was that drink made them ribald and bolder even than they were when sober.

The wineshop keeper saw his chance now for revenge and when Induk passed with the child clinging to her back he pointed at her with his forefinger and shouted, "There goes a Christian and the wife of a teacher in that Christian school where the students cried out yesterday against the noble Governor-General! I have even heard her cry out *Mansei* herself!"

Upon this the soldiers shouted for the village police who came running. Since police were always Japanese they and the soldiers surrounded Induk there in the middle of the street while the people went into their houses and shut their doors in terror so that they might have no part in whatever took place. Induk was alone then, with the child on her back. Seeing herself surrounded by angry faces, the child began to cry, whereupon a policeman snatched her from Induk's back and threw her aside upon the stone-cobbled street. Other police seized Induk herself and held her hands behind her back.

"Have you ever cried *Mansei*?" a petty officer among the soldiers demanded.

His face was red and his eyes glittered. His short black hair stood erect on his head and he lifted his gun as though he were about to strike her with the butt. Induk was desperate and frightened, the screams of the child wracking her ears, and she did not know what to do. She remained silent, looking from one face to the other until her eyes caught the sight of the wineshop keeper.

"You," she faltered. "I beg you—we are Korean, you and I—"

He laughed loud coarse laughter. "Now you beg me," he chortled. "Now you are a beggar—"

"Take her to the police station," the officer ordered. "Question her and get the truth from her. Did she or did she not shout *Mansei*?"

Induk's heart all but stopped its beat. If she were in the police station where none could see what might happen, then she would be lost. She made haste to confess whatever would help her.

"It may be," she faltered, her mouth so dry she could scarcely speak the words, "it may be that at some time, long ago, before I understood—it may be that I did cry *Mansei*, but I promise you—"

It was enough. The soldiers yelled and clapped their hands and the police seized her and hustled her down the street to the police station. Now Induk was all mother and she fought and kicked at the men and tore their faces with her nails.

"My child," she gasped. "I cannot leave my child here alone—"

The child had run after her, screaming and sobbing, but a soldier seized her and thrust her down to the ground and threatened her with his bayonet. At this Induk was beside herself when suddenly a door opened and a woman ran out and took up the child and ran back with her into the house. Then Induk was quiet. She wiped her face with the hem of her skirt, but before she could speak the police seized her again. They bound her hands behind her back with a strip of cloth and forced her on. In a few minutes she was at the police station, surrounded by men. Terror filled her mind and her body. Her blood ran slow and cold in her veins, her eyes blurred, and her breath stopped in her breast.

As she entered the door of the low brick building a man who stood behind her, whether soldier or police she did not know, stretched out his leg and gave her a strong kick and she fell forward into the room. She struggled to get up but her bound wrists held her down and before she could do more than lift her head a policeman put his foot on her neck and began to beat her with his club. Then he hauled her to her feet and unbound her hands. No sooner had she drawn her breath and smoothed back her hair than the Chief of Police, who had entered the room meanwhile, ordered her to undress. She stared at him, unbelieving. She knew that many times women had been seized thus and made to strip themselves naked, but now that it was herself, she could not move. She only stood staring at him, as though she had not heard.

"Take off your clothes!" he bellowed.

She found her voice somehow. "Sir," she stammered, "sir, I am the wife of—of—a respected man—I am a mother— For the sake of decency—do not—do not—"

With a strange howl the men rushed forward and tore off her garments. She clung to her undergarments but they were torn out of her hands. She tried to sit down to hide herself but they forced her up. She turned to the wall, trying to conceal herself from the many men in the room but they forced her to turn around again. She tried to shelter herself with her arms, but one man twisted her arms and held her hands behind her back and the others beat and kicked her. Bruised and bleeding, she would have fallen to the floor but they held her up to continue the beating until her head fell forward on her breast and she knew no more.

In the village word of what was happening flew from house to house. Among the villagers some stayed in their houses from dire fear, but others gathered in the street in a fury and outrage, and the hotbloods among them were for attacking the police station and rescuing Induk. Others declared that this would only mean that they and their families would next be attacked. After such argument two among them who were Christians were chosen to go to the police station and protest against the stripping of women.

Some hours had passed before this decision was come to, and when the two went to the police station, both old men and near the end of their days anyway, they found no women there. Wherever Induk was, they did not see her. Instead the Chief of Police received them courteously, sitting behind his desk in his office. When they spoke against the stripping of women, declaring it unlawful, the Chief of Police was only cold.

"You are mistaken," he said shortly. "It is not against our law. We must strip prisoners to see that they carry no illegal papers."

The older of the two men spoke up bravely. "Then why do you strip only young women? And why do you not also strip men?"

To this the Chief of Police made no reply. For a long moment he glared at the two old men in their white robes and tall black hats, staves in their hands to support them, and they looked steadily back at him and showed no fear. He turned then to a soldier who stood in the room with his bayonet fixed.

"Show these men out," he ordered.

The soldier put down his gun and seized each old man by a shoulder and led them out. As soon as he opened the door, however, he saw that a crowd stood there, angry and defiant.

"Where is the woman?" one shouted.

"Let the woman come out free!" another yelled.

"Put us in prison, too, or release the woman!" others cried.

Such shouts went up that the Chief of Police rose from his seat and went to the door and made himself stiff and straight and hoped thereby to frighten them into silence. Far from this, they shouted more loudly than ever. He hesitated a moment and then shouted back at them, whereupon they shouted still more so that he could not be heard. He hesitated and then turned back into the room.

"Let the woman go free," he muttered. "One woman is not worth so much time and trouble."

The crowd waited, the two old men standing in front, side by side. In a few minutes two soldiers came out with Induk hanging between them. She was conscious, but she could not speak. Blood had dried on her face and half-clothed body, but under the dried crust fresh blood, bright red, flowed out slowly. A great moan rose from the crowd. A strong young man came forward and took her on his back and carried her away. The crowd followed, the men groaning and the women wailing. Last of all the woman came who had sheltered Induk's child, and so they took Induk and the child home again.

. . . When Yul-han came home at the end of the day as usual, his son with him, Ippun met him at the door, her hand on her mouth for silence.

"Where is my son's mother?" Yul-han asked, for Induk was always at the door to meet him and take off his shoes.

Ippun led him aside into the kitchen. "My mistress was beaten," she said in a loud whisper, her garlic breath at his nostrils.

He stepped back. "Beaten?"

She began the story and he listened, unbelieving and yet knowing that what he heard was true. He did not wait for Ippun to finish.

"What can we do when a decent woman is not safe outside her husband's house," he muttered and he hastened to the room where Induk lay on her bed. Ippun had bound her head and washed her many wounds, and she lay there stiffly, her lips puffed and her eyes swollen shut. He knelt down beside her.

"My wife, my heart, what have they done to you?"

Tears came from under Induk's purpled eyelids, thick tears like pus.

"Tell no one," she whispered.

"Let me fetch my mother," Yul-han urged.

"No one—especially no woman—not even my own mother," Induk whispered.

"Then I must get the American doctor immediately."

So saying, he went again to the city, only stopping long enough before he went to bid Ippun not to tell his parents.

"I will tell them myself later," he said and made haste away.

Neither he nor Ippun noticed that Liang had heard everything, for she was in the kitchen again, feeding the little girl, who clung to her now that the mother could not care for her. When Liang saw his father gone, he went to his mother's room and stood in the doorway, and stared at the fearful sight. This was his mother! He put both hands to his mouth to stop his sobs and then he ran outside and into the bamboo grove and threw himself down against the earth.

First Yul-han went to the missionary and told him what had happened to Induk and then the two went together to the American doctor, and Yul-han told him how Induk was wounded and swollen by blows. The two Americans looked at one another.

"How long can we be silent?" the doctor muttered between his teeth. "Are we not to defend these people whom we came to serve?"

He put his tools together and with no more talk he went to Yul-han's house. Skillfully the American washed all wounds, and he gave Induk a drug to breathe which put her to sleep and he took needle and thread and stitched shreds of torn flesh together again.

While this went on, Liang had come to the door and stood looking in. At first he was frightened, and he covered his mouth with his hands to keep back a cry. Then as he saw his mother peacefully sleeping he tiptoed into the room and came to his father's side and slipped his hand into his father's hand, all this in silence.

When the doctor was finished he saw the boy and smiled at him, and Liang was encouraged to ask a question. He came near and looked up at the American with grave eyes.

"Will you tell Woodrow Wilson to help my mother?"

Yul-han hastened to explain how Liang had made the American President his idol. The doctor listened as he gathered his tools again and nodding toward Induk, who still slept, he spoke to Yul-han.

"Your wife will be well again in a few days but she must rest. Lucky that she did not lose what is in her."

Then he paused for a moment before Liang, who still stood straight and tall and watching all he did.

"Better not to have idols," he said and a sad smile trembled about his mouth as he went away.

Late that evening when Induk was still sleeping under the drug which the American had given her, and while Ippun fed his two children and put them to bed, Yul-han went to his father. Il-han was already in his night garments, and when he opened the door, a candle in his hand, the flickering light spread uncertain shadows and Yul-han saw for the first time how age had gripped his father. All his life he had leaned on his father. Even when he was distant from him because of some argument it was only for a while and soon he came back again. Now he stood irresolute. Should he put his woes, too, on his father's back?

"Come in," Il-han said. "The candle gutters in the wind."

Yul-han demurred. "It is too late."

"No, no," Il-han insisted.

His need was so great that Yul-han could not resist. He came in and Il-han led him into the library and put the candle on the table.

"Sit down," he said.

He sat in his usual place but Yul-han was too restless to sit. He stood, looking down at his father, thinking how to begin so that his father would not suffer shock. Suddenly his throat was caught in such a knot of sobbing that he could not say anything. However he tried to control himself he found his body shaking, his face twisting. Il-han was alarmed indeed. This calm son of his!

"Speak out," he commanded. "Else something will break in you."

The sound of his father's firm voice had its old power over Yul-han now as when he was a child, and abruptly, in jerks and pauses, he told the bare story of what had happened to Induk. Il-han listened, his eyes wide, his lips pressed together, and he did not once interrupt. It was soon told. Yul-han felt the lump in his throat melt away. He was able to breathe. He sat down and wiped his face with his white silk kerchief.

"Father," he said, "I must join the people. I can no longer stand apart."

"We must both do that which we have never done before," Il-han replied. He hesitated, debating in himself whether he should not now tell Yul-han of his elder brother, and then he knew he must.

"Son," he went on, "you spoke of a man who hides behind the name of the Living Reed. That man is your brother."

"I know, Father," Yul-han replied, and went on to tell of how Yul-chun had come to him in the night, and Il-han related the details of the trial that he had seen with his own eyes. He told Yul-han why he had not shared his knowledge with him then, nor even with Sunia, for if she had known she would have found ways of taking food and fresh clothing to him in his prison cell, which might have endangered all their lives.

The night wore on toward dawn, and it was a blessing that Sunia had gone early to sleep, else she would have been in and out time and again to ask why they did not go to bed and whether they would have food or drink. But she slept soundly and they talked on, nor was it idle talk. The two men came slowly to a vast resolution, set firm when Il-han suddenly slapped his two hands on the table before him.

"I will go again to America," he declared. "I will go to see Woodrow Wilson myself. Face to face, I will tell him what our people suffer. He will put a stop to it. He has ways. He is the most powerful man on earth."

Even this did not astonish Yul-han overmuch, in his present mood. He considered for a moment and then had a sudden thought.

"Father, you speak no English! You have forgotten after these years even what you used to know."

Il-han would not be discouraged. "Put it that Woodrow Wilson speaks no Korean! No, no—it will not be difficult to find a young Korean to go with me who speaks both languages. Nothing is easier than to learn a language. It is only that I have no time now to learn again. I must go at once. It is not only for the sake of these here in our own country. Everywhere in the world our exiles are waiting for the day of freedom—two million and more abroad, waiting to come home! A million in Manchuria, eight hundred thousand in Siberia, three hundred thousand in Japan, and who knows how many in China, Mexico, Hawaii and America? America. I go there as an old man, a father. Woodrow Wilson will respect my gray hairs."

"I will go with you," Yul-han declared.

"You must not," Il-han retorted.

"But my mother will not hear of your leaving home at your age to go so far!"

"I allow your mother much freedom," Il-han said with dignity, "but not to decide what duty I am to perform. If evil is to befall me and I die in a strange land, then all the more reason that you, my son, should be here to take my place in our family and our nation. Do not oppose me, my son! The war is near its end. The peace must be carved out for the future. I must have my part in it—why else do I live?"

So the two men came to agreement and Yul-han rose to depart before the sun came up over the wall. The sky was lit already with a rosy opaline light when he bade his father farewell. If they could do all they planned, Yul-han to discover a young man to accompany his father and Il-han to prepare for the journey, within seven days they would be on their way.

"And tomorrow," Il-han said to his son as they parted, "I will tell your mother. It will exhaust me, but I shall not allow her to change my mind."

. . . Yul-han knew the next day that his mother had somehow heard of what Induk had suffered for she came to his house in a quiet solemn mood, such as he had never seen in her before.

"Come in, Mother," he said when she stood in the doorway.

"What of the child?" she asked Yul-han.

Yul-han supposed she spoke of his daughter. "She seems unharmed, and she is with Ippun."

"No, no," Sunia cried at him, "I mean the one not born!"

"She holds it safely in her," he said, and led the way to Induk's bed.

Sunia had never been affectionate with her son's wife, but now she knelt on the floor and gazed tenderly at Induk, her tears flowing down her thin cheeks. She took Induk's swollen hand and held it gently, and she sobbed once or twice before she could speak.

"How is it here?" she asked softly and laid her hand on Induk's belly.

"I shielded myself," Induk said, her voice coming faintly. "I turned myself this way and that when the blows fell."

"To think that we women go on bearing in such times," Sunia sighed.

They said little more, the two women, but in the silence they came nearer together than they had ever been, and Sunia rose after a little while, saying that she was brewing a special ginseng soup with whole chicken broth and when it was done she would bring it.

"Sleep, my daughter," she said, and went away again.

And Induk did sleep, for she could not keep herself awake. Part of her drowsiness was her body's need to escape but part was the foreign drug which the American doctor had left.

Sunia went to the outer door then, Yul-han following her, and on the threshold they paused for a few words.

"Has my father told you what he will do?" Yul-han inquired.

"He has told me," Sunia said.

"Can you bear it?" Yul-han asked.

"No," Sunia said, "but I must."

With this she went away, and Yul-han watched her as she went and saw how bent her body was these days as though it bore a heavy weight, the head drooping and the shoulders dropped. He remembered her straight and slender and her head held always high.

Yet when she was gone, his mind returned to its work. Whom should he send with his father? He cast about for someone he knew and reflecting upon this one and that his mind fixed on his fellow teacher, Sung-man, and he sent word to him by his father's servant, inviting him to meet in the teashop where they had met before. He had pondered whether this was the safest place to discuss dangerous matters, but so vigilant were the police that he dared not seem to do anything hidden. Wherever he might go in secret with Sung-man some spy would discover it, either Japanese or a traitorous Korean.

The servant brought back word that Sung-man would meet him the next evening and so they met. In the midst of the full teahouse, and all the busy noise of men coming and going and servants running everywhere with tea and food, Yul-han put it to Sung-man whether he would go with his father to America. Sung-man, who seemed always careless of everything except his food, listened while he guzzled a bowl of noodles. Without changing the careless look on his face or the careless grin he wore as disguise, he filled his mouth and swallowed two great gulps and then, as though he told a joke, he said that he would go whenever Yul-han wished. Moreover, he could provide the money, for although he himself had no money beyond what he earned, yet he knew where money was.

"Are you a member of that—"

Yul-han put the half question, for he would not say the New Peoples Society, but Sung-man nodded.

"They are also in that country you have named," he added.

The fighters for Korean independence were also in America! Yul-han received this news with surprise and comfort. His father would be among his own countrymen, there would be persons to welcome him and see that he was safe. He looked at Sung-man's silly face with new respect. How much was hidden behind that grotesquerie!

"There remains only the matter of how to leave one place and enter another," he observed.

"You are a Christian," was Sung-man's quick reply. "You can enter through the missionaries," and laughing, as though he was telling a joke, Sung-man lifted his empty bowl and pounded the table and bawled to a waiter to fill it again.

. . . "They can't go straight to America," the missionary said to the doctor.

They sat together with Yul-han in the vestry of the church. He had feared that they would not help him, for he knew the order from their superiors abroad was that they were not to mingle in the affairs of government. Yet these two Americans sat here in homely fashion, talking as calmly as though they discussed a matter of business. Looking from one plain face to the other, hearing the hearty voices, perceiving the good sense, which was their nature, he knew that whatever they were in race and nation, they were his friends and the friends of his people. He listened while they planned how his father and Sung-man would go to Europe and from there secretly to America, and how when they reached their destination, they, missionary and doctor, would see that the two Koreans were met by Christians and taken to private homes. Everywhere they would be met by Christians and sent on to others, and so all was planned to take place immediately.

"How can I thank you?" Yul-han said when he rose to leave.

The missionary clapped him on the back and made him wince. Never could Yul-han be used to such friendly blows, accustomed as he was to the tradition of his own countrymen that one did not lay hands on the person of another.

"We are Christian brothers," the missionary shouted.

Yul-han went home, much moved by what had taken place, and he found Induk able to sit up, although she could not bear to move from her pillows so sore was her whole body. He knelt beside her and sent Ippun away and he told her everything. She listened, and then she put out her bandaged hand and he took it.

"This is why I was put to such suffering," she said. "Out of evil good has come."

He knew she spoke from Christian faith but he was still too new a Christian to believe that it was necessary for one to suffer in order that others might be saved. Yet he would not distress her now with his doubts. Let her have the comfort of her soul, and so he sat holding her bandaged hand.

"The American President is here," Sung-man said. "We are fortunate. He leaves tomorrow for Boston."

Il-han drew a deep breath. All morning he had sat waiting in his cramped room in a cheap hotel in Paris, where he had arrived two days ago from India. They had heard contradictory news. Wilson had already gone, he had not gone. He was failing in the Peace Conference, he was not failing. The Fourteen Points were being changed by the Allies, yet he was fighting bravely. No, he was not fighting bravely, he was allowing himself to be swayed. No one knew what was happening. Koreans, exiled in France as they were in many countries, had come together in Paris, anxious and trying to sift out the truth.

Il-han, listening the night before in their meeting here in

his room, had said nothing until the end when he had heard everything. Then he had spoken firmly and quietly.

"I will go myself tomorrow, wherever the American President is, and face to face—"

He had been interrupted by half a dozen voices. "Do you think we are the only people? Every small nation in the world has sent its people to speak to Woodrow Wilson! And what will you say that they have not said?"

Il-han was unmoved. He felt dazed by the distance from home, he missed Sunia with a dull ache in his breast which he could not forget, he was homesick and ashamed of it, and yet his will held firm to its purpose. He must see Wilson face to face and tell him—tell him— What would he tell him? Sleepless in strange beds raised high from the floor so that he was afraid to turn himself over lest he fall to the floor, he had tried to plan what he would say.

"When I am face to face with him," he had told them doggedly, "I shall know what to say. The words will come of themselves out of my heart where they have long been pent."

So high he looked, indeed so much the noble yangban, that the younger men could say nothing. Sung-man took his part always.

"I know that what our father-friend says is true. He is of the same generation as Wilson and in courtesy Wilson will hear him when he might hurry past us."

They had agreed to meet early the next morning and wait for Wilson in the lobby of the Crillon Hotel, where he was staying. Again Il-han was restless all night until at last Sung-man rose and lifted the mattresses from the two high beds and laid them on the floor and took away the soft hot pillows and laid two books under the bottom sheets instead, and toward dawn Il-han drifted into brief sleep. He woke early and with the urgency of the aged he pressed Sung-man to rise, and so too early they were waiting in the lobby. Yet early as they were, some had come before them. A handful of Polish peasants in their garments of homespun wool embroidered in designs of scarlet were already there, wearing on their heads high hats of black fur. They had brought with them a priest who could speak French, and so could explain that in the new boundaries which had been made by the war, the corner of Poland where they lived had been given to Czechoslovakia, and they wanted their land to be in Poland and not in Czechoslovakia. They, too, in their far part of the world, had heard that the American President was in Paris, he who had said that people should be free to determine for themselves by whom they should be governed. They had lost their way, the priest said, and so they had inquired of a Polish sheepherder, who knew the stars and the way to go. When the sheepherder learned their purpose, he left his sheep and came with them since he too wanted to be free and he watched the stars and pointed out the path. When they reached Warsaw, Polish patriots gave them money and sent them on to Paris and they had come straight down the wide boulevards to this hotel where they were told Woodrow Wilson was staying.

With these Il-han and his fellow countrymen waited, and soon they were joined by still others, all wearing the garments of their own people, refugees from Armenia, land people from the Ukraine, Jews from Bessarabia and Dobrudja, Swedes who yearned to get back the lost Aaland Isles, chieftains from distant clans in the Caucasus and the Carpathian mountains, Arabs from Iraq, tribesmen from Albania and from the Hedjaz. All these and many others who had lost their countries, their governments and their languages now came to the American President as their savior, impelled by the need to pour out upon him their manifold sufferings.

He came at last, the tall thin man, his face desperate with weariness. That was what Il-han saw first as Wilson came through a door, his face, desperate with weariness. He paused, irresolute, he spoke in a low voice to those who were with him. They argued, but he turned and went out through the door by which he had come. A young man spoke to them in English and Sung-man translated for Il-han.

"We are asked to come upstairs to the President's private rooms."

"I will walk," Il-han said. "I will not go up in that small climbing box."

So he and Sung-man went up the carpeted stairs and into a great room. Wilson stood there by a long table waiting for them, and Il-han, pressing toward the front, saw how his left hand trembled. He was very white, the paleness of his face enhanced by his knee-length black coat and his dark gray trousers. His hair was nearly white, too, and his face was lined. But they all pressed forward, and the peasants kissed the hem of his coat and knelt until their foreheads touched the floor.

Wilson said nothing at first and a man spoke for him, asking that each group put its case through its leader, and they would then proceed in order of the English alphabet, and he begged them to speak as quickly as possible for the Peace Conference waited upon the President. They tried to do what he wished and when it came to Il-han's turn, he pressed into Wilson's hand a long paper he had written which Sung-man had translated into English, and he said in his own language, "Sir and most Honored, we have come from Korea. Our people are dying under the invader's rule. Sir, our country has a written history of four thousand years, and we have been a center of civilization for the surrounding nations, surviving all invasions until now. You—only you—are our hope in all this world and for the ages to come."

While Sung-man translated, Il-han looked into the sad blue eyes of an aging man, he saw the firm mouth quiver and smile and the lips press themselves together again. Before he could reply, Wilson stumbled as though he would fall and two young men on his staff stepped forward to support him.

One of them said in a low voice to Wilson, "I hope you won't speak of self-determination again, sir. It's dangerous to put such an idea into the minds of certain races, I assure you. They'll make impossible demands on you and the Peace Conference. The phrase is simply loaded with dynamite. It's a pity you ever uttered it, Mr. President. It will cause a lot of misery."

Sung-man took Il-han aside and translated for him and

hearing it, Il-han felt a misery creep into his heart and his belly. He turned his head to see what Wilson would say. The American's face had changed to a greenish hue and he was stammering in a broken voice.

"I am ill—I'm very sorry—I must be excused—"

His young men caught him by the arms then and led him away. When he was gone blankness fell upon them all. They had been strangers at first, these people from many countries. Then for a brief moment they had been comrades in a common cause. Now they were strangers again.

"Let us go home," Il-han said. "Let us go home."

Yul-han listened in silence as his father told the long story, his eyes upon his father's face. Neither he nor his mother had dared to put into words the great change they saw there. Il-han had left home looking a man of his years, thin as all were thin nowadays who were not traitors, but healthy. Now he had come home an old man. Yet he would not allow anyone to blame Wilson.

"He is wise beyond his times," Il-han declared. "He did not know the world—true, I grant that. He did not know how tyrants rule, and how many long to be free. His dream will shape the world, nevertheless—not for us in our generation but for your children, my son—perhaps for your children. I regret nothing. I looked in his face. I saw a man stricken by his own pity for us to whom he could not fulfill his promises."

Induk was there, and Sunia, and Induk spoke softly. "He is a man crucified."

She was well again but she had lost her calm good looks. Across her neck and face lay a great crimson scar, and Il-han regarded her with a tenderness he had never felt before.

"It has been a lesson for me," he said. "I know now that we must trust to ourselves only. No one will help us."

Induk looked at him bravely. "Father, let us trust God!"

"Ah, I do not know your God," Il-han replied. And thinking the reply too short he added in courtesy, "Ask for his help, if it will comfort you."

. . . While his father had been away Yul-han had steadfastly

carried out his determination to become a member of the New
Peoples Society, but he did not tell Induk. Her nature was
timid and delicate, and the torture to which she had been
subjected increased these qualities in her. She became even
more devoted in her religion, spending much time in prayer,
and she began to visit her childhood home. It was not usual
for a daughter to cling to her blood family, but Induk now
did so, since they were Christian and she found in their
presence a support and strength which she did not find elsewhere. Her father was an officer in his church while earning
his living by a small silk shop. Her mother was a lady of good
family but she had not learned to read until she became a
Christian, and then she made great effort so that she could
read the Christian Scriptures. Since Induk's torture, her family
had doubled their hours of prayer, and in their despair and
terror of what might happen next they became more than
ever devout, beseeching God in constant prayers to save them
and save their country. To know that Yul-han had become a
member of so dangerous a company as the New Peoples Society would have overwhelmed them and he would not tell
them.

This company, as he knew, was spread into many countries and had created centers everywhere to work for the
freedom of Korea. In America a Korean government-in-exile
was in preparation for the day when they could declare themselves free. Secret news of such matters flew around the world
by printed page, by written letters, by spoken words. In
Philadelphia—

"Where is Philadelphia?" Yul-han asked his father.

The time was evening, at twilight, in a day unseasonably
mild for the second solar month of that Christian year, nineteen hundred and nineteen. Four days ago snow was melted
and the buds were swelling on the plum trees. Tomorrow it
might be winter again.

Il-han had taken to smoking a bamboo pipe since his return from abroad and he paused to draw a puff or two while
he searched his memory.

"Philadelphia is a city in the eastern part of the United

States near the sea but not on the sea," he said. "A largish city, yes, but what I remember is a great bell there. They call it the Liberty Bell. I believe it was struck to declare American independence. It stands in a building—a hall named Independence. We were taken to see it."

"Our people in America are planning a great meeting there," Yul-han said. "They are writing a constitution which they will read in that hall in the presence of the great bell. And here we have written a Declaration of Independence. I have committed it to memory and destroyed the paper. So we have been commanded to do. Each of us knows it by heart."

He closed his eyes and began to chant under his breath.

" 'We herewith proclaim the independence of Korea and the liberty of the Korean people. We tell it to the world in witness of the equality of all nations and we pass it on to posterity as their inherent right.

" 'We make this proclamation, having behind us 5,000 years of history, and 20,000,000 of a united loyal people. We take this step to insure to our children for all time to come personal liberty, in accord with the awakening consciousness of the new era. This is the clear leading of God, the moving principle of the present age, the just claim of the whole human race! It is something that cannot be stamped out, or stifled, or gagged, or suppressed by any means.

" 'Victims of an older age, when brute force and the spirit of plunder ruled, we have come after these long thousands of years to experience the agony of ten years of foreign oppression, with every loss to the right to live, every restriction of the freedom of thought, every damage done to the dignity of life, every opportunity lost for a share in the intelligent advance of the age in which we live.

" 'Assuredly, if the defects of the past are to be rectified, if the agony of the present is to be unloosed, if the future oppression is to be avoided, if thought is to be set free, if right of action is to be given a place, if we are to attain to any way of progress, if we are to deliver our children from the painful, shameful heritage, if we are to leave blessing and happiness intact for those who succeed us, the first of all necessary things is the clear-cut independence of our people. What cannot our twenty millions do, every man with sword in heart, in this day when human nature and conscience are making a stand for truth and right? What barrier can we not break, what purpose can we not accomplish?' "

Il-han listened, his head bowed. Over his heart and into his mind a great peace descended. The purpose of his people had been carved clear and plain in stately words.

Days passed and Yul-han was seldom at home in the evenings. He told Induk that he had new work to do but what it was he did not say, and she feared to know and would not ask. She spent her evenings alone, reading the Sacred Scriptures and praying often, her children asleep beside her while she waited for the yet unborn. She kept her candle lighted for Yul-han's return but if by midnight he had not come, she obeyed his command that she go to bed and leave the house in darkness.

He could not have told her where he spent his evenings, even if he would, for he was never in the same place twice. He and his company met in open fields, under the darkness of trees; they met in caves in the mountains, in hidden gullies and behind rocks. He learned to walk in the black of the night, feeling the path with his feet, guided by a star hanging in the east over the dying sunset sky. He learned to know when another human being came near without a sound. He knew what the rustle of a bamboo meant, and how to give no sign when he felt a paper, folded small, thrust into the curve of his hand. He learned not to look up or to speak when a servant in a teashop gave him a message with his pot of tea, or a student in his class wrote words between the lines of an essay. He thought nothing of getting messages from any country in the world where his countrymen gathered their strength into one great dream.

Yet even here in their hearts, single for independence, there was division. One leader was for violence, declaring himself for an armed uprising inside their country, while another protested that such an uprising could not succeed since the invaders were far stronger and they would only make excuse that they were compelled to use force to quell the rebels. No, that leader said, the nation must resist without violence, protest but not by arms, and this protest must take place on some national occasion. This man prevailed, and Yul-han was with him. Prudent he was and wise beyond his years and he, too, believed that an armed attack against the rulers could only lead to defeat.

What occasion could there be? The Governor-General forbade all gatherings of the populace in public places. Even in churches there were always spies present, and Yul-han had more than once been called before the official who had let him be Christian to answer questions as to who was Christian and who was not and whether one Christian or another belonged to the New Peoples Society. He learned to lie easily and without conscience if a life could be saved by lies.

It was the old King who inadvertently came to their aid, and in this fashion. After the great war, the Japanese rulers, foreseeing that Korea would ask for independence, had written a petition to be signed by Koreans, saying that they were grateful to the Emperor of Japan for his good and kindly rule and that they were asking of their own free will to become a part of the Japanese nation. This petition the ruling Japanese had presented to the old King, now deposed, for him to sign. He had shown no courage during these years and his people had all but forgotten him, but, confronted with the heinous sheet, he summoned his strength and refused to sign it. His people were amazed and for the first time they acclaimed him and in his consequent agitation he had an apoplexy and he died. Since all knew he was thin and bloodless and since he had died two days before his death was announced, rumors flew about, one that he had been poisoned, and another that he had killed himself rather than give permission for his son to be married to the Japanese Princess Nashimoto. Whatever the cause, he was dead and Yul-han and his company seized the King's death as an occasion for the announcement of the freedom of Korea. They disputed bitterly as to whether there should be a bloody uprising or a peaceful demonstration of what was now called the Mansei Revolution. The Christians were for peace instead of blood, and among these Yul-han was the leader. Nor were the Christians the only ones who so declared themselves. The sect of Chuntokyo, who believed in a God who was the Supreme Mind, and the sect of Hananim, who combined the Christian doctrine of brotherhood with the Confucian ethic and the Buddhist philosophy, joined with the Christians. These together had written the Declaration of Independence and Yul-han had spent long nights in a dark cellar under a temple, the monks assisting, while he and his fellows printed the Declaration from hand-carved wooden blocks upon thousands of sheets of papers. The sheets were sent throughout the country to every city, village and hamlet, to every farmhouse and every factory, and to Koreans over the whole world. Lovers of freedom in every country seized upon the sheets and treasured them.

And while this work was being done, thirty-three men, fifteen of them Christians, were preparing in secret the day of announcement of independence. In every township they set up a local committee, each committee knit to the next, and this though spies were everywhere. Meanwhile the leaders, in the name of the people, besought the rulers to allow them a day of mourning for the dead King, and the request was finally, though most unwillingly, granted. The first day of the third month was the day allotted and toward that day all worked together. The plan was this: crowds were to assemble everywhere, and the sign, village to village, was to be fires blazing on the mountains as beacons, until over the whole country people were ready to gather at the same hour to hear the announcement made of their independence. Then the crowds were to parade the streets of every city and town and village, waving their national flags and shouting the national cry, *"Mansei! Mansei!"*

. . . Somehow the secret was kept, the instructions carried in loaves of bread, in the coils of men's hair, under their hats, in the long sleeves of women, until every citizen knew that on the first day of the third month, which was the seventh day of

the week, at two hours past noon, all were to gather in their
own streets. The Japanese rulers, still aware of nothing, had
nevertheless feared what might happen, and to every hundred
Koreans over the nation they had appointed a policeman and
had added many hundreds of spies to those already at work.

At noon upon the chosen day the thirty-three signers of the
Proclamation gathered to eat their noon meal together in the
Bright Moon Restaurant in the capital city. As soon as the hour
struck two, they rose and walked together to give themselves
to the police, and this without violence or any resistance.
Among them Yul-han walked first, his steps measured, his face
calm.

The police at first were dazed when the men stood before
them. They hesitated, not knowing whether they should arrest
these ringleaders. In doubt they accepted them, but left them
in a room in the police station, free except for two soldiers as
guards, while they went to ask for orders from their superiors.

"These guards are not necessary," Yul-han told them as they
went. "We have no wish to escape. It is our purpose to go to
prison."

The police were further confounded by such words and
fearing some trickery and shaking their heads, they went on.
Meanwhile all over the nation the people were obeying instructions and the streets were crowded everywhere with singing,
shouting people, waving flags and crying *"Mansei."* But the
thirty-three sat waiting with the two guards for many hours.

At the end of that time the police still had not returned, and
going toward the window, Yul-han saw a strange small commotion. The glass was so clouded with dust that he could not
see through, but as he watched, and he had learned to watch
small signs without speaking, he saw a round place washed
clean, and he saw that this spot was being washed clean by
Ippun wetting her forefinger in her mouth and then rubbing
the glass. To the clean spot she applied one eye and a part of
her face, enough for her to see Yul-han and to motion to him
violently with her finger crooked. The guards by this time were
careless and drowsy, and without sound he went to the door,
tried it and found it not locked and so he went out. It was

twilight and to the east he saw a glow that lighted the sky.

East? Then it could not be the sunset.

"Fire!" Ippun breathed hoarsely at his ear. "They have set the church on fire. Your daughter is there—and her mother—"

He did not wait for more. Through the crowds still milling in the streets he ran, past the bellowing police and the soldiers everywhere beating and berating the people, stooping to crush himself between legs and pushing bodies out of his way. Now he knew why they had been left so long with only two guards. The whole city was under attack. Hundreds of men and women and children were lying in the streets, bleeding from the blows of clubs, dead from the bullets of guns. He stayed neither to look nor to ask. He ran to the church and saw it ablaze. He ran up the steps and tried the doors. They were locked. From within came cries and wailing and yet above all he heard the sound of human voices soaring through the flames, singing the words of a Christian hymn.

"Nearer my God to thee—"

"Induk!" he shouted. "Induk—Induk!"

He remembered the vestry and the little door there that led into the church. That door they may have forgotten to lock! The flames were only on the roof. She might still be alive and he could snatch her out of the fire. He ran through the glittering brightness, the blackening shadows, the clouds of smoke to the rear of the church. Ah, the door was not locked! He was choking and coughing in the vestry, feeling his way to the door into the church. He felt the knob. The door opened and he flung himself into the shadows streaked with wild and livid light. At the same moment he heard a thunder of falling beams, a booming crash and human voices screaming in agony. The blazing roof had fallen in. For one instant he knew, and then he knew no more.

. . . Outside, Ippun waited. Now she saw and she covered her ears with her hands and shut her eyes and ran through the night. She ran without stopping, her arms flailing like wings at her shoulders to speed her way. Through the unguarded city gate she ran, and down the country road until she reached Il-han's house. Still without stopping, stark-mad with fright and horror, she ran into the house where Il-han and Sunia sat side by side. Before them on the ondul floor Liang played with a vehicle he had made from a paper box. He had built wheels to it, and he was working with a broken wheel.

Upon these Ippun burst, her hair streaming down her back and her face a grimace, the wide mouth stretched, the eyes ready to burst from their sockets. She pointed with her shaking forefinger at the child.

"That—that one," she stammered, her voice a high strange whine, "that one—he is all you have left—"

And she fell upon the floor unconscious.

All, all was lost. Before the night had passed, Il-han knew that thousands lay dying in the streets. In every city, town and hamlet they lay dying. Before the days had passed he knew that villages blazed against the night sky and other Christian churches were burned, many with their congregation inside. The deadly stench of roasted human flesh hung about the streets of the capital.

. . . Meanwhile the beatings continued of those who had been taken prisoner. The missionary haunted the streets like a white ghost to prevent what he could, and an American, hired to be adviser to the Japanese, could not restrain his horror though he dared not give his name. What he wrote to his own countrymen and what was printed in America was printed also on the small sheets which Il-han still found under his door:

> A few hundred yards from where I sit, the beating goes on, day after day. The victims are tied down to a frame and beaten on the naked body with rods until they become unconscious. Then cold water is poured on them until they are revived, when the process is repeated many times. Men and women and children are shot down or bayoneted. The Christian Church is especially chosen as an object of fury, and to the Christians is meted out special severity.

Il-han read this as he read all else that was brought to him by his servant or told to him by those who passed his house, and his heart was cold as death itself. His mind knew, but his heart no longer felt. Sunia, too, neither spoke nor wept. She moved about her house slowly as though she were very old, beyond seeing or hearing or feeling. Her only thought was for Liang, and she stayed by him night and day and he was never out of her sight. Ippun, without request or permission, came to live with them, and she did the work of house and garden and they let her.

Some explanation must be made to his grandchild, Il-han told himself, yet what could he say? For the first few days he said nothing. Then he went to Sunia.

"What shall we tell the child?" he inquired.

She looked at him with lackluster eyes. "I will feed and clothe him, but do not ask me to do more."

Yet the matter could not be put off, for Liang began to press.

"Where is my father?" he asked. "Why shall I not go home?"

He forgot to eat, and he sat with his chopsticks loose in his hand.

"When I go home—" he began again and then he paused. "When shall I go home?"

Il-han was hard put to it until he remembered that the Christians believed that all good souls went to heaven, and he seized upon the thought.

"Your father and your mother and your little sister have all gone to heaven," he told the child.

Liang had heard of heaven, and he listened to this with a grave face. "Is heaven far?" he asked.

"No," Il-han said, "it is no more than a minute away."

"Then why do we not go, too?" Liang asked.

"We cannot go without invitation," Il-han said. "When we are sent for, we go."

"Shall I go with you and my grandmother and Ippun?" Liang asked.

"Yes," Il-han said. "We will go together—"

All this he considered a lie, yet the more he considered it the more he was not sure whether it was altogether so. Who knew what lay beyond death's horizon?

"Meanwhile," he told the child, "we will live together."

He had still one great comfort, his secret that now began to spread through the company of the underground, that the Living Reed had escaped. The cell in which he had lived so long was small, it was said, only a little larger than a coffin, the floor of stones laid close one upon the other. Yet one day guards found it empty. Empty? No, for up through those stones a green young bamboo shoot had forced its way!

Among the people the news spread, a ray of morning sun breaking through the darkness of the night, and nowhere was this light more bright than in Il-han's heart. He still had a living son.

PART III

"WHY do you follow me?" Yul-chun demanded.

He bent over the small refractory hand press. It was too old, this press, worn out years ago in an American newspaper office in a country town in Ohio. Without it, nevertheless, the *Independence News of Korea* could not be published. As it was, the sheet appeared irregularly, although he had been able to keep it weekly after the Mansei Demonstration had been put down at the end of the World War. It was well that the press was small for he had to move it from place to place now that the revolution had to go underground again. Only in America could the Koreans continue openly in rebellion against the invaders.

The bitter tonic of anger and disappointment had invigorated him and others like him. When he left Yul-han's house that night, he had not gone to China as he had said he would. Somewhere, by someone, he had been betrayed. As he stepped into the street, he had been seized in the dark by rough hands, and bound. He never saw the face of his captors but he knew by their muttered words that they were Japanese although they spoke in Korean. They had beaten him with the butts of their guns until he was insensible. When he woke he was once more in a cell in an old prison, lying on a floor of uneven stones laid on the earth. He did not know why he was not dead, why they had not killed him. No one was within sight or hearing. He heard no sign of voice or footsteps except that once a day a guard brought a bowl of millet and a gourd of water. He saw nothing of this guard except his hands, sliding open an aperture in the iron door. Slowly he had recovered until he was able to think of life again, and escape. Yet perhaps he could never have escaped had it not been for the

337

madness of the Mansei Demonstration. He would not have escaped then except that the guard, handing in his food as usual, handed in a steel file, and still without a word. A steel file! The guard could only be a Korean, a traitorous Korean whose conscience was moved for some reason. He had taken the file without a word and had compelled himself to eat the miserable food to which he was sternly accustomed. He must have time to think. Was the file a trick to tempt him to escape? Were his murderers waiting outside the window?

Then he had heard, far off, like the surf of a distant ocean, the uproar of human voices. That had decided him. He must chance his escape. He worked all day on the thick iron mesh of the hole in the wall that served for light and air, an aperture too small, one would have supposed, for a human body, but he was bone-thin, a collapsible skeleton, he had told himself grimly, and he had forced himself through it in the night, tearing the flesh from shoulders and hips. Immediately he had lost himself in the swarming crowds and then had hid in a ruined temple outside the city walls, where old and toothless monks were his faithful watchmen. From here he sent out the small printed sheet. Another young rebel, disguised as an acolyte, helped him here in the temple, sleeping by day and at night distributing the sheets throughout the city and to others throughout the country. Others, monks themselves, were also his messengers and his news-gatherers.

On this day, now drawing near its close, Yul-chun was making haste to finish his task, a warning to his fellow patriots that they were to take no heart in the proposals of Woodrow Wilson that there should be a League of Nations.

"If we cannot trust one nation, will twenty be more fit to trust?"

He was setting the type for these words when the girl appeared at the door. He had met her at a secret meeting, a strong slender figure in man's trousers and jacket, and she had followed him from then on, appearing wherever he was, obedient, speaking little, persistent in offering herself to him. He would not have noticed her except she moved swiftly to obey his commands. Today she came in a blue cotton skirt beneath her jacket instead of trousers. She did not speak when he looked up. She was simply there at the door, and he remembered now that he had asked a question and that she had not answered. He straightened himself, pushed back a lock of hair and left a smudge of black on his forehead.

"Well?" he said impatiently.

She came in and stood leaning against the wall, her arms folded across her breast.

"You said you needed someone to help you."

"Not you," he retorted. "Not a woman."

"Man or woman, it makes no difference in our work."

"It makes a difference when it is you."

"Can I help being a woman?"

"You can help pursuing me."

She made her eyes wide at this, great dark eyes, the whites very clear.

"I have chosen you," she said simply.

"I have no wish to be chosen," he retorted. "I have too much to do. Ah, this wretched machine!"

He had worked as he talked, and now the press stopped. Ink ran over the paper in black streams. He tore out the paper, threw it on the floor and set the line of type again.

"I know how to set type," she said.

He seemed not to hear her, absorbed in his task, his mind busy. He had to think far ahead now. The revolution must never fail again. Nothing must be wasted in petty effort, and that it might not, he and his fellow rebels must join with others like them in every country. The mistake had been that here in Korea they had thought they could win alone against their own aggressors. He knew now that they could not. Revolution must be world-wide. Wherever the most immediate need was, there all must attack, until country by country the people were free. Divided, the revolution would always be crushed by the stronger foe. Nothing could be done now in Korea.

"Never hit a Japanese, even in retaliation." Yul-chun had sent the advice into every part of Korea, and he had watched it obeyed. Now was not the time to strike, he had said, and he had seen his fellow patriots tortured and some of them die, but had not lifted a hand to strike back. How long it could go on he did not know. Six thousand fresh soldiers had been sent from Japan. Yet less than two months after the Mansei Demonstration, through his printed sheets he had summoned representatives from every province and they had organized again a secret Korean government. They had elected a president, a young man surnamed Yi. There had been meetings in China and in Siberia, too, to support the secret government. Then Yi had gone to America to meet with Koreans there, but Woodrow Wilson had forbidden his State Department to issue a passport to the Korean, saying that a passport to such a person would disturb the Japanese whom he did not wish to disturb now, since he planned to build peace in Asia upon the foundation of Japanese power.

When this news was brought back to him, Yul-chun had bared his teeth in grim laughter.

"Peace? Can peace be built upon Japanese power politics? War is certain—another world war! It will begin in Germany as it did before, but next time Japan will strike at America."

At this moment he felt her hand on his shoulder. She stood beside him, but he went on working. The sheet was coming through at last.

"When you go to China, take me with you?"

"I am going to Russia."

"I will go to Russia."

"Perhaps I am going to China."

"China, then."

He shook off her hand and stopped the press. "Where I am going you cannot follow," he said bluntly.

"Where are you truly going?" she demanded.

"To many places."

"Where first?"

"To Kirin in East Manchuria. Is that a place for a woman?"

She knew Kirin as well as he did. When the Korean soldiers were disbanded by the Japanese years ago, thousands of them went to Kirin. There they had built a military school to train guerrillas. Since then some had come back, one by one, few by few, to fight in the mountains of Korea and in the city byways. Not only soldiers but many Korean landfolk had gone to Manchuria, a million and more, and these supported the army. Besides these men were those who had gone to China when the Manchu dynasty ended, and they were not a few millions. In every country in the world he supposed there were at least some Koreans in exile.

"I am as woman what you are as man," she was saying.

He ignored this. She was always stressing their difference— she a woman, he a man.

"From Kirin I shall go on foot through China to the center of the revolution now shaping itself in the southern provinces."

"I can walk," she insisted.

"I may even go into Russia, to see what their new techniques are for training the landfolk."

"I have always wanted to go to Russia."

He struck his hands together in desperation. "Hanya!" he exclaimed. "You know that I have sworn never to marry. I have no life to give a woman. I have no home."

"I have not asked you for marriage."

"Well, then love, if that is what you mean! Such love always ends in quarrels and hatred. I have no time for women, I tell you!"

"I am only one woman," she said stubbornly.

He exploded. "I will not have myself weakened and distracted by emotions!"

"You are a man. You have desire—"

"I am a man, yes, but not an animal! I can control my desires and I do."

He looked at her, his eyes hard. "What sort of woman are you that you would force a man?"

She returned his look, her eyes as hard. "I am the sort of woman you men have made nowadays. You tell us we must take our share in the struggle for independence. You say that we cannot be soft, or think of childbearing, or living safely in houses. Yet I am still a woman."

"Is it your need to pursue me?"

"If you do not pursue me, I must pursue you."

"I have told you I will not allow myself to love a woman. If a man loves a woman, whether he marries her or not, he loses his freedom."

"If you cannot love me, then—"

"I am not saying I cannot. I am saying I will not."

He went back to his work. She stood in silence, watching him.

"When are you going away?" she asked after a while.

In the rattle of the machine he pretended he did not hear her, but she knew his silence intentional and she came close to him.

"If you are going away, when will you go?"

"As soon as possible."

"Tomorrow?"

"Perhaps."

She stood looking at him, again in silence. She let her eyes linger on his body, on the straight shoulders, the bare brown arms, the strong neck, his clipped dark hair, his thighs, his brown legs bare beneath his upturned rolled trousers, his feet in sandals—how many miles those feet had walked! She loved even his feet and she could have cradled them in her arms. She yielded to the strange sweet enchantment of his body, the attraction of his flesh. She longed to spring at him as once she had seen a female tiger in the mountains spring at her mate, forcing herself beneath him, but she dared not. He was capable of such rage that he could throw her on the ground and trample her. A deep rending sigh shook her and she turned and went away.

He knew when she had gone but he continued steadfastly at his work. When it was finished he bound the sheets into bundles and hid them behind a corner of the wall. With them he left a printed message, unsigned, that he was going away. He needed to say no more. Someone would take his place. Then he took up his knapsack and strapped it on his back and walked away into the darkness, heading north for Siberia.

He had not been in Russia before but he would be no stranger there. When the Japanese occupied his country many

Koreans and their families in the north had crossed the short boundary between Korea and Siberia. They had been welcomed and had settled on lands allotted to them, or if they were scholars they had gone to Moscow and Leningrad. Koreans had taken part in the Russian October Revolution and in the Civil War and through the disturbances of the intervention. Lenin himself had taken advantage of the Korean struggle against the Japanese invaders, declaring that in Korea the people understood better than the Chinese the necessity for learning the methods of revolution. Yet Yul-chun had never been to Siberia or to Russia. It was his intention now to go there first and to discover for himself at the purest sources what the new Communism was and how it was succeeding. He would learn the techniques and master the logic. In his knapsack he carried Karl Marx's *Das Kapital* and a copy of the *Communist Manifesto,* and Lenin's *State and Revolution,* all translated into Korean. This was not to say he had any love for Russia or Russians, but simply that now when Japan was the enemy, it was time to make Russia a friend. Long ago Taiwan-gun had played the same game, hating both countries meanwhile. Reflecting upon history in the long days while he walked and in the lonely nights when he slept in a village inn or under a mountain rock, Yul-chun remembered well that twice in his lifetime Russia and Japan had met in secret to divide his country between them at the 38th parallel, and they had been prevented from announcing such division only because they feared the Americans and English.

He walked by night and slept by day until he reached the high mountains. Then, as the danger of meeting Japanese soldiers and spies grew less, he walked at dawn and after sunset, sleeping through the small hours under some rock. His was a country of mountains, four-fifths of the land area in high terrain, and he loved the heights. To rise when the first pale light broke over the lofty crests still black against the silvery sky, to breathe in the mists from the gorges, to hear the splash of waterfalls and the echoing voices of singing birds, cleansed his mind and renewed his spirit. Alone as he was, stopping near a house of a village only to buy food, he could not but remember Hanya, however unwillingly, and he reflected upon his relation to her. That there was a relation he could not deny, although he had never so much as touched her hand. Yet a man cannot hear a woman declare her love for him without knowing that a relationship is established, and this though he will not allow himself to respond or indeed wish to respond. He had a strong natural desire for women, and this he knew, but he would not yield to it. He had remained virgin in spite of much teasing and ribaldry among his fellow revolutionists, who took women wherever they went and left them behind. Sejin, for example, who was like a brother to him, had often argued women with him.

"It is dangerous for you to continue a virgin," Sejin declared. He was a tall slim young man from a seacoast village, and he could swim in any sea and dive deeper than any woman abalone diver. "You are defenseless, you saint among men! You are afraid of love, but the only defense against the one great love is women-women-women! To have many makes it impossible to have only one. It is the one who is the tyrant. If you have many women they are all your slaves, rivals, and therefore eager to please."

"Not so," Yul-chun had replied. "A single love may be a tragedy but it is not a day-to-day, bit-by-bit destruction."

"Ah, you innocent," Sejin had retorted. "I agree that we should not marry. None of us should marry when we have a revolution to make. But it is not we who are destroyed, it is love that is destroyed. I daresay I could love one woman and write poetry and live obsessed, as you will do if you are not careful, but my safety is that when I think of many women, I lose the possibility of the one—and the dream. Thus I keep my freedom. You still dream, and even your dream enslaves you."

Yul-chun had listened but remained unchanged, reflecting that it was Tolstoy who decided his mind and gave him strength to deny all women, even Hanya. He had been inspired by Tolstoy and when he discovered that Tolstoy had created his greatest novels only when he had ceased to occupy his time and his energy with women, he had determined to renounce women from the first. Why waste any part of his life? Nevertheless, he was too honest not to acknowledge to himself that in spite of resolution he found himself curious about women and what their place was, however he might decide that they had no place in his individual life. In the society of the future it was scarcely sensible to believe that a woman could be allowed only to do the slight work of her own household and her own few children. The problems and labors of the times were immense, and was it just that all solutions and labors should devolve on men while women were permitted to busy themselves with the small affairs of single households? But why was he thinking of women? He would not think of any woman. Since he had sacrificed everything for his country, he would also sacrifice desire.

. . . He walked northward through the mountains to Antung, a city at the mouth of the Yalu River but on the soil of Manchuria. Here he planned to rest for a while and learn of what was taking place in Russia before he made the long journey northwest. Since Antung was a city where many travelers met, he would hear news. He arrived at Antung in early summer and found many Koreans there, some in families eking out their livelihood as petty merchants and traders, but most of them solitary men like himself, restless and searching for a means to free their country. All advised Yul-chun against going to Russia.

"Go to China," they told him. "The revolution is finished in Russia. In China it is only beginning. The Chinese leader, Sun Yat-sen, has invited Russians to help him, since Western powers have refused him help, and you will see their tactics. We Koreans are more like the Chinese than like the Russians."

He followed this advice and after staying long enough in Antung to learn what he wanted to know, he packed his knapsack again and went deeper into Manchuria. In Manchuria he stayed with the escaped soldiers, and found them not dismayed by the failure of the Mansei Demonstration. Instead they were training themselves for the next world war, which they said was surely coming, for Japan was making ready to conquer China now while confusion was increasing in that country. A great new revolution, they told him, was shaping itself like a thunderhead out of the south.

"Sun Yat-sen needs an army," they told Yul-chun, "and Russia is training Chinese soldiers for him. When all is ready they will make a second attack, marching along the Yangtse River to the southern capital of Nanking and then they will seize the country and set up a new government."

Yul-chun listened to this and much more, and then without telling anyone where he went he headed south again to China.

. . . It was nearly winter before he reached Peking and there he was halted by a fierce storm, the wind blowing out of the cold desert and driving the snow in drifts along the country roads. Half frozen and his money gone, he was compelled to stay for a while in the city and he sought out the Koreans he had once known and who had fled there. Most of them were gone, some killed in the south, some killed or in prison in Korea, but he found one whom he had known, a monk who came first from the Chung Dong Monastery on the island of Kanghwa and later had gone as a mendicant monk to the Yulin Monastery in the Diamond Mountains.

The monk was also a Kim but not of Andong and he remembered Yul-chun from earlier days when they had worked together in their own country. Now when Yul-chun stood at the door of the small, poor house where Kim and his fellows lived in the Chinese part of the city, they cried out in joy each at the sight of the other.

"Come in, come in!" Kim cried. He shut the door quickly to bar the great drifts of snow that blew in with Yul-chun. "Say not one word until you have taken off those wet garments," he went on, "and I daresay you have had nothing to eat all day."

"I am empty as a bag," Yul-chun confessed, "and a penniless beggar besides."

As he changed into dry garments and ate the hot noodles that Kim prepared, they talked, exchanging news and hopes. In the year of Mansei, the young monk had become a member of the Monks' Independence Movement, and with his fellows, some three or four hundred, they too had printed a declaration of independence. He had traveled among villages, wearing his monk's robes, but when he came to the capital he was too late for the day of Mansei, and he was seized by the police and put into prison for a year. When he was free again he went on with his work. While he was in the capital he fell in with the young men and women who were reading Russian books, and so he read Karl Marx, for which Hegel, he said, had prepared him.

Last year, with seven fellow monks, he came here to Peking so that he might learn more about revolution, but after a few months, five of the seven monks returned to the monastery, where they said life was more pure and more safe than among these revolutionaries.

"What shall we do now?" Kim asked.

Yul-chun, remembering his printing press, made reply. "We must publish a magazine."

"There has been one called *The Wild Plain.*"

"We will make no poetry," Yul-chun said bluntly. "We will call ours *Revolution.*"

Long into the night they talked and they ate again and at last they went to sleep. Before he slept, however, Yul-chun made up his mind that he would stay in Peking at least for a time and return to his best loved work, that of creating new literature for the revolution, his home here with his fellows. For this he needed only a pallet for bed, and he had in his knapsack his lacquer rice bowl and the silver chopsticks and spoon which his grandfather had given him a hundred days after he was born. He was happy again, safe among his kind, and he set himself to his chosen work.

"You make yourself blind!"

The sound of Hanya's voice struck a blow across his brain. His hand, holding the chisel, hung motionless above the stone. He did not turn his head, but he knew that she was crossing the brick floor, though her straw-sandaled feet made no sound. She came to his side and snatched the chisel from his hand.

"They told me you were doing this stupid thing," she cried. "Do you imagine yourself a god? Can you make miracles?"

"Give it to me," he muttered between his teeth.

He put out his hand to take the chisel from her but she held the tool behind her back.

"I would not believe it when they told me," she went on with the same passion. "'He is making himself blind,' they said—'writing the magazine with his own hand, all of it,' they said, 'and then carving the letters into stone—'"

"I am compelled to use lithograph because I can find no printing press in the city, at least none that I can buy," he retorted.

"So you will be blind because there is no printing press in Peking that you can buy!" she mocked. She threw the chisel on the floor and took a magazine from the table of rough unpainted wood. "Thirty-two pages! Twice a month! How many copies?"

"We began with eight hundred, but now we have more than three thousand. It goes to our own country, but also to Manchuria, America, Hawaii, Siberia—"

"Be quiet!" she cried. And stooping she took up the chisel, and walking to the door she threw it as far as she could into the street.

He was too surprised to move, not imagining that she could do such a thing. Then he sprang at her and twisted her out of his way but she clung to him and would not let him go. Try as he would, he could not rid himself of her. Arms about his neck, legs around his thighs, she clung, catching his arms when he flailed at her, kicking him when he pulled away. They fought in silence, their breathing hard, their faces set in angry grimace, their eyes furious.

He was shocked at her strength. Passive he had always said women were, passive and negative, weak frail creatures at best, but this woman he had to fight as though she were a man. He paused for a moment to get his breath and she seized the instant to wrap her arms around him under his shoulders and then he felt her teeth bite into his neck.

"You—you tiger," he panted. "You—you—dare to—"

"Your blood tastes sweet on my tongue," she murmured against his neck.

And he felt her lips soft against the spot where an instant

before he had felt her teeth. He stood motionless, suddenly aware that she was no longer fighting him. Her body relaxed, she lay against him, yielding, her face in the curve of his shoulder. She was drawing him down slowly, gently, and he felt his head swim. She reached out her hand and between thumb and finger she pinched the wick of the candle by whose light he had been working, and they were in darkness. In darkness she drew him down until they lay on the floor, she beneath him. His whole body was warm and fluid, his will gone, his entire being one swelling urge toward her.

. . . This was the story of their love thereafter. He yielded to her and he fought her. When she insisted that he must stop printing the magazine he declared that he was by nature a writer, and never so happy as when he wrote, and he was fortunate that the revolution needed writers. He insisted that he would never yield to her and daily he did yield to her until in desperation he decided to leave Peking and go south again. This he did because she told him one day that she would have a child.

He forbade her to come with him. "There will be war," he told her. "It will be dangerous for you. And I must not be hampered by a pregnant woman. I would think of you instead of the battle."

They had been living together for more than a year, here in Peking and in villages of North China and Manchuria to which they wandered from time to time, but he had never ceased to believe that it would be better if he were alone and to tell her so. When she said that a child was coming, her black eyes soft with joy and her whole being radiant, he felt a strange new anger against her, a surge of love mixed with hatred, and he cried out now, against her joy.

"You know I said we must not have a child! You use this trickery to compel me to think of you—you and the child—you divide me! I am to pity you and the helpless child. You make a triumph of it."

She heard this, her eyes wide, and she looked at him as though she had never seen him before. "You are not a man," she said, her very voice wondering. "I have not wanted to believe it, but now I know. You are not a man, and I have loved you, thinking you were a man, believing that in your heart you loved me."

She studied his angry face, dwelling upon its every feature. "How I have loved you," she said, still wondering.

And with these words she turned and left him standing there in the room which for this short time she had made into a home.

. . . He waited for her through twenty-three days and nights and he could not believe that she would not come back. When day passed into night and night dragged endlessly toward dawn again, he began to understand that she was never coming back. Then he had himself to battle. He longed for her. He yearned to go in search of her. He dreamed of taking her with him to Korea to his father's house and staying with her at least until the child was born. He had told her of that house and of his family. Lying quietly side by side in the night after they had made love, she had often asked him to tell her about his childhood. She asked him of every small thing, as though she herself had lived in that house.

"Did you sleep in the room next to the kitchen, or in the one next your father?"

"We spread our beds in whatever room we wished," he explained, "but never in my father's room. My tutor slept with my brother and me, after we no longer needed a nurse. My brother was a good child, but I was not good."

She laughed when he said that. "You are still not good!"

"Yet it is I who am alive," he retorted, "and my poor brother is dead." For Yul-chun knew, as all Koreans knew, how his brother and Induk had met their end, and with them their daughter who would not be separated from her mother and so Induk had taken her to the Christian church that day.

"Prudent and careful and good, it was he whom they killed," Yul-chun now reminded Hanya. "You see why I say a man should not have a wife and children?"

"Be quiet," she told him.

It was her usual rejoinder when he said what she did not like to hear. It had come to such a pass of love between them that what he had once said seriously he said at last in play, for he believed she knew that he loved her although he would never tell her so. Part of the play, or so he thought, was her pleading to be told and his refusal.

"Tell me you love me—tell me only once so that I have it to remember!" This was her plea.

"I will not," he always replied, "for if I do, I have no defense against you. You will get so far inside me that I shall never be able to root you out. Words are like iron nails hammered into hard wood."

"You do love me?" she coaxed.

"What do you think?" he asked, biting back the words that would say he loved her.

"I think you do," she said in the same soft voice, "and since you do, why not tell me so?"

"Ah ha," he had cried, "you nearly caught me, but I am too clever for you."

So he had never said he loved her and now she was gone and he could not tell her if he would. He waited seven days more, sleepless with longing, his body demanding her presence, but he would not yield to his own demand. If he went after her, then he would never be free again. He rose one night in the small hours, desperate with weariness and longing, and he packed his knapsack and set out for the south on foot and alone.

. . . He traveled three thousand miles, on foot and on horseback, and lived through many months before he reached the city of Canton in South China. He lingered here and there on the way to see how the people lived and whether there could be reason to expect revolution, for he was too just by nature to believe that they should be compelled, nor would he allow himself to use these Chinese land people to strengthen the cause of freedom for his own people. He was not able to make up his mind as he walked the country roads and passed through villages and slept in small inns. The people were a cheerful, cruel people, accepting hardship and dealing hardly with any whom they thought unfriendly, too gay for suffering, although they spoke robustly against the times, grieving that they had no ruler in Peking now that revolutionists had destroyed the imperial throne.

"Oh, that we had our Old Buddha again," they told him. "She was our father and mother. While she lived, we knew we were safe. Now who knows what will happen to us?"

They spoke of the Empress Tzu-hsi. She had died many years ago, yet such had been her power over their minds and hearts that he came upon villages where the people did not know she was dead and when he told them, they were afraid. The difference between the Chinese and his own people was that the Chinese were still free. If they had no government, as indeed they had not, for Sun Yat-sen with all his followers had not been able to set up a new government in the vast and ancient country, at least the people were free to govern themselves according to family tradition and habit, which they did, so that the country was at peace except for the war lords battling among themselves for a chance to rule, and the revolutionists who were young and full of discontents. In spite of all, the land people farmed their fields and the sea people caught fish, and the river people lived in boats, crowding the canals and rivers and the coastal towns. He doubted much that the vast continent and the countless people could be roused to revolution or indeed whether they should be roused. Their lives were stable in custom and tradition and they were not starving and no one oppressed them except here and there a greedy landlord. He heard laughter and lively wit in the teashops where men gathered, and children were fat, and women were busy. Against whom then could they rebel? They asked only to be let alone, and more than once some old man or young would quote to him the ancient saying of Lao-tse, that the governing of a people was like the cooking of a small fish, it should be done lightly.

The further he traveled the more he marveled that one country could be so vast and contain such variety in landscape and people. Desert in the north and northwest spread into rich plains, and here the fields were wide and the land people grew wheat and dry crops and they ate wheaten bread and millet and they were tall and fair-skinned and they reeked of garlic, for the favorite food of the countryfolk was a thin sheet of un-leavened bread rolled around stalks of garlic. The northern cities were busy with shops of every kind, the markets plenti-ful and the streets wide. The people wore cotton garments, in winter padded with cotton, and if one wore silk, he covered it with a cotton outer robe.

In the central part, above and below the Yangtse, a river as wide as a sea for a thousand miles, where steamships of many countries came and went and foreign warships kept watch at treaty ports, the country grew mountainous, but not as his country was. Here the mountains were green and gentle and the valleys were spread in fertile plains between. The people were tall but not so tall as those in the north, and there were many cities, richly crowded with shops. The people were less simple, too, than those of the north, indeed they were often crafty and worldly, even shrewd, but they were gay and full of talk and laughter, the women lively and free in coming and going as they liked, except for the ladies in rich men's houses who stayed inside their walls.

One whole winter he spent in the city of Shanghai, for here he found some three thousand Koreans gathered and he soon made a place for himself among those who printed a magazine called *Young Korea*. Yet again he discovered his compatriots divided, and this time into two main groups, those who still favored Americans—and these were for the most part Chris-tians and educated in the United States, and believed in non-violent revolution—and the second group who were for the Russian method of revolution and were all for direct attack against the Japanese now ruling in Korea. Both groups re-ceived money secretly from Korean patriots in Korea and the exiles elsewhere.

Yul-chun lived at first among those who still believed in Americans, and from them he learned much that he had not known of those people who had befriended his country through their missionaries and then had betrayed it through their politicians. He hated them for the betrayal, but as he learned of them through the leader of Koreans who had spent many years in the United States, it was not the history or the nature of the Americans that moved him to relinquish some of this hatred. Instead he was moved by their songs. While he was in school in the United States, this leader had learned many songs, especially the songs of the black people who were slaves there, and he had returned to Korea with these songs in his soul and had taught them to schoolchildren. Now, exiled in the vast, heartless city of Shanghai, he taught the songs to his fellow exiles. In the evenings as they gathered in the shabby room they had rented as their meeting place, these Koreans sang the songs of the African slaves in America.

Yul-chun at first refused to sing, partly because he did not know the songs, but also because he feared anything which might soften his heart so that he could feel pain. Yet in spite of his determination, his heart did soften as he listened to the voices of his fellow exiles, singing the mournful music of slaves. He was haunted by the melodies in the songs, "Old Black Joe," "Carry Me Back to Old Virginny," "Massa's in the Cold, Cold Ground." Melancholy music, tragic words, which somehow comforted their sad hearts, and one night Yul-chun found himself weeping as he sang.

This weeping frightened him. He had not wept since he was a child in his father's house and he had long believed that he could never weep again, for he had seen too much of torture and danger and death for weeping. He resolved that he must put such music far away from him, knowing how music could seduce his people. And to this end he left these exiles and joined the terrorists, a small secret group here in the city who had dedicated themselves to killing and destruction.

It was not the first time that Yul-chun had been with them. His childhood tutor, the gentlest of men, who had trained him in the nonviolence of Confucius and in the merciful compassion of Buddha, when he joined the Tonghak, had become the most reckless of terrorists. It seemed that this kindly and mild young man was compelled to make a sacrifice of himself, and again and again he had committed the most ruthless acts. He had emigrated to Siberia and had formed the terrorist group called The Red Flag, and from there he had gone to Manchuria to take part in the assassination of Prince Ito, after which he himself was captured and put to death.

Now in Shanghai Yul-chun approached the second terrorist group, the Yi Nul Tan, or Society of Brave Justice. He was with them but not of them—not yet. He could not as yet commit himself wholly to death and destruction as the only weapons of revolution and especially when among these single-hearted young men he found division. For in this winter of the Christian year 1924, the Society of Brave Justice was split into three parts, Nationalist, Anarchist and Communist. He watched this division with growing cynicism, and the more because the most violent of the terrorists were also the most corrupt as men. They wore western dress, they oiled their hair, they made a cult of their appearance, and since most of them were tall and handsome young men, women sought them, and among these the most passionate were women of mixed Russian-Korean ancestry, the daughters of exiled patriots in Siberia.

One night in early spring Yul-chun walked in the park in the French section of Shanghai where the exiles lived, and he saw how these members of the Society of Brave Justice made rendezvous there with the women, how boldly they exchanged the acts of physical love, how wild these exchanges were and how promiscuous and how quickly forgotten. The fires in his own flesh were strong enough to be stirred and he could understand how young and desperate men, daily face to face with death, were compelled to find relief in brief and violent passion. But this was not his way. His eyes were on the goal of independence for his people and a wise and sensible plan for life. It was time for him to be on his way again, therefore, and he left Shanghai before the spring grew warm, and went south again.

. . . He arrived back in the city of Canton in the autumn of the year, at the time of the rice harvest. The fields were gay with cheerful harvesters, the crops were good and food would be plenty for the winter. Again he doubted that these Chinese people could be stirred to rebellion unless there was a war from outside, which was to say unless Japanese military men again dreamed their dreams of empire. Then he reminded himself that he was here for a greater cause than this. He was here to find those who could help him make Korea free.

. . . "You have come at last. And alone?"

This was Kim's greeting and question. When Yul-chun had given up the magazine at Hanya's insistence, after he had been ill with a heavy cough, Kim had left Peking in some disgust because, he said, Hanya had spoiled Yul-chun for a revolutionist. With several others he had come to Canton, they had rented two rooms in a house which was in a narrow crooked street where workers in ivory lived and plied their crafts. Tusks of ivory came whole from the jungles of Burma and Malaya and were sold to the craftsmen, who cut them and carved the pieces into ivory gods and goddesses and figures of men and women, into boxes and jewelry and every sort of object for use and beauty. Among these many families the exiles came and went unnoticed, all wearing Chinese dress.

"Alone," Yul-chun replied.

He threw down his knapsack and shook off his worn sandals. The soles were in shreds and he had a stone bruise under his left instep. He sat down, nursing his foot in his hand, while Kim stood looking at him.

"Did she leave you or did you leave her?"

"She left me," Yul-chun said shortly. "And I did not go after her," he added.

"You look hungry," Kim said next.

"I am not hungry," Yul-chun replied in the same short voice. "I have been well fed all the way, especially in Shanghai."

"Then you have another hunger," Kim said, laughing. "Easily satisfied, comrade! Though how you could leave Shanghai with that sort of hunger—but we have many comrades here, too."

"Who could believe you were ever a monk!"

Yul-chun nursed his painful foot as he spoke, and looked about the bare room. "Can you put a few boards on two benches for another bed?"

"I have been expecting you," Kim said. "I have kept space

for you here. No woman could satisfy you forever. I knew that I had only to wait."

"How many Koreans are in Canton?" Yul-chun asked.

"Only about sixty," Kim replied, "and they belong to the Yi Nul Tan."

"Again! I have only just left them in Shanghai."

"Russian advisers here are teaching them new methods, and it may be we shall need them in our own country when the time comes."

"I have no confidence now in terrorists," Yul-chun retorted. "They enjoy their work too much—and they leave fury behind them."

"We can use them," Kim said. He was dragging his bed to one side of the room and arranging a place for the other bed.

"Have you joined the Communists?" Yul-chun asked.

"Yes! If I am a revolutionist, let me be complete! And you?"

"No. I must be convinced that it is the best means for getting independence."

"You cannot know until you become Communist yourself. Faith first, and then conviction."

"That is the difference between us. You must have a faith. Not I! I have no faith in anything or anyone. And I am convinced that the Japanese will never be content with our small mountainous country. What they have been saying ever since the time of Hideyoshi is still true. For them Korea is only a stepping-stone to Asia. And now that I have seen China with my own eyes, the richness of its soil, their great cities, the skills of its people, I am convinced that whoever holds China holds Asia—and perhaps some day the world."

He spoke with eloquent energy, and Kim listened, enchanted. "You should talk instead of write!"

But Yul-chun was not finished and did not hear. He went on, his eyes blazing his thoughts. "Who can prevent this island dream? Who but us, an independent Korea, blocking the aggression? Who else sees the danger? China is no more than a watchdog, what has she done to prevent Japan? What has any other power done?"

"You should be a terrorist, my friend," Kim said. "You would make a good one."

And he rose and went to the open door and stood looking out into the growing darkness.

Behind him Yul-chun sat in silence. Then, overcome with exhaustion sudden and profound, he threw himself on the bed.

. . . "The real war," Yul-chun complained to Kim, "is the war we wage among ourselves."

For Yul-chun, after only a few months, discovered that the Korean revolutionaries continued here the feuds they had brought with them from their own country. Those who believed in terror were against those who believed in nonviolence. Those who came from the north were against those who came from the south. Some were Communist and believed that only a total change in ideology could save their people; some were against Communism, saying that an ideology was only an obstacle when independence was the goal. Those who had come from Manchuria separated themselves from those who came from Korea and both were against those who came from Siberia. Beyond such internal division among his compatriots, Yul-chun discovered the enmities between the sects and clans and the Chinese groups, especially the single-minded Chinese Communists who, under their Russian advisers, felt that they should control all, and were cruel to those who did not follow them.

"We destroy ourselves," he continued despondently.

They worked all day at their chosen tasks, Yul-chun again at writing and printing, but at night he and Kim and many others gathered in a large old teashop which they had rented for their meetings. The numbers of exiles grew daily until now hundreds had come to join the Chinese revolutionaries. In a few months there were eight hundred Koreans alone, some four hundred from the Army of Independence in Manchuria, a hundred and more from Siberia, and the rest from Korea. They were all young, under forty years of age, and some as young as fourteen and fifteen. Among them a lad named Yak-san attached himself to Yul-chun, and the two became friends. This boy had put aside the name his family had given him and had chosen the name of a famous terrorist, Kim Yak-san, who had once tried to kill a Japanese Governor-General in Seoul, by the name of Saito. According to legend, the terrorist had borrowed the garments and the mailbag of a follower who earned his living as a postman. In the bag he hid seven bombs and on a day when he heard the Governor-General was to meet in his office with other high Japanese officials, he went there and threw the seven bombs into the room. The officials had already left, but the bombs destroyed much of the building and other Japanese were killed. Meanwhile the terrorist disguised himself again, this time as a fisherman, while the police looked for him in every part of the country. After a few days he escaped to Antung and from there he went to Manchuria.

When the lad Yak-san heard Yul-chun's family name he went to him eagerly.

"Sir, are you Kim of the Kim Yak-san?" he inquired.

"I am not," Yul-chun replied. "I am a Kim of Andong, and I am not a terrorist."

The lad's face fell, but he stayed with Yul-chun, nevertheless. For Yul-chun, Yak-san was like the younger brother he remembered in his father's house, and for Yak-san, Yul-chun was both elder brother and father. Yak-san's father, the boy told Yul-chun, had been killed by police in a northern city of Korea. He was an only child and, left alone, he had joined others who escaped to Manchuria where he heard the story of the terrorist. With the terrorist he went as far as Shanghai where he had lost him.

"He did not love me," the lad said bravely. "He told me not to follow him, and when I said I could not help it, he moved to another part of the city and I could never find him, though I tried for many days."

"He could not love anyone," Yul-chun said to comfort him. "He was afraid that if he let himself love he would not be able to kill."

The boy looked thoughtful for a while. Then he spoke. "May I follow you?"

"Certainly you may," Yul-chun replied.

Now in the teashop he sat beside Yul-chun on a low stool and listened to all that was said.

"We must achieve unity, at least in the core of our group," Yul-chun went on. "We should gather together those who believe in unity as we do and make the core."

"And thereby create only another clique," Kim retorted.

"To be a terrorist is most simple," Yul-tan, the present leader of the terrorists, announced.

"When you have killed everyone," Yul-chun argued, "what will you have? Terrorists who will then begin to kill one another!"

"Nevertheless," the terrorist maintained, "we are the most unified of all the groups. We agree among ourselves that all our enemies must be killed, one by one if necessary. Houses must be burned, palaces destroyed, governments overthrown, armies deceived."

As usual, they talked far into the night. Indeed, there were times when Yul-chun believed that talk was their chief occupation. Yet through the interchange of thought and argument slowly, as form is shaped from stone, he perceived that a certain unity was built.

After a year of such argument and still against his doubts, Yul-chun at last accepted the terrorists as the center of this unity, since they were the only ones who agreed upon one simple principle of action, that of destruction, and it might be true that destruction there must be before construction could take place. He would not accept them without compromise, however. He demanded that the terrorists promise, for their part, to give up their name of Yi Nul Tan and take instead the name of Korean National Independence. Through this core of unity Yul-chun maintained connection with all other Korean independence groups in many countries, in preparation for the day when their country could be free. That day, it was now finally agreed, could only be after the next great world war, already appearing upon the horizons of time.

He might have grown a heart as hard as stone during these years had it not been for the lad Yak-san, and two others, a man and wife who worked together in the group. Yak-san followed him like a young faithful servant, listening to what he said, obeying his every wish, and watchful that he ate his food and drank tea when the day was hot. Unwilling as Yul-chun was to allow himself to feel emotion, yet he could not but be touched by the loyalty of this lonely orphan boy. Something of the old family feeling stirred in him again and he wondered if his own child had been a son. He would be beyond babyhood now, a boy of four years. Had Hanya told him who his father was and who his grandfather? He had never heard of her since she walked away that day in Peking, he had not received a letter, nor did he know where she was. He might not have thought of her except that among those with whom he worked there were also these two, husband and wife by the name of Choi, who taught him unwittingly by their devotion what love could be between man and woman. Both were Korean, the woman a young widow whose old merchant husband had been killed on the day of the Mansei. The man was the son of a landowner, and he had been in the streets and part of the battle when he came upon the young woman, trying to lift the body of her dead husband. He had helped her, and together they brought the dead man into his house, and later he helped her to find a burial place and to buy a coffin. When the funeral ceremonies were over, he asked the young widow if she had loved her husband and she had said simply that she had not, but she wished to do her duty to him nevertheless. He asked if this duty meant that she would always be a widow and she replied that she would like to love a man. Moreover, she had no family by marriage since her husband's parents were dead and he had been an only child. Nor had she children, and her own family had moved away to Siberia. She had begged her husband to go there, too, but he had refused, saying that since he was only a merchant and his business good, it was not likely that he would be mistaken for a rebel. On that day of his death, however, he had been so mistaken and a Japanese soldier had shot him through the head because he went into the street to see where the crowds were going.

All this Choi heard with lively interest and when she had finished he asked her if she could love him. She had looked at him thoughtfully, his tall frame, his handsome head and brilliant dark eyes, and then she said that she thought she could love him. He took her by the hand and led her away and they were married by the new code and had remained together in perfect happiness ever since, living first in Siberia and Manchuria and then coming south to help the Chinese.

These two, as he saw them always together, persuaded Yulchun into new reflection upon marriage and he allowed himself to remember Hanya and to wonder about her. In his desire to remain free he had asked her nothing about herself. Whatever she had told him had come from her in the few times of peace between them. At night after love, she had curled herself against him and out of her quiet would come now and again fragments of her memories.

"Such peace as this I used to feel when I climbed the mountain behind my father's house," she told him. "To climb, to climb, and then to reach the crest of the mountain and know I could go no higher—that was peace. I lie on my back upon the rock and I gaze into the blue sky. Up there the sky is very blue."

He listened and did not hear, drowsy with his own peace.

"My father was shot," she said one day.

She was making *duk*, a steamed bread such as one could not buy in Peking. He had been impatient when she spent time on such cookery, but now he remembered with a reluctant tenderness how she had bought glutinous rice and pounded it to flour and steamed it in a sealed jar, and then pounded it again and rolled it out and cut it into circles which she filed with sweetened crushed beans, and how carefully she had brushed each cake with sesame oil. He had complained when she brought the cakes for him to eat to celebrate a holiday, but she had laughed at him.

"You eat them—you eat them," she had exulted.

"My stomach is stronger than my will, and that pleases you but it does not please me," he had retorted.

He had blamed her in his heart because this was, he

thought, another of her wiles to imprison him in a house and home. Only later did he recall that she had said her father was shot, and he was about to inquire of her how it had come about, and did not for fear she might bind him to her through sympathy and her need for comfort. Her father had been some sort of official in the Regent's court, that he knew, for she had a seal that had belonged to him, a piece of jade carved in Chinese letters giving his name and rank, and she kept this jade with her, tied in a square of silk. She had two brothers, he also knew, for sometimes she spoke of their games together in a large garden somewhere and how she was stronger than they, and this made them angry.

"I am too tall," she sighed.

When he had not replied to this, she looked at him side-wise, her beautiful eyes longing.

"Do you not think I am too tall?" she had coaxed.

He denied his own impulse to lie. "I have never thought of it," he said.

Now with time and distance between them, he wished that he had told her the truth, that she was not too tall, since he was the taller. And one day, consumed with longing for her, he asked his old friend Choi if marriage was not a hindrance to him, and hoped to hear him say it was.

"Not only in matter of time that a woman demands," Yul-chun added, "but in matter of the occupation of a man's thoughts, the division in him between devotion to his country and to her."

Choi laughed. "You spend more time thinking about women than I do, I swear! No, my brother, when you have a woman of your own, you no longer think of women. You do not think even of her. She is simply yourself, in you and with you. She makes you free. Moreover, she shares your work, if she is the right woman. Then, to, it is pleasant to have your clothes clean and your food cooked, and she takes care of your money so that it is not spent foolishly. You are always better off when you have a good wife."

Yul-chun put such replies in his heart and slowly his heart changed his mind and he ceased to resist the thought of

Hanya. Some day, he even thought, half dreaming, he might go north again and find her and his child. Not yet—not yet, whatever his longing, for he must stay by the revolution until in triumph he and his comrades entered the imperial city of Peking. Then he would return to his own country, for with their help, whom he had helped, his people too could be freed.

He saw Yak-san grow from a child to a youth, hard and brave and ruthless. The young were always ruthless, and Yulchun saw himself again in Yak-san. At fifteen Yak-san had a new hero, the terrorist Wu Geng-nin, who led the attempt to kill the Japanese General Tanaka when he came to Shanghai to continue his plans for empire after he had written the memorial of demands upon China. The terrorists had arranged for attack from three directions as Tanaka came down from the ship which brought him from Japan. Wu was to shoot him with a pistol. If he failed, Kim Yak-san was to attack with a bomb. If the bomb did not kill, a third terrorist, He Chun-am, was to hack him with a sword. An American woman passenger, however, came down the gangway before Tanaka and when Wu fired she became afraid and grasped Tanaka. He, seeing what was happening, pretended to fall dead, and Wu, believing he had killed the enemy, turned to escape. He leaped into a taxicab but the driver would not drive him, and Wu threw him into the street and tried to drive himself but not knowing how to drive, was arrested before he went far by British police, who gave him to the French, since he lived with the other exiles in the French concession, and they in turn gave him to the Japanese. He was locked in a tower with several Japanese, one of whom was an anarchist. A Japanese servant girl pitied Wu and brought him a steel knife and he cut the lock from the door and with the anarchist he escaped to the house of an American friend who hid him until he could get to Canton to tell his story.

The young Yak-san sat at his feet, not only for the sake of Wu himself but because his other hero, Kim Yak-san, had been part of the plot. Wu was kind to the youth, and unknown to Yul-chun, he argued for terrorism to Yak-san, so that Yak-san's heart was divided between the two men who befriended him.

In the next year the founder of the Chinese revolution, Sun Yat-sen, died in Peking and all revolutionists were cast into deep sorrow and gloom. Yet what could they do but persist in what had been planned? With Russian advisers an army was built under the headship of a young soldier, Chiang Kai-shek, who came back from military training in Japan and Russia.

A second revolution was soon in readiness, its armies trained to march north to the Yangtse River and proceed down that river to Nanking where a new capital was to be set in the heart of the ancient city. Yul-chun, now detailed to make translations of Marxist books from the Japanese, began to doubt more and more whether the Chinese revolutionists understood fully the hardships that lay ahead if they were to fulfill this dream of conquering their vast continental country. Their people were still firm in old ways, they were not yet discontented enough for revolt, and finally tradition took the place of government. They were poor but they did not know it. Their landlords oppressed them but not to despair, or if to despair, they rose up and murdered the landlord with knives and pitchforks. Yul-chun perceived that his own countrymen understood reforms far better than the Chinese revolutionists did, because of the long oppressions of the Japanese in their own country, forcing Koreans to rebel, and because many young Koreans had been educated in Japan, where they had learned of anarchy and Karl Marx.

In an early spring the Second Revolution set forth on the journey northward, Kim, the ex-monk, still irrepressibly full of optimism and faith in mankind, among them.

"We will help our Chinese brothers, and then they will help us," he told Yul-chun as they packed their knapsacks.

Yul-chun could only smile. His faith in the Chinese was dim, and he was no longer an optimist even about revolutions. On the last night before they were to leave the city he did not take part in the meeting of celebration. Instead he went to see three foreigners. One was an English labor leader, Thomas Mann by name though he was not related to the German writer. He was an old man, cheerful and in the loneliness of age affectionate with all the revolutionists whatever their group. Now when he saw Yul-chun at his door he took him by the arm and drew him into the small room which was his home.

"Come and have a cup of tea," he coaxed. "Good English tea with a bit of sugar and milk. And I've some Huntley biscuits from England."

Yul-chun sat down on a chair beside the small iron grate of coals. He drank the English tea which reminded him of Tibetan buttered tea he had drunk in Manchuria, and he listened for an hour to the old man's rambling, casual talk of how the English people had achieved independence under their own kings. "Killing a king only when absolutely necessary, you know," he said, chuckling. "In an odd sort of English way we rather like them, you know! It was our own government, after all, and we shaped it into a democracy. It wasn't easy— Have another biscuit!"

Yul-chun, his school English taught by Americans, was puzzled by the strong English accent, but he could follow, and so he was moved to trust the benign old man, at least to trust his good heart, if not his mind, invincibly hopeful in his old age.

He was not so sure of the American, Earl Browder, whom he next sought. He had heard him make speeches against American imperialism and while they were clear and easy enough to comprehend, and were much applauded, yet Yul-chun felt an instinctive distrust of a man who accused his own government while he was in a foreign land and among foreigners from many countries. He watched Browder as they sat together in a hotel room. The man had the look of a scholar, but scholar or not, Yul-chun resolved never to trust an American again. As for Borodin, whom he visited last, this man was a short, stocky Russian, middle-aged, slow in speech, practical. He looked like a successful businessman rather than an ardent revolutionist, a man with a mind for organization, a father to the young enthusiastic childlike men whom he led.

The youthful Chinese trusted this Russian, but for Yul-chun trust in any Russian was impossible. Too long Russians had been on Korean soil, too many plans they had laid for possession. Yes, the Czar was dead, but did a country change its soul because it changed a ruler?

He returned to the room he still shared with Kim and found that Yak-san had finished packing his knapsack for him and had gone to bed.

. . . What might he have become, Yul-chun sometimes wondered, had he not kept within himself the smoldering fire of his hope that some day he would find Hanya and return with her to his own country? He dreamed how it would be, and he set the dream into words for Yak-san sometimes, when they were encamped before battle. When others slept and he kept himself awake from duty, he would talk to Yak-san thus:

"When all this weary fighting is over, when the cause is won, then we will go home, you and I, to my father's house. Somewhere on the way we will find my wife and my son, and together we will all go home. First we will rest a few days, say for a month, and then we will take up war again, but for our own and in our own country."

Home was now the word that held the dream, and he would not let himself think of it except at such times or in the night after the day's bitter warfare. For the year was only one long war. He was proud of his countrymen. They fought with dashing bravery and dauntless leadership. They were eloquent in persuasion of the landfolk and city dwellers among whom they marched and the Chinese generals sent Chinese-speaking Koreans first to prepare the way. The new revolutionary army swept northward, victory upon victory, they reached the Yangtse River in central China, and still victorious, marched on to Nanking.

Then they were betrayed. Their leader went past the city, leaving it to his second in command, while he went with his own army to Shanghai in secret to set up a counterrevolutionary government. The news came at the very hour of this triumph, when the city gates were battered down after three days of siege, and the city taken.

It was not to be believed. They looked at one another, unbelieving. They gathered in crowds in captured buildings to talk. It was true, nevertheless, and when they were compelled to believe, the armies retreated up the river to Wuhan, there to set up a government of their own, and with them went every Korean exile, except those who were killed in battle.

But Yul-chun began to draw apart from the revolution. He knew that sooner or later he must leave the Chinese. Cruelty —cruelty was what drove him away, and hardened though he was, he was not cruel. He saw Chinese killing Chinese, "purges," they were called, but for him purges were murders, young men, young girls, accused by rightists of being leftists, landfolk and merchants accused by leftists of being rightists. In one day, in one hour, within the space of a few minutes, he made the decision. The day was hot, the air humid and heavy, and the men were as quarrelsome as angry bees in midsummer. A mighty battle was looming, for the great city of Changsha was next to be taken. All were anxious and discouraged as they faced battle for, although the Russian advisers had directed every battle, the revolutionary army had not won a victory since the split in Nanking. Moreover a young revolutionist, Mao Tse-tung, rejected by the Communist Party because he had declared that Russian tactics would not serve in China where the mass of the people were landfolk and where there was no true proletariat, this man now came forward and declared that no battles could be won without the help of the landfolk. Scholar and peasant, according to Chinese history, he declared, could overthrow a dynasty, but separately they could never win a battle. He predicted failure in Changsha, and this frightened the revolutionists while it angered the Russians.

Alas, the prophecy was fulfilled. The men fought bravely, but they could not prevail against the landfolk who swarmed in from the countryside in all four directions to aid, not the revolutionists who announced themselves as their saviors, but the old magistrate and all his court. Many revolutionists were killed, among them not a few Koreans, but this alone would not have changed Yul-chun's mind. What compelled him was that in retreat to the northwest the revolutionists in angry despair grew mad with despair and they fell upon any hapless peasant who came into sight.

Thus Yul-chun saw before his own eyes the monstrous murder of an entire family in their own farmhouse. Innocent and prudent, they had stayed at home and barred their gate. The retreating men paused to rest, and seeing that the farmhouse was larger than most, they beat on the gate. The family within hesitated long enough to draw a few breaths, wondering, doubtless, whether they should pull back the bar. In that instant the irritable anger of the men burst forth. They broke down the gate and swarmed into the house and destroyed it utterly. The old grandparents they hanged from the beams of the roof, the peasant and his wife they shot and butchered, the young daughters were raped by many men and left bleeding and dead, the sons were cut to pieces in savage joy, except for one small boy, whom Yul-chun saved, and in this fashion.

He had at first tried to prevent the men by reasonable persuasion, but the soldiers were beyond reason and their ears were deaf. He stood helplessly by, and yet he forced himself to stay, for he must know what these men were with whom he had cast his lot. He must know the worst, for what they did now they might do again and again if ever they came to power. Thus he saw the full horror of what they did and what they could do. Cruelty was in their blood and being. Suffering, perhaps, had made them cruel, but cruel they were, whatever the reason, and as he saw, he changed. No, these too were not to be trusted, and all the fine talk of saving the people could not make him trust them. Whatever the government, it could be measured only by the quality of the men who administered it, and these men could not be good rulers.

"Come," he said to Yak-san who had stood near him, taking no part but staring his eyes out while he watched.

They were about to turn away when a child fell at their feet, an infant boy, naked and bleeding, tossed there on the point of a bayonet by some soldier. Yul-chun stooped and took the child into his arms and ran, Yak-san following, and in the noise and madness none saw them go.

"What to do with this child!" Yul-chun exclaimed to Yak-san.

"We must leave him with some farm family," Yak-san suggested.

This they did that same evening. They came to a small quiet village beyond the range of battle, and Yul-chun, asking for shelter for the night, told the story of the child to the villagers as they sat on their benches around the village threshing floor in the cool of twilight. When he asked if any one of them would accept the child, a young farmwife came forward.

"Look at me," she said, pointing at her bosom. "My breasts are dripping full of milk, for my own child died two days ago of the ten-day fever, and there is no one to drink my milk."

Her jacket was wet with the milk overflowing from her bursting breasts, and she took the child and let him suckle.

Those were the years of a strange imprisonment. Mountains were the walls of the prison, and they, the vanquished, were the prisoners. At first Yul-chun fell into an empty despair. What could be useful to him in this wild region? He was cut off from the mainstream of the revolution, even from life itself, and far beyond the reach of the underground messengers with whom until now he had maintained connection, however infrequent. Nor was the despair only his. The remnant that was left of the revolutionary armies after the long march north sank into a desperate weariness of mind and spirit far beyond the fatigue of body. Weeks and months passed and in the bitter cold of the winter they did little beyond forage and beg for food and fuel. They sheltered themselves in a deserted temple, they built huts of mats and scraps of wood and tin, they lived in caves, they slept by day as by night to preserve their feeble strength.

So it was until spring came and brought renewal and awakening. They began to stir, they looked at one another in a daze, they went out to find green weeds for vegetables, and to mix with the millet which was their chief food. And Yul-

chun was the first to come to himself. By luck he had found
shelter with a Chinese farm family, as poor as any; the house
had two small rooms shared with the ox, two pigs, and a few
hens. Poor as they were, they had a lively interest in Yul-chun
because he came from another country and he whiled away
the long dark days when snow fell by telling them stories of
his people and telling them, too, of all that had taken place
here in their own country, of which events they were altogether ignorant, since they could not read, nor, had they been
able to read, were there any newspapers.

Yet Yul-chun was amazed by their wit and intelligence, and
it seemed unjust that they were compelled to remain ignorant.
He conceived a purpose then to teach them to read. Out of
this came a people's school, for once he taught the one
family, many others clamored to learn, men, women and
children, until he found himself the head of a school, a lowly
one, for there were no books and he wrote his lessons in the
dust of a threshing floor. Their eagerness was such that many
soon could read simple words. Then he found there was
nothing for them to read. He was compelled to write small
books for them, a few pages in each, and through these little
books he was able to teach them the doctrines of better ways
of living, and how to govern themselves according to the
revolution.

The joy of the people when they found they could read and
even write a little became the source of new inspiration for
Yul-chun and all his companions. New policies were made,
new plans, based upon the people and their cooperation with
the revolutionary army. And the people were ready and
eager.

"You have opened our eyes," the elder in a village declared.
"Whereas we were blind, now we see. The wisdom in books
is now our possession."

By this means a strong unifying interest in the villagers took
hold and the leaders of the revolution learned how to win the
people, who in turn fed and supported them.

"We help you," an ardent farmer had shouted. "We help
you for you are the only ones who have ever helped us." Then

he cursed and swore against the rulers they had had, and spat into the dust to show how he despised them.

In this way time passed swiftly for Yul-chun. One year followed another, until one day he knew he must find his way home.

"We must travel alone," he told Yak-san that day. They left the friendly village that night and the next day they went on, by foot and by horseback, until they came to a railroad where, by following the tracks, they came to a station and so entrained for Peking.

The scent of pines hot in the August sun mingled with the scent of incense in the small room where Yul-chun sat at a table, writing. A cicada burst into rasping song, mounted to a crisis of midsummer frenzy and exhausted sank into quiet. From some distant place in the temple the monotonous chanting of Buddhist priests provided an atmosphere of peace in contrast to the statistics which Yul-chun was compiling for record. The Korean exiles, what were left of them, lived here while they waited out the years and watched for the hour when they might return to their own country. This was Yul-chun's room in which he slept and worked. Yak-san shared a room with three other young men, but Yul-chun, because he was now considered among the elders, had this cell to himself, a pleasant place opening upon a narrow court on the edge of the mountain. Beyond the pine tree tops the mountains rolled down to the plains and in the distance were the walls of Peking.

He returned to the counting of the dead, their names, the places where they came from in Korea. He counted not only these who had died in China but the many who had been exiled in the long struggle for independence since the Japanese came to Korea: in the Christian year 1907, seventy thousand men of the Korean army scattered and forced into exile; in 1910 more than a million Koreans driven across the Yalu River and wandering to Siberia and China and Manchuria, and countless others in Europe and the Americas; in Korea itself in 1919 after the Mansei Demonstration, fifty thousand prisoners and seven thousand killed; in Japan after the great earthquake of 1923, five thousand Koreans, one thousand of them students, massacred because some had said that the earthquake was punishment on Japan by the gods for the crimes committed in Korea; in Manchuria in 1920 more than six thousand Korean exiles killed by Japanese troops there; and three hundred Korean terrorists killed by Japanese in Shanghai; of the eight hundred young Koreans who joined the Chinese revolutionaries in Canton, almost all were now dead, two hundred in Canton alone, and in 1928 in Korea, the Japanese killed one thousand young men in Korea as Communists, although less than half of them were Communists. Yet who could count or even know how many Korean exiles had been killed in Siberia under the Czars, in China under war lords, in Japan, and even by the French and British in Shanghai! And who could know how many had died in prison cells under torture or with minds deranged! Who knew, who could ever know, the loss Korea had suffered in these, her best and most brilliant young men, who only asked that their country be their own!

Yul-chun put down his pen. Yak-san was at the door with his noonday meal of vegetables and rice, for in the Buddhist temple no meat was eaten.

"I have news," Yak-san said, putting the tray on the table. He leaned to whisper. "The Japanese will seize Manchuria within ten days!"

Yul-chun dropped the chopsticks he had taken into his right hand.

"We must leave here tomorrow," he exclaimed. "We must be out of Manchuria before it belongs to Japan. I must know what will happen to our own country if—"

He broke off and went to the door and stood gazing across the mountains and the plain.

"Elder brother, your food is growing cold," Yak-san reminded him after a few minutes.

Yul-chun did not turn. "Take it away," he said. "I have no appetite. The entire world will be at war once more before long, if the news you have brought is to be trusted."

They left as soon as Yul-chun could prepare others to take his place. Kim, the ex-monk, had long been his aide and to Kim he entrusted all that had been his own responsibility. The few Koreans who still remained gathered around him as he prepared to leave. All were homesick and yearned to go with him, but they would not.

"It would be unthankful if we were all to desert our Chinese comrades now," Kim said, "before their war is won. Remember that we said we would stay until they entered Peking in triumph. Alas, the world war must be won before we can hope for that victory."

"I will go home first," Yul-chun said, "and I will tell you when you must follow. I will find out how matters are in our country and, if war comes, what we must do."

With these words, Yul-chun bade them farewell and took up his knapsack and went down the mountain, Yak-san following.

On the long journey toward the north, which they made on foot or horseback since Japanese had seized all trains, Yul-chun had many days and nights in which to review these years during which he had lived among Communists, had known them well, had believed in their honesty of purpose and in their devotion, and many he still thought of as friends. He had not regretted leaving the Chinese Communists, but he wished now to distinguish between Communist and Chinese. The Chinese could be very cruel and for that reason he had left them. But need Communists be cruel? In the coming divisions of a world war, Japan and Russia would become even more bitter enemies than in the past, and if Japan were on the losing side, Communists would be on the winning side, and they would become strong in his country. He trusted no one, but must he distrust Communists? Evil men there were among them, yet these were punished and cast out when found. Some were even killed. In Canton he had sat in tribunal more than once to try a comrade who had betrayed them by dishonesty or by personal cruelty and oppressive behavior. He had more than once raised his hand to signify his approval of the death sentence and though he had never fired the last shot, he had stood by to see it done. Nor had he refused to take part in the judgment of greedy landlords and evil magistrates and conniving tax gatherers. These, too, he had judged worthy of death and he had seen them killed and he had remained silent. He had even shouted the slogans of the Party, LAND FOR THE PEASANTS, FOOD FOR THE POOR AND THE WORKERS, PEACE FOR THE SOLDIERS, and he had helped to write the principles agreed upon by the Sixth Congress of the Comintern to establish a government to be called a Workers' and Peasants' Democratic Dictatorship.

He was walking side by side with Yak-san in the even swift stride that had become habit. The scent about them was one of peace. Autumn had come, harvests were gathered and the fields, quiescent in waiting for winter, made an ordered pattern, broken only by the low thatched roofs of villages where the landfolk lived and had lived for thousands of years. The immense land spread of China and Manchuria belonged to these folk. Even the landlords knew in their hearts that the land was not theirs in truth, whatever the purchase price. And landfolk could be cruel. Unless Communism made them gentle, they could be very cruel.

"The scene is peace," Yul-chun said to Yak-san, "but there is no peace. I do not speak of the battles among war lords in China but I speak of the war of centuries. Do you remember the young man who was killed in Hailofeng, the one I tried to save?"

"I remember," Yak-san said. "We were the same age."

They said no more, for they had learned in the dangerous years not to speak if silence were more safe and they had become taciturn by habit. But Yul-chun remembered. The landfolk of the region had that day brought to the revolutionary court of judgment a young man of handsome and frank countenance. He wore the ragged garments of the poor, but the landfolk accused him of disguise.

"He is not one of us!" they had shouted. "Look at his skin —like a woman's! He is as white as a foreigner. Surely he is one of our enemies."

Yul-chun, who that day sat in the court, had taken pity on the young man. It was not too hard to see old men killed whose faces told the story of their evil lives and he had learned to watch such deaths, impassive and silent. But this man was young and intelligent and one who could perhaps be won to the revolution. The landfolk, however, were implacable.

"He is our enemy," they insisted.

"Do you know his name?" Yul-chun had inquired.

"His name does not matter," they had replied. "He is our class enemy."

And they clamored for his death.

When no hope was left, two women, one older, one younger, came from the waiting crowd, also dressed in poor garments. It was easy to see that they too were not landfolk. Each took the young man's hand, right and left, and side by side the three walked to the wall of execution and there all were shot. Of the many whom he had seen thus killed, Yul-chun could not forget the faces of these three, kindly and intelligent and pure. Now the memory came freshly and he allowed himself to wonder whether the revolutionists had been wise in following the Communist pattern. Alas, it was too late for China to decide but for his own country there was still time. And he remembered what Kim had told him of the retreat to the northwest. Kim and the remaining Koreans had marched with the Chinese Communists until they heard that Yul-chun was in Peking, and they left the Chinese there and gathered in the temple. Days and nights they had talked, telling Yul-chun all that had happened.

The Chinese Red Army had fought bravely, they had suffered starvation and sickness, but the Nationalist troops had outnumbered them a hundred to one again and again. Only when the landfolk began to help the Red soldiers with food and clothing and new straw sandals were they able to escape from constant defeat. Their great mistake at first had been to meet the enemy in battle. Face to face they had always lost.

They had lost count of time in days of danger and suffering and hunger, in nights when they halted beside river or brook and washed their wounds and buried their dead. They had been forbidden to rob the landfolk of food as the enemy did, and yet they starved if they did not, or begged. They had eaten sweet potatoes roasted in coals or boiled in soup, they said, until never again would they willingly eat sweet potatoes. And what of the days when they marched through heat and long grass, their blood drained by huge mosquitoes, so that they were weakened for months thereafter by the chills and sweats of malaria, for which they had no remedy! They took off their white summer garments lest they be seen by the enemy and crawled on their hands and knees, and they dared not cough lest the sound betray them to the hovering enemy. They slept by day and walked by night and they learned to sleep as they walked. There were days upon days of which now they could remember nothing except that they waked in the house of some merciful peasant, hidden in a village whose name they did not know, and then they walked again. Sometimes they found fellow Koreans and again each was alone and lost among the Chinese. Many they never saw again and they thought them dead.

"I thought Kim was dead," one said, "until once on a city street my hand was clutched and I knew I felt Kim's hand although I could not recognize the face I saw!"

Here Kim broke in. "I saved myself by lying under the water of a rice paddy, only my nostrils above water, and thus I hid for several days."

The long march was ended, the Chinese Communists were in the far northwest, the Nationalists were in Nanking. But none of this was important now, in Yul-chun's mind. He had left it all behind. He was going home. Home! The word, so long unused, summoned Hanya again. It was time now to find her, to find their child, and take them with him, home.

Yet so committed was he that he could not prevent himself from lingering on the way to set up people's schools here and there. His way was to find one man or boy who could read a little, or if he could not read, possessed a good intelligence, and teach him how to teach others, and so begin a school.

To the landfolk, he said, "This one is your teacher, but if he is to teach you, then you must find him shelter, and two suits of clothes, one for summer, one for winter."

This they were willing to do, and so wherever Yul-chun went, he left behind him centers of hope and enlightenment, small indeed, but each a light in the surrounding dark of ignorance. His journey was lengthened by years beyond what he had planned, and often in the lonely nights he reproached himself for delay. Yet he could not harden his heart against these eager, good landfolk of China, whom none had heeded or helped for a hundred years. And so he lingered and so he stayed, chafing and longing all the while to be on his way.

It was more, too, than love of his own people and his own country. He was no longer a youth and in the lonely nights he thought of Hanya and their child. In each place Yul-chun made inquiry about her. Few remembered her. Even in Peking where they had lived together, he and she, he had been unable to find any trace of her. It was only when they came to a dust-ridden village in Manchuria where he and Hanya had once lived for a few months that he heard of her. Here he and Yak-san went to the home of a Korean who had known Kim when he was a monk, and after Yul-chun was washed and rested, he went into the streets and to the market, everywhere that he and Hanya once were known. The faces now were strange and people shook their heads, and after six days of such search, unwillingly he began to believe that perhaps she was dead.

Then, the last night before they were to rise early and begin their walking again, an old woman came to the gate of the Korean's house.

"A beggar woman," he said, "but she pretends she knows you. It is a ruse for begging."

Yul-chun rose, nevertheless, and went to the gate and recognized the old woman as one from whom Hanya used to buy cabbages for kimchee. The years had changed her from a buxom countrywoman to a wizened hag. She put out her withered hand and seized Yul-chun by the sleeve.

"I hear you are looking for your woman," she said in a hoarse whisper, the spittle flying from her toothless gums.

Yul-chun drew back. "What have you to tell me?" he asked.

"She stayed with me after she left you," the old hag said. "She came to my house on her way to Siberia and she stayed half a moon of days. I sold her cabbages cheap and she sold them again in the markets and got herself some money for her journey north."

"How can I believe you?" Yul-chun asked, not believing and yet longing to believe.

"She gave me this," the hag said.

With this she reached into her scraggy bosom and pulled out a filthy string, at the end of which was a small amulet, a little silver Buddha, which he remembered now that Hanya had kept in a box with a few treasures she had saved from her mother—a pair of jade earrings, a thin silver bracelet, a thimble, and two brass hairpins.

"Now do you believe?" the hag asked.

"I believe," he replied. "Only tell me where she went."

"She said she went to her brother in Siberia," the hag replied.

"She had no brother," Yul-chun declared.

The hag showed hideous broken teeth. "This is your misfortune," she cackled.

She held out her hand, and poor as Yul-chun was he put into her dry old palm a piece of money.

Northward again they went and Yul-chun stopped in every place where he found people of his own country and inquired of any one who might remember Hanya. None remembered. She had walked alone and kept to herself, it seemed, and he knew that was her way. Before he reached Mukden he and Yak-san both put on Chinese garments, gray cotton robes, so that they appeared as two scholars who come to visit a city. They put their hands in their sleeves and hunched their shoulders as such scholars do, and the Japanese police thought them men of Peking and let them pass. Koreans they arrested, for they knew Manchuria had many Korean exiles, all of whom were rebels against Japan, unless they were traitors.

It was not possible, however, for Yul-chun to pass through Manchuria without being known. By this time more than a million landfolk from Korea were exiles here and they worked as farmers for wealthy landlords. Yul-chun delayed, and with him always Yak-san, until he could inquire into their plight. When he found it was hard and that they were poor, he met secretly with leaders of the Chinese peasants, hiding themselves in the fields of tall sorghum as though they were bandits, as many of the Chinese were, and in this way he united both Chinese and Koreans—the Koreans the leaders, for the Chinese peasants had no unity. The new group was called the Korean-Chinese Peasant Association. The young Korean scholars had their own secret group which was called the Korean Revolutionary Young Men's League, in which the leadership was Communist. These Korean Communists were poor and hungry and many of them were ill. They had no homes and they slept under trees and in crevices of the earth, in caves in the mountains, wherever they could, and this in winter as well as in summer, the bitter winters of a northern land. Yul-chun was determined now against Communism, fearing that for his country this would mean exchanging one tyranny for another and he drew aside from the Communist young men, much as he pitied them and praised them, too, for their courage.

What was his surprise then when one day Yak-san came to him and asked to remain in Manchuria with these young men!

"You desert me!" Yul-chun exclaimed.

"Let me remain with these young men," Yak-san replied.

"I said I would take you to my own home," Yul-chun argued.

"I am an orphan, so destined by fate, and I must avenge my parents," Yak-san replied.

"How will you avenge them?" Yul-chun demanded.

Yak-san looked away. He scraped his bare toes in the dust of the road, for they had stopped in the middle of the day to rest under a date tree and gnaw their dried unleavened bread.

"I know you do not wish me to say this, Elder Brother," Yak-san said at last, "but the Communists will help me."

Yul-chun tried not to be angry. "You believe in them?"

"I believe in their ways," Yak-san said. "I care nothing for their faith in this or that, for or against, but I like their ways. When they meet an enemy—" He drew his finger across his throat.

"You think this settles everything?" Yul-chun demanded.

"I have two enemies," Yak-san replied in the same slow steady voice. "One killed my father, the other killed my mother. My father was crushed to death under the butt of a gun. I know the man who did it. I know his name, I know his face. He is not dead. My mother died from a stab in the belly with a bayonet. She carried a child in her—my brother, ready to be born. I know who stabbed her and who killed my brother before he could draw his first breath. I shall kill that man."

What could Yul-chun say? A dozen years ago he would have leaped to his feet and cried out that he would go with Yak-san. Now he knew that merely to kill a man did not end the evil he had done or that others like him would do. Only to kill was not enough.

"You long to have the comfort of revenge," he told Yak-san.

"Say so if you like," Yak-san retorted.

At the next center of Koreans, in Antung, on the border of Korea, Yak-san left him. A coolness had grown between them, but when the last moment came, they looked into each other's eyes, and suddenly they embraced. They parted then and without looking back each went his way.

. . . At Antung, Yul-chun was tempted to go without further delay to his father's house. During the years of his youth he had never been sick for home, but now he was. He longed for the safety of the old house about him, and this though his mind told him there was no safety even there. He longed for his lost chidlhood and even for his mother's cookery. He remembered his tutor, their walks in the gardens along the country roads, the many stories his tutor had told him and read to him, and the poetry he had recited to him, the ancient beautiful poetry. His tutor had a sweet singing voice, neither deep nor high but warm with love of country, and as a child he, a stormy, restless boy, would sit in the cool of the evening and listen to this singing, and feel a brief and melancholy peace. Who could have thought in those quiet days and nights that the young poet would have joined the terrorists! His own first doubt of death as a weapon had begun then, when he saw his gentle tutor so changed, a dagger in his hand instead of a lute. It is not only the stabbed who die. He sighed at such thoughts and turned away from his home. No, he would continue his way northward to Siberia. If Hanya were alive he would find her and find his child. If he made a center of his own, he could begin again.

He rested in a small inn for three days and told himself that he would soon set forth on his long and lonely journey into the wide plains and eternal forests of Siberia, forests of pine and birch, stretching endlessly beyond all horizons. But now he waited, making inquiries of any Koreans, as his habit was, to know whether one had seen or heard of Hanya. Some replied with laughter and teasing, asking why he still yearned for a woman he had not met for many years, to which he replied simply that she had his child, who might be a son, to which they replied in turn that any pretty young woman would willingly give him a son. He smiled without mirth, knowing that none could understand his need for Hanya and his own child. And yet after so long a time, would not both be strangers to him? He was irresolute again and lingered still longer in the inn, divided by his longing to return to his father's house and his wish for his own. He was angry with himself, too, for surely this was no time to indulge his private family longings.

And while he lingered thus, time passing, he perceived that every year, every month and at last every day the ingredients for war were more near to boiling and again in Germany. An ancient and demonic spirit was combining them with present discontent, a mixture resolving into a concentrated surge toward violence and power, waiting only for the voice of some one man to be the vent. The man was found, and in Europe the old turmoil began, the rush and halt, the protests and the justifications, the talk of peace while peace became impossible. All made him know that war was near again, world war, and he must not go north to Siberia, for it was too late and he must not linger.

And yet he did linger, making excuse at last that he should start some schools in the countryside around Antung. The landfolk here were as ignorant, as good and as eager as any he had found in China, and he might never return, and they would in that case remain forever unable to read. In one village and another he set up such schools.

One day in spring he walked back from a village school to the city. Something of the softness of the spring crept into his blood and bones, the lovely and reluctant spring of a northern climate. The Yalu River swelled with spring floods, fruit trees blossomed and weeds grew green on the roadsides. The land women and children came swarming out of their villages to dig the fresh weeds for tonic food. He wandered into the country one day in his irresolution, and an impudent old woman looked up from her digging to remark his good looks.

"Here is the man I look for," she cackled, "no longer young and not yet old," and she thrust out the tip of her tongue until it touched the end of her flat nose. Her wicked old eyes twinkled at her companions and they burst into ribald laughter.

Yul-chun smiled. "I might accept your favors, Mother, except that I have a wife. True, I have lost her but I look for her—and for my son."

Womanlike, they were ready to hear such talk, and they squatted back on their heels and tossed out their questions. "Where did you lose her?" "Is she young?" "Is she pretty?" "How long ago and why did you let her go?"

He answered, half absently, half playfully, making a romantic tale of it partly for their pleasure, partly to satisfy his own heart. He could not speak of Hanya to his fellows except to say he searched for her, but to these old wives, whom he would never see again, he could speak.

"I lost her long ago," he said, "and yes, she was young, and yes, she was pretty, and she carried my son in her. I know it was a son. And I lost them both because I did not know I loved her. I thought my duty was elsewhere. She went away one day and I did not go to find her. Why? Because I thought she would surely come back if she loved me so well."

"Ah ha," the old woman said, "there you were wrong. When a woman loves whole and is not loved, she must leave the one she loves, or see her heart break slowly day by day. Better to leave him and have it broken, clean and forever."

Here a small crumpled woman piped up. She had not spoken before but had kept on busily at her weed-digging. "There are many who look for those they have lost—wives looking for husbands, sons for fathers, daughters for sisters and mothers. In these times many are lost and many are looking, especially here in this region between one country and another."

"Have you heard of a wife looking for her husband?" Yul-chun asked.

She looked up at him sharply and down again. "Not for a man like you," she said. She sat back on her heels and stared at him. "There is a young man—very young—who comes here in the winters and in the summers he turns north again. It may be that he is already gone north. Coming or going, he passes through our village since the road north runs through it."

"How old is he?" Yul-chun asked.

She pursed her dry old lips. "Eighteen—say—or something more."

He refused to believe that any good fortune could be his. Nevertheless he put the next question. "Do you think he has passed through to the north yet?"

"I have not seen him," she said slowly, still staring at him. "I have not seen him since autumn. But he does not look like you."

Yul-chun put his hand into his pocket and drew out a piece

of money. "I am at the inn at the corner of the first street to the left of the city gate. Bring him to me if you see him, and I will give you twice this much over again."

He gave the money to the old woman, scornful of himself that he did so. The money was not his to give. It was the scanty precious store that his fellow Koreans sent him from time to time, knowing that he kept watch for them while he lived here in Antung, between Manchuria and Korea, a likely place for news, and he was wise in knowing what such news meant.

"Take this," they said when they gave him money. "Use it for the cause." Well, he would pay it back double for the cause some day, when the world war was won.

He returned to the inn, still scornful of himself for dreaming even the smallest faintest dream that this youth might be his son. Yet it was true that many people were looking for others lost and Antung was the place of meeting. Many stayed as he was staying, in hope. He refused to hope but he stayed. He tried to make himself hopeless, it was urgent that he go home, and he stayed on, clinging to his dream of taking Hanya with him and his son. And dreaming of his son, he thought often of his brother's son, that child, that babe, that matchless boy who, springing into his arms and embracing him as though he had found one for whom he had long searched, had so astounded them all, that one must now be a young man. Yul-chun's first question when he heard of his brother's death, through a spy, had been to ask of Yul-han's son.

"What of the boy?" he had cried.

"He was safe with his grandparents. He is with them now," the spy told him.

And there he must be now, growing into that grace and strength that only such a child can have. No, he would wait a few days more. And these days grew into weeks.

Then suddenly, on a midsummer day, war broke across the Western World. Now Yul-chun knew he must go home, even childless, and he prepared himself toward that end and in haste he taught others how to do what he did. He gave a thought or two as to whether he should find the old woman once more. He had seen her every month at least twice, had asked her if—and when she shook her head and cracked her knuckles, he gave her a coin and let her go.

He could not believe what he saw therefore when, a few days before the day he had set to begin his journey, the old woman came to his door holding by the sleeve a tall bone-thin young man who needed to have his hair cut. Long and straight his black locks fell over his forehead and down his cheeks, and he wore Russian clothes, full trousers and high boots and a tunic belted at the waist.

"Here he is," she said, mumbling through her broken teeth. "He came through our village late this year, after I wasted many days watching for him—good days of work I have missed—and I told the guard at the village gate to wake me if a young man came by, and he must be paid, too, that guard!"

Yul-chun was lying on his bed when she came in, his hands folded under his head, reflecting and regretting, perhaps, the time he had spent here in waiting and watching, and wondering if he should have gone into Siberia to look for Hanya. Many times he had been about to go and had not gone, prevented by his fellow Koreans who said that since it was well known that he had refused to be a Communist, he would be killed if he went upon Russian soil.

"Dead, you will never find your woman," they argued.

"You must think of your country first," others argued.

And so he had not gone as he had thought he would when he left China, and now would never go. Yet while he had lingered here, he held together the exiles through the news sheets he printed wherever he went. Thus only he had told the others how the Japanese were victorious in China, and how a month ago in Canton seven thousand Korean conscripts had turned against their Japanese officers and killed them.

Now when he saw the old woman he rose from his bed and went toward the young man she led. He saw no likeness in that sullen face either to himself or to Hanya. Let him be prudent lest he commit himself to a stranger!

"Do you look for someone?" he asked.

"This old woman," the young man answered, his voice lusty and strong, "this old woman has dragged me here, saying that you are my father, but I see no likeness to what my mother told me."

They looked at each other with mutual distrust.

"Nor have I reason to think that you could be the son I have never seen," Yul-chun rejoined.

The old woman set up a clamor. "Where is my money?" she screamed and she thrust her dirty palm up into Yul-chun's face.

He was on the point of saying that he owed her nothing since this was not his son, then he remembered that his bargain had not included such certainty. He had said that she was to bring the young man to him wherever she found him, however long the search, and he had given up the search. Yet here the young man was! He could only reach into his pocket again and take out two coins and put them in her black-lined palm. She looked at the money coldly.

"Come," she said, "for how many days I have not worked, spring and autumn, watching at the city gates for this fellow! And because this year he was late, I watched through summer, too!"

At this the young man took umbrage. "You!" he shouted. "You bring me here for nothing! I am set back in my journey. This is not my father. My father is a young man, taller than I am, very handsome—his skin white as milk, my mother said!"

So shouting, he took the old woman by the shoulders, spun her around twice and sent her flying from the door. Then he closed the door and barred it. "These land people," he complained. "They are too greedy and altogether ignorant. They need a power above them to compel them."

Yul-chun was not listening.

"Your mother said your father was young—and handsome —and his skin was white? How many years ago did she say that?"

"Many years," the young man said. "She died," he added.

He gnawed at his lower lip and mumbled. "Died? She was killed."

"Killed?" Yul-chun's lips went dry. He sat down on the bed. "How was she killed?"

The young man sat down on the bed beside him. "We lived in a hut on a Russian peasant's land. It was not his land, but we helped to till it. A nobleman owned the land. Long ago that was—long ago, and everything is changed now. But in those days the winters were endless and we were always hungry before spring came. We dried berries and roots and mushrooms but we always ate everything too soon. That is— I ate too much. I was young and I did not see that she gave everything to me. One day in the spring she stole into the forests of the nobleman to find some early mushrooms, or a few green weeds. She said she knew a hollow where the sun shone warm and where there was no wind. There she went and I followed. She told me to hide among the trees, and so I hid, but where I could see her. It was a quiet place, scarcely the birds were there. Suddenly I heard footsteps and a great crackling of broken branches on the ground. I saw a big man in good clothes, high leather boots and trousers of leather and a loose jacket belted in at the waist, a bearded man, with a whip in his hand. He shouted at my mother that she was a thief and she tried to run but he laid hold of her—and—"

The young man faltered and bit his lip and then went on.

"He beat her when he was finished with her and she did not get up again. She fell in a drift of late snow under a thick pine tree. She did not move when I called. She did not answer. Her eyes were open and staring at nothing. I was afraid and I ran away. I left her there and I never went back. Nor did I ever tell what had happened to her. And I do not know why I tell you now, for no one can do anything."

"What was her name?" Yul-chun asked.

"I do not know," the young man said. He frowned. "You will think I lie, but I only called her O-man-ee. And we knew no one except the Russian peasants. They called her Woman!"

It was on the edge of Yul-chun's tongue to ask the next question. Did she not tell you your father's name? But resolved against hope, he would not. At this moment the young man shook his hair back and it fell away from his ears. Yul-chun stared. The lobe of the left ear was not perfect. It was the same ear with which his brother Yul-han had been born!

"What is your name?" Yul-chun muttered. His voice would not come out of his throat and his heart beat hard enough to make him faint.

"Sasha," the young man said.

"Sasha!" Yul-chun exclaimed. "But that is a Russian name."

"I was born in Russia."

Yul-chun looked at him with reluctant certainty. The young man got to his feet. "I must be on my way," he said.

"What is your haste?" Yul-chun asked, to delay him.

"I am a trader," Sasha said. "I bring furs and woolens here to Antung and I take back brass and silver goods and sometimes a rich man orders celadon dishes and lacquer chests from Korea."

He was set on going, and Yul-chun could think of no other way to delay except by telling the truth.

"It may be that you—it may be—you are my son," he stammered.

Sasha paused at the door.

"How do you know?" he demanded.

"You bear upon you a family mark," Yul-chun replied. "My blood brother had that same ear you have. It cannot be accident that there should be two such ears."

He came near to Sasha and lifted the lock of his hair and looked at the ear.

"It is the same," he said.

But Sasha pulled away from him. "That cursed ear," he muttered.

"Not cursed, but perhaps most fortunate," Yul-chun retorted.

"Fortunate? Unfortunate," Sasha exclaimed. "Too many men tease me for my ear. Did a Russian bear bite me—what woman loves you too well—such things, all stupid!"

Yul-chun, fearful and hopeful, tried to laugh but Sasha looked at him gravely. For an instant the two men exchanged a speculative gaze.

"Do we part?" Yul-chun inquired at last. When Sasha did not answer he stepped back. "It may be you are right. The lobe of an ear—it is no proof. Who knows how many people in the world have the same defect?"

Now it was Sasha who hesitated. Then he spoke. "My mother had something of jade which she valued above all else. Though we starved, she would not use it. What was it?"

Yul-chun answered instantly. "It was a seal of red jade which was once her father's, before he was killed."

Sasha could not hide his astonishment. Speechless, he put his hand in the bosom of his tunic and brought out the jade seal.

Yul-chun gazed at it and nodded. "I saw it last in her hand," he said slowly.

Suddenly he could not hold back his tears. He threw his arms about his son.

"Now we will go home," he said. "At last—at last!"

. . . He was a silent young man, this son of his. He must be wooed and coaxed, it seemed, for he could let hours pass in silence. But Yul-chun's heart melted into constant warm-flowing talk, so moved he was by having his son. For the first few days he held back nothing. He drew his son into his own life and into the life of the Kim family. When he found how ignorant Sasha was of his own people and his own country, he talked of the early history of the Korean people, and how they came to be living here on this long mountainous strip of land hanging from the Russian mainland like fruit upon a vine. He told of the struggles of their people to keep their independence and how they had been compelled through the centuries to play one nation against another, lean first toward this one, and then toward that.

"I tell you, Sasha," he began earnestly one day as they walked side by side, and then paused as he spoke the name. "Sasha?" he repeated. "How can I take you to your grandfather with that name? I shall give you another. Yes, I have it—you shall be another Il-han. Your grandfather's name will honor you, and may you honor him."

His son did not say yes or no, but as the days passed, Yul-chun saw that he would not accept the new name. Unless he were called Sasha he did not answer. For a few days, as they traveled on, Yul-chun inquired of himself whether he should not argue the name, and then decided he should not. It was too soon. The bonds which should have been between father and son since birth must be knit now as carefully as though his son were newly born to him, as in a sense he was. He returned then to the Russian name, and still Sasha said nothing for or against. Studying that closed handsome face, the high forehead, the broad cheekbones, the small dark eyes under flying black brows, the full stubborn mouth, Yul-chun puzzled as to what sort of man his son was. Closed against the world, secretive, brooding, and yet sometimes suddenly impetuous, how could Sasha be revealed to him? He had told Sasha everything and Sasha told him nothing.

"Will you not speak to me of yourself and your mother?" he said at last one day.

They were well into Korea now, walking through high mountains, treading narrow footpaths that clung to the cliffs and wound in and out among the rocks.

"I have nothing to tell," Sasha said. "Every day was a day of work on the land. At night we went to political meetings. There was nothing more."

"But after Hanya—after your mother died, what did you do?"

"I was put into a Russian orphanage."

"And then?"

"Nothing."

"You were sent to school?"

"Of course. All children are sent to school."

"Were they kind to you?"

"Kind? I had enough to eat and a place to sleep."

"But someone was—someone took the place of your mother?"

"No—there was no need for that."

"You missed your mother—being so young."

"I do not remember."

"Are you—have you ever been in love?"

"Love? No!"

"How is it you are a trader?"

Yul-chun put the question innocently, and he was surprised to see that Sasha turned suspicious eyes on him.

"Why do you ask that?"

"Why? Because you are my son."

Sasha waited an instant, then answered. "I am restless. I like to wander. Since I am Korean I am not forced—that is, I am free. Also my mother told me to find you if I could, and especially to look for you in Antung. If you returned to Korea you would pass through Antung, she said."

"Did she say I would return?"

"Yes."

"Is that all?"

"Yes."

"Surely there is more," Yul-chun urged. "What are your dreams? Where are your hopes? Every young man has dreams and hopes."

"Not me," Sasha said stubbornly, his eyes on the path ahead.

"Have you known terrors that make you silent?" Yul-chun asked next.

"There are some things I will never tell you," Sasha said.

Yul-chun felt a desperate reluctance to reach home with this son until somehow he had discovered how to open his heart. If Sasha could not love him, the father, how could he love his grandparents, or even his country? Moreover, there was no haste. The Japanese had strong hold everywhere, and the time for revolt was not yet. Why, then, Yul-chun inquired of himself, why should he not linger here in villages as he had in China and Manchuria and near Antung, and sow the seeds of the people's schools? It would be difficult, for Japanese police would be watchful, but he would be wily. He would teach the people Japanese words by day, but at night he would teach them Korean.

He told Sasha of his plan, and begged his help. Sasha listened, unmoved. "The government should do this," he said.

"It is not our government," Yul-chun replied.

Sasha shrugged and said no more. Thereafter he sat watching while his father labored earnestly with new and old scholars and then a young student, teaching them the way to teach the unlettered landfolk.

"Son, will you not help me?" Yul-chun asked one day.

"I read only Russian," Sasha replied carelessly.

Yul-chun's jaw dropped. It had not occurred to him that though Sasha spoke he could not read or write Korean, his ancestral language.

"How is it you did not tell me?" he demanded.

Sasha shrugged again. "I am not one for books," he said.

"Nevertheless I must teach you," Yul-chun said firmly.

And he did so from that day on. Each night, wherever they slept, Yul-chun taught his son. Sometimes in the day, too, if they were in a lonely place, he stopped and gave Sasha a lesson.

As for Sasha, he learned well enough, neither willingly nor unwillingly, and unmoved as ever. No, not by touch or word was this son's heart moved. Days passed and months, for Yul-chun continued his building of schools, as slowly they went southward, until almost two years had passed, and Yul-chun, at first wounded, had learned to accept Sasha as he was.

This was the son he had found, a slim, silent, grim young man, who hid himself even from his father. Urging and persuasion only made him draw the invisible cloak the more tightly about him. Somehow he must be won, but not by force. Thereafter Yul-chun used every device that love and pride could conceive. For already he loved this son. The human feelings he had so long repressed emerged powerfully now from his strong nature, and finding no other object they centered on Sasha. Often in the evening when they sat resting after the day's travel on foot or in some passing vehicle a landman offered, he longed to put out his hand and touch the warm brown flesh of his handsome son. He did not yield to the longing after the first time. Sasha had endured the touch and then had moved away and Yul-chun let his hand drop. No, not by contact nor by word was this son's heart to be moved, if indeed it could be moved. Yul-chun, wounded, could only sigh and try to remember himself when young. He, too, had not welcomed the touch of his father's hand. Now that he had this son, he began to understand how often he must have grieved his own father, and from his present hidden pain he spoke one day, as he and Sasha came out of the mountains and into the foothills below.

"I hope that my old father still lives when we reach home. I have not seen him for many years, nor have I written a letter, fearing that such a letter from me might bring him into danger. But now, as we walk together, you and I, I think of my father, and I remember many times when my coldness and my abrupt speech must have cut his heart. He never told me so and I was too young to know."

To this Sasha made no answer. The thong of his sandal broke and he stopped to mend it while Yul-chun waited.

And again on another day Yul-chun spoke. "My mind in those days when I was young was altogether engaged in the sorrows of our people. I thought only of our freedom, of our independence as a nation, and I wished not to yield any part of my being to our family or to any claim from the past."

He said this and waited for Sasha to say that he too had such feelings, but Sasha did not say so. He looked at his father as though he did not know what had been said, as though he heard a foreign language, as though he listened to a dotard.

Yul-chun gave way then to silence. In silence they went except for the small necessities of daily life, and the questions of food and drink and a place to sleep at night were all that passed between the two. Yet every day they walked side by side, or one following the other if the path were narrow, but still together, and every day they saw the same landscapes, the magic of the unchanging beauty of blue sky and sea and gray rock and green field, and the stately procession of the tall and handsome people to whom they belonged. Even the poor, even the beggared, had beauty, and Yul-chun himself saw his people with new eyes. He had lived long among the squat dark people of southern China and he had forgotten how different his own people were, different in the very build of the bone, in the fairness of skin, in the eyes brown, not black, in the hair softly dark, not stiffly black. He longed to tell his son how proud they could well be of their people, how gay they were, in spite of all hardship, witty in their talk, lighthearted singers and at the same time hardworking and thrifty and brave, but he bit back such words, knowing that this, too, the son must discover for himself.

Soon, to his joy, Sasha did one day speak of his own will and not in answer to a question.

"I have grown so used to the flat plains of Russia that I did not know how fine the mountains are. As for the sea, what I have heard is not the half of what I now know by my own eyes."

They were never out of sight of mountains and seldom out of sight of the sea. They walked nearer to the west than the east, and when they lost the sea for a while suddenly they came upon it again in bay and cove, for the western coast was deeply indented with bay and cove and these were narrowed between cliffs so steep that the tides ran always high.

This that Sasha said revealed to Yul-chun that his son's heart was alive somewhere in the depths of his being. He could feel beauty, and he was observing what he saw and not walking without seeing. If Sasha could not be won by the natural feeling of father for son, then it might be that he could be won by the strong beauty of his country. Perhaps through love of country other loves could be aroused. For the ability to love, though a natural gift, may be stifled before it can grow, and what had there been in Sasha's life to teach him love? His mother had died when he was a small child, he had grown up one of many children in an orphanage, and until now his father was a stranger. As for women, he had yet to know more than the clamor of his male impulse. He did not know how to love, or even that he needed love, and his ability to love human beings could only develop when he came to know them.

At night, therefore, when they stopped at some inn or in a landman's house, Yul-chun did not allow himself to sleep early. Instead he sat with the others and led Sasha to do so with him. In this way Sasha could learn something more about his people than he had by mere trading. More than this, Yul-chun too could learn of what was taking place in the underground in Korea and elsewhere. Thus he learned that Kim Yak-san, the terrorist, was still alive and in China, and he had gathered Koreans in the central part of that country into a volunteer corps against the Japanese. The Chinese Nationalists feared this group as revolutionary, and sent them to the front to face the Japanese. Yet many Korean conscripts deserted from the Japanese armies, and helped the Chinese. And he heard that in the heart of China, in Chungking, the city to which the Chinese Nationalist leaders had fled, Koreans had united several factions into one independence society, and Korean exiles came from many countries to join that society and fight the Japanese. The Chinese Nationalists welcomed them at last, and a Korean Independence Army was formed.

In Korea itself, Yul-chun heard, the Japanese rulers were using every means to change Koreans into Japanese. With his own eyes he read in newspapers that the new Governor-General, a military officer of high rank, insisted that "Japanese and Koreans must blend to make one harmonious whole."

"It is impossible," Yul-chun exclaimed to Sasha.

He threw down the newspaper he had been reading. As he did so he caught a strange secret look in Sasha's black eyes.

"Why do you say impossible?" Sasha asked.

Yul-chun exploded. "Ask yourself! If it were possible, why do the Japanese need twenty thousand regular police here in our country, and two hundred thousand auxiliaries? Why do Korean workmen get paid only half what Japanese are paid? Why do Koreans cross the Yalu River again as brigands to attack Japanese?"

Sasha shrugged his shoulders. "You make yourself too hot."

Heat went out of Yul-chun and he felt suddenly cold. "Why do you never call me Father?" he muttered.

When Sasha did not answer, he hid his hurt, saying, "Never mind. It is better that you are honest. It will come. I can wait."

. . . They continued their journey southward day by day and there were times, now and then, when Yul-chun felt some hope that he and his son could some day come together in heart and spirit as he took pains to guide their path through those places famous for beauty, the tombs and temples, the castles, and ancient fortresses. Thus while they traveled along the western coast Yul-chun turned aside often to see the ancient tombs, and while they were still in the north he showed Sasha the dolmens made of great flat stones set on rude stone pillars so that they looked like tables for giants. In reality they too were tombs and within each vast structure was the tomb chamber. While he showed the treasures Yul-chun told of the great men of the past who were buried here, and he told of their great deeds and their high dreams and how their lives too were spent in the struggle to keep their country independent and apart from those who sought always to enslave its people and seize its wealth.

Temples Sasha would have none of, nor would he so much as step over the threshold of any temple. The guardian gods in the entrance hall only made him laugh in derision.

"There are no such beings as gods," he declared, and if a monk came out from the temple he would shout at him rudely. "Are you a man? Or are those women's robes you wear?"

Yul-chun passed all temples after this without stopping, and soon he found that the fortresses were where Sasha lingered, the stone fortresses of the early days when the hordes of Manchuria invaded and were driven back, the fortresses attached to great old castles, the fortresses of old palaces, all these Sasha studied with lively interest and he asked many questions of wars and victories and when he heard of defeats he scowled and swore that once the present invaders were sent out, never again must other invaders be allowed.

"But how?" he demanded one night when they stopped for the night in a village inn, "how shall we rid ourselves of these invaders?"

He talked easily now with his father, never of himself or of the past, but always of the present and always of their country. The country was winning him, the beautiful country that he was coming to believe was his own. He was still shy with people, but he was ardent with love—yes, perhaps it was love —for the land and the sea and the sky.

Yul-chun, rejoicing, was careful to seem cool. "When this present world war is over," he replied, "the Japanese will be vanquished, at least for a generation. We must seize the moment. The instant they surrender, we must step forward and take back the throne and claim our country. The western world is fighting for us now except Americans, who still hold themselves aloof, and though we cannot take our share in the war, yet our enemy is the common enemy and we have a right to our share of the victory. We ask no spoils, no land belonging to others. We ask only for our own country back, which is our independence."

He was watching Sasha's face as he spoke, and for the first time he saw something of what he wanted to see and heard what he longed to hear. His son's face lighted, his son's hand was outstretched and his son's voice spoke with unusual ardor.

"I will be there, at that moment—with you—" He paused and then spoke the one word which Yul-chun had waited so long to hear.

"Father—" Sasha muttered, his voice low and still reluctant.

Yul-chun could not reply. His heart swelled into his throat and he put out his right hand and clasped his son's hand. For the moment the two were in communion.

. . . Three days later the news flashed over all Korea and crept into every village and byway: Japan had attacked the United States. Yul-chun and Sasha were a dozen miles from the capital. Arriving in a small town in the twelfth month of that year toward the end of the seventh day, Yul-chun had decided to stop there for the night, for he had not wanted to go immediately to his father's house. He and Sasha were travel worn, their garments soiled. Moreover, he had put aside some money to buy Sasha other garments than the Russian ones he wore. Thus they could appear with dignity as members of the Kim clan. And no sooner had they entered the inn of this town than they heard that on that very day in the morning while Christians were meeting in the churches, Japanese airplanes had swarmed over Honolulu and dropped bombs on the American warships in the harbor. The innkeeper told them, his voice a whisper, his eyes exultant as he put his hand before his mouth.

"Have you heard—"

"I cannot believe it," Yul-chun exclaimed to Sasha. "Even the most arrogant Japanese officer could not dream of victory over the United States."

Sasha was stuffing his mouth with good Korean bread. They sat at a table in a small room.

"Believe because you must," Sasha said. "It has happened."

Yul-chun did not hear. His mind ran ahead in hope renewed. Now the Americans would enter the war in all their power. Now the mighty industries of the United States would be put to work against Japan, and what was against Japan was for Korea. For the first time in how many years he dared to hope again. When the war was won, when the Japanese were vanquished, his country would be free. Victory—victory!

He leaped up as though he were a young man again. "Come, my son!" he cried. "Not a moment's delay now! We must go instantly to my father's house. We must prepare for independence!"

Sasha stared at him, his mouth full. "But—but you said I must have new clothes tomorrow!"

Yul-chun was suddenly impatient. "Your cousin will lend you something. Come—come!" And with this urging, sooner than words could tell he had paid the innkeeper, who in consternation asked why they left so soon and what was it they did not like in his inn and only tell him and he would make it right. Yul-chun assured him his inn was good, the food good, but the news hastened him, and in less than an hour he and Sasha were on their way again.

. . . It was after midnight when at last he stood before the well-remembered gate, Sasha at his side. There was no moon and in the darkness he felt the path under his feet for a rock and with it he pounded the barred gate. After a long few minutes he heard the gateman's cracked and drowsy voice.

"Who is here at this hour?"

"It is I, your master's son," Yul-chun replied.

The gateman would not open at such easy answer. He mumbled while he lit a lantern and then he opened the wicket and peered through. Yul-chun put his face close to the opening and smiled. "It is I," he said, "older by many years, but your master's elder son, nevertheless."

The gateman gave a shout then and opened the gate, the same gateman, young when Yul-chun was a child, and now old.

"Come in, young master," he cried. "Welcome home, young master! But I must wake your father slowly, or he will die of joy."

"Do not wake him," Yul-chun said, stepping into the courtyard. "Let him sleep until morning. Are my parents well?"

"Well except for the ills of old age, which we all have," the gateman replied, "but who is with you, young master?"

"My son," Yul-chun said proudly.

"Your son," the old man echoed and lifting his lantern he let the light fall on Sasha's dark and handsome face.

The old man gazed at him for a lingering moment. Then he let the light fall. "Now there are two of them in the house," he muttered.

"How two?" Yul-chun demanded.

Before the gateman could answer, the lattice of the house slid back and a young man stood there, slim and tall and naked except for a towel about his middle and in spite of the winter night, in which a few snowflakes were already falling.

"Who is there?" he called.

"In the name of the gods," the gateman cried, "do you come straight from your bath into the snowy night?"

"A minute," the young man cried, and in an instant was back again, wrapped in a quilted robe.

The gateman beckoned with his left hand, the lantern held high in his right. In the path of light the young man came toward them and the gateman turned his head to Yul-chun.

"Behold your brother's son," he said to Yul-chun. And to the young man he said, "Behold your uncle who we thought was lost. He has come home. And here is his son. Now there are two of you."

Yul-chun could not take his eyes from the young man. Yes, this was Liang. Yul-chun knew him. The glorious child had grown into this young man. Glorious? Yes, the eyes were the same, larger, luminous, benign, the mouth smiling, the head nobly shaped and held high.

"Do you recognize me as once you did?" Yul-chun asked.

He felt his heart beat, inexplicably quickened as Liang gazed at him intently.

"I do recognize you," Liang said and his voice was deep and kind.

"Is it possible that you remember? You were very young," Yul-chun said.

"I cannot remember, but I recognize you," Liang said.

He spoke with calm confidence in the largeness of his soul, understanding and expecting understanding, and Yul-chun felt the same reverence now that he had felt when he held the remarkable child in his arms. There were indeed two of them, as the gateman had said, two of this new generation, two young men to take the place of the dead and the old, two for the struggle ahead, two for the victory that must be won.

He reached for his son's right hand and for his nephew's right hand and he bound them together in his own hands.

"You two," he said, "you must be more than cousins. You must be brothers."

He left them then and went into the house alone, the gateman leading the way with the lantern. At the inner door an old servingwoman stood and the gateman told her who Yul-chun was. She knelt then and took off Yul-chun's worn leather shoes and put slippers on his feet.

"Sir, I am Ippun," she said when this was done. "I have served your honored brother and his lady." She hesitated and then she said proudly, "It is I who have cared for their son."

He inclined his head. "How can I thank you?"

He said no more but went to the room where he had slept as a child, and she took the mattresses from the wall closet and laid them on the floor and spread the coverlets. Then she went away and he undressed and prepared for rest. Yet weary as he was, he paused to look from the window into the main room of the house. There he saw the two young men sitting on opposite sides of the table, the candle flickering between them. They were talking, talking, and they had forgotten the hour. He gave a great sigh as though a burden fell from his shoulders, and then he laid himself down to sleep.

. . . He was wakened in the morning by Ippun coming in with a basin of water for washing and fresh garments.

"Our old master sends these for you. He asks you not to make haste after your long journey. He has waited a long time, he says, and it is nothing to wait until you have washed and eaten." She bowed and went out.

He lay for a moment, collecting himself out of deep sleep, realizing that he was in his old room. Nothing had changed. Only he! He rose at last and washed and put on the fresh garments. Ippun returned with a tray of tea and small sweet cakes. She set them on the low table.

"Eat a little, drink a swallow or two," she coaxed.

While he ate and drank she put away the mattresses and the silken quilts into the wall cupboards, and when he was finished she handed him a cloth wrung out of hot water to wipe his hands, bowed and took the tray away.

He stood a moment, preparing his spirit, then went into the main room. His old parents were standing side by side waiting for him, and behind them stood Liang and Sasha. His parents stretched out their arms to him as he entered and he fell to his knees as their son. They lifted him up then, tears on their cheeks, and he felt their arms around him, he put his arms around them, first his father and then his mother. How thin and small their bodies were, how piteously shrunken to the very bones!

"Have you not had enough to eat?" he kept saying. "No, you have not had enough to eat! While I have been wandering you have grown so thin—I shall never leave you again!"

They tried to laugh, his mother sobbed and his father held his hand. "We are only old," Il-han said, "we are very old, and it is time for us to die, but we had to live until you came home again."

"And you bring us this fine grandson," Sunia sobbed, pointing to where Sasha stood at one side. "Thanks be to all the gods—and we must all have something to celebrate—I made some special—where is Ippun? I told Ippun—"

She hurried away, tottering slightly as she walked, but the two young men pressed forward.

"Grandfather," Liang said. "Sasha and I, we must go to the city immediately. There may be more news."

Il-han stretched his head. "Must you go? The police will be savage today, puffed up with pride for what was done yesterday. When they find that your uncle is here—do you think the Living Reed can be hidden?"

Sunia heard and came running back as fast as her old feet could carry her. "Not both of you," she wailed. "One of you must stay, lest an evil come about and—if we lose one—"

Il-han made apology for her to Yul-chun. "So used has this poor soul become to the loss of one or another of our family and clan—"

The two young men spoke together.

"I will not stay—"

"Nor I—"

"Safer for two—"

"Go," Yul-chun said. "I will stay. And do not think of me. Whatever your duty is, do it."

As he spoke he noticed that Sasha no longer wore his old garments. Instead he wore Korean robes that Liang, doubtless, had lent him. Strangely they did not suit him. His dark face and black eyes and hair, his bold profile and arrogant bearing, made him look foreign in the long white robes, somewhat too large for him at that, for Liang was the taller.

"Go," he said again, "and if there is time, buy yourself some clothes. You cannot always wear those. Here is enough money."

The two young men went away then and while they were gone, Yul-chun stayed with his parents and he told them of all that had befallen him, even of Hanya and of how Sasha was born, and he heard the long story of their lives here in the grass roof house. They ate of the dishes that Ippun brought in on trays and set before them, but Sunia did not eat with the men. She had never eaten with menfolk and she did not now, whatever young women did. She bade Ippun set her tray to one side so that the two men could talk. She listened, nevertheless, and she put in her part from time to time, and while they waited for the return of the young men, Yul-chun, from one parent and the other, was able to discover much that he had not known before of all that had happened and was happening in the lives of their people.

"And now," Il-han said at last, "we can only wait until the Americans win this war. Then we will ride in on the wave of victory."

"Father," Yul-chun exclaimed. "I hope you do not mean what you say. There will be no easy riding on any wave. We must be ready with the machinery to take over the government and administer it in modern and efficient ways. Without delay we must study Western government and choose from each those elements which best suit our people. The President must choose the cabinet, the whole structure to offset the Communist structure—"

He saw that his father was listening without comprehending, his eyes fixed on Yul-chun's face, as he leaned forward to hear.

"Why do I trouble you with such matters, my father?" he said in love and pity. "You have done your share. Tell me about Liang."

Here was a subject upon which his parents could not say enough, his father carrying the tale and his mother putting in such bits as his father forgot.

"After the fire died down from the burning of that church," Il-han said, "all who had lost relatives went to find relics and bones for burial. Of Induk and the little girl we could find nothing, for who could sort out such bones as were mingled with the hot ashes?"

Sunia broke in. "I always did say that scrap of blue cloth was a bit of Induk's skirt. Ippun said she wore a blue skirt that day—"

Il-han continued without pause. "Your brother's body was not burned—not altogether. I was able to—"

Here Il-han's chin trembled under his thin white beard, but he put up his hand when Yul-chun tried to urge him not to say more.

"No, no—I must tell you. It is your right to know. The police stood by while we searched, and they allowed me to—to—see—we had taken a—a coffin with us, the servant and I, and we were able to—we gathered the parts—a beam had fallen across his back, but the face—it was he, I—I couldn't mistake him. Yes, it was he—and we—we had—a funeral—"

Sunia was sobbing softly. "We buried him beside his grandfather. Such a rainy day—the rain falling like waterspouts, though the fortuneteller said it was a lucky day—and a yellow frog hopped out of the grave and I thought of your old tutor and the story of Golden Frog, do you remember, my son?"

"I remember," Yul-chun said.

"And whatever became of that tutor's wife?" Sunia mused in the easy diversion of the old. "Not his wife altogether she was, for he went away somewhere before the wedding day and never came back, and they sent his distant cousin here to ask where he was, but how could we know? He had left us, too, and the poor young woman went into a nunnery since she had no husband and was too virtuous to marry another."

Il-han waited with some impatience while she talked on and now he could wait no longer. "It was of Liang that we were speaking, I believe! A god watched over him that day the church was set on fire by the police. He—"

"No god but his mother," Sunia put in. "She knew the child loved you, his grandfather, and she sent him to us."

"Well, well," Il-han said, "at least he was here. Let us agree on that. And he has been here ever since, our hope and our comfort, for we feared you dead, too, my son!"

"As good as dead," Yul-chun agreed. "I dared not write letters to you. A price has been on my head, as you know, since the day I escaped from prison, after the Mansei—"

Sunia broke in. "And was it true that a bamboo shoot sprang up between the stones of the cell after you escaped?"

Yul-chun smiled. "Is there such a legend?"

"No legend," his father retorted. "There were many who saw it, and the police, discovering the reason why they came to the jail as though on a pilgrimage, dug the bamboo up by the roots."

"Did they do so?" Yul-chun said and fell into musing. "So the green bamboo was gone, root and all!"

"But," Il-han went on in triumph, "they could never get all the root. Up the green shoot came in some other corner! And at last to stop the people's joy when they saw it, the police poured cement over the floor."

"There is bamboo everywhere," Sunia said.

Yul-chun turned to her. "True, my mother, and so let us talk of Liang."

Il-han leaned against the back rest of his floor cushion and prepared to enjoy himself again.

"This grandson of mine, before he was three he knew his letters. At five he could write very well. At seven he was beyond my teaching him anything except the old classics, and I sent him to an American school, although privately I taught him, too. He speaks English well and reads English books. He speaks French and German and he studied Latin for his medicine."

"Medicine?"

"He is learning to be a physician in both foreign and Korean medicine. He is also a surgeon, for he says no one can be only one in such times as we suffer."

"But why a physician?" Yul-chun inquired.

"He says that he can at least heal the people's bodies," Il-han replied. "It comforts him, he says."

"Is he Christian?" Yul-chun asked.

"No, and yet yes." Il-han said.

"How no and yes?" Sunia demanded. "No, he is not Christian." She had left her corner and now sat with them, her eyes still lively in her withered face.

Il-han yielded. "He is not Christian, true, yet he behaves as though he were. He is not Buddhist, but he is like a Buddhist. As for Confucius, Liang reads the classics and he observes correctness."

"You have taught him well," Yul-chun told his father.

"I have taught him nothing," Il-han insisted. "He learns without being taught."

"I wonder," Yul-chun said, reflecting. "I wonder how he will like Sasha."

"Sasha—Sasha—what name is this?" Sunia demanded.

"His mother gave it to him," Yul-chun said shortly. He saw weariness on his father's face and he rose. "Rest now, Father. I have tired you."

"You have only blessed me," Il-han replied, and his eyes followed Yul-chun out of the room.

"It is better than Moscow," Sasha said. He stood on a low hill above the city and gazed down upon the palaces and parks, the wide streets, the massive buildings of universities and new department stores. Liang had brought him to show him the city before they entered it.

"You have been in Moscow?" Liang asked.

"Once," Sasha replied. "Our school sent us there at our graduation. Moscow is also very fine, but—" He swept his right hand over the vista. "Still I do not know whether I go or stay."

"Stay," Liang said. "At least stay until you know us well."

A western wind had cleared the sky in the night and his

face, open and benign in the clear sunlight, expressed an inner radiance. Sasha felt an unwilling admiration.

"You are very busy with your work."

"Yes, I am busy," Liang said. "I finish my internship at the American hospital next summer. But I have time when I am off duty."

"Is it a Christian hospital?"

"Yes—a missionary hospital."

"Are you Christian?" Sasha's question was curt.

"No," Liang's voice was amiable, "I am not Christian."

"All religion is bad," Sasha declared. "It is an opiate for the people."

"I believe in God," Liang said quietly. "Where there is law as there is in the natural world, there must be a law-giver. Yet I do not believe, as Christians do, that we can be saved by a passive acceptance of God. We must save ourselves by doing what is godlike and we will become godlike."

Sasha protested. "I see no sense in what you say. How do you know what is good? How do you know there is a god? I say there is none."

Liang did not reply at once. When he did it was with a firm gentle authority.

"In the beginning, Sasha, our people were sun-worshipers. History tells us so, and it is reasonable, for our ancestors came from the cold and windy lands of Central Asia. The winters were long, and in the deep valleys between high mountains the sun shone for only a few hours a day. It is natural that our ancestors loved the sun and went eastward to find the sun. This is how they arrived at our country. But their longing for warmth and brightness, their heavenward yearning, persisted. They dreamed of a kind and powerful friend, a father-being, who lived far beyond their reach and because they could not reach him, they dreamed that he reached them, and he sent his son to become a man. Everywhere in the whole world there is such a dream. The Christians thought they brought it here —but we had it already. True, the manner of his birth varies. The Christians say he was born miraculously of a virgin. We have a legend that he was born of a union between bear and tiger—"

"Bear and tiger?" Sasha had sat down on a rock, brushing away the light snow, but now he suddenly stood up.

"Yes," Liang said, "and so we Koreans have kept the mountain tiger as our national symbol."

"Bear is the symbol of Russia," Sasha exclaimed.

Liang laughed. "Let us not stretch symbols too far! Some of our patients say the tiger has nothing to do with gods, that it is our national animal because the map of our country looks like a sitting tiger. Some say it is because we tell the other peoples to leave us in our lair and we will not disturb them, even as the mountain tiger will not attack unless he is attacked."

Sasha did not answer. He lay back on the cold rock, hands clasped behind his head, and gazed into the purple sky. Too much was happening, and too fast. He was Korean, and among the Russians he had felt alien. Now that he was here, he felt more alien than ever. Yet this was his family, his cousin, his father, his grandparents—those grandparents, like two ancient dolls in their old fashioned garments! And this cousin, so handsome that it made a man jealous to look at him, and yet this air of being saint, poet, scholar, all that was remote and impractical except that he was a doctor, a surgeon, and wanted to practice among the poor!

"I wish I could remember my mother better," he said suddenly.

"Tell me about her," Liang said.

Sasha stared into the sky. "I should remember her better," he said, "but she worked day and night for our food, and she never talked much. And I was too young to ask the questions that I wish now I had asked. She came of landfolk. I think she did, for she read no books. But how came she to have a jade seal? Yet here in this scholar's family, I feel out of place."

Liang rose as he spoke. "Rather, you have been out of place until now. Come—we must buy those clothes. And I have taken half a day's absence, but I must be back at the hospital and you may come with me—after you are dressed in your own clothes!"

And suddenly he went running down the mountainside like a boy, Sasha following.

. . . "Dr. Blaine, this is my cousin, Sasha."

The American stopped in the corridor of the big new hospital. "I didn't know you had a cousin."

He put out his hand. Sasha looked at it and Liang laughed.

"He has not known Americans. Sasha, put out your hand, please, like this!"

Sasha put out his hand and felt the warm, strong, foreign hand. The American turned to Liang.

"Did you take that throat culture yesterday, Liang? The woman's fever is up this morning."

"The report is on your desk, sir."

"Good."

He hurried away, and the two young men went on. Sasha had never been in a hospital before but he was too proud to say so. He looked at everything as though he had seen such things, until at last they came to a ward of young men.

"This is my special ward," Liang said. "I am responsible for these men. They are all wounded either by accident in some industry or in a political battle."

"Battle!" Sasha exclaimed.

"Many battles," Liang said. "We have our underground war. This patient, for example—"

He stopped by the bedside of a haggard boy of seventeen or eighteen. "How were you wounded, Yu-sin?"

"I am a student, sir. Our school went on strike with the factory workers—who get paid only half what Japanese workers get—we were marching—they attacked us with bayonets—we had only sticks we held over our shoulders, symbols of the guns forbidden to us."

"He has a fractured skull, his right arm broken, three ribs—and a strip of flesh torn from his right hip."

They went from bed to bed, Liang telling one story after another. In one bed a man lay near death and Liang sent for a nurse and a hypodermic, then called his superior. It was too late. The man ceased to breathe. Liang covered him with the sheet.

"No one knows who he is," he told Sasha when they were outside again. "He was in the underground and would give no name, either his own or another."

"How will they know he is gone?" Sasha asked.

"They know," Liang said. "And another has already taken his place."

Yul-chun seemed to live in idleness for many months after he returned to his father's house. This was partly to deceive the Japanese police and partly to allow himself time to decide what he should do. It was true also that he found himself weary after so many years of danger and hardship. He had been plagued by pains in his joints while he walked south with Sasha, but he had not spoken of it, knowing he was under surveillance, and now he decided to return to writing while he waited for the war to end with victory for the western nations, as end it must since the Americans were using their vast national machinery for war. It was a bold decision. As long ago as the end of the war with Russia, Japan had forbidden such Korean newspapers as were not favorable to Japanese. When she annexed Korea in the Christian year 1910, all Korean newspapers were stopped. Only the underground newspaper upon which Yul-chun had worked during the Mansei Demonstration could not be stopped. Ten years later, however, three newspapers were allowed if they did not speak of political matters. The year before the bombing of Pearl Harbor, these were stopped. There were now no newspapers in Korea except those Japanese. He prepared to publish as soon as possible not a newspaper but a magazine, wise, clever, subtle, which to an ignorant Japanese would show no hint of subversion, but to an intelligent Korean would convey information. It was not to be a magazine for the merchant, the trades, the landfolk or the seafolk. It was for the intellectual, for the thinkers, for the planners. He would take time for its conception, its preparation. He would choose his associates carefully, and none should be of his own family.

Yul-chun now assumed the life of a recluse and a scholar, traditional for one who had retired from public and political life. He put aside his western clothes and the trousers and jacket of the Chinese and wore the white robes of the Korean gentleman. He bought a horsehair hat, he let his beard grow, he seldom left his father's house.

Il-han could only be delighted. He assigned two rooms for Yul-chun's use and gave orders to the household that his son was not to be disturbed, which orders Sunia disobeyed whenever she felt that Yul-chun should be given food and tea. They were poor these days, and she had trouble to arrange for the delicacies she wished him to have, but Ippun was crafty and when she went to the markets she brought back more than she paid for, and Sunia asked no questions. In these times theft was right and lies were necessary.

The household settled itself around the two newcomers, and outwardly all was well enough so long as they were careful not to seem concerned with government. For Il-han this was easy. Age was creeping into his bones and marrow, and he lived in the past. He was typical of his people, conciliatory and peaceful, inclined to resignation. He quoted old proverbs more and more often to express what he could not put into words.

"Can one spit on a smiling face?" he inquired; or he said, "Vengeance cannot last a night's sleep." His only reproach to a lazy servant or an idle farmer on the land was a handful of gentle words. "The man who lies under a persimmon tree with his mouth open may never get food, however long his patience." Most of the time he slept—the sudden short slumbers of the old. Only Sunia did not sleep or rest. She grew old and very thin, but the handsome outline of her bones gave strength to her face and bearing. Only her voice did not change. Clear and strong, scolding or tender, to hear that voice without seeing her one would say she was a young woman.

Among these three, the young men lived a life of their own. The difference between them, Yul-chun reflected, was of communication. Sasha could not explain himself to others, nor could he understand beyond the sound of their words to him. But Liang moved in total comprehension. There was a genius in him, and it sent forth a shaft of light between him and every human being. He scarcely needed to speak, it seemed, for in the wholeness of his comprehension of the feelings, the thoughts, the very being of others, they gave him their confidence in return. Enlightenment, the Buddhists called it, and had Liang been Buddhist he would have been a high abbot, or if Tibetan, then a Dalai Lama, an incarnation. The result of this difference between Liang and Sasha was that Liang lived in peace and without apparent struggle, as though when he was born he had already climbed his mountain, while Sasha, imprisoned within himself, fought against the bonds of his own wayward moods, and could not climb beyond himself.

Yet Yul-chun was troubled. The joyful recognition which Liang had given him in babyhood was not renewed. Open as Liang was with him, ready always for talk or service, the special moment did not come and Yul-chun found himself waiting for it as though for ascension.

. . . In his quiet room in the house of his ancestors Yul-chun now began to spread the net which was to cover not only his own country but other countries as well. His purpose was twofold; first to prepare the Koreans for victory so that when the moment came and the Japanese were expelled, the nation would have its own government ready to function; and second, he planned to hasten victory by rousing the Koreans in other countries, and especially in the United States. Somewhere in the periphery of his mind and consciousness was the warning that Russia must be watched. For hundreds of years Russia had wanted Korea for its seacoast, its treasures of metals and minerals hidden in the mountains, its fisheries, the power of its rushing rivers and high tides. He did not believe that the heart of Russia was changed. Her ambitions might even be sharpened and intensified by a new government of hungry men, whose ancestors had been half-starved peasants. It was now their turn to grow fat and grow rich.

How was he to achieve such immense purpose? He pondered long on the question. He was too well known and he did not doubt that the vital men and women of the underground knew he was at home and were only waiting to reach him. There were many small but important signs of their knowing. Rude drawings of young bamboo appeared on the walls and gates. Certain products of daily use were named Bamboo. Poems about spring and growth were scattered in the streets, none mentioning his name but some using the words "living" and "reed." He maintained a steady silence, nevertheless, knowing very well that the Japanese authorities understood such signs and knew where he was and were watching him.

He could only conclude as months passed that he must have help. It would be foolish to risk his life and lose hope for his purpose, and after further thought and with reluctance he decided that he would talk with Liang. He hesitated to do so, for he knew that he might involve and imperil his nephew who would some day be the head of the family, and perhaps soon, since his own life was always in peril. Yet so far as he knew, Liang had no interest in politics or government. He seemed absorbed in his hospital, in his patients, in his people. He came and went freely, greeting Japanese as easily as he did his own countrymen, and speaking Japanese without accent. He had many patients among the Japanese who did not trust Korean doctors but did trust Liang. He had graduated with high honors from a Japanese university in the capital yet he had never gone to Japan, saying when he was invited that he was too busy, and that some day he would go when his internship was ended. To the American doctor he behaved as a son, speaking English perfectly and working with warm affection.

Yul-chun observed this universality and hesitated for a matter of weeks before he approached Liang. Could it be possible that a man beloved by all was really to be trusted? Who knew where his secret heart was? In the night he was beset by doubts and questions, but in the morning again, he had only to see Liang's open face and hear his voice, clear and confident, and especially hear his laughter, to trust him again. At last, compelled by his necessity for help, he decided that he would indeed speak. He waited for the opportune moment.

It came one day in winter, upon the second anniversary of the day when the Americans entered the war. It was evening. The old couple, his parents, had gone to bed early for they felt the cold, and Sasha had been in the city all day and had not returned, might not return, perhaps, for he was restless and often away. Liang was not on duty at the hospital that night and Yul-chun, putting all these signs together, made up his mind to speak after their evening meal.

"I need advice," he told Liang when Ippun had taken away the dishes and had filled the teapot again.

Liang smiled. "You flatter me, Uncle!"

"No," Yul-chun replied, "I have been too long away from home and I cannot remain idle."

With this, he outlined for him his twofold purpose, and thus continued: "It is not difficult for me to communicate with our countrymen abroad. I know all the leaders. Of these the most important are in the United States, and the next in China. The first group must shape American opinion and persuade the American government to recognize our right to independence and to realize that we are able to govern ourselves. Our provisional government is still in existence, its officers now in the United States. Through them we must work, and it is our task from here to keep them informed in both countries of what is taking place. They must keep us informed in return so that proceeding together we shall be ready to take back our country at the moment the Americans arrive upon our shores in victory."

To his surprise, Liang's whole being changed. The moment returned, that moment when as an infant he had recognized the man. His face was illumined, his eyes shone, an electric force beamed from him. He put out his hands and grasped Yul-chun's hands.

"I have been waiting ever since you came back," he exclaimed. "I thought you would never speak, yet I knew you would, I knew you must."

Yul-chun was amazed and overjoyed and yet half afraid. This was what he had hoped for, this was what he needed.

They talked long then, Liang assured yet modest, his mind quick and clear. He listened to the long story Yul-chun now told of his life in China, and how he had fought wholeheartedly side by side with the revolution there, and had learned the technique and the tactics, had maintained his work of writing and printing, and then had left, repelled by cruelties and driven by his fear of new tyrannies.

"There is no guarantee of freedom merely because a new power arises in a nation," Yul-chun concluded. "We must be prepared against such power. We must still distrust those who have been our ancient enemies. It is true, I have trusted the Americans. Yet of all the nations, we must count them as our only possible friends. They have betrayed us—yes, but it was in ignorance, not greed. Perhaps they have learned now. If not, we must teach them. That is what our fellow countrymen must do—teach them, so that when victory comes, they will know what to do with it. Let us forget the past. Let us remember only that the Americans among all nations have not seized our land or tried to rule us. And I do not forget their Christian missionaries. I am not Christian and I doubt religion, but they have opened hospitals and schools and they have been friends to us, these missionaries, and they have spoken for us and it is not their fault that they have not been heard. Governments are deaf and blind. Therefore I accept the Americans! They are our only hope. I was bitter against my father once because he said these very words. I am not bitter now, I am in despair. I know that in the world we face after the war there will be the same enemies, and the same passion to rule. We must have friends—and our only hope is the Americans. Above all, we must find someone who will go to America, and soon."

Liang listened to this speech with quiet attention and again Yul-chun felt the comfort of his total understanding, so complete that he had the illusion that he need not have used words. It was a strange feeling, one that he could not analyze or compare to any other, but it permeated him.

"I know one who can help us," Liang said. "She is a woman."

Here he stopped. He filled his uncle's tea bowl and his own, then went on.

"A few months ago I would not have hesitated to bring her to you. Now—I hesitate!"

Yul-chun proceeded cautiously. "Is this woman young?"

"Very young."

"And beautiful?"

"Very beautiful."

"A friend? Or something more?"

"Let us not speak of what she is to me—only of what she is."

"Then what is she?"

Yul-chun leaned against his back rest and fixed his gaze on Liang's face. He imagined that he saw a cloud there.

"She is a famous dancer," Liang said.

"A dancer!" Yul-chun exclaimed. His voice expressed what he thought. A dancer? How could she be trusted? Above all, could it be possible that Liang was like other men, his calm beautiful face merely a trick of birth?

Liang smiled. "I know what you are thinking and I agree with you except in this one person. She is not merely a dancer. She is—everything."

"How is it you know her?" Yul-chun demanded.

"She came to our hospital two years ago, from Peking. Since she is partly Japanese the Chinese had arrested her as a spy and tortured her."

"Partly Japanese!"

"And partly English. Her grandfather was an English diplomat in China and he fell in love with a beautiful Manchu girl, the daughter of a prince. They had to escape from China to save their lives. Nor were they accepted in England, and so they went to Paris, and there Mariko's mother was born."

"How is she Japanese?" Yul-chun inquired.

"Her father," Liang replied. "Her father was the Japanese Ambassador to Berlin, and on a holiday he met her mother in Paris. They were married, and came back to Japan, where Mariko grew up until she was twelve when her father was sent as Special Envoy from the Emperor. She speaks five languages equally well, but first of all she is an artist."

Artist, he said, not woman! Yul-chun put his next question.

"And why is she here?"

"She is dancing in the Japanese theatre."

"How can she be of use to us?"

"She is going to the United States to perform."

"And you trust her?"

"As I trust myself."

Yul-chun sighed deeply. He had known no dancers except the simple girls who danced in the Communist propaganda plays used for the landfolk in China and Manchuria. Cynic though he considered himself, of women he knew nothing, and a dancer, he believed as all Koreans did, was woman at her lowest level. He did not speak these thoughts lest he offend Liang, but Liang answered as though he had spoken.

"You have been so absorbed, Uncle, in your devotion to our cause that you have not had time to realize the change in the world. I assure you that she is a woman of dignity as well as beauty. Many men pursue her, of course, but I insist that she is trustworthy."

"I must take your word for what she is," Yul-chun retorted. "It is not likely that I shall ever be able to judge for myself."

"Many men have also confided in her," Liang replied. "She has been the confidante of prime ministers and kings. She listens, she keeps their confidence, she is partisan of none."

"I wish to meet this paragon," Yul-chun said drily.

For the first time Liang hesitated. "It would be easy enough," he said slowly, "for she wants to meet you. She has heard of you, as who has not, and she has several times begged me to bring her here—it must be in secret, for she has the confidence even of the Governor-General—"

Yul-chun felt a chill at the heart. How could such a woman be trusted?

"There is one difficulty," Liang was saying. "Sasha is in love with her."

Yul-chun cried out, "Sasha! Does she respond?"

"She says no, but there is something of yes in the way she says it," Liang replied thoughtfully. "Perhaps she feels something of both. Perhaps it is not love at all. Sasha is impetuous —importunate—very handsome—"

Impetuous—importunate!

"I see I do not know my own son," Yul-chun said quietly.

Silence fell between them. He yearned to discover whether Liang also loved this woman, but he could not ask again. The young man had such natural dignity, with all his ease and grace, that the elder man could not cross the delicate barrier between the generations.

"Perhaps we should think of someone else. This young woman seems too complicated."

Liang laughed. "Ours are complicated times, Uncle! She is not simple, but nothing is simple. No, she is the only one, and I will bring you both together somehow."

He rose as he spoke, and whatever his inner mood, he appeared his usual benign self. The change had been only for a moment and he had restored himself. As for Liang, he bowed and left the room. At the same moment he heard a noise at the outer door, and Ippun's voice scolding Sasha.

"Little master—little master, you are too late! There is mud on your coat."

"I fell." Sasha's voice was thick.

"You have been drinking," Ippun scolded.

"It is not your business to tell me!" Sasha shouted.

Liang went to the door. Sasha was leaning on Ippun's shoulder, unable to walk.

"I will take care of him, Ippun," Liang said. "See that the door is locked for the night. Make my uncle's bed, and then go to your own."

He put Sasha's arm about his neck and half carrying him, he led him to the room which was now Sasha's own. Ippun had made it neat, she had spread the bed and lit the night lamp on the low table at the head of the bed—and had put a thermos of tea there and a bowl. Liang lowered his cousin to the bed and then poured the bowl half full of tea.

"Drink this—it will help you."

Sasha obeyed without protest and still without protest he let Liang undress him to his undergarments. Then he threw himself down and slept while Liang covered him with the quilt.

Liang sat in his usual seat in the theatre, in the middle of the fourth row. Somewhere in the shadows behind him he knew that Sasha was watching the performance, too. He had seen Sasha at the ticket window when he came in, but the crowd was dense and Sasha had not, he believed, seen him.

He gazed intently now at the flying figure on the stage, Mariko in the closing scene. Her long sleeves waved like a bird's wings and then whirled as she whirled, the slow rhythm quickening as she approached the climax. Clever, clever these ancient dancers, seemingly religious, seemingly reverent, and underneath the delicacy and the grace all the dark passion of mankind! And no one understood this better than Mariko. He had known her now for two years and still he had not fathomed her. She was a child of many races, the human emblem of mixed cultures, holding within herself the hostile drives of her ancestral past, brilliant and willful, lawless and tender, never to be trusted for the next emotion, the next impulse, the next decision to act, and yet she was deeply trustworthy because she could never be partisan. Such was Mariko. She would do nothing for a cause, of that he was sure, but she would do anything for him.

She was closing the dance. Slowly, slowly the silken wings of her wide sleeves descended to the dying movements of the end. He caught her eyes, those startling eyes, shining and dark, and he knew that she was telling him that he was to come to her. Not to her dressing room—

"Never come to my dressing room," she had told him when they first met. "That is for everybody. Not for you!"

He had not known what to make of her directness, her boldness he would have said, except that it was not bold, only exquisitely shy and childlike, and he said nothing because he did not know what to say.

To his startled look she had replied. "We have no time, you and I. I must leave Seoul in twenty days, and I have never seen you before. There are only these twenty days. Then I fly to New York, London, Paris. I may never come back—who can tell? I thought I was safe in Peking because I have a Chinese godfather there, but when the Japanese came, the Chinese called me a spy. And in Tokyo I was nearly thrown into prison because I speak Chinese so well—I speak the language wherever I am. But I was never a spy. I cannot care enough about any country to be a spy. I dance. I am an artist. If I do anything else it is for a human being—not for a country. I belong to no country—and every country."

All this she had poured out in her soft hurried voice, stripping off her costume as she spoke, revealing a skin-tight undergarment which she slipped from her shoulders before she drew a western dress over her head. He might not have been there for all she cared, it seemed, or he might have been a woman, except from the instant their eyes met they shared the knowledge that she was woman and he was man.

They had not met often since then. He had never made an advance toward her, nor she toward him. Yet when they were alone for the first time in her house, without invitation or hesitation they had embraced, though without words. They had never spoken of love but they were in the state of mutual love. To have put it into words would have been to enclose it and belittle it and define it.

Once when he had visited a monastery on Kanghwa island, he had called upon the abbot, and they had fallen into deep conversation. He had listened while the abbot explained the mysteries of Buddhism, of which he was not ignorant, for he had studied well the books in his grandfather's library. Of all religions he was most drawn to Buddhism, and yet he had no wish to become Buddhist. There again he refused definition. To belong to one was to deny himself the privilege of belonging to all.

"And beyond this," he had said when the abbot had finished, "there is the difficulty of Nirvana—the difficulty for me, at least. You tell me that Nirvana is the ultimate goal of the human spirit—or the soul, if you wish. But Nirvana is non-being, and I have no longing not to be. On the contrary, I long for all-being."

The abbot had replied, "You mistake the meaning of Nirvana. It is not non-being. True, it is the absence of pain, the absence of sin and wrongdoing, the absence of passion, and even of temptation, but not because of non-being. Not at all! On the contrary, it is that very all-being of which you speak. It is total awareness, total comprehension, total understanding, so that we do not need words to communicate. We simply know. We know because we are Nothing is hidden from the mind and the spirit that dwell in Nirvana. The absence of suffering, of pain, of passion, of temptation itself, is the result of already knowing and therefore understanding, aware of all that exists in this eternity which we call time."

When the abbot spoke these words, Liang had felt a relief and release in himself, a complete peace pervading not only his mind but every part of his body. His muscles, his heart, his inner organs, all moved into a harmony which was peace. He had waited for many minutes while he assimilated this peace. Then he was ready to return to his life.

"Thank you, Father," he said to the abbot. "What you have said is true. I feel it in my whole being. Now I understand what is meant by Nirvana. I shall know as I am known. Yet—and I hope that this will not hurt you—I do not wish to become a Buddhist."

"Why should you be Buddhist?" the abbot replied. "In Nirvana there is neither Buddhist nor any other division. These classifications are not needed when we reach the state of total awareness and total understanding. Go in peace."

With this the abbot had blessed him and Liang came down from the mountain and went home at once. The abbot's words came back to him when he first saw Mariko alone. It was the evening after Japanese bombs had fallen on Pearl Harbor. He had had no intention of going to the theatre that night. The evening had been spent with others of his own age, young men from the university. They had argued and discussed the news, searching it over and over again to know what portent it held for Korea. He had been about to go back to his room in the hospital when darkness fell, and passing by the theatre on his way he had lingered, he did not know why, except that he was reluctant to return to his solitary room and was disinclined for study. His mind, usually calm, was still disturbed, for the attack on Pearl Harbor had been altogether unexpected and he had not been satisfied with the conclusions his fellow students had reached. Yet he could not reach his own. Restlessly, senselessly he had thought at the time, he had stopped at the theatre, and noticing that the beautiful dancer who had been treated at the hospital was to perform, he had bought a ticket and gone in.

The place was half empty. People had stayed at home to ponder and to talk and to guess the future. He sat in the middle of the first row, close enough to catch the scent of Mariko's robes as she danced, close enough to see her lovely face. She was small, her face oval and pale and her eyes large and glowing with exhilaration and joy in the dance. She was as light as a bird, her shoulders moving with every movement a separate grace and elegance, and this not only of the body but of her inner being. She had a rhythm of her own, expressed with elegance, and the master drummer followed rather than led. She appeared to stand still while she moved, and yet when she was still she seemed to move with inner exhilaration. Her performance that night had been the Fairy Dance, its story that of a fairy who was bathing in a lake when a woodcutter stole her clothes, so that she was compelled to marry him and live on earth. Liang had never seen it performed with such artistry, and watching her gossamer garments floating about her like mist, he forgot for a little while the tragedy of the day. And afterwards did what he had never done before. Driven it seemed by a spirit in his feet, he had gone backstage. Although usually her door was crowded, no one was there that night, and she had opened the door herself, still in her costume, and they had stood looking at each other.

"Come in," she said. "I saw you in the front row. It was for you I danced, after I saw you."

He came in and she closed the door.

"I was not sure whether you saw me," he said at last.

"You know I did," she said simply.

"Now I know," he had replied, and remembered what the abbot had told him. Total awareness, total understanding! This was what he and Mariko had, each of the other, from that first moment face to face.

She was leaving the stage now, and he rose before the crowd filled the aisles and walked rapidly through the lobby. There he saw Sasha making his way to the stage door, but again Sasha did not see him. He left the theatre and walked westward past the Bando Hotel for ten blocks until he came to the gate of her house. The gateman let him in and he sat in the moonlit garden until she could arrive, although the night was chill. He did not like to enter her house until she came home, lest it seem a presumption that he was her lover.

"Shall I bring your tea here, master?" the gateman asked.

"If you will," Liang replied with courtesy.

What the two servants thought of his presence here he did not know or indeed care. He was scrupulous, leaving always within an hour after she reached home. The ritual was the same. She changed into Japanese or Chinese dress, as her mood was, preferring Chinese, and then she took a light supper which he might share or not as he pleased. They had never spent a night together, yet each knew that at some time this was inevitable although when it would be neither knew. They had discussed it only once and quietly, as they had discussed marriage, without conclusion. He supposed that in the past she had had lovers, but he was sure in the state of total awareness in which he lived, that she had no lovers now.

He heard her car at the gate, a Rolls-Royce, and he put down his tea bowl and rose as she came into the gate, still in her theatre costume but a coat of Russian sable wrapped about her. When she saw him she came to him and took his hand between both her own.

"I am late," she said. "Sasha insisted on staying after the others were gone."

"Sasha!" he exclaimed. She dropped his hand and laughed uncertainly and without mirth.

"It is cold in the garden tonight, is it not?"

She spoke unexpectedly in English and he was aware that she was afraid.

"Sasha has threatened to follow you," he said.

"Yes."

She linked her fingers in his and drew him with her toward the house. At the door her woman servant knelt to take off their shoes.

"You told him he could not come?"

"Of course. I told him I had a guest."

"And he asked if the guest were I?"

"Yes, but I lied to him. I said it was Baron Tsushima."

She could lie as easily as a child and confess it in the same breath. He was puzzled, for he himself could not lie, and yet he understood the necessity of lies in her complicated life, where men continually pursued her, and he did not reply to this. They went into her sitting room, the wall screens were closed, the curtains drawn, and on the low table steam rose from silver dishes of food.

"Excuse me," she said, "and please sit down."

She drifted out of the room so gracefully that she seemed not to walk and he waited. A maidservant entered with a Japanese robe and took off his coat and helped him to slip into the robe. He sat down then, only to rise when a moment later she came in wearing a soft French negligee of green chiffon, the full skirt floating about her.

"Ah, you are too polite," she said, smiling. "Rising to meet me? It is only you who persist in such courtesies."

"Let me have my way," he replied.

They sat down on their floor cushions, opposite each other as usual, and were alone. The first moment was always the same. Each searched the other's face. This, she said, was to learn what each was feeling, and what had passed since they last met. Then she put out her hands, palms upward and he clasped them. Into each palm he pressed his lips and as he did so, she took his palm, one after the other, and pressed her lips there.

She drew back her hands after this and she laughed softly.

"Now I know," she said, "and all is well with me, too. Let us eat. I am hungry. The dance was difficult tonight. I felt there were too many people. They crowded onto the stage behind me. I have forbidden it, but still it happens. Then I feel caught between the crowds in front and the crowds behind."

"They love you," he said gently.

"Yes, they love me, but it means nothing to me," she said quickly. "So much love—from nameless persons, none of whom I shall ever know!"

A small silver pot filled with hot soup stood before each of them, and he poured the soup from hers into a silver cup, and then poured his own cup from his pot.

"Better than hate," he said.

"Oh, I have had hate, too," she retorted. "In Peking I saw a theatre full of people suddenly hate me. I had to escape for my life while they screamed after me that I was Japanese. You don't hate the bit of Japanese in me?"

"I hate nothing in you. I love everything in you," he said gravely.

A long moment hung between them, luminous and silent. He broke it unwillingly.

"Drink your soup while it is hot. Meanwhile I must tell you I have a duty tonight. I have made a promise concerning you, which you are not compelled to keep."

She lifted her delicate eyebrows at this.

"When you go to the United States next week," he said, "I ask you to carry some messages."

"Yes?"

"Of two kinds," he went on. "My grandfather has a few American friends. And the missionaries we know have also relatives and friends. Our government-in-exile is there. You will take messages to them."

"Yes?"

She held the silver cup in both hands, warming them, the delicate eyebrows still uplifted above eyes so glorious in size and shape and depth that he was all but stifled by the breath caught in his breast.

"Please—" he said, his voice low. "Please do not look at me like that until I have finished!"

She laughed sudden clear laughter and changed her look. That face of hers, so exquisite, so mobile, quivering and alive —he looked away and went on.

"The purpose of these messages is to prepare everything here in our country for the coming of the Americans—and to prepare the Americans for us, when they come."

She put down her cup. "The Americans!"

"They will come, I assure you. If there is any danger to you here, because of the messages, then stay away—stay in America or in France, wait until the victory when we have taken back our country. Then I shall arrange such a welcome for you as a queen would have. My grandfather loved a queen once, and my grandmother is jealous to this day. But no one knows that I have a queen of my own!"

He looked up at her now. They leaned across the narrow table and kissed. She had taught him the kiss.

"Touch my lips," she had said to him suddenly one evening as they sat like this across the table.

He had been stupid and only stared at her.

"Like this," she had insisted, and taking his hand she had kissed it.

"But how your lips?" he had inquired.

"With your lips," she had whispered, and had pursed her lips into a waiting flower.

He had of course seen kisses in western motion pictures but he had taken it as a strange western custom. Nevertheless at her bidding he had leaned forward until his lips rested on hers, and had let them so rest for a short space. Then he had sat back.

"Pleasant?" she had inquired with mischief.

"New," he had said reflecting, "very new—"

"You are not sure you like it?" she had inquired.

"Not quite," he had confessed, somewhat embarrassed.

"Shall we try again?"

She made this suggestion in so calm a voice that he had tried again and had made conclusion.

"Very pleasant!"

She had laughed outrageously at him then and the scene had made cause for laughter many times thereafter. He would not allow many kisses in an evening, however, and tonight not until he had finished his duty. He had no wish to use her as a prostitute. It might be that she had been so used but he had never inquired. In the reserve and delicacy of his spirit he did not want to know. What had been could not be changed. She was what she now was and he had complete faith in her. His comprehending instinct discerned no impurity in her.

"I shall not be able to refuse Sasha forever," she said suddenly.

He waited, aware of a quick anxiety. She helped herself to chicken and with a pair of silver chopsticks put a tender bit into his bowl.

She went on when he did not speak. "What shall I tell this cousin of yours? He is very fierce—not like you—" She broke off.

He spoke out of a fear such as he had never felt. "How can I answer until I know how you feel?"

"I am afraid of him," she said in a low voice.

"Why?"

She shook her head. "He has a power in him."

"Over you?" he asked.

A long pause then, while she ate, bit by bit, daintily, not lifting her eyes. Then she put down her silver chopsticks.

"I feel him," she confessed, "and I am afraid."

"Of him?"

"Of myself, too."

He met her pleading eyes gravely. "I have not finished my duty. Do we speak now of Sasha or shall I go on with what I must say?"

She sat back and folded her hands together. "Please go on."

Against all his being he went on. "You are to take certain letters to certain persons whose names and addresses I will give you. Do not entrust the letters to anyone else, but put them yourself into the hands of those who should receive them."

"Are these persons Americans or Koreans?"

"Most of them are Koreans but a few are Americans. It is essential that the important persons in Washington should know that we have a government ready to perform its duties and that when the American army arrives it is we who will receive our country from their hands and not our Japanese rulers."

She listened closely and without coquetry or graceful movement until he had finished. "Must I know all this?" she asked.

"You prefer not to know?"

"It is safer for me not to know. Let me be the innocent bearer of these messages."

He had now to face the truth. He was putting her life into danger. Upon the slightest suspicion of what he was asking her to do she might be arrested or, more likely, simply shot when she came on the stage, or as she left the theatre or in her own garden or anywhere in the world where she happened to be, in any country, in any city.

To such death they were accustomed. An unknown assassin, a murderer never found, meant that no attempt need be made for justice. And who more reasonably killed than a beautiful woman whom many men loved?

He groaned aloud. "What man was ever compelled to make such a choice—between his love and his country!"

She smiled and suddenly was all woman again. "Do you know," she said softly, hands clasped under her chin, "I have never seen you troubled. Now you are troubled—and for me! So I know you love me. And I shall be safe. Do you know why? Because I shall be very careful—very, very careful—to come back alive and well and safely to you. I will take no chances. So you need not make the choice. I will take the messages. I will deliver them, but I will not know what is in them. I do not ask. I will only see that they are received. It will not be difficult. I have many American friends. Some are famous and powerful. They will all help me. Say no more—say no more! Some moment before I leave, at one o'clock six nights from now, after my performance, give me the letters. Let me go alone to the airfield. There will be many people there to see me off, but you must not be there. And now that is enough."

She looked at him sidewise. "If this is not the night, sir, my love, then you had better go."

She tempted him heartlessly and with all her heart every night, and every night he went away. There would be a night when he stayed but it was not yet and it was not this night. He trusted to the clairvoyance he knew he possessed but which he could not explain. Somewhere far away, but still within the realm of his own being, he had instincts that he believed were old memories for he felt them rather than knew them. He heard no voices but he was directed through feeling and he had learned long ago as a small child in his grandfather's house that when he disobeyed this feeling he was sad, and when he obeyed, he lived in harmony with himself. He did not think of it as evil or good but as harmony or disharmony.

Now with all his strong and passionate nature he longed to say to her that he would stay and he did not, for he knew indeed the time was not yet. They rose together, he went to her side, hesitating, not trusting himself to touch her lips. Instead he took her hand and pressed his lips into the warm soft palm, scented as her whole body was always scented, with Chinese kwei-hua, a small white flower of no beauty except in its undying fragrance.

. . . He slipped through the gate and into the quiet street. The hour was late and if he met a watchman he would be questioned. There was always that danger. He braced himself then when at the left turn of the street a man came toward him through the twilight of a clouded moon. Then he saw that it was no watchman but Sasha, wrapped in a capelike cloak. They met and stopped and he saw Sasha's face, pale and staring.

"What is it, Sasha?" He made his voice calm and usual.

"I followed you," Sasha muttered. "I have been waiting for hours."

"Why have you waited? Why did you not knock on the gate and come in?"

"It is you," Sasha said in the same muttering. "You are why she would not let me come! Baron Tsushima! What Baron are you? You and she—you and she—"

Liang stopped him. "Sasha, what you are thinking is not true. We are not lovers."

"Then why are you with her in the night?" Sasha demanded.

Liang waited for a long moment before he replied. Then it became clear to him what he must say. He took Sasha's arm.

"Come with me!"

In silence the two men walked the dim streets, empty except for beggars who crept through the night looking for refuse or shelter. Of these there were more than a few but they did not accost the young men, fearing these two, well dressed and strong. By law, beggars were forbidden and it was only at night that they could prowl about the streets, knowing that the Japanese were asleep and the watchmen were Koreans. On the two walked until they came to the hospital where he had his room. Many nights Sasha had stayed here with him, sometimes in sleep, sometimes in talk. They were cousins, but they were not always friends. Something new, something strange, was in Sasha. Whether it was the ancestry of his northern mother, whether it was the rudeness of his upbringing and the harshness of the Siberian climate, Liang did not know. With his peculiar genius, he understood Sasha, but not as part of himself.

"Sit down," he said when they had closed the door. The building was modern, and his room had a wooden floor, a table, two chairs and two cot beds.

Sasha flung off his coat. Like other young Korean men he now wore western clothes. He sat down on the cot bed and began to unlace his shoes.

"Tell me that you stay half the night with a dancer and do nothing but talk and I will not believe you."

His voice was sullen, his face dark. He kicked off his shoes and threw himself back on the cot.

"Believe me or not, it is true," Liang said quietly. "And it was not only a dancer with whom I talked. It was a famous artist, who happens to be my friend."

"A dancer," Sasha insisted in the same sullen voice, "and if you have not heard what else she is, you are a fool, and I know you are not a fool. I could tell you what she said to me tonight—yes, we spoke, she and I." He sat up and stared at Liang with flashing eyes. "I wait for her every night at the stage door. Sometimes she lets me go home with her."

He watched Liang to see what the effect of this might be. Liang was sitting in the chair by the table, and there was no change in his face.

"You don't ask what she said?" Sasha cried.

"No."

He was about to say more. Then he did not. She had told him she was afraid of Sasha. In a woman fear of a man may be the under edge of admiration, and admiration the upper edge of love. He wondered why he was not angry with Sasha, or even with her, but he was not. The gift he had been given was sometimes heavy to bear, the ability always to understand why the other person was as he was. Wounded, yes, but never angry, and there were times when he longed to feel fierce personal anger. Now, even now, he imagined that it might be possible to strike Sasha a hard blow, wrestle with him in combat, shout at him that Mariko was not to be fouled by his desire and suspicion.

"She is afraid of you," he said suddenly and was shocked. He had no intention of such revelation.

A strange secret look stole over Sasha's handsome face. His eyes narrowed and he smiled.

"She told you that?"

"Yes."

"It is enough—for a beginning."

Sasha lay back again, his hands behind his head. As clearly as though his eyes could penetrate that skull, Liang knew what was taking place there. A hard simple core of ruthless desire was shaping into a plan. A woman who fears, Sasha was thinking, is a woman who can be taken by force. No more pleading —no more waiting at stage doors! He would enter her house. When she came home he would be there. He would enter by force.

This was what Liang saw as clearly as though it had already taken place. He felt a sudden uplift of power in him. Was this anger at last? Was this how a man felt when he could strike another man? He leaped up and felt his hand curl into fists. He saw Sasha leap up to meet him. They stood staring into each other's eyes. As suddenly as it had come, the impulse died in Liang's body.

"It cannot be done, Sasha," he said. "She has guards in her house. You will have to find another way."

He sat down again. The loneliness of Sasha, a boy who saw his mother dead under a tree in the forest, whose home was the coldness of an orphanage in Russia, a youth, wandering here and there to earn his living, who found his father only to know that they could never meet, a man who had never known what love was in parent or friend or lover. Of what use was it to strike such a man as Sasha? A blow could never change him.

He felt this as clearly as though he were inside Sasha's skin, Sasha's blood running through his veins, and by the instinct in himself which he could never understand, he knew that he must tell Sasha that Mariko now was embarked upon a most dangerous mission.

"The reason I went to see Mariko Araki tonight was a secret one, but I will tell you what it is. You are a Korean, Sasha, and you are a Kim of Andong. Above all other things that you are, you are first of all Korean of the clan of Kim. Our blood is the blood of patriots. At this time we cannot think of ourselves. We must think of our people, our country. Our grandfather has spent his life for our country. He saved our Queen when she was about to be killed and his lasting grief is that he could not save her in the end. My father died because he was a patriot and my mother suffered and died. And your father has been an exile since his youth, and now he is about to begin the most dangerous work of his life. We, the Kim, are staking all we have and are on the moment when victory is declared and the Americans come to our country. We must be ready for that moment. We Koreans must not be divided as we have been, fighting each other, in the open as we did in the past or in secret as we still do. We must be ready with a united government able to take over our country from the defeated Japanese. The Americans must know we are ready. It is for this that I went to see Mariko. She is to take letters to America."

Sasha stood listening, his hand hanging, his mouth ajar.

"Why Americans?" he demanded. "What have the Americans ever done for us?"

"They have never taken our land," Liang replied. "They have never dreamed of empire. Whatever they may have done or may not have done, they are the only people who have declared the ideals of which we have only dreamed. True, we were not saved, but an American, Woodrow Wilson, declared self-determination of peoples."

"I never heard his name," Sasha retorted.

"He is dead," Liang said gently, "and I think he died when he found how large his promise was and he knew he could not fulfill it. Yet though dead he lives."

Sasha turned away. "You are being religious." He threw himself on the bed and yawned.

"Nations, like individuals, can only learn by their own individual experience."

Yul-chun paused in his writing. The snow was falling softly but heavily into the garden. It had begun only a few minutes ago, but if it kept up there would be a foot of snow by twilight. The house was silent and he was alone. Yul-han's house was now his own. He had found himself cramped in his father's house, and at the mercy of his mother, coming in too often to see if he were cold or hungry or feverish or had he not worked too long, and he had asked for this house. There was also Sasha. To his surprise, Sasha after months of idleness had wished to go to the Christian school so that he might improve his English and go to America. Sometimes Sasha came home at night, sometimes he did not. Last night he came home early with his books, and after he had his meal he went to his room. On the whole, Yul-chun reflected, Sasha was improving, although of late he had shown a sudden hostility to Liang which the latter seemed not to notice. Yul-chun sighed and turned his thoughts resolutely away. Deeper than his longing had once been for Hanya was the constant troubling anxiety he felt for his son. Hanya had been a stranger, but Sasha was part of himself, though how often he too was a stranger!

Resolutely he took up his pen. "We cannot learn to govern ourselves as a modern nation while we are ruled by another. Yet we must be able to defend ourselves at the moment of victory, lest defenselessness invite new invasion. We must be willing to be poor in order that we can build a navy to protect our shores. On the north we must build bastions and fortresses and maintain a heavy defense to prevent the age-old threat of Russia. To the incoming American Military Government, let me recommend immediate recognition of our provisional Korean government. It was our hope that our own brave Korean soldiers, now in China, could have helped the American army against Japan, our common foe. We would have saved many American lives thereby. Bitter indeed was our disappointment when this was not allowed."

Someone knocked and looking up he saw Liang at the door, and with him a small slender woman wrapped in a sable coat, snow glistening on her dark hair. They bowed.

"We disturb you, Uncle," Liang said.

"No—no, I was just finishing an editorial," Yul-chun replied.

"Uncle, this is Mariko Araki," Liang said.

Yul-chun bowed once, not too deeply, and Mariko bowed deeply several times. Then she allowed Liang to take off her coat. Underneath she wore Korean dress, a short bodice of pale gold brocaded satin, tied at the right shoulder with a bow, and a full skirt of crimson satin. Under the skirt he saw the upturned toes of her little gold shoes and he gazed at her frankly from head to foot. This was the dancer!

"Come in," he said. "Seat yourselves. I have some western chairs. Sometimes I sit in a chair myself to promote circulation in the legs."

Mariko laughed. "I do it by dancing!"

"Ah," Yul-chun said. "It is a resource, but not for me."

She sat down on a chair and Liang took another. After a moment's hesitation, Yul-chun resumed his seat on the floor cushion beside the low desk.

"Apologizing, Uncle, for sitting above you," Liang said with his usual good nature, "but these western clothes allow me too little freedom."

He wore a western suit which made him look slim and tall.

"We shall all be sitting in chairs when the Americans come," Yul-chun replied.

Liang and Mariko exchanged looks, and Liang began again. "Uncle, Mariko is leaving tonight for America. I promised that I would bring her to see you before she went. Yet I have put it off until today, I suppose because I have been—I am fearful for her. But she is very brave. She will help us."

"I am not brave," Mariko put in. "I do not want to know anything. I wish not to answer questions. But if you put something in my hand, sir, I will put it in the hand where it should be. That is all."

Yul-chun listened, appraising her as she spoke. He was experienced in such appraisal. How often had he not searched one who must be entrusted with a message of life or death! He was satisfied now with what he saw in this charming face. It was an honest face, frank, mischievous perhaps, but a child's mischief born of gaiety and not of wile.

"Why are you willing to do this?" he asked.

She did not hesitate. "I do it for someone I love. He is Korean and so I do it for Korea."

She did not look at Liang. Was it he? Yul-chun asked of himself. Was it Sasha? Liang inquired of his heart.

"That is to say I am only a woman," Mariko was saying, "and being a woman I do something for a man, not for a country—unless it is his country."

Yul-chun waited, still expecting to hear who this man was, but Mariko was finished. She composed herself, folding one hand over the other, her small hands pale against her crimson satin skirt. He opened a drawer in the desk and took out a silver key. With this key he unlocked a compartment hidden in the back of the drawer, and from it he drew three letters.

"I have already written them," he said, his voice low and solemn. "They are addressed to—"

He held out the letters for Liang to see. Liang nodded and Yul-chun proceeded.

"In case the letter to the President does not reach him, I have this friend—" he pointed to the second letter—"who will then go personally to Washington. He has access to the President. This is essential, for the President does not know our history, else how could he have suggested two years ago that Korea be placed under the international trusteeship of China, the United States and, he said, one or two other nations? We, who have been a nation for four thousand years! What if that one other nation were Russia! In my letter to him I have explained the fearful peril of Russia."

Here Yul-chun felt compelled to pause, so great was his

agitation. He set his lips, he cleared his throat and heaved up a sigh from the bottom of his heart. Then he continued.

"I repeat to both of you, who will outlive me, the day may come when we will look back to these years under the Japanese rulers and call them good. At least the Japanese have prevented the Russians. I say this, although I have known the torture of my flesh and the breaking of my bones under the hands of a Japanese torturer."

They listened to him in silence, motionless, their quiet expressing their respect and their awe. They loved him for the legend that he had become in their country, the Living Reed, and for what he was now, heroic, selfless, a tall powerful man, worn with suffering, his face noble and bold but lined too early with pain, his thick dark hair already gray. Suddenly Liang spoke.

"Uncle, I told Sasha that she was going to the United States with letters. Did I do wrong?"

"You did very wrong," Yul-chun exclaimed. Then realizing what he had said, he turned to Mariko. "My son is not evil. I am sure he is not evil. He has not lived in his own country and now he seems somewhat lost here. We must win him to our family. Liang, I cannot blame you, but—"

The door to the right opened, and as though he had heard his name Sasha came in. He was dressed in western clothes, a hat in his hand, a coat over his arm. He looked at the three, surprised. Or was it pretense at surprise? Liang could not decide. Yul-chun spoke immediately and too quickly.

"Come in, my son. Liang has told you. We are sending the letters. I have made them very brief but firm, very firm. As for example, to the President I—this is the copy, I kept it for our own records. Now that you know—I am very glad you know —Liang, I change my mind, it is well that you told him. I would like Sasha to become part of us—"

Yul-chun was fumbling among papers in the secret compartment. "Yes, here it is. Yes! To the President as follows—"

And again Yul-chun lifted the paper and read in his loud clear voice. "We in Korea have been deeply disturbed for the past two years. Those few words agreed upon by you, Sir, and the British Prime Minister and the Nationalist Chinese ruler Chiang, haunt us day and night. I repeat them, Sir, lest you have forgotten what we can never forget. 'The aforesaid Powers, mindful of the enslavement of Korea, are determined that in due course Korea become free and independent.' These words, Sir, are carved into our hearts and they bleed. 'In due course.' Sir, in the space of these three small words Korea is doomed."

When he heard this, Liang had one of his moments of foreknowledge. He could not explain the prophetic weight, he tried to escape it, he shrugged it off. He rose and walked about the room, but could not escape. Doom! The heavy word resounded in his ears as though he heard near him the single heavy beat of a great brass drum, and the echoes reverberated into the future.

Behind him, afar off, he heard Sasha's voice. "I am going into the city, Mariko. The carriage is at the door. Come with me."

Liang turned. Mariko rose, unwilling, and looked from one to the other bewildered. Her asking eyes rested on Liang's face. He nodded as though she had spoken and she bowed to Yul-chun and followed Sasha from the room.

"But here are the letters," Yul-chun exclaimed.

"I will take them to her tonight," Liang said. "It is better that she does not have them with her now—"

. . . She was in the house directing the packing of her costumes for her tour when he went to her that evening. Japanese kimono, narrow Chinese robes slit boldly up the thigh, French evening gowns, English tweed suits and Russian furs were piled on the mat-covered floors. Three maids worked silently and without rest under her command. She sat in a deep chair, frowning with decisions made quickly and without argument. At the sight of Liang she rose and went to the other room and closed the wall screens.

"But at last," she exclaimed when they were alone. "Where have you been? I thought I would have to leave without seeing you."

"I came by horseback," he said. "The snow is a foot deep. I

inquired at the airport to know if the planes were stopped, but they are not."

"Are you coming to the theatre tonight?"

"Yes, but not to your room. And not to the airport. We shall not meet again until you return."

She stood motionless as a deer stands, suddenly afraid. "How has Sasha so much money? Those new clothes!"

"I do not know."

"Are you afraid of Sasha, too?"

"No, I am afraid of no one."

"Why, oh why did you let him take me away?"

"It is not the time to quarrel with him. And you must not be afraid. You are an artist. No one can destroy you unless you destroy yourself by fears."

"Let us not speak of Sasha," she said with resolution. "Have you the letters?"

"Yes." He took them from his pocket and she thrust them into the bosom of the Japanese kimono.

"Tell Sasha not to come to the theatre!'

"If I see him."

They stood looking at each other, suddenly speechless, the abyss of being parted already between them.

"When you come back . . ." he said and stopped.

"When I come back," she repeated. "Oh when I come back —yes—yes—yes—"

"The war may be over. And we—"

"Yes!"

The word was a yearning sigh. He put out his hands and she clasped them in hers and then loosed them and pressed herself against him. He bent his head and kissed her deeply. They stood for a long moment, until the maid called from behind the wall screen.

"Mistress, shall I put the gold dress into the box for Paris, or is it to be worn in New York?"

She tore herself away, gave him a pleading look, and left him, and he knew he would not see her alone again.

. . . Whether Sasha went to the airport Liang did not know. He did not see his cousin at the theatre and he returned to the hospital. The next day he performed a difficult and new operation alone for the first time, the American doctor at his side but taking no part. The necessity for concentration helped the hours to pass, and Liang finished his task at noon, his patient still alive and likely to live.

"Good work," the American exclaimed. "I thought for a moment that the artery might slip from your hand. But you're a born surgeon. I never saw better hands for it."

The patient was a young man who had been stabbed, the lung pierced and the heart damaged. Liang knew how it had been done. He recognized the man as a leader of the new terrorists. Now he would live again to kill others!

Liang pulled off his rubber gloves. "Thank you, sir," he said to the American. "You have taught me all I know."

"I'd like to send you to Johns Hopkins," the American said warmly. "Some such great hospital, anyway. Techniques for heart surgery are improving every day. Say, I never saw an artery tied like that, though!"

"A Korean knot," Liang said, taking off his white coat. "It holds fast, but a touch can release it—if you know the touch!"

"You sure have the touch."

The American clapped him on the shoulder and Liang smiled and went to his office.

By now Mariko must be nearly halfway to New York. The first letter would soon be safely out of her hands. Those little hands, so supple, so graceful in the dance! On that last night she had made her farewell program of old Korean folk dances, the Sword Dance the climax of the evening. All knew that it was not by chance that she had chosen to perform the story of the famous boy dancer of the ancient Silla Kingdom who perfected himself in a dance, holding a sword in each hand. His fame spread over the whole peninsula until he was summoned to appear before the King of Paekche, the enemy of Silla. There before the throne he danced so well that the audience cried out, beside themselves with pleasure, and the King rose from his throne. At that moment the dancer leaping forward thrust his sword into the King's heart. He was killed, of course, but by his courage he had inspired his own people in Silla and in his memory they preserved the Sword Dance. Mariko had performed it with classical style, even to wearing the mask of a boy's face, her dance-swords, the blades connected by wires to the handles, striking in rhythm with her flying feet. When she had finished, the audience rose shouting to its feet. She had snatched off her mask to show her own lovely face, and bowed again and again, her eyes fixed, as Liang knew, upon his face. Then she had run away, the ends of her wide golden sash flying behind her, and he saw her no more.

The endlessness of time until they met again! For the first time in his life he, the light of heart, felt his heart heavy in his breast. "Attachment," Buddha had said, "is the cause of grief." He pondered the saying, and that night in his room, he wrote it down. After a time he made a poem.

> Buddha was both right and wrong.
> Attachment, with all its pain,
> Is now my deepest gain,
> My inward Song—
>   Life long!

He copied it carefully and without writing his name beneath it he put it in an envelope and addressed it to Mariko in New York. They had agreed it would be too dangerous for them to write. But what could a Japanese censor make of a poem?

The American President died suddenly one spring day. The news echoed around the world and into every city and village in Korea. Liang heard it in the hospital and hastened home to announce it to his grandfather and uncle.

Yul-chun drew him aside. "Do you know whether the letter was delivered?"

"I have heard nothing," Liang replied.

"We cannot know in any case whether the one who takes his place will see the letter," Yul-chun said, downcast.

"We cannot know anything," Liang agreed. "We can only wait."

. . . Spring passed and summer entered. Liang worked day and night at the hospital and saw little of Sasha until the school year ended. Silence filled the land, a tension of waiting. The end of the war was inevitably near, the world knew it, and yet the mechanism to force that end could not be found. In Seoul the police grew every day more oppressive and all controls were tightened throughout the country. Jails were filled and schools put under surveillance. Germany surrendered and the tension increased. Every Korean now knew that Japan must surrender and every heart was impatient because there was no surrender.

"A blind and stubborn people, the Japanese," Yul-chun declared.

"The people know nothing of what goes on behind the military screen," Liang replied.

It was midsummer and they were in the garden for respite from the heat. Sasha was teasing a puppy by dipping it into the goldfish pond, and Liang could not bear to see the small creature's fright. He walked abruptly to the pool and took the shivering dog into his arms and Sasha threw pebbles into the water to scare the fish.

"I am going to Paris," he announced.

They heard this in silence. Then Il-han spoke. "I was in Paris once, to see Woodrow Wilson. Many people were there from many countries. He was surprised to see us pressing around him, each begging for his help. I know now he was frightened."

"Of you?" Sasha asked idly.

"Of himself," Il-han said.

A roar of thunder rumbled from the mountains to the north, and a naked flash of lightning forked across the twilight sky.

"Come into the house!" Sunia cried at them from the door.

They went in slowly, reluctant to leave the coolness. Sasha lingered alone in the doorway. Suddenly he saw the puppy under a bush and dragging it forth he dropped it into the pool.

. . . The summer days wore on, hot and long. Liang still heard nothing from Mariko and there was no announced surrender, although the Japanese were losing on every front. People were weary with waiting. Yet they could only wait. One night a man with a gunshot through his leg was brought into the emergency ward and Liang's duty was to tend the wound. When it was cleaned and bandaged, the man pressed a small square of folded paper into his hand. Accustomed to such messages, Liang said nothing. He turned his back and unfolded the paper. It was addressed to the Japanese people but signed by Americans and it gave the conditions of surrender, warning them also that if Japan did not surrender, eleven cities would be bombed.

He returned to the wounded man now lying on the bed and leaned over him, pretending to adjust his pillow.

"Were they bombed?"

"Six cities."

"We have not heard of it here."

"I am just back from Japan."

"No surrender?"

"None. The Japanese government is split. The peace party has asked Russia to mediate. They ignore the American warning—with scorn."

"The other cities?"

"They will be destroyed. Millions of leaflets have warned a second time."

"The people?"

"Dazed, immobile, waiting."

"What next?"

"The Americans have a new and terrible weapon. It is next —unless Russia acts."

"Will Russia—"

"No."

A nurse came near and Liang went away. He hastened to his room, took off his western garments and put on Korean robes. Thus disguised, he left the hospital and the city and returned to his grandfather's house.

. . . In the house, meanwhile, there was already confusion. Yul-chun had received a secret message, carried by a fruit vendor from the north. Among his apples and peaches the man had hidden certain objects which could only be Russian, and Yul-chun in the garden recognized them as the man bargained. The man nodded mysteriously when Yul-chun inquired, then drew near to whisper.

"The Russians are pouring into the north!"

These fearful words fell upon Yul-chun's ears and he hastened to tell them to his father. Il-han was lying in a long chair of woven rattan, smoking his long bamboo pipe as he listened. He knocked the ash from the small brass bowl at one end and filled it with the strong sweet tobacco he enjoyed in his old age.

"Father!" Yul-chun exclaimed. "Do you say nothing?"

"What is there to say?" Il-han replied. He lay back and drew hard on the pipe and two streams of smoke came from his nostrils.

"Then I must go into the city," Yul-chun exclaimed, more than a little angry with his old father. "I must get in touch again with the underground—"

"Calm yourself," Il-han told him. "You will only get yourself killed. Do you think the Japanese are not watching for you? They are waiting to see what you will do."

"Why do you say this?"

"Because they know everything, and nothing you can do now will save us. Pretend you are ill. Go to bed. Declare that you have a fever. I will tell everyone you are not expected to live. We must wait. Then when the Japanese surrender we must all be ready to seize the power.

"But if the Russian troops—"

"There will be a brief moment, a few hours between the surrender and the arrival. Let us hope there will be the brief moment—the few hours—"

They were interrupted by Sasha bursting through the gate. His eyes were wide, his whole face exploding with what he had to tell, too impetuous for greeting his elders.

"A new bomb, a new bomb has fallen! The whole sky lit in Japan—a city burst into flames. This morning—it was early morning, just as schools were opening and men going to business—"

It was at this moment that Liang reached home and, following upon Sasha, heard what was said. "The military will not surrender, even though the Emperor wishes it," he exclaimed.

Sasha gave a loud laugh. "They will see another bomb! Another bomb will fall!"

They were startled by his laughter, they looked at him and at one another, and none spoke. No one, not even his father, knew Sasha well enough to reprove him for such laughter, yet all were frightened by it.

Il-han spoke. "Russia will now declare war on Japan."

"Let that war be declared," Sasha said joyously. "What the Americans have begun the Russians will finish!" He laughed again, that loud cruel laughter, and the other three hearing it, could only be silent as he went into the house.

"How did Sasha know of the bombs before any of us?"

They looked at one another and none could answer.

. . . Two days later Russia declared war on Japan. The news leaked out. Everyone knew and no one talked. Still Japan did not surrender. Russia moved her troops into Manchuria, and still Japan did not surrender. On the third day the second bomb fell on the city of Nagasaki. How many bombs did the Americans have? On the fourth day Japan sent an offer of surrender, stipulating only that the Emperor be left upon his throne.

These blows fell, and the men in the house of the Kim—Il-han, his son and his two grandsons—prepared themselves. The orders from the secret Korean government were that all must wait for the coming of the Americans. Until then there must be no move from Koreans, no reprisals against the Japanese, no sign of rebellion. Let all wait quietly in their houses. Their hope must be in the Americans.

In obedience Liang did not go to the hospital and Sasha stayed, too.

"When will they come?" Yul-chun groaned.

He was the restless one. Il-han was calm with the deep philosophic calm of the old. He watched Yul-chun with something like amusement one day as that one walked from house to garden and garden to house, unable to sit or to read or even to put his hand to a useful task when Sunia suggested the mending of the roof where a few tiles had fallen in a windstorm a few days before.

"You should write a book," Il-han said. He sat on a bench in a corner of the garden to catch the noon sun.

"A book?" Yul-chun repeated.

Il-han knocked the ash from the small brass bowl of his bamboo pipe.

"I wrote a book."

Yul-chun paused before him. "When?"

"Years ago when I was restless like you. The Japanese had come, and I was a prisoner here, as you are now, and I wrote a book in which I put down every evil act of the invaders. Thus I made history and thus I vented my fury."

Yul-chun was astounded and diverted. "Let me see this book, Father," he said.

"Follow me," Il-han said.

He rose and went into the house, Yul-chun following, and opening a chest of polished wood bound in brass, he lifted from it a thick manuscript wrapped in silken cloth.

Yul-chun received it in both hands. "What labor!" he said. "Am I to read it?"

"As you will," Il-han replied. "There are good bits in it," he went on. "You will even find yourself in it. I wrote down faithfully all about your trial, to the last detail of how you looked."

"You shame me," Yul-chun muttered.

He did sit down then, as his father returned to the garden and filled his pipe again, and forgot his restlessness as he read the careful polished sentences in which the elder had reported every evil of the times, murder and massacre and assassination, rape and looting and arson, chicanery and deceit. He read day and night until the book was finished, and he had given it back to his father.

Then his restlessness fell on him with double weight, for he knew beyond doubt that all his father had written was true. When would his people be delivered? He began to doubt the

Americans, although Il-han remained calm and the two young men were confident, Liang because he trusted the Americans, Sasha—who knew anything about Sasha?

Only Yul-chun, the one between, could neither be calm nor confident. Hope and fear stirred him in equal measure and made him restless day and night, while the slow formal steps were taken between governments, the victor and the vanquished. Meanwhile the Russian soldiers were indeed already pouring into the north. It was no longer the secret of fruit vendors. Six days before the final surrender they had come on foot through Siberia and by sea from Manchuria. The people were too dazed to protest or to move. Only the few had heard that Russia would share in the booty of war, and now like hares before hounds, they stood stricken and silent as the rough soldiery crowded the country roads and villages and swarmed into the cities.

"Where will it end?" Yul-chun demanded. "Will they cover the whole country before the Americans come?"

But they were not to cover the country. Someone, some American officer, somewhere, who knew where, drew a line across a map. The Russians were to stop, the people were told, at the 38th parallel. Where was the 38th parallel? Some remembered that the Russians and Japanese had talked of dividing Korea there. In sickening foreboding men and women studied maps in old schoolbooks their children had once used, to discover whether their homes were to be under Communist rule. If the answer was yes, they gave themselves up to despair and many killed themselves. If the answer was no, they prayed for the Americans to come quickly. Where were the Americans?

"They are asleep," Sasha declared with laughter.

"They will come," Liang said steadily.

They did not come.

Yet more days passed, one after another while the people waited in agony, and the Americans did not come. What if the wild Soviet soldiers swarmed even over the boundary that had been set for them? Already there were stories of pillage and robbery and rape. In the grass roof house Liang

cleaned and loaded two old rifles he had bought in the city.
There were no young women here and for that let all be
thankful, but it was well to be ready. How thankful, too, that
Mariko was now safely in Paris! He had followed, through
newspaper reports, her path of glory.

"Something entirely new from Asia, yet something we can
understand. The tincture of her Western ancestry—"

Only Sasha was scornful. "I know the Russian soldiers," he
said. "They are bold and they are young like me, most of
them, but they are not worse than other soldiers. If they come
I will speak Russian to them and they will not harm us."

And he poured out a stream of Russian to show what he
would say. The others listened to him, half fearful, then Sunia
told him sharply to be silent.

"In this house," she said, "we speak only Korean." And she
would not heed Sasha's furious sullen look.

But all were easily impatient in these few bitter days, when
searing anxiety burned in them like fever. Then suddenly it
was announced everywhere that on the ninth day of the same
month, the ninth of the year, at last, at last the Americans
were coming! They were to enter at the port of Inchon, and
learning the news, the people everywhere prepared banners
and Korean flags, flowers and gifts. None dared yet to leave
home, nevertheless, for the Japanese Governor-General had
asked permission from the Americans to maintain police control lest Koreans make reprisal on the six hundred thousand
Japanese now living in that southern part of Korea, many of
them having fled from the north when the Russians appeared.
Permission had been granted. Koreans remained in their
homes and no reprisals were made, the people being too
proud in any case to take such petty revenge.

Then another command came from the Japanese Governor-
General. Koreans were forbidden to meet the Americans.

"This we cannot obey," Yul-chun declared.

. . . On the appointed day therefore, Il-han and his son and
grandsons came to the docks at Inchon, wearing Korean robes.
Sunia had cut flowers from her garden and Il-han carried a
bouquet in his right hand to present to the Americans, but

Yul-chun carried the Korean flag, hidden for all these years, and Liang held an American flag. Only Sasha was empty-handed.

When they arrived at the docks they found some five hundred Koreans already there, leading citizens who had been chosen in secret to represent the people in receiving the Americans, all bearing in their hands gifts and flowers from those who could not come and waving banners of welcome and Korean flags. The day was hot but fair. The sun poured down upon land and water, making the green more green and the sea as blue as heaven. The great American ship, her flags flying, was anchored in the harbor, and all stood silent and motionless as the gangway was let down. To the right were the Japanese officials in full uniform, the Governor-General in front, his sword at his side. To the left were the Japanese police holding back the Korean crowd of some five hundred persons.

Yet they could not be held back. When the American General appeared on the gangway, the five hundred pressed forward, waving their flags and banners, to greet the American General as he came down the gangway from his ship. At this same moment the Japanese police lifted their guns and opened fire. Five Koreans fell dead, and nine fell wounded, and gifts and banners were wet with their blood.

What Il-han and Yul-chun and the two young men now saw was not to be believed, but they saw it and were compelled to believe what their eyes told. For that American General, descending from his ship, did not reprove or stay those police or even blame them for what they had done. Instead he commended them for "controlling the mob," as he put it, whereupon the Koreans who had come to welcome him were scattered by the police and the waiting Japanese officials became the hosts. With their eyes Il-han and Yul-chun and the two young men saw this and with their ears they heard the American General declare to the Japanese officials that they were to keep their posts until he could form a military government to take over the country. He neither spoke to the Koreans nor seemed to see them. While they heard and saw this, the four of them, Il-han and Yul-chun, Sasha and Liang, were standing crowded together in a doorway of a house. The door was barred, but they had taken shelter there under the roof when the police dispersed the welcoming Koreans. They looked at one another, the flags and flowers hanging limp in their hands.

"What shall we do now, Grandfather?" Liang asked.

"We go home again," Il-han replied. He threw the flowers into a ditch. "Fold our flag," he told Yul-chun, "we will take it home with us and put it away for a another day."

This they were about to do when Yul-chun turned, irreso-lute until he saw the American accept the sword of the Governor-General. He heard him speak affably to the Japa-nese, ignoring the fleeing Koreans. He saw the flags and the banners trampled in the dust as the Koreans ran, the flowers crushed. And suddenly he went mad. He ran back, waving the Korean flag and shouting, *"Mansei—Mansei!"*

He was not allowed to shout more than this. Guns were instantly raised, shots sounded in the air and he fell into the dust, dead.

It was Liang who ran back to him, and what might have happened to him, too, cannot be told, for he was saved by his superior at the hospital. Among the Koreans but somewhat apart from them were a few Americans, missionaries and teachers and doctors, and it was the doctor who ran to meet Liang.

"Go back," the American whispered. "Go back—go back before they shoot again! Leave him! I will take him to the hospital—but hurry—hurry—I am in their bad graces—I can't save you—"

Liang could only obey, for he saw Il-han had fallen and could not be lifted, although Sasha was holding up his head. Together the two young men lifted the aged man and they carried him to the hospital to await the coming of Yul-chun's dead body, Liang comforting his grandfather as he went.

"My uncle would have chosen a death like this."

But Il-han refused comfort. "Am I to be comforted? Be silent!"

There was no silence, nevertheless, for behind them came those who were left of the crowd, weeping and groaning because the Living Reed was dead.

"Who will take his place?" Il-han inquired.

It was the day of the funeral and they were home again, but Yul-chun lay now on the hillside beside his grandfather. From everywhere people had come to bow before his old parents and to him.

"No one—no one," Sunia sobbed. "We have lost our sons."

They were in the main room, waiting for Ippun to bring them hot tea. Suddenly from the garden they heard angry voices.

"How dare you go to the north?"

"Can that be our Liang?" Sunia whispered.

"Hush," Il-han said. They sat side by side on their floor cushions, and he put out his hand to take Sunia's hand while they listened.

In the dark garden the two young men sprang at each other. The two old people heards pants of rage, the grunts and snorts of young men embattled.

"Sasha will kill our Liang," Sunia muttered. She got to her feet with effort and tottered to the door.

"You two!" she screamed in her high quavering old voice.

They did not hear her and Il-han came to her side.

"What are they fighting about now?" he inquired.

"Who knows?" Sunia said. She peered out from under her hand. They were struggling in the dust, locked together. She began to sob. "Our Liang will be killed!"

But Liang was astride the fallen Sasha. He had him by the shoulders, shaking his head against the hard earth.

"You!" Sasha was shouting between chattering teeth. "You have no pride—you—you—live here—under the—the insult of these Americans—no shame—take your—your hands away —my throat—"

Il-han suddenly pushed Sunia aside. He strode on his shaky legs to the two young men and with all his strength he tried to pull them apart.

"Must I see you against each other, you two in my own house? Are we forever to be against each other?"

At the sound of Il-han's voice Liang suddenly came to himself. He got up and drew his breath in great sobs. "Grandfather," he began and could not go on.

But Sasha was on his feet, too. He stopped to take up a knapsack where it had fallen from his shoulder, his old knapsack, and Il-han saw he had put on the clothes in which he had come, the full trousers, the high boots, the belted tunic.

"Traitor!" Sasha now screamed at Liang. "Soft—silly—full of love—stupid love! Dog's filth! I spit on you—I spit on all of you!"

He spat into the dust at their feet and shouldering his knapsack he ran through the open gate.

Liang stooped then and picked up a small sheet of paper from the earth.

"It was this that sent him mad," he said to his grandparents. "It was this, after he had seen his father buried. Too much—I know that. And why did I—how could I—it is myself I cannot understand."

Il-han took the bit of paper from his hand and spelled out the words in the light of the stone lantern. It was a cablegram from Paris: ARE YOU LIVING?

He shook his head. "I can make nothing of that," he said and he gave it back to Liang.

"Come inside the house," Sunia called.

But Liang did not heed. He sat down on a stone seat and held his head in his hands. Nor did Il-han heed. He went to the gate and peered into the night beyond, the night into which Sasha had plunged himself.

"What is independence?" Il-han inquired but of no one. He paused and then made his own answer. "Independence? It was a happy thought!"

"Come in!" Sunia called again and she went out and taking his hand, she led Il-han into the house.

"Come, my old man," she said, soothing him. "Come, my dear old man."

She helped him to his cushion, and Ippun came in with the teapot and lit a candle.

Outside in the garden Liang came slowly to himself. He felt his soul return into his body. He felt the night wind cool and he heard an early cricket call. Sasha would never come back. They had lost Sasha. He had feared it when he saw Sasha's face as the coffin was lowered into the grave. He knew it when Sasha, sobbing, had elbowed his way through the reverent crowd. He had followed as quickly as he could, but Sasha had reached home first and had snatched Mariko's cablegram from the gateman's hand, the message she had sent from Paris. Sasha was waiting at the gate to spring at him in jealous fury, to accuse him, and suddenly they were trying to kill each other!

The crumpled paper had fallen from his hand. He saw it lying there and took it up and smoothed it out, and read it again.

"Are you living?" These were the words. She had sent them in jest perhaps, or perhaps in love. Safe enough, those words she had chosen by accident, perhaps, in a mood of gaiety or loneliness. Then suddenly conviction rose in him like a voice, though he heard no voice.

Are you living?

Living! His uncle was the Living Reed. Even as he lay in his grave people had murmured the words, and some told again the legend of the young bamboo pushing up between the rough stones in the cell from which he had escaped so long ago. From his coffin he could not escape, and the people mourned. But only a few days ago, Liang now remembered, his uncle had reminded him, almost shyly, of his return one night in secret to see his younger brother, and of how he, Liang, then a baby, had seemed to recognize him, although they had never met before.

"You sprang into my arms, you put your hands upon my cheeks, you knew me from some other life—"

He could almost remember the moment itself. And he recalled other times when Yul-chun had talked of the heritage of Korean patriots.

"In the spring," he could hear his uncle saying, "in the spring the old root of the bamboo sends up its new green shoot. It has always been so and it will be so forever, as long as men are born."

". . . Come into the house," his grandmother was calling. "Come into the house, Liang, and shut the door!"

He rose and went no further than the door. He stood there, himself again.

"I am going to the city, Grandmother. Grandfather, I must ask my friend to send a message for me—my American friend."

"What message?" Il-han asked.

"That I am living," Liang said.

"It is late," Sunia complained.

"Not too late, Grandmother," he said, "not while I live."

And bowing to them he left them to Ippun and went his way alone. In the sky beyond the gate a new young moon held fullness, and beneath the moon there shone a star, the usual, steady star.

Epilogue

It was high noon at Pusan, on a fine autumn day, two years ago. I had traveled the length and breadth of South Korea, by motorcar, so that I could stop when I liked. The road was often narrow and rough, the bridges over the many brooks, bombed during the war, had not yet been rebuilt, and we rattled over dry stones or splashed through water made shallow by the dry season. I had enjoyed all of it, marveling afresh at the noble beauty of the landscape and treasuring afresh the warm welcoming kindness of the people. Now I was at Pusan, at the southern tip of Korea. It is a port famous in history, but I had not come here for the sake of history. I had come to visit the place where men of the United Nations who died in the Korean war lie buried, each nationality under its own flag. In the cool autumn wind all the flags were flying bravely.

I laid the wreath I had brought at the foot of the memorial monument and I stood for a few minutes of contemplative silence. The scene was matchless. On three sides was the surrounding sea, a sea as blue as the Mediterranean. Behind were the severe gray flanks of the mountains, the town nestled at their feet. The cemetery is as beautiful as a garden, kept meticulously by devoted Koreans. On either side of me stood two young Korean guards in military uniform, silent as I surveyed the scene. My eyes rested on the American flag.

"I would like to walk among the graves of the Americans," I said. "I knew some of them."

The guard on my right replied, "Madame, we are very sorry —no Americans are here. All were returned to your country. Only the flag remains."

I had a feeling of shock. No Americans here? How this must

have wounded the Koreans! Before I could express my regret, a tall Korean man in a western business suit approached me. The brilliant sun shone on his silver-gray hair, his handsome intelligent face. He spoke in English.

"Do not be distressed, please. We understand how the families of the brave Americans might feel. It is only natural that they wished to have their sons safely home again. Our country must seem a very remote place in which to die."

"Thank you," I replied. "All the same, I believe that if my fellow countrymen had known, had understood, they would have been honored to leave their sons here, among their comrades."

"Ah yes," a soft voice put in. "I have been in your country— I know how friendly your people are."

"My wife," the tall Korean said.

I turned and met face to face an exquisite woman in Korean dress.

It was the beginning of a friendship and from these two I created the characters of Liang and Mariko. From them also I learned what happened after the ending of my book. I had read, of course, of the events, how the American government had done its best to correct the first misunderstandings. But through my new Korean friends I came to my own comprehension of all that had happened.

"We misunderstood, too," Liang said one night, a week later, as we lingered over dinner in his house in Seoul. "Koreans were angry and disappointed when the first Americans came. I am sure that your soldiers during the days of the occupation, in those years between 1945 and 1948, must have had many bad experiences. We were not at our best after half a century of ruthless Japanese control."

"Even the Japanese did some good things," Mariko reminded him. "Don't forget your hospital."

We were sitting on the warm ondul floor around the low table. It was a pleasant room in a delightful house, Korean but modern. Next door was the excellent hospital where Liang worked. He had done graduate work at Johns Hopkins and was a skilled surgeon.

"I remember the good as well as the evil," he now replied, and went on: "But we Koreans are determined to be a free and independent nation. We will never give up that struggle. It is in the beat of our hearts, in the flow of our blood. And we look back and wonder how different our lives might have been if that treaty between our two countries, yours and mine, had been honored—that treaty of amity and commerce, ratified by your country in 1883, that gave us the promise of your assistance if we were invaded. In return we were to give you our trade. But your Theodore Roosevelt was prudent—he did not wish to become embroiled in the rivalry of Japan and Russia for possession of Korea. William Howard Taft, who was then your Secretary of War, went to Tokyo and on July 29, 1905, signed a secret agreement giving Korea to Japan, if Japan would promise not to keep your country out of Manchuria and not to attack the Philippines—"

Mariko rose from the table. "Liang, why do you speak of old things? Let us speak of how Americans sent their sons here to die for our freedom."

Liang responded instantly. "Yes! You are right."

We all rose then and went into the living room and Mariko played the piano and she and Liang sang together, most beautifully, old Korean songs and new American songs. I remember they sang a duet version of "Getting to Know You" from the Rodgers and Hammerstein musical.

Looking back, I know that both Liang and Mariko were right. Yes, the mistakes of history bring relentless reprisals. There is a direct connection between that secret agreement signed in Tokyo by Taft and Katsura and the young men of many nations who died on Korean soil. Korea is divided today not only by the 38th parallel, but also by the Korean men and women born in Russian territory when their parents fled their country at the time it was occupied by Japan. These children grew up in Communism, as Sasha did, and believed they were "liberating" their country when they went to Korea. American lads died at their hands.

But, as Mariko says, why speak of old things? Let us remember, rather, that a tie binds our peoples together. Brave young American men climbed the rugged slopes of Korean mountains and fought in homesickness and desperate weariness for the sake of a people strange to them and for reasons they scarcely understood, even when they yielded up their lives. With such noble impulses and final sacrifice, let the past be forgot, except for what it teaches for the future.

PEARL S. BUCK